gleau

gleau

L.A. Collins

TATE PUBLISHING
AND ENTERPRISES, LLC

Published by Tate Publishing & Enterprises, LLC
127 E. Trade Center Terrace | Mustang, Oklahoma 73064 USA
1.888.361.9473 | www.tatepublishing.com

Tate Publishing is committed to excellence in the publishing industry. The company reflects the philosophy established by the founders, based on Psalm 68:11,
"The Lord gave the word and great was the company of those who published it."

Book design copyright © 2013 by Tate Publishing, LLC. All rights reserved.
Cover design by Arjay Grecia
Interior design by Deborah Toling

Published in the United States of America

ISBN: 978-1-62902-026-6
1. Fiction / General
2. Fiction / Christian / General
13.09.25

PART I

Before Dawn

LEE WINSLOW MADE A MENTAL list for the day, Wednesday, August 10, 2011, noting that today would be a good one. It was also the day after she'd seen her first white squirrel. Not an albino, but a white squirrel with dark eyes and nose. She had been on this earth for over fifty-five years and had seen thousands of gray, red, and even black squirrels, but never a white one, which proved to her that the world still held mystery.

Dressed in a white cotton slip gown, she surveyed her bit of the world, appreciated the cool of the predawn morning, and wrapped both hands around a mug of potent coffee. Lee was living her dream in the near nightmare the world had become. A patch of earth, a barn full of animals, and privacy made it her heaven on earth. She did her best not to dwell on things beyond her control, which was just about everything, including what tomorrow would bring: the Bad Day. From where she sat on the bench next to the kitchen door, it was obvious the wax beans needed picking again before market on Friday. *And it wouldn't hurt to go gather eggs once more either*, she thought. Semi took a seat next to Lee and placed a paw on her forearm.

"Mornin', Mr. Blue Eyes."

Semi patted her arm in response, flexing his claws ever so slightly.

Semi had no clue he was just a cat, and sometimes Lee wondered if perhaps he was more. At a glance, he would be seen as a Siamese variety. His points were seal, and his eyes were icy sapphires. His light coat hadn't darkened as many Siamese do with age, and Lee suspected it had something to do with his unusual genetic circumstances. His mother was a calico barn cat Lee rescued from the pound, and his father was a traveling salesman, identity unknown. Semi had three alley cat siblings, and he was completely white at birth; and until his markings began to appear, Lee assumed he was just a white cat. As his points developed, so did his curious personality and their mutual devotion. He became her shadow, companion, and frequently her confidante. It was quite obvious too that he preferred, beyond all other creatures, the company of his petite human female with auburn hair that hung to her waist and eyes that matched his. When it came time to assign him a proper name, Lee had already determined that he was more a Semi-ese than a Siamese, and the tag Semi stuck.

Lee sipped her coffee and drank in the promise of terrific weather for the day ahead, a promise that ultimately wouldn't be kept. "Well, where should we start? Friday is market day, you know," she reminded Semi as she stood, stretched on tiptoes, and stifled a yawn. Eyes wide, Semi stared at her intently as if waiting for instructions. She didn't bother to inform him that tomorrow would be a bad day, as if by not informing him she could avoid it. Looking down at her helper, Lee added, "Let me throw on some clothes, and I'll be right with you." Lee gave her feline buddy a stroke from head to tail and gave the screen door latch a tug. They both climbed the two steps from the landing to the kitchen entry. The kitchen was by far the largest room in the small single-story farmhouse, more than enough housing for Lee and Semi, but it did have two small bedrooms in case either of them had guests.

Heading to the bedroom, Lee was redirected when her phone began ringing. Semi led her to it, which was hidden under a rumpled throw on the living room sofa. "Thanks, Semi. We should add bloodhound to your list of talents," she added as she retrieved and flipped open the phone.

"Hello?" Reception was never great in this part of rural Minnesota, but the crackle and hiss was bad enough that she checked to make sure she was still connected. Without her glasses, it was difficult to recognize the incoming call number, but she frequently got calls from her son in Afghanistan, so it wasn't unusual to receive an unknown number. Again she asked, "Hello?"

The static cleared.

"Hello? Are you there?"

Almost instantly, Lee got a reply. "I'm home," the male voice stated. Before Lee could say anything in response, the call ended.

"Hmm. That was odd." Semi stared at Lee with catlike concern. "Probably a wrong number." And she was more than likely correct, but she thought she heard something more. It was a déjà vu experience.

Lee checked the received call number, and none was recorded. She gave Semi a serious look and shook her head. "Nothing like modern technology, huh, boy?" Semi followed her to the bedroom while she pulled on a pair of jean shorts and a paint spattered T-shirt. As she slipped on a pair of manure-stained flip-flops, donned her glasses, and refreshed her coffee, thoughts of the phone call were buried under a list of chores that refused to be ignored. Semi scooted out the cat door to lead the way. The sun was barely above the eastern horizon, but Jax, the Golden Phoenix rooster, had been welcoming dawn for the past hour. The laying hens—Lee called them her girls—were waiting at the gate of their run to be set free to forage. Coyotes, martens, and other carnivores were a constant worry at night when Bomber, the Shetland sheepdog, was in the barn. Even he was no match for a pack of coyotes, so she confined him nightly with the regular barn dwellers.

"Come on, ladies," Lee spoke, swinging wide the gate, and the multihued flock spilled out in every direction. On her way to the barn, she felt the phone in her pocket and thought about calling her daughter, Emily, and telling her about the unusual phone call. It was only a little past seven in the morning, which meant Emily was in morning mode with her tribe of five. Lee would call her later. She stopped at the pump house to turn on the water and made her way past bellowing steers and two very pregnant Texas longhorn cows staring holes through her. Like iron filings following a magnet, all eyes followed Lee to the barn, including Semi, who puffed himself up in anticipation of the Sheltie's release. The door to the barn was pulled open, and Bomber shot out, giving his signature central-axis spin. He paid no attention to a silly cat with static cling as he had many important things to pee on. Semi regained his composure and followed Lee into the barn.

While pouring feed into respective troughs, Lee considered what brought her to this paradise of manure and subzero winters. Farmwork wasn't beyond her ability, and it did test her physically, but it gave her what she needed most—a sense of capable independence. In less than a year's time, her thirty-year marriage ended because of sordid adultery; her only son, Nick, joined the Marine Corps; and her closest friend of twenty years was killed by an unlicensed driver running his truck through a stop sign. Tragedy wasn't fair, and neither was life. Then again, tragedy was nothing new. She was only six years old the day her parents were killed, and it was her aunt Jan who coined it the Bad Day.

Considerations of the past dissolved as barn chores neared completion, and Lee unlatched the gate to the pigpen while toting a five-gallon bucket of feed and pushing her way to the trough through half a dozen noisy feeder hogs. Semi kept his distance during this process, waiting outside the fence as pigs are notorious tail biters. When they were tiny piglets, Semi enjoyed their games of cat and giant mouse, but once they grew to over fifteen pounds, the tables were turned. Once upon a time, he had been treed for over two hours inside their compound until Lee heard his pitiful cries and rescued him from the pack of porcine demons. It was the end of the cat-pig friendship.

"Come on, furball," Lee remarked to Semi as she hung the bucket on the fence post and headed to the henhouse. She grabbed a wire gathering basket on her way through the henhouse door and was surprised by the generosity of her tiny flock.

As she counted and carefully placed each egg in the basket, she marveled at not only the bounty, but the delicate coloring of each egg. Her mixed bag of Araucana, New Hampshire Reds, Black Australorps, crested Polish, and Cuckoo Marans were the jewels of the barnyard as well as a source of income. Lee was entertained daily by their frantic glee while chasing a grasshopper or diligent scratching and inspection, like a group of feathered prospectors digging for gold.

As the pair made their way to the house with a basket of nearly four dozen eggs, Lee looked down at her shadow in a fur suit and remarked, "It's a good thing we checked the nests, huh, Semi?" Before he could agree, Lee's pocket began ringing. She placed the basket on the step and dug the phone from her short's pocket. It was Emily's number.

"Good morning, sweetie. You must have ESP."

"Good morning, Mom. Why would you think that?"

"I was going to call you earlier, but I figured you would still be delivering children. Not literally, of course," she joked.

"Very funny, Mom. Five is my limit. What's up that you were going to call?"

"Nothing dire. I got an odd call this morning. Did Nick call you today?"

"Odd how? And no, he didn't call me."

"It was probably just a wrong number. After I said hello, a man's voice said 'I'm home' and then hung up."

"Doesn't sound too sinister. Any heavy breathing?"

"No, silly, and don't I wish!" Lee laughed.

"I think you're right. More than likely someone had the wrong number or was just leaving a courtesy message."

"That makes sense. It just creeped me out a bit."

"Well, 'tis the season. That's why I called. How are you faring?"

"I was better before that call, but I'm okay. You have to remember, I've been dealing with this for nearly fifty years."

"Forty-nine to be exact. And I know you prefer to deal with it alone, but are you sure you wouldn't want to come for dinner tomorrow night? We're having—big surprise here—spaghetti."

"I have to get ready for market on Friday, so as tempting as your offer is, I'll have to take a rain check. Oh, Semi and I collected forty-six eggs this morning. Do you need any?"

"Sure. I could always use another dozen. The girls like the pink ones if you get any."

"I'll tell the hens. Okay, sweetie. Thanks for the call."

"You're welcome. If you need me tomorrow, don't hesitate, okay?"

"I'll be fine. Semi and I will get a good night's sleep. Bye, hon. Love you much."

"Love you too. Bye."

Smiling, Lee closed the phone, slid it back in her pocket, and made her way into the kitchen where Semi sat in his padded rocker, looking at her with his "what took you so long" look. "Don't get too comfortable there, Mr. S. We've got beans to pick as soon as I get these eggs cleaned up and put in the refrigerator." Semi closed his eyes to slits, indicating that he would sit this one out. Lee understood. She didn't have to wear a fur coat in the summer sun.

The day went by far too quickly for Lee to get everything on her list completed. A late afternoon thunderstorm dropped some needed rain and stalled her progress, but it was a good day all in all. The quarter-acre garden yielded almost a bushel of late wax beans, a half bushel of both yellow squash and gray zucchini, and three baskets of roma, beefsteak, golden, and green zebra tomatoes. With the fourteen dozen eggs she had, it would be a profitable market day. The barn was secured, the hens were in the roost, and Lee did her best to keep thoughts of the Bad Day at bay. It was coming, and there wasn't anything to do but get through it as gracefully as possible. Emily was right. Forty-nine years, give or take six hours, Lee had struggled through this day.

And she would do it again tomorrow. A cool shower and a hot cup of tea might help. On second thought, nothing was going to help, but the shower and tea would still be pleasant. She had traveled so many avenues of distraction, hoping that something she could do would short-circuit this annual torment. Nothing worked. There was nothing left to do other than crawl between cool lilac-scented sheets, open a good book, and fall asleep with Semi at her side and await the dream. The dream that ushered in the Bad Day was always the same. Until tonight.

August 11, 1961

*L*EE GARRETT DRAGGED HER TOES through the warm powdery earth beneath the swing. She looked up at the cloudless blue sky and thought about all the new friends she would meet when she started school in less than three weeks. First grade was real school, not like the kindergarten she attended in the basement of the local church. It would have desks and chalkboards, and first grade meant she wasn't a baby anymore. Now Jase was the only baby in the family. The screen door creaked, and daydreams disappeared. Momma was calling her.

"LeeLee, keep an eye on Jase please. I'm frying chicken, and Daddy will be home in about an hour, and we'll eat early, okay?"

"Yes, Momma," she called back. The screen door creaked again as Momma disappeared into the house. The prospect of her favorite fried chicken was a tether that would keep her from wandering very far; that, of course, and the added responsibility of looking after her baby brother, Jase. Anyone big enough to go to first grade was big enough to watch a baby, she thought.

In the long shadow behind the modest rental home of Paul and Anna Garrett, Jase was entertaining himself in his playpen. From the swing, Lee had to squint, and it took a few seconds for her eyes to adjust from the contrasting brightness, but the top of his bald head was barely visible above the tangle of toys and blankets. She hopped off the swing and dutifully marched over to check on her charge. As she peered over the top rail of his cozy maple prison, Jase smiled up at her with his wide black-eyed Susan eyes. That's what Momma called them, black-eyed Susan eyes. They were the lightest blue-gray rimmed in black with yellow petals radiating from the pupils. Even from a child's perspective, they were quite striking.

"What are you up to?" Lee asked her obviously delighted little brother. With a mouth full of stuffed animal, he pulled himself upright and steadied himself by grasping the top rail. "You can't eat Duggie, silly boy," she giggled. Duggie was a stuffed blue-and-white gingham dog that Lee won for him in a game of chance at last summer's state fair. Lee took great pride in the fact that it seemed to be his favorite indulgence. She playfully scrubbed the top of his head. "Now you be good. I'm going to swing, and Momma's cooking chicken." Satisfied that she had done her duty, Lee walked back to her swing and reengaged thoughts of school.

No sooner than she settled on the seat of the swing, a voice startled her. "Hello, Lee-Lee."

Standing a few feet in front of her was a person she didn't know. Shyly, she answered, "Hi. Who are you?"

"Just a friend, and I need to tell you something."

The person began to speak, but Lee noticed that the words she was hearing weren't coming from his mouth.

"How do you do that?" she asked and suddenly realized she had responded in kind.

"It's just easier this way and more fun, don't you think?" replied the stranger.

"Yes," she had to agree. It was fun.

"Okay, I need to tell you something very important," continued this person.

As Lee listened, she was hearing two distinct conversations. One was lighthearted small talk, and the other was quite serious in nature. Lee shook her head in agreement to what was being asked of her without hesitation. As the conversation grew to a close, Lee considered asking this person to stay for a fried chicken dinner, but the back door opened, and Momma was calling her again. She looked toward the house, and when she looked back to extend the invitation, the stranger was gone.

"Where'd he go?" she asked aloud. Lee jumped off the swing and looked around the yard to see where the person had gone.

"Lee-Lee, where is Jase?" Momma asked

"In the playpen," she responded with assurance.

"I don't see him." Momma descended the three steps and began pushing things aside in the playpen.

"He was right there when I checked on him just a minute ago," Lee insisted.

"You didn't take him out, did you?" her mother inquired.

"Nope. Just talked to him," Lee responded openly.

Momma was looking very serious. "Stay right here. I need to go turn the stove off." She disappeared into the house, shut off the gas flame under the chicken, and a few seconds later reappeared and directed Lee. "I'll check this way. You go around the other way and look for him, and I'll meet you out front."

"Okay, Momma."

Momma was calling loudly for Jase as she rounded the north end of the house. Lee followed her example and started calling for her little brother. They met at the front steps. "You didn't see him crawl out, did you?"

"No, Momma. He was just playing with Duggie."

The look of worry on her mother's face was obvious but perplexing to Lee. She knew Jase was fine and he would be back, but she had no idea why she knew this to be true.

"I'm going to Mrs. Wright's. You stay right here in case he comes back," her mother instructed.

"Okay, Momma." Lee sat on the step as her mother ran across the yard and through the boxwood hedge to the neighbor's yard. She guessed they wouldn't be eating an early dinner after all.

Momma returned at a brisk to frantic pace with Mrs. Wright in tow, trying to keep up. Mrs. Wright was a grandmother, trusted neighbor, and friend who treated all the small children in the neighborhood as though they were her own. Momma flew past Lee into the house. A bit out of breath, Mrs. Wright carefully eased herself down to the step next to Lee. "We'll find him,

Lee-Lee. Not to worry, munchkin!" She patted Lee's knee with a careworn hand.

"I know," Lee replied nonchalantly, much to Mrs. Wright's surprise. "He'll be back, and he'll be fine."

"Now that's good attitude, dear." Lee wasn't listening to Mrs. Wright. Lee could hear Momma on the phone. Her last word before she hung up was, "Hurry." The front door opened, and Lee's mother, now with cheeks flushed and tears past brimming, asked Mrs. Wright to stay with Lee while she checked the other neighbors' yards. "Of course I will, dear. You go ahead," Mrs. Wright assured.

From that point on, things started happening so fast that Lee had difficulty comprehending why all this was necessary. Just as Momma returned, Daddy's car pulled up in the driveway, and right behind him was a police car. Then people from the neighborhood, some she knew and others that she didn't, had begun to congregate and ask what they could do to help. Another police car with different writing on the side pulled into the grass in the front yard, and a man and a big dog on a leash got out and followed Daddy to the backyard. Mrs. Wright gathered with other ladies, and they all tried to calm Momma. Momma was crying. Lee wished she could make her mother understand that Jase was fine and he would be back.

"Lee-Lee?" The question made her look up.

"Hi, Daddy!" Lee jumped off the step and hugged her father. She felt a hug in return and then a firm but gentle hand on her shoulder.

"Lee, I need you to remember everything that happened today and answer some questions if you can."

"Sure, Daddy."

"This is Officer Gale. Anything you can think of might help us find Jase." Her father stepped aside, and the policeman who brought the big dog stepped toward Lee.

"Where's your dog?" Lee asked.

"He's in the backyard doing his job," Officer Gale explained.

"What's his name?"

"His name is Shogun, but right now I need to do my job too, and it would help us both if you could answer a few questions for us. Is that okay?"

"I'll try."

"Good enough. Where was Jase the last time you saw him, Lee-Lee?"

"In his playpen in the backyard."

"Do you remember what time it was, Lee?"

She was six and didn't own a watch. "It was before Momma turned off the chicken."

The officer realized his mistake and asked another question. "When did you see that Jase wasn't in the playpen?"

"When Momma told me. I tried to see where the little guy had gone, but I couldn't find him."

The officer looked confused. "When you say the little guy, you mean Jase, right?"

"No. The little guy I was talking to when I was on the swing."

Now instant alarm showed on Officer Gale's face. "Are you telling me there was someone else in the backyard with you?"

"Yes. I tried to find him, but Momma made me help look for Jase."

Officer Gale stepped away for a moment to confer with Lee's father. With a brow creased with concern, her daddy now needed find out what Lee knew.

"Was this someone you know, Lee-Lee?" Daddy asked.

"No."

"Was it someone Mommy and Daddy know?"

"No, I don't think so."

"Can you describe them for me? Was it a man?"

"I think so." Lee did her best to picture the person who had talked to her by the swing.

"Was this man big like Daddy?"

"No, he was littler. And he had no hair like grandpa, so I guess he was old too."

Daddy turned to the officer. "A short old bald guy."

"What color were his eyes, sweetie? Did you notice?"

"No. He had on big sunglasses."

It was summer, so wearing sunglasses wasn't unusual. "Can you describe them any more for Dad?"

"They were like yours, Daddy. Alligator glasses!"

Her father turned to Officer Gale. "A short old bald guy wearing aviator sunglasses." Back to Lee again, he asked, "Did he say anything to you?"

"We talked…" Lee hesitated, deciding not to reveal *how* they spoke. Then she brightened and continued, "About school and stuff."

Lee went on to tell them his clothes were gray pants and a white shirt, no mustache, and no moles, tattoos, or facial hair. He wore no remarkable jewelry, had no emblems on his clothing, and she didn't remember his shoes at all. Satisfied that all useful information had been gathered, her father again began speaking with the police officer. Lee was grateful for her release from answering questions that in her mind didn't need answers. She had the answers. Jase was fine, and he would be back. The only question she had was why she knew this.

"Hey there, my Lee-Lee!"

Ah! It was Aunt Jan to the rescue. Lee jumped up and met the solid embrace of her mother's baby sister. Aunt Jan was the anchor. When the bovine effluvia hit the fan, Aunt Jan was the picture of calm, stability, and practical thinking, all of which were in great demand at this moment.

"Give me a minute to talk with Mom, and I'll be right back. Okay?"

"Sure," Lee answered.

Aunt Jan met her sister's open arms, and after a short conversation, they hugged again. Lee was watching as Aunt Jan left her mother's side and walked toward her, the look of concern replaced by a wide smile. "How would you like to come spend the night at the farm with your cousin Lisa?"

"Really? Right now?" Her enthusiasm was hard to suppress given the circumstances, but Lee figured the grown-ups knew best. In less than two minutes, she was in and out of the house with an overnight bag and prayed no one would inspect its contents.

"Now that was fast," Aunt Jan said with as much amazement as praise. "Go tell Mom and Dad good-bye, and I'll be waiting by the car."

Lee hugged her distracted parents then turned to Aunt Jan and held up a "just a minute" finger and disappeared around the corner to the back of the house. In short order, she reappeared and made her way to the waiting station wagon, her expression suggesting serious six-year-old thought. As the passenger door was opened and her bag was deposited in the backseat, Aunt Jan asked, "Why the look? Couldn't find something?"

"I guess Jase took it with him."

"Took what with him, hon?"

"Duggie. He was in there earlier but not now. "

What Jan wanted most was to distract her niece from the torturous thoughts with which even adults had trouble coming to grips. "It will be okay. I'm sure they'll both turn up just fine." Before Jan could suggest a stop for ice cream on the way home, Lee replied nonchalantly, "I know."

Jan put the wagon in reverse, and Lee looked past the throng of people in the yard to study the simple contours of the green asbestos–shingled house that she knew she was looking at for the last time in her life. Then she heard the thunder.

Awake

LEE AWOKE AS IF SHE'D hit the bottom of a dry well. Eyes wide open, the world had disappeared, and she was adrift in the barren vacuum of space. Another thunderous crash, and she hit the bottom of the well again, this time acknowledging the flash of lightning and the reality that surrounded her in the darkness of her bedroom. As the paralysis of sleep abated, Lee took stock of the fact that she was indeed in her own bed, and the storm had caused a power outage. Another lightning flash caused Lee to let out a startled "Ooh!" as Semi was only inches from her face in an attempt to make his presence known.

"Geez, Semi!" She reached into the darkness and stroked him reassuringly. "You scared me, Mr. S."

Under the distant rumble, Lee heard a steady thumping that seemed to slow as she maintained contact with Semi's soft warm body. Instinctively, she fumbled in the pitch-black for her phone on the nightstand. *Now would be a good time for some lightning*, she thought. On cue, a distant flash lit the room momentarily, and her phone was in hand. Flipping it open, the precious illumination had a calming effect she hadn't expected. Feeling a little silly, she realized the thumping she'd heard only moments before was her own heart knocking on the door to consciousness.

"Well, I'm awake now," she said aloud. Retrieving her glasses from the stand, she noted the time on the phone. It was here. The Bad Day had begun, but never like this before. It was eleven minutes past one in the morning on the eleventh day. The Bad Day. Semi positioned himself at Lee's side to verify the information on the phone. Okay, so this wasn't how things normally played out. Lee blamed it on the storm and made her way to the bathroom via phone light. Her thoughts drifted back to the dream she was so rudely awakened from and realized it wasn't just another dream, or even the right dream for that matter. It was a memory. And it was a memory she didn't often revisit because it put her in a state of melancholy she preferred to avoid. It was the last time she saw either of her parents alive. Her mother crying, her father distraught, her baby brother was missing, and nothing made sense. It was exactly fifty years ago to the day, hour, and minute that her world exploded.

Lee finished in the bathroom and "Helen Kellered" her way back to bed. The storm was subsiding, and crawling back into bed made her feel safe again. But she knew no one was ever really safe. Not really. Lee had been sent to Aunt Jan's that day so she would be safe. And she was safe, but her world wasn't. She could remember falling asleep in bed with her cousin, Lisa, while they were discussing school shopping—something Lee had never done before. Sometime after midnight, the sounds of adult voices from down the hall had awakened them both. Lisa went to investigate while Lee stayed in bed watching the flicker of colored lights filter through the eyelet curtains from outside. She could remember being very tired and concerned about what her parents were going through, but she was confident that her brother was fine. He would be back. It was a promise. A promise made so long ago and, as yet, not kept.

As Lee arranged the bedclothes around herself to get back to sleep, the memory she did her level best to suppress demanded acknowledgment. What she had spent years keeping in a protective fog came rushing into focus. Aunt Jan was at the breakfast table, her face buried in her hands. Lee said, "Good morning," and hearing that, Aunt Jan dried her eyes with fists and gathered Lee in a tight embrace.

"I wish it was, sweetheart, but I need to tell you something."

Lying there in the dark, Lee physically stopped breathing for a moment as they both had done standing in that kitchen all those years ago. "Mommy and Daddy went to heaven last night." Aunt Jan continued, "I'm so sorry, sweetie."

The anguish in her aunt's voice and the weight of the reality she'd just been handed should have crushed an innocent child with ease, but even now, Lee had difficulty reconciling her response to her aunt's news. "It will be okay, Aunt Jan. I can stay with you. And Jase will be back. He's fine."

Lying there in the dark listening to the growl of the retreating storm, Lee wondered what had made those words come out of her mouth or why she could never remember shedding even a single tear. She would love to have thought that she possessed some divine wisdom giving her the strength to comfort those around her, but she knew that wasn't true. Not until years later would she have even the slightest curiosity about the event that took the parents she loved so dearly in the blink of an eye. The newspaper headline stated, "Three Dead in Gas Explosion: Child Still Missing."

It was Officer Gale who had thought to look in the crawl space for her brother. Lee could recall that it was forbidden to go near those outside wooden doors that led to the small dirt-floored cellar. To a child, they were a sliding board or a hill to climb. It was eleven minutes past one in the morning when Officer Gale and Lee's father descended the wooden steps. No one knew for sure, but something sparked an apparent gas leak, and the result was a devastating explosion and fire. When Aunt Jan passed away in the mid-1990s, the coroner's report containing the harsh details of the fatal injuries her parents suffered was among the papers left for Lisa to sift through. When asked if it was something Lee might want to have, she asked her cousin Lisa to hold on to it for her. Lee now wondered if Lisa had indeed kept it.

"No more of that. My brain is tired," Lee mumbled to Semi, now curled up on the pillow with one paw on Lee's hand. As she rescrunched the pillow and settled herself for sleep, the soft glow of the digital clock returned, signaling the end to the power outage. Within moments, REM had kicked in, and the business of the night continued.

Sunrise

FOR THE FIFTIETH TIME, LEE stood facing an unfamiliar horizon. A length of sandy beach stretched as far as she could see to either side of where she stood on a dune facing an expanse of ocean she knew only from this unconscious dreamscape exposure. Looking straight up, she saw the last remaining star of the night. Then focusing on the horizon line, she waited for the elusive green flash that preceded the dawn. As always, the flash appeared, and her walk began. Green meant go.

Barefoot, she strode through the wind-smoothed sand of the barrier dune and down a small incline to the high-tide line. Blemished only by ridges of the retreating waves, pebbles, and bits of shell, the surface here was more resistant and cooler. Turning north as she always did, her stroll began. The breeze was soft, and as she moved forward, she was captivated by the smooth deep-green water that gracefully rolled and somersaulted into a spiral until it reached her path as a liquid sheet of glass. More interesting was that when she stopped walking to watch this spectacle, its motion ceased, becoming a freeze frame that defied time and gravity and every other law of nature and physics; a frozen spectacle as captivating for its beauty as its singularity, but she couldn't linger. A storm was brewing.

As much as she feared the unknown ahead, Lee focused her attention on the apex where sky met the converging beach and ocean and continued her march forward. Black clouds were gathering and as if by noticing this, a strong wind rose from their direction, telling her to turn back. From the previous experience, she knew that if she did, panic would ensue upon discovering that she had left no footprints to follow back, and she would awaken. Resisting the urge to turn back, a figure appeared, walking toward her from the darkening end of the beach. This was new. She had always been alone before.

At this moment, fear and curiosity were at odds with one another, but Lee was determined to find out what all of this meant, if anything. Slowly, the distance between herself and the human figure closed. As it did, Lee could see that this was a man dressed in cutoff jeans and a T-shirt. He had dark hair and a healthy five o'clock shadow. When he was within a rock's throw away, she could see that he was smiling, and a warm calm settled over her. She had never seen this individual before in her life, and yet there was something so familiar, almost familial about him, that she stopped walking and let him continue toward her. He progressed to within the distance of a handshake and stopped. For what seemed like forever, but was probably the span of thirty seconds, they stood there smiling at one another.

Finally, Lee gathered the courage to ask, "Do I know you?" Never before had she spoken a word during her walk on the beach, and she noticed that the question was posed purely in her mind. The man didn't answer immediately but instead held out his hand in a gesture to take hers. She responded by placing her hand in his, and as she felt the warmth of his grasp, she heard, "I'm home."

Awake, Again

STILL FEELING THE REALITY OF the hand she'd taken, Lee found herself sitting bolt upright in bed with Semi sleeping soundly in her lap, his head draped neatly over her right hand. Light entering the bedroom windows told her that morning was well under way, and she was late attending to her chores. Semi opened his steely blues and yawned lazily. A knock at the kitchen door prompted a flurry of bedclothes being dispatched, and covering herself with a barn jacket, Lee greeted Mr. Verne, a regular egg customer, at the door. Apologies for the delay were exchanged as well as two dozen eggs, and when that immediate business was done, Lee remembered that today was the Bad Day. But this was different. The traditional doom and gloom, fearfulness, and paranoia of the Bad Day were gone.

Lee checked the clock. It was nearly eight, but she decided the chickens could wait until after coffee. Filling the pot, she turned to see Semi staring intently at her. "So sorry, Semi. Didn't mean to roust you so rudely." Semi's eyes widened, and he sashayed across the kitchen and gave Lee's legs an affectionate brush. Lee couldn't remember what her daughter's schedule was, but she had to share this good news with someone. Retrieving her phone from the nightstand, she scrolled to Emily's number in her contact list and hit Send. The phone rang only twice, and Em answered.

"Hey, Mom, what's up? You okay?"

"Hey, sweetie. Yes, I'm fine. Better than fine, really."

"Oh?" Emily was silent for a moment. "What happened?"

"Nothing and everything," she stated, still not sure exactly what was happening. "Something changed last night, and there are some things I need to investigate, I think."

"Changed how? Are you sure you're okay? You almost sound happy."

"I am happy, but not sure why. I just know things are better, and I finally think I'm supposed to find out why. I need to call Aunt Lisa. I hope she'll have some answers for me."

"About the dream? Or something else?" Emily knew that her grandparents were killed in a house fire when her mother was only six, but it was a subject rarely, if ever, discussed. And some things were left unspoken entirely.

"It's about my brother."

"Your *brother*? You had a brother? Mom, you never told—"

Lee cut her short. "I know, I know. I'm sorry. I never told you about him because I never knew what to tell you."

"Well, what happened to him? Where is he? Geez, Mom, I can't believe you didn't tell us we had an uncle."

"You did," Lee stated as simple fact. "But what happened to him is still unsolved as far as I know. He just disappeared."

"No one just disappears, Mom. How old was he? Was he kidnapped, or—"

"It's a little complicated."

"Now there's an understatement!"

"Well, it was more than I could handle when I was six. It happened the same day your grandparents were killed, and he was almost two. I'm not sure what was ever determined about his whereabouts, but now I need to find out." Lee could tell her daughter needed answers as much as she did. "Hold on, hon. Let me call Aunt Lisa, and I'll be over this afternoon to bring you up to speed. Okay?"

Reluctantly, Emily agreed to wait. "All right. But I want to know everything. Everything! I still can't believe this just slipped your mind, Mom. What was his name? You can remember that, can't you?"

"Yes." The name came to her instantly and was familiar to them both. "His name is, or was, Jase Albert Garrett, after his two grandfathers."

"Mom! No wonder you insisted! You knew!"

"No, I didn't know. At the time, it just felt right."

"Wow. I have an uncle Jase. Just wait till Nick calls!"

"No, no. Don't mention a word to Nick. Let me tell him."

"Okay, but call me back as soon as you're done talking to Aunt Lisa, or I'm calling you back in thirty minutes."

"Will do. Love you, hon. Bye."

Emily hung up after a quick good-bye with the escalating sounds of one small child attacking another with a mace, but Lee knew this sound well. It usually amounted to one child not relinquishing something deemed a dire necessity by another. Emily and her husband, Matt, lived in a mere crossroads of a town called Cedar Mills where the bars outnumbered the churches three to two, but more folks patronized the latter. Lee made a mental note to take pink eggs.

The phone still in her hand, Lee went directly to her contact list, found Lisa's number, and hit Send. While waiting for an answer, it flashed through her mind that she had never discussed in detail the conversation that took place while she was on the swing. Surely after five rings the voice mail would pick up, but before Lee heard a recording, she heard a female voice full of sleep answer. "Okay, who died? And if no one died, this had better be good, or you'll wish it was you. This is LA, you know."

"Sorry, Lise. I know it's early, but this is kind of important."

Recognizing her sister's voice, Lisa was quick to lighten. "Ah, and good morning to you too, Your Eggcellency. Did one of your flock finally lay a square one?"

"Geez, are you always 'on'?" Lee laughed.

"You call this 'on'? Let me get some coffee going, and I'll show you 'on'. What's up, sis? You okay? Kids okay? And what the hell time is it?"

"Answering in reverse order here. Kids are good. I'm fine. It's eight thirty my time. And I just need some information, as soon as you get coffee, of course."

"Of course. Let the caffeine get me firing on all synapses, and I'll give you any and all information I can retrieve. Holy crap!"

"What's wrong?"

"It's six thirty!"

"I know. I'm sorry," Lee apologized and stifled her amusement.

"This had better be good. My hair doesn't get up until ten. I'll have to drape the mirrors to prevent breakage."

"I'm hoping it is good." Though laughing at her sister's remarks, Lee got right to the point. "Do you still have your mom's papers about the Bad Day?"

"Somewhere, I'm sure. What's up? Oh dear God! That's right. Today is the day, isn't it!"

"Yes, it is. But it's okay."

"Really? Cool. Or I think it should be. Anyway, I've got to ask the obvious question here. Why is it okay now?" Before Lee could answer, "Damn, Lee, you were one spooky kid for too many years for this to suddenly be okay. Not that I'm not happy for you, of course."

"Of course. And I guess I was a little spooky. Sorry."

"A little? No need to apologize, but you were a major spook on this day when you were a kid. Not that you had any control over it, but you had all the pros stumped."

"I did? Geez, I don't remember all of that. It was just sad, and too many people asked too many stupid questions."

"Hold on, let me pour the water in the coffeemaker, and I will embellish."

Lee could hear water running, and then her sister was back. "On that day—this day—you would change. I'll do my best to describe what I remember."

The first time it was apparent that anything seemed amiss was when Lisa's mom told little Lee the grim news of that August day. Lee's reactions were not those of a six-year-old child. Instead, what she exhibited was a perceived unnatural control. She was calm, settled, not closed off, but she refused to demonstrate what the experts deemed a natural reaction to trauma. She wasn't hysterical or prone to teary displays of grief. She was accepting of the events and would engage in discussions of the reality, but never to the satisfaction of certain adults. Aunt Jan acknowledged this oddity, but it never raised any red flags of concern. What did stand out were Lee's unusual abilities on the Bad Day.

On the first anniversary of the tragedy, while Lee played in the yard with Lisa, a neighbor came to the house in a genuine gesture of concern and asked how the family was doing. A gift plate of cookies prompted the brewing of a pot of coffee, and conversation ensued. Aunt Jan thanked her for her kindness and mentioned that all was well considering the lingering consequences. Every attempt had been made to follow up on the disappearance of Lee's brother, but the burdens of work, the death of Officer Gale, new family responsibilities, and very little evidence to follow up on made progress in the case come to all but a grinding halt. The case remained open, but life went on without any substantive gains.

When Lee and Lisa entered the kitchen, the conversation stopped. "Lee smelled those cookies," Lisa announced, rather surprised to see a plate of cookies on the table.

"That's quite a sniffer you have there, young lady," the neighbor added.

"Thank you," Lee replied, reaching for a cookie. "Oatmeal is my favorite, especially with cinnamon and extra vanilla."

"Why, you are right. This is my special recipe." The neighbor and Aunt Jan exchanged looks of wonder.

Finishing half her cookie, Lee spoke up again, her gaze meeting both women equally. "Don't worry about Jase. He's fine, and he'll be back." The women were speechless. "I heard you worrying, but don't. It will be fine."

"Well. I'm glad you're positive about it," said the neighbor, now wide-eyed as she stood, leaving her coffee half-full. Aunt Jan stood also and thanked her again as the kindly neighbor nearly knocked over a chair exiting the kitchen by way of the back door.

"Wow, she was in a hurry, but glad she left the cookies," Lisa said, a cookie in each hand.

Coming back to the table, Aunt Jan directed a question to Lee. "Could you really hear us talking from all the way out there in the yard?"

Before Lee could answer, Lisa answered for her. "Yeah, I couldn't, but she could. And you wouldn't believe how far she can see, Mom. Layton's black Lab was walking the tree line across the back field, and she could read his collar tag while we were on the swings!" It was nearly a mile to the said tree line.

On the phone, Lisa took a breath and prodded Lee's memory. "Do you remember that day? I think that neighbor was Mrs. Castle, and I know for a fact she never brought us any more cookies. You scared the crap out of that poor woman!"

"I didn't mean to, and I do vaguely recall that day, but nothing that happened that day stuck out as unusual to me."

"That was what made it so weird. The day before and the day after, you were your normal goofy self, but on the Bad Day, you were someone else, but still you. Like an older version of you. You had a way of looking at things that they said was beyond your years."

"Who is 'they'?"

"The shrinks or—excusez moi—the child psychologists Mom had to drag you to. I think you ticked them off." Lisa laughed.

"Oh yeah. Geez, I remember that, parts of it anyway. They asked some of the dumbest questions, and as I'm remembering it now, they did get upset when I didn't give them what they wanted. One guy, some little skinny balding man, asked me if being jealous would ever make me do anything violent to my baby brother. I have no clue where this came from, but I told him to ask his sister Beverly if she liked having her hair pulled. He got right up, marched me out to the waiting area, and told your mom I had serious problems and should be on medication or perhaps institutionalized."

"And he wasn't the only one. Mom's only concern was the hyperaesthesia," Lisa continued.

"The hyper what?"

"Hyperaesthesia. Your heightened senses. It only ever happened on that day, but that's why I say you were spooky. You were suddenly able to see, hear, smell, and sense things that those around you couldn't. I actually thought it was kinda cool. Mom just wanted to rule out anything physically wrong. You know, like a brain tumor or something. Anyway, after the physical tests revealed nothing but health and the psychos wanted you drugged all year for a single day's worth of difficulty, Mom figured you were fine and told the docs to pound sand. She said everyone was entitled to a bad day every now and then, and yours wasn't without reason."

"Thank God for your mom and her common sense."

"Yeah, I miss her too. Do you have it now?"

"Have what now? The hyperwhatever? I'm not sure. Frankly, I never realized I had it before."

"Well, if you've got it, today is the day. Look around. Anything seem odd?"

"Not that I'm sensing physically. I guess the only odd thing is that I'm happy."

"Hmm. Come to think of it, that would be odd. Like I said, you were a more grown-up version of you, very serious and to the point. And I wouldn't say you were ever unhappy, but you were, more or less, devoid of any emotional expression." Lisa poured a second cup of coffee and continued. "Yep, I'd say being happy is a difference. One I wouldn't question either, just enjoy."

"Thanks, Lise. I plan on doing just that. But there is one more thing."

Without missing a beat, Lisa replied, "Oh God, you're not pregnant, are you? Tell me you're not!"

Lee couldn't answer until her laughter subsided. "You nut! I'm not that weird."

"What can I say? One word for you: Octomom. We've even updated Murphy's law out here. If it can happen, it will in California."

"I won't argue with that." Lee chuckled. "Meanwhile, back on Planet Earth, do you still have any of the paperwork your mom kept concerning that day?"

"I'm way ahead of you. Just dragged out the file from the back of the bottom drawer. Let me blow the dust off and see what's here."

After confirming the existence of a birth certificate, police report, a handwritten book of notes, and several letters of response from various government agencies, Lisa found a short note and receipt from the *Independence Review* concerning a submitted photograph they obtained from Lee's parents.

"Shoot. I guess the photo was never returned, but they probably didn't know to whom it should be returned after your parents died," Lisa added regrettably.

"Maybe they still have it. It would be nice to have since it was possibly the only photograph that survived the fire."

"Could be. I'll get this stuff in a padded envelope and mail it to you today."

"Thanks, Sister Lise. "

"You make me sound like a nun! What are you trying to do? Get me thrown out of the state or just ruin my hard-earned scarlet reputation?"

Lee was laughing again. "My god, it's good to talk to you. I haven't laughed this much in ages."

"My pleasure. I miss you too, Lee. I'll try to make it out for Christmas this year, weather permitting."

"Fantastic. I'll have the wine chilling."

"One more thing. For what it's worth, I do know that your brother was never officially declared dead. So maybe you were right."

"Right about what?"

"That Jase is fine and he'll be back. If I heard you say that once, I heard it a hundred times."

"I'll let you know when I find out. Thanks again. Love you."

"Talk later. Love you too. Bye."

Lee's hopes were high that she could find some information in the archives at the local newspaper office if, in fact, they had archives and they went back that far. Paper files had given way to microfiche and then converted to disc storage. Maybe she would get lucky. In the meantime, she phoned Emily, gave her the short version of her conversation with Lisa, readied herself in short order, grabbed two dozen eggs, and headed for Cedar Mills.

Lee pulled behind the home she helped her son-in-law build and was met by the three oldest of Emily's chicks. These beautiful little girls were instant reminders of all that is truly significant in the world.

"Nana! You brought us eggs, I see. Any pink ones?" queried eight-year-old Pamela.

Lee gathered them all in her arms and breathed in the sweet, earthy fragrance of human kittens. "I'm sure there are a few in there. Some blue ones too. Do you want to carry them in for me?"

"Sure." Pamela handed the second dozen to Lorelei the six-year-old, and they raced toward the back door. Lee looked down at the remaining child, Joy, who placed her tiny hand in Lee's and pulled her toward the door. Lee was met at the door by Emily balancing the next to the youngest of her brood on her hip.

"Come on in, Mom. I put coffee on, and you're not leaving until I know everything."

Lee hugged the standing pair and kissed baby Matthew on his downy head. "Well, hello to you too." Lee laughed as she made her way through the laundry room to the kitchen. Seating herself at the bar, she never tired of admiring the cabinetry of solid walnut with book-matched makore veneer and ebony inlay trim—a hallmark showcasing her son-in-law's talents.

"Okay. You know most everything I know, but I am going to tell you something I've never told anyone else about, and much of it is still a mystery to me." Lee hesitated. "I'm not sure if this is a beginning or an end, but I definitely need to find out where I am between the two."

"Spill it," Emily said in a matter-of-fact tone.

Her mother had her full attention as Lee described the scene recalled from the night before. She detailed the apparent mental telepathy the stranger employed and relayed the visual to the best of her recollection. "When I was six, I had no idea what telepathy was or that it wasn't something normal. I just knew, even then, that it would be a source of questions, and it would be wise to avoid discussing it." That much was true. "And Aunt Lisa reminded me of something I told nearly everyone who broached the subject of your uncle's disappearance."

"Which was?"

"That he would be fine and he would come back."

"Maybe that's what this is all about. Some sort of intuition that he's alive."

"That's definitely part of it, but there's more, and just what more, I have no clue. I'm going to the *Review* office and see if they have any information that I don't. They may even have the photograph given to the police for identification when Jase went missing."

"You want me go with you? For moral support, maybe?"

"Sure, if you don't mind. You can be the Abbott to my Costello." Lee laughed.

"You're dating yourself, Ma. What time and where?"

"Market ends at two o'clock. Meet me there at half past, and that will give me time to pack up."

"Sounds like a plan." Emily hugged her mother as she unseated herself to leave. "I'm so glad this seems to be ending for you."

"For us. And I hope you're right."

"About what?"

"That it's ending."

"No worries, Mom. See you tomorrow."

Lee saw herself out, and the short drive home was a blur as her mind was swirling with questions. Reality came into sharp focus as she entered the farm lane and was greeted by Semi perched atop a rock-retaining wall like a sentry. As if transported by Scotty, he greeted Lee when she opened the door to the truck. "You need to teach me that transporter trick, Mr. Kitty. Ready for chores?"

They spent the remainder of the day seeing to all that needed doing, including packing the truck for market. By five o'clock, Lee was all in and ready for a light meal and a celebratory glass of wine. She opened a bottle of Running with Scissors Petite Sirah and threw together a salad harvested from the garden. Semi's bowl was filled with his evening ration, and they dined together. It was a good day after all, and she smiled as she made a toast.

"Here's to all the small things that make life big." Semi looked up from his dish. "And to cats who smile back!"

Pulitzer Dreamer

BRETT HUME HAD LEFT EARLY from home, not so much to get a jump on work, but to get to the farmer's market while the selection was at its best. To the best of his judgment, he procured everything requested and a few things that weren't on the list that just looked good to him, including two dozen multicolored eggs. If it hadn't been for the throng of customers at that particular table, he would have been inclined to strike up a casual conversation with the attractive lady selling the eggs. He did, however, note that an address and phone number were included on the carton label. Perhaps that avenue would offer a more suitable opportunity for a proper introduction to this petite redhead with an inviting smile and hands unadorned by symbols of attachment.

The newspaper office was only a half a block away from the park and was located in a storefront building that had once been a ladies millinery shop, among other things, and Brett had another twenty minutes before they were open to the public. He took this opportunity to stow his market bounty in the office refrigerator and then do a reverse search on the telephone number on the egg carton. The search revealed a match to the listed address on the carton, and he was hoping the name Lee was attached to the lady in the park rather than some nonadvertised male.

Then the phone rang. "*Independence Review*. Brett Hume speaking. How may I help you?" The day had begun.

The Review

EATHER WAS PERFECT FOR A brisk market. Lee's eggs vanished instantly, and she made a note to plant more fingerling potatoes in next year's garden. By half past one, the crowds in the town park had thinned, and it was bargain time. Lee had learned that the sorts of customers who shopped in the late-day market fell into rather distinct groups. It was easy to spot the resell brokers who tried to buy for pennies on the dollar anything a vendor didn't care to take back home and sell it for a considerable markup in the Cities the following day. More to her favor were the bargain-shopping elderly and young mothers stretching a weekly budget to cover a month. She let them know what a favor they bestowed by saving Lee the labor of transporting unsold goods back home.

As Lee stacked the last empty box and folded her table, Emily arrived right on time.

"Ready, Freddy?" Emily asked after rolling down the driver's window on her minivan, a.k.a. kid-transport vehicle.

"Let me lock up, and I'll be right there." Lee hopped in the front passenger seat of the van—the only one not occupied by a child-safety seat—and buckled up. "Who has the kiddos?" Lee asked, noticing the quiet.

"I twisted Matt's arm," Emily joked. "Actually, he was working on estimates and project layouts in the office, and I put in movie for the tribe, and the two little ones are napping. They'll be fine with their dad till I get back."

"You're a lucky woman, Em."

"This I know, Mom," she said with a smile. "The *Review* office is only a couple blocks away," she continued. "I googled it last night, but the online archives only go back eleven years, and they don't list a publication inception date on a proper masthead, so I hope there's a human being at this office who can help."

"Me too."

The pair took off, making two left turns to put them on the main drag, and half a block later, Emily pulled into a parking spot directly in front of their destination. "Lucy, I'm home," Emily said in her best Desi Arnaz voice as she put the van in Park.

"Geez," Lee remarked, gathering her purse and unbuckling her seat belt.

"What?" Em responded.

"You just reminded me of that creepy phone call I got the other morning."

"It wasn't that creepy, Mom. Unless of course it sounded like Desi!"

⁘⸰⸰Ⓜ⸰⸰⁘

The day was a short one, and as Brett readied to make his last call of the day before returning home, a buzzer sounded, indicating someone entering from the street entrance. Assuming his Friday dual role as receptionist, he entered the small lobby and greeted a pair of women, one he recognized instantly.

"Hello," he said, extending his hand in a professional greeting that Lee accepted automatically. "Brett Hume. How may I help you ladies?"

"Hi, I'm Lee Winslow. I'm hoping you can help me locate some information."

"I'll do my best." Bingo! She wasn't a he Lee.

"Your online archives don't go back far enough for what we need," Emily spoke up. "Do you have an accessible source for previous editions?"

"What date were you looking for?" Brett answered, still focusing his attention on Lee.

"The year would be 1961, the week of August the eleventh, to be precise," Lee answered, hoping this wasn't a dead end.

"Wow. More than a few years ago." Brett went immediately to a sizeable wooden cabinet filled with large bound copies of the paper, each occupying a shelf with the years in a brass tab identifying them. "This only goes back to two thousand. Let's check in the back storage area."

Lee and Emily followed Brett through a swinging wooden gate, past the reception area and an office space of desks topped with computers and phones. Lee surveyed the room and noticed the high-pressed metal ceiling and heavy ornate crown moldings that had been painted office white. As they neared the back of the room, an archway opened in to a short hallway with doors at either end. The door to the right opened into a large well-lit room with high windows. The walls were lined with shelves and filing cabinets full of print and photographic documentation, encapsulating the lives and times of the local residents for the past hundred years or so.

"You said 1961, right?" Brett confirmed.

"Yes. Thank you."

In the center of the room was a vacant oak table with two chairs. While Brett searched the stacks for the desired year, Lee and Emily each pulled out a chair.

"Here we go," Brett announced as he pulled the volume from the pile and brought it to the table.

"Here goes something, I hope," Lee remarked as she carefully opened the large book filled with yellowed pages. Without saying a word and each nearly holding their breath, Lee and Emily turned the pages while hovering above the chairs pulled out, but not sat in. Emily glanced behind her and noticed Brett standing behind them, watching. He did not return her glance, paying more attention to the activity before him, or was it the person standing in front of him that required his notice?

"Ah. Here we go. August 12, 1961. Now let's see if there are any answers," Lee wondered aloud. There was the headline she remembered: "Three Dead in Gas Explosion; Child Still

Missing." The article on the front page was accompanied by a photo of the volunteer fire crew extinguishing the fire, but anything relating to her brother was continued on page 3. Carefully, she turned the page, and there he was. The photograph under the small headline "Missing Child" was cropped from a family picture, as the background of her brother's picture was their mother's lap. "There he is," Lee said in nearly a whisper. "Your uncle Jase." Tears began to well in Lee's eyes, and it was something she hadn't anticipated. Instinctively, Emily wrapped an arm around her mother, drawing her closer while she continued to read the article.

"Someone you knew?" Brett's question broke the silence and the mood. Self-consciously, Lee erased her tears before turning to make a reply. "Yes, my brother," Lee stated, having regained her composure.

"Sorry to hear that," Brett apologized

Lee couldn't believe what came out of her mouth next. "No apologies necessary. He'll be back."

"Really?" Brett asked with a note of surprise.

Upon hearing what she couldn't believe she'd just heard, Emily turned from her finished reading and interrupted. "We don't know that, Mom. But I guess it doesn't hurt to be optimistic." Lee met her daughter's glare and quickly realized her mistake.

"I will always have hope," Lee directed to Brett.

Catching the exchange between mother and daughter, Brett decided to break the tension that so quickly filled the room. "Hope is a good thing."

"And so was your help, Mr. Hume. I'm grateful for your time and assistance," Lee answered formally.

"Please, call me Brett. And thank you for the beautiful eggs this morning."

"I thought you looked familiar. Thanks for your patronage."

Once again, Emily took the lead. "Okay, everyone has been thanked for everything. You ready to go, Mom?"

Not quite understanding her daughter's rush but accepting the opportunity, Lee gathered her purse and followed Emily from the room. Brett escorted them out to the lobby.

"If there's anything else I can help you with," Brett said, leaving the offer open-ended.

Lee turned, and Emily proceeded to the door. "I do have one more question. Does the paper retain submitted photographs?" Not waiting for a reply, she added, "Because I think the photo in the paper was taken from the one submitted to the police."

Brett thought for a second. "Ordinarily, with our current policy, no, we don't. But considering the time frame and the fact that it was a police matter, I'll check it out."

"Thanks," Lee responded as Emily waited impatiently for her mother to exit through the door she held open. "You know where to find me."

Once outside, Emily went into full-protective daughter mode. "Yeah, I bet he'll check it out."

"You're too suspicious."

"And you aren't suspicious enough. I saw what he was checking out, and it wasn't anything to do with what was in the paper," Em stated with authority. Lee tried to ignore the inference, but her daughter continued. "Mom, we were in a newspaper office, and you trust too easily."

"Yes, but what does being in a newspaper office have to do with me trusting?"

"Good grief, I'm amazed I didn't end up walking the streets on Hennipen Avenue in the Cities!"

"It was named after a Jesuit priest, you know," Lee added, trying to derail Emily's lecture.

"No digressing. Newspaper people are the nosiest people on earth, and you don't need any more complications in your life."

"My life, complicated?"

They were both laughing as they got in to the van.

Before the doors were closed on the departing van in front of the office, Brett began to pore over the article that had garnered so much interest from his last two visitors. Maybe there was more to today's events than just a serendipitous meeting between a single man and the single lady who caught his eye. There could be a story here. Perhaps it wasn't on the scale of a new world order, but it had enough mystery and a human interest angle to make it intriguing. And if he also got the girl, that was a bonus. "Cold Case" and "The Locator" episodes featuring his story were tossed around in his brain for a moment. For the first time in forever, he was excited about an unknown. Unknowns weren't always good, but at least this one was all his.

Brett jotted down as many particulars as he thought were necessary and decided he could research this on his laptop at home. He bagged his market purchases to take home, made sure the doors were locked and the alarm system was set, and headed for home and to the lady in his life: Barbara.

Graceful Fall

IT HAD BEEN TWO WEEKS since Lee's visit to the local paper office and a week since a large manila envelope arrived in the mail from Lisa. Several evenings Emily had come to visit and sift through all the documentation of the events of 1961, hoping to discover something that would bring closure to the whole business. As far as Lee was concerned, until she knew what happened to her brother, closure wasn't possible. Still, something told her that the mystery, in some form or fashion, would be solved. For that reason only, she was willing to forego impatience and wait for what she felt was inevitable.

Emily, protective pit bull that she was, knew that the newspaper dude had become a regular customer at the farmer's market, and it had nothing to do with an appetite for free-range eggs. She didn't trust this man and wasn't going to be shy about it. Lee thought nothing suspicious of his continued visits to the market, and often, in the middle of Emily's misgivings, Lee could clearly hear Julie Andrews crooning "Don't go in the cage tonight, Mother darling." After all, Brett had been to the market *before* Lee had ventured into his place of business. Maybe he should be the one to be suspicious. None of this justification swayed Em. She knew all things round and brown weren't always chocolate truffles, and this guy didn't pass the sniff test.

The first week of September signaled the end of the market and subtle hints of the winter to come. Hay was stockpiled, feed stores were being replenished, stock tank heaters and heat lamps were brought from storage and checked. Manure had been spread on the garden plot, and the small planting of pumpkins and gourds was ripening along the turn row. Lee's life had taken on the rhythm of a steady heartbeat while the rest of the world seemed to be constantly on the verge of cardiac arrest. The daily barrage of news alerts and breaking stories were often negative, but Lee waded through the media muck to stay minimally informed about situations possibly affecting her son. Even though Nick was on the other side of the world in a place known only to Lee from the photographs he brought back between tours, Lee didn't hesitate to put her baby's safety in hands far more capable than her own. She looked forward to November because Nick would be home and in her arms again.

As September turned to October, the soybeans and corn planted in her rented fields were ready for harvest, and Lee looked forward to one of her favorite times of the year to engage Emily's brood. It was her privilege and honor to plan, design, and construct Halloween costumes for her grandchildren. The youngest two wouldn't object to hand-me-downs from previous years, but the oldest three had definite opinions. For the entire month, the kitchen and spare bedroom were piled high with materials and accessories meant to turn imagination and fantasy into reality. Semi, suspicious of a pile of fake fur near his rocker in the kitchen, temporarily puffed and gave the invader a wide birth as he made his way to his food dish.

Halloween fell on a Monday, so the parties and parades were all scheduled for the weekend prior to the official day. Lee prepared for Emily and the gang to arrive for their final fittings on Thursday evening. Two pumpkins sat on the bench outside the kitchen door, waiting to be turned into jack-o'-lanterns, and Lee wanted them both carved and lit when everyone got there. The costumes were finished and hung in the spare bedroom awaiting approval; candied apples and bat-shaped sugar cookies were piled on huge plates, and a bottle of Rex Goliath Giant 47 Pound Rooster Pinot Noir was chilling for the aftermath.

At shortly before three o'clock that afternoon, Lee grabbed the larger of the two pumpkins and made quick work of turning it into a smiling simpleton. As she set the finished pumpkin on the edge of the deck, she turned to go back to the kitchen with the smaller gourd. Out of the corner of her eye, she caught movement. She turned, fully expecting to see Semi or Bomber, but instead, about fifty feet away, walking up the driveway toward her was a man. She was used to having new customers arrive unannounced to buy eggs, so she tempered her initial surprise with a greeting.

"Oh, I'm sorry. I didn't see you at first. Here for eggs?" Anticipating his response, she added, "I'll be right with you." Entering the kitchen entryway, she set the pumpkin on the floor and reached up to lower a set of attic steps above the landing. She lowered them just enough to expose the hiding place she used to safely stow her Ruger Mini-14. The clip was installed, and she relaxed immediately. Ordinarily, it was used strictly to dispatch coyotes that threatened her animals, but as she lived alone, it served as personal defense if necessary. She stepped back outside, and before letting the storm door close completely, she yelled back into the empty house, "I'll be right back in. I have a customer." Satisfied that she had set the stage in her favor, she turned to face the man now standing only eight feet away at the edge of the deck.

"Hi. Are you Lee?"

"Yes, I am. Do I know you?" If Lee had ever met this individual before, she did not recall the time or place or his name. His hair was very dark, thick and wavy, but cut short. He was about six feet tall, had a slim but sturdy build, and wore jeans and a tan Carhartt jacket. He stood with his hands clasped behind his back. And he was smiling at her.

"Sorry if I startled you," he said, looking down.

"No problem. I was just expecting my daughter to arrive. Is there something I can do to help you?"

Just then, Semi exited the house through his cat door and walked past Lee to inspect the visitor. Semi was very cautious with newcomers, and if anything was amiss, he would let her know. Lee watched in amazement as Semi approached the stranger. Looking up at the man, he stopped only briefly and then began brushing himself against the man's legs, purring loudly.

"Wow. I guess he knows you." Lee laughed.

"All cats like me," the man replied. "And you do know me, or I should say we've met before."

Lee thought for a moment. "From the market?"

"It's been a while," he answered.

As Lee searched her memory, a little embarrassed that she couldn't place him, he brought his hands from behind his back.

"I know you'll remember this." What he held in his hands made an instant connection. Before the "what is that" thought could become words, her second question made its way into the atmosphere between them.

"Where did you get that?" She held out her hand, and the object in question was handed to her without hesitation. Feeling the need to sit down, Lee backed up and lowered herself to the bench beside the door, never taking her eyes from what she held. Again she asked insistently, "Where did you get this?"

"You gave it to me."

His answer prompted no immediate reaction as Lee inspected the small blue-and-white gingham stuffed animal with frayed ears. "This is impossible," Lee whispered.

"Nothing is truly impossible," the man replied, knowing full well the tsunami of thoughts now going through his sister's mind.

She looked up and studied the face before her. Semi sat braced against the man's leg, purring contentedly. Rising to get closer, the man stood motionless and let Lee approach. She stared into his eyes for an answer, and it came.

"Black-eyed—" she began.

"Susan eyes," he said, finishing her reply. "And his name is Duggie."

Lee had so much to say and so many questions to ask, but at this moment, only a single word escaped her being in search of confirmation. "Jase?"

"I'm home," he answered.

Homecoming

"**L**OOK AT NANA'S PUMPKINS ALL lit up, guys!" Emily announced to her captive passengers as they drove up the lane and parked next to Lee's truck. It was a few minutes past six and just dark enough for candlelight to shine brightly. As she helped her small herd disembark, Semi poked his head out the cat door. Rather than being strangled by pulling his head back in, he shot through the door and made a U-turn, escaping the indignity of being treated like a plaything.

The three girls were already in the house as Emily opened the screen door with Mathew holding one hand, a baby carrier in the other cradling her youngest son, and a purse and diaper bag each slung on a shoulder. Lee was always impressed by how her daughter managed to make mothering five children look almost organized. Emily escorted Mathew up the three steps to the entry and heard something amazing: silence. At the doorway to the kitchen, the girls stood motionless, as if an invisible force field stopped their progress.

"What's the holdup, ladies? Move it," Emily urged. As she neared the doorway, it was apparent what immobilized the girls. All three were staring intently at this man sitting at the head of Nana's kitchen table with Semi lying over his left shoulder staring back at them.

Busy at the counter pouring water in the coffeemaker, Lee heard them come in. "Come on in, girls," she directed, noting eyes as big as saucers riveted on Jase. "I've made bat cookies for you," she added, trying to persuade them to step foot into the room. Pam, obviously her mother's child, said aloud what the others were thinking.

Directing it to her grandmother, she asked, "Who's *that*?" while aiming an index finger at the figure seated in the chair.

"I was waiting for you all to come in to make introductions. Girls, Nana got a surprise visitor," Lee answered with a forced smile. The girls cleared the doorway and made their way to the plate of cookies. "Everyone," she began, "this is Nana's cousin, Jase." She then looked directly into her daughter's face and gave her a wink. Emily responded with a look of half wonder and half concern.

"Are you our cousin too?" asked Lorelei.

"I'd like that," Jase answered. He carefully peeled the purring Semi from his shoulder and gently lowered him to the floor. As he did, Joy appeared at his side, offering a cookie. "Thank you," he told the smiling four-year-old. As he received the gift, she immediately sidled up to him, indicating her approval. The older two accepted Joy's judgment, and suddenly Jase was the center of attention.

Emily took this opportunity to request Lee's help in situating Mathew with a basket of toys and releasing a sleeping infant from his carrier. As the girls pelted Jase with questions, Emily had a few of her own to throw at her mother. They knelt in the floor dissecting the octopus of safety straps, and Emily began, "Are you sure? When did he arrive? And where has he been?"

"He came walking up the drive this afternoon. I'll let you know where he's been when I know, and trust me, I've never been more sure of anything in my life. He is my brother."

"Well, that tells me a lot," Em replied, heavy on the sarcasm.

"I can't explain it right now. Just trust me on this, and follow my lead. For reasons of privacy, he's my cousin. Okay? You can know. I just don't want the girls broadcasting it."

"Fine by me, but you still have some 'splainin' to do, Lucy."

Lee laughed at her daughter's tenacity to know all and at the same time was grateful for what she knew was an expression of love; a little twisted, but love all the same. Lee gathered the sleeping baby to her chest, and they both turned their attention to Jase and the girls.

"Good Lord," Em announced, seeing Jase with the two youngest in his lap and Pam draped around his neck like a human scarf.

"Can we keep him?" Pam pleaded, snuggling her face into his neck.

"If you don't chase him away by jumping all over him," Emily half scolded.

Wanting a chance to greet his niece properly, Jase suggested the girls try on their costumes so he could see them. "Yeah! A fashion show!" Pam added with enthusiasm. Lifting the two from his lap, they raced into the spare room where the clothing mayhem could begin. Jase stood and walked around the table to where Emily stood next to her mother. "You have beautiful children."

"Thank you," Emily responded flatly, still not sure what to think of this sudden appearance.

"I'm your mom's brother, and I'm so happy to meet you." Jase extended his hand, and Emily took it, expecting a simple polite handshake. What she experienced was far more. The flood of emotion and the instant knowing cut through Emily's suspicions instantly. What began as a handshake ended as a full-fledged bear hug that imparted unconditional love and one very unmistakable truth. This was family.

"Okay, Lucy, you're off the hook," Emily told her mother. "I understand now," she admitted.

"Thanks, Desi. I knew you would," Lee agreed. The look of awe and contentment on her daughter's face was one Lee had seen five times before when she welcomed each of her children into this world. From the living room, little Mathew walked into the kitchen and wrapped himself around Jase and Emily's legs. Jase kissed his niece on the cheek and knelt down to make Matt's acquaintance.

"Hi, Matt. I'm Jase."

The child put both hands on either side of Jase's face and, smiling, said only one word, "Eyes," and then threw himself around Jase's neck.

"Wow. Now that's new. He's my shy one, and he's never done that before," Emily informed.

Jase stood, scooping up the child, and cradled the three-year-old in both arms. Lee moved closer to the standing pair, a sleeping baby cradled in her arms. "Last but not least, this is the youngest member of the Benson family," Lee began.

Deliberately, Matt pointed to his little brother and then to Jase, repeating his single utterance, "Eyes, eyes!" Grinning from ear to ear, Matt again gave Jase a ferocious hug. As quickly as the bonding procedure began, it ended with Matt declaring, "Okay, I love you. Down." Jase lowered Matt to the floor, and he disappeared into the living room.

"Decisive little character, that one is," Jase remarked, half-laughing.

"You are right about that. He definitely has a mind of his own," Lee agreed. "And this little fellow probably will too. I'd like you to meet Albert Jase Benson," Lee said proudly, handing the still sleeping infant to Jase.

Lee and Emily both smiled broadly, watching Jase admire his tiny namesake. At that moment, an angel smile appeared on the baby's face, and he opened his eyes. Staring back at Jase was another set of black-eyed Susan eyes.

The evening progressed in a normal chaotic fashion with costume hems being adjusted, the customary issuance of tears drawn by childish insult and quelled by forced parental apology, a short-lived barrage of flying bat cookies, and slight drama when Lorelei got a candied apple stuck in her hair. When the frustration was complete, popcorn was popped, and the children were settled in the living room for some Halloween cartoon fare, and the adults opened the wine and the photograph albums. Jase was enjoying it all and wished it could be like this forever, but he knew it would remain a wish. A storm was brewing.

Brett Hume missed his Friday market visits, and Barbara missed the free-range eggs.

"The address is on the label, right?" Barbara asked, hoping Brett would be willing to go out of his way for this particular item.

"Yes, it is. And for you, my dear, nothing is too much to ask."

Barbara laughed at his exaggerated gallantry and added, "You do spoil me, big brother."

His sister's expression of delight with his humor was something he never tired of. It was the natural order of things for these siblings to share lives closer than most. Eight years older than Barbara, she was only fifteen when her big brother, Brett, married Rosemary, a Cities girl, and returned home to put his degree in communications to work at the local newspaper. For the first two years, life was good for all the members of the Hume clan, then as often happens in life, circumstances arose that required change. Failing health, both mental and physical, forced his mother to hospitalize Brett's father. Caring for both her husband and Barbara proved to be an undue strain, so Brett accepted the responsibility of caring for his sister. This new situation did not sit well with Brett's new wife, and the marriage ended a year later. As far as Brett was concerned, it was for the best. Assuming the role of patriarch in the family due to his father's deteriorating health, Brett didn't want to stand in the way of Rosemary's pursuit of happiness, nor did he want to abandon his duties to his mother and sister. He accepted, with no regrets, what life had given him and what it took away. It was a lesson he'd learned from Barbara.

"You don't fool me a bit, Brett Hume. Those are good eggs, but I don't think eggs alone are responsible for this new joie de vivre you're sporting."

"I have no idea what you're talking about," Brett responded, smiling broadly.

"If I didn't know better, I'd think you liked the egg lady as much as the eggs."

"Well, you do know better, but if anything changes, I'll let you know."

"Touché, bro, but you know I can see right through you."

They both laughed at this absurdity. Brett often wished his sister could see herself through his eyes. He had difficulty deciding where more her beauty resided, inside or out. Slightly over five and a half feet tall, she had long wavy hair, the color of bitter chocolate, that framed the face of an angel. Fawn-set eyes, closer to amber than brown, had an intensity that could see into the soul.

"I'll have you know I've been doing some research for Ms. Winslow, so I guess your assessment is valid."

"Research? Really? About what, may I ask?"

Brett's tone got more serious as he described Lee's ordeal as a child. "I've asked Will Koch, the detective I know, to check things out for me, and this morning he gave me a call. When I go get your eggs, I'll let her know what I've found."

"How sad, to suffer such a loss as a child. Makes you wonder where the lesson is in that."

"Your guess is as good as mine, but believe it or not, the case is still open, and I think Lee still has hope her brother may yet be found."

"Not hope," Barbara interrupted.

"Why not hope? If the case is still open, I don't think that's too unreasonable."

"Faith. She has faith. It takes more than hope to hang on this long, don't you think?"

"I guess so, Barb, but faith is more your gig than mine."

"I have faith in you, big brother, even when you act like a donkey's hind end," Barbara replied, giggling.

"Isn't that being redundant?"

"Go get me some eggs," she said, ignoring his bait. "I love you."

"Love you too. I'll be back a little after noon. Any later, I'll give you a call."

"Thanks. And you do know we're getting our first snow—"

"Do not speak its name," Brett stopped her, holding a finger in the air. "It only encourages it. And yes, I'll be careful driving."

Mid-November brought the first snowflakes to the barnyard, covering the frozen ground in a thin white sheet. It was nothing worth firing up the tractor to clear, but it did manage to make intersections interesting for every teenager with a new driver's license. And from past experience, Lee knew it was possible she wouldn't see bare ground again until the following March. But this year, things would be different. Instead of looking ahead to a slow succession of days illuminated by soft gray light on a landscape asleep under a blanket of ice, she saw a dream coming true. Nick would be home on leave shortly before Thanksgiving, and Lisa, as promised, would arrive the day after Christmas. It would be a family holiday gathering unprecedented in her lifetime.

From the pair of north-facing kitchen windows, Lee watched Jase cross from the chicken house to the barn, Bomber trotting along as his escort as he completed morning chores. When he emerged again from the barn, Lee started the coffee and returned to the window to watch him stride slowly toward the house. After a little more than three weeks of patient silence, Lee decided today would be a good day to point out the eight-hundred-pound gorilla sitting in the room.

Jase entered the kitchen walkway and removed his coat and boots, and Lee asked, "How many eggs?"

"Oh. I forgot to get them. Where's the basket?"

Lee laughed and stopped his thought. "No, no. I meant how many eggs would you like for breakfast? I'll go roust the girls later."

"Oh, okay. Three, thank you." Jase pulled a chair out and sat at the table. As Lee cracked eggs into the pan, Jase unlocked the door to conversation he knew Lee wanted to open. "I know you have questions for me, Lee."

"Perceptive, aren't you, or did you just read my mind?" Lee remarked as she placed a plate of eggs and toast in front of Jase.

"I did forget to pick up the eggs," he reminded her.

"Well, that just assures me you're human. I think," she chided.

"Rest assured. I'm human." Jase laughed. "Now, go ahead and ask me what you want to know."

"Everything. I want to know everything. Not that it makes any difference, but where did you go, and where have you been all this time?"

"I've been somewhere safe, and as promised, it was time for me to come home."

Lee stared at him, now more confused. "I'm a little fuzzy on the whole 'somewhere safe' thing. Could you be a bit more specific?"

"If I gave you a specific place, do you think it would it change the fact that I'm here?"

Lee thought for a moment. "I guess not, but it might explain why you were taken."

"Those are both relevant questions, but the answers aren't mine to give, not right now anyway. Remember, I wasn't even two years old when this happened. Hardly in charge of my own destiny at that point. But I'm here now, and for as long as I can, I'll be with you." Jase could see by the look on his sister's face that his answers fell short of what she wanted to know. "I'm not trying to be evasive, but when the time is right, you will understand."

"Okay." Lee stared at her plate, wishing her frustration would wane. "I'll accept what I have to accept. And you're right. I don't really care what the circumstances were, and knowing more isn't going to change what's truly important to me. You are here now. But—and this is a big but—I've gone over every scenario my imagination can conjure up, and nothing fits. If you can't tell me what happened, you can do me one favor."

"I'll give it my best shot."

"Tell me you weren't abducted by aliens, or kidnapped by some illegal baby theft ring, or used as some CIA experimental group, or raised as a sex slave in some deviant's cellar bunker, or—"

Jase was laughing.

"It isn't funny. Believe it or not, since you got here, all of these thoughts crossed my mind."

"I'm sorry. I'm not laughing at you. And no, none of those things happened to me."

Somewhat relieved but still curious, Lee responded, "Good to know. I just hope Emily buys the whole somewhere safe thing." They both started laughing at that prospect, and then it was cut short by a knock at the kitchen door.

Lee got up from her chair. "I'll get it. Probably an egg customer. Eat your eggs before they get rubbery."

Lee went to answer the door, and Jase could hear Lee greet someone she obviously knew.

"Oh. Hi," Lee managed to say as the door was pulled open from the outside.

"Good morning, Ms. Winslow. I've come to buy some eggs, if you have them, and bring you up to speed on what my research has produced," Brett announced, fully expecting to be invited inside to get out of the snow.

"Good morning, Mr. Hume, isn't it?" Lee was trying to think of every reason not to be hospitable without causing suspicion. "Sure, I have eggs, how many would you like?"

"A couple dozen should do it." Before Lee could disappear to get the eggs, Brett added, "Mind if I come in? I do have some news to share."

To avoid awkwardness, she responded automatically, "Sure, come on in. Care for some coffee?" She made her way into the kitchen quickly and put a finger to her lips as soon as she caught

Jase's attention. Semi, sleeping on his favorite rocker, suddenly came to life and stood in the doorway to the kitchen, putting himself between Lee and this possible invader. Jase turned to see a man removing his cap and brushing the snow from his shoes on the rug placed at the inner door. He stood from the table to see what the shushing had been about.

"Oh, I'm sorry. I didn't realize you had company. Please sit. I don't want to interrupt your breakfast." Brett was clearly surprised to see a man in Lee's kitchen, especially one that seemed so at home.

As Lee was pouring a cup of coffee, she made the introductions. "Brett, this is my cousin, Fred." Turning to "Fred" and trying not to roll her eyes, she said, "Fred, this is Brett Hume, loyal customer and reporter for our local paper, the *Independence Review*."

The two men shook hands, and Semi returned to his rocker, satisfied that the intruder was no threat. Lee pulled out a chair for Brett to sit and placed his coffee on the table. "How do you take it?" Lee asked.

"Oh, black is fine, thanks." A brief moment of silence ensued until Lee placed two dozen eggs on the table near Brett. "Thanks. How much do I owe you?"

"Three should do it, thanks," Lee replied, settling herself into her chair. Turning her attention to Jase, Lee described how Brett had helped her find the story that was originally published in the paper about the accident at her parent's home. She also explained that Brett had offered to see what he could uncover about the disappearance of her brother.

Jase turned to Brett and said, "That was kind of you, Brett."

"It was nothing, really. Just doing what I can to help." Brett couldn't quite put his finger on it, but something about this situation wasn't quite what it appeared to be. His spidy senses were tingling. "Not that I know Lee as any more than a business acquaintance, but I didn't know she had extended family other than her daughter in the area. You live locally?"

"I've just relocated from back east. Brought my truck west to work in the Dakotas," Jase fabricated.

Lee was impressed. There was a need for trucks working both the opening oil concerns and the booming reservation construction.

"Interesting," Brett lied back. "I didn't see your truck when I pulled in the yard. You drive a belly dump?"

"No, a quad Pete, converted it myself. Left it up north to have some work done. Things are slowin' down now, and I figured I'd come visit Lee."

In Lee's mind she heard the referee, "Point! Score 1–Love."

"Nice that you have relatives in this area. Considering moving here?" Brett persisted.

"I'll see how the work holds," Jase answered, hoping his ambiguity would put an end to the inquisition.

"You said you had some news to share," Lee jumped in.

Brett hesitated, reconsidering what he would share based on this new player in the game. Nonchalantly, his left hand felt for the folded envelope in his back pocket. At that moment, he decided he'd keep his ace up his sleeve. "Just wanted to let you know I have a friend of mine, a detective, checking the case files for me. He'll let me know what he finds," Brett lied.

"That's great," Lee said, trying to sound like it was. "I just don't want anyone going to too much trouble." Brett gave her a weak smile that immediately turned her stomach. At the same time, Semi raised his head and locked both eyes on Brett.

"No trouble. None at all," he assured her. "Not for me anyway."

Without another word, Brett stood, placed three one dollar bills on the table, picked up his eggs and his cap, and headed for the door. On his way out, he bid them an insincere good-bye. "Nice to have met you, Fred."

"Same here," Jase replied. At the same time he heard the outside door close with a heavy hand.

The pair seated at the table stared at one another and listened to the rumble of an engine start. As the sound faded into the distance, Jase began laughing.

"*Fred?* I'm Cousin Fred?" Jase said, still highly amused.

"He made me nervous, and it was the first thing that popped out of my mouth." Lee was still nervous. "I'm just glad he's gone."

"Don't worry about him. He's harmless," Brett tried to assure her.

"He's a reporter, for cryin' out loud. That makes him the worst kind of busybody with attitude there is. Today's so-called journalists think they have a right to be nosy and invade people's privacy." Lee could hear Emily's words in her head.

"He may be curious, but he's something else that you've overlooked." Jase was grinning and shaking his head.

"And what would that be?" Lee asked openly.

"He's a man."

"Oh, for heaven sakes, now you sound like Em." Lee had to admit, a personal interest was not something she had considered. Right now, the only thing that concerned her was Brett's interest in Jase, not her. "He may be putting things together more than we think, and that's not good."

"Relax, Lee. I've got this covered. Trust me."

"Fred. Yeah, right. Fred my butt," Brett muttered as Lee's farm disappeared from his rearview mirror. He had no clue who this interloper was, but he was going to find out. The man did bear a slight family resemblance, but Brett wasn't convinced. If this guy wasn't good ol' Cousin Fred, exactly who was he, and why did he get the impression that Lee wanted to hide his identity? *And now, I'm not supposed to go to any trouble? Guess Barb was wrong about the whole faith thing.* Whoever he was, he was either competition or a relative with something to hide, and right now, Brett was betting on competition. Coming to the first intersection where he would turn right to head back home, he applied his brakes and heard the grind of the antilock system kick in. The snow was only a couple inches deep, but it was just enough to cause problems if a driver was distracted. And this situation had Brett distracted.

After fifteen minutes of careful driving, Brett pulled into the driveway of the modest bungalow on Kouba Avenue. He pressed the garage door remote and pulled into the single space. With two dozen eggs under his arm, he entered the house through the laundry room entry and closed the outer garage door with the push of a button. Music was playing as he entered the kitchen, but in his present state of agitation, it was beyond him to appreciate the lovely strains. Barbara was seated at the kitchen table enjoying both her tea and the music when she heard, "It's me" coming from the laundry room entrance.

"That didn't take long," she said, hoping for a positive response.

"Got your eggs, and I'll be busy with some work for a while. What time is rehearsal today?" Brett asked absently.

"It's Saturday, Brett. And who pooped in your sandbox?"

Her question snapped him out of his mini funk. "Your radar is working well today." He chuckled. "Sorry. I'd blame my crabbiness on the weather, but it isn't that."

"Well, whatever it is made you forget today is Saturday, and Monday is a recording session," she mentioned, attempting to draw him into her world.

"Oh yeah, and how's that going?" he asked, happy for the topic change.

"Great. You should come to a concert sometime. You could bring the egg lady."

Brett did his best not to think about what he just heard. After all, Barbara had no way of knowing what had transpired less than an hour ago. "That's a thought," he agreed and continued, "And what piece are you working on now?"

"Tchaikovsky's *Nutcracker Suite*, my favorite for obvious reasons." Barbara was a keyboardist with the Minneapolis Metropolitan Orchestra. She began playing piano as a child, to this day played the piano and organ at church, and was introduced to the celesta when she became a member of the orchestra. It was a rare treat to step into the shoes of a percussionist, but it was the sound that captured her heart. To Barbara, it was as its name suggested a heavenly tone. "And then we have a section of Beethoven's works we're recording, regular Friday night performances, and an assortment of holiday concerts, so it will be a busy season."

"Sounds very busy," Brett agreed.

"Thanks for the eggs, Brett."

"Don't mention it. I put them in the fridge, right-hand side, second shelf from the bottom."

"Okay. Enough is enough. What's up?" Ordinarily Barbara wouldn't press on insignificant matters, but this heaviness was palpable.

"Probably nothing. It's a little complicated."

"The uprisings in the Middle East are complicated. Is it worse than that?"

"Of course not." Leave it to Barbara to put things in perspective and bring his concerns to a sharable level.

"Then give," Barbara instructed.

"When I went to get the eggs, there was a guy there."

"I knew it!"

"Just hold on there, Bat Girl. Don't get too impressed with yourself. She introduced this guy as her cousin, Fred."

"So she has a cousin. What's wrong with that?"

"Nothing, if that's who he really is." Brett recounted the entire visit and admitted he'd withheld the photograph Will Koch had given to him.

"Now why would you do that?" Barbara asked.

61

"To tell you the truth, I'm not sure why. I just have this feeling something isn't right."

"You really do like this Lee, don't you?" Brett didn't say a word. "Give me the car keys," Barbara demanded. "I'll drive right over there and straighten this out!"

Brett burst into hysterical laughter. "You crack me up, Barb!" Brett was visualizing his sister driving to Lee's house demolition derby style. Blind since birth, other than drive a car, there wasn't much her lack of vision prevented her from doing, but echolocation at fifty miles per hour passed the limits of safety and sanity. Still, Brett thought it would be a hoot to see her try.

PART II

In the Shadows

The Farmer

FOR ALL INTENTS AND PURPOSES, White Swann Mushroom Company seemed to be just a successful agricultural enterprise providing a quality product. Making use of abandoned mines and providing needed jobs as well as providing compost for other farming concerns made it a green endeavor despite the absence of chlorophyll in its main product. Even though their product line had gone well beyond the simple white button, they kept their research and development division busy finding an alternative to the currently patented process of growing morels commercially, fortifying an outward appearance of legitimacy. For the owner of White Swann, maintaining a façade grew into a remarkable business that showcased crimini, oyster, shiitake, maitake, portabella, and enoki fungi while perfectly disguising both his base of operations and his intentions. Unlike several of his other ventures, the mushroom company demanded shade but was not the least bit shady.

Associated by name only and keeping a strict distance between him and the actual operation, Mr. Swann delegated all aspects of the farming to competent managers, lawyers, and public relations individuals. Their loyalty may not have been earned, but it was certainly bought and paid for. Though never mentioned, his employees all knew where the buck stopped, and it never stopped in the hands of the one paying them to be responsible. Then of course, on the rare occasion when being in the public arena was a forced necessity, assuming the role of the "aw, shucks dirt-under-the-fingernails, hip-deep-in-manure" farmer was handy. It made him invisible and harmless. Thus, the White Swann Mushroom Company was perfect sheep's clothing, and the guise provided all the access and camouflage necessary for Sturmisch Swann to move mountains undetected.

On this particular day, standing in the backyard of his modest Kent Island vacation home on Maryland's eastern shore, Sturmisch Swann contemplated the destiny of the speck of rock he stood upon as it spiraled through the cosmos. His eyes took in the Chesapeake Bay landscape before him, but his thoughts were elsewhere. It wasn't the multihued sunset or the pair of graceful canvas backs returning to their nightly roost that inspired his awe. It was, instead, the coming to fruition of his goal in life.

With deliberate leisure and keeping his attention focused on the unregistered grandeur before him, Sturmisch carefully removed the gold cufflinks from the sleeves of his shirt and pocketed them. First the left, then the right sleeves were turned back with precision until the task was complete. A slight itch on his left forearm first alarmed him and then calmed him as he looked where the itch directed and saw only an adornment of his youth. A small Ouroboros, stitched neatly in black ink, had faded in the last fifty years. To anyone else, it would appear to be a capital *O*, but the faint outline of a serpent's head was still obvious to Sturmisch. Sturmisch was the serpent's head, consuming all before him and all that followed was him, or so it was in the doctrine of Sturmisch Swann.

Giving Thanks

I T WAS WEDNESDAY, THE TWENTY-THIRD of November, and Lee watched the day unfold like a dream coming true. Jase and Emily's girls were handling the chores in the barnyard, and Lee had the kitchen to herself. The main attraction for tomorrow's feast was chilling in the basement refrigerator. When he was a member of the flock, his name was Goobler, but with a prayer of thanks and the swift falling of a hatchet, he was now renamed Delicious. For the first time in forever, Lee added both leaves to the dining table and recruited extra folding chairs from the closet to accommodate all of tomorrow's guests, including her son Nick whom she was expecting at any time. Semi, perched atop the secretary in the corner of the kitchen, chose to oversee rather than participate in these activities beyond his understanding. As long as his dish remained untouched, his world was fine, and they could rearrange all the furniture they wished.

The squeak of the storm door handle marked a brief stay in Lee's progress as Pam, Lorelei, and Joy entered with the serenity of a marching band.

"Nana, we got eggs!" the three announced, nearly in unison.

"Fantastic, and thank you. Did you count them?"

"Six blue and four white. The rest are brown," Pam volunteered.

"There are thirty-two brown," Lorelei spoke up.

Joy cradled a single egg. "Pink!" she stated with glee.

The door handle squeaked again, and as expected, Jase joined the group, but he wasn't alone.

"Look what I found wandering around outside."

Instantly, Lee was across the kitchen and encircled her son with both arms. Only seconds elapsed, and she released him with an apology. "Good grief, at least I could let you put down your things and get comfortable before attacking you." Lee laughed, unable to restrict tears of pure joy.

"Not a problem, Mom. But you're right. Let me put this stuff down so I can hug proper." It had been eight months since she was in the company of her second born, and her first impression was that he that he had lost weight and gained wisdom. From past experience, the initial meeting was always overwhelming, and though Lee tried, it was impossible not to remember this grown man as the precious child she held in her arms nearly thirty years before. His embrace was that of a man now, sincere and solid, no longer the awkward and forced obligation of youth. Unsure exactly how it was conveyed, Lee felt new strength, gratitude, and humility emanating from her son's soul. She breathed in the scent of him and felt the calm of a mother whose offspring were once again, secure in the nest. And in the speed of thought, she thanked every source for his safe return and blessed every parent deprived of a moment like this one.

Understanding his mother's needs, Nick placed his hands on her shoulders and faced her. Kissing her on the cheek, she heard the words that allowed her to release him back into the world. "Good to be home, Mom."

"I'm so glad you're here. What can I get you? Coffee, beer, pop?"

"I'm fine at the moment, thanks."

Lee backed away, and the girls descended upon him. "Uncle Nick!" was exclaimed a dozen times, and he greeted each with hugs and acknowledgments about how big they'd gotten. Nick put his things in the spare room and finally settled at the table with Lee and Jase and the offer of coffee.

"Well, Mom, any more relatives hiding under a rock around here you want to bring into the family fold?"

Lee shook her head and said, "I wasn't hiding him, and how did you find out? Did Em blab?"

"No, can't blame this on Emily," Jase volunteered. "I introduced myself outside."

"Yeah, and I had to ask if he was an uncle in the euphemistic sense or what." Nick laughed. "Then he told me he was your brother, which kinda threw me for a loop. Before I could ask any more, he said you would explain this all to me." And Lee did, or to the extent that she could until Emily and Matt arrived, and a full-out family get-together began. In the process of making a pile of sandwiches, Lee listened to the symphony of voices in her kitchen, the crescendo of laughter and thought—this has to be what heaven sounds like. Smiling at the thought, she glanced to her right and saw Semi atop the secretary shaking his head in affirmation.

It was shortly past ten that evening, and Lee was preparing to stuff the "bird du jour." Emily and Matt left with their worn-out crew an hour earlier and would return at one o'clock the following day with appetites and pies. Nick retired to the living room to rest after nearly twenty-eight hours of travel, and Jase took on the task of chopping onions and celery for homemade stuffing. An armada of casserole dishes lined the countertop to receive favorite family recipes, and the kitchen was full of the fragrances of sage and cinnamon.

Shortly before eleven, Lee's phone rang. Finding it hard to imagine anyone calling at this late hour, it occurred to her that Emily could have a cooking question. Without checking the incoming call number, she answered.

"Yes?"

"You were expecting my call?" the male voice responded with a chuckle.

"Oh no, I'm sorry. I thought you were my daughter."

"Hardly." The man laughed. "And you're not my mother either," he added, now more amused than before.

Not wanting to offend a potential customer, Lee decided to remain on the good-natured side of things. "I'm so sorry. I don't recognize your voice. Who is this?"

Lee noticed there was music playing in the background and the din of voices was present. "You don't recognize my voice? I guess I should be insulted."

Lee didn't like the tone of this conversation and was beginning to suspect that the caller was drunk. "It's not my intention to insult anyone, but if you can't say who you are, I'm going to end this call."

"Now don't get upset, missy. Lemme talk to Fred," he slurred.

Immediately, Lee knew the identity of the caller. "Mr. Hume, leave my family alone."

Jase interrupted his task and turned his attention to Lee.

"Now that's a switch. First you ask for my help, and now you tell me to mind my own business. I know what yer up to."

Resisting the urge to defend herself, Lee decided to take advantage of his inebriated state and find out what he knew. "Yes, I suppose you do. And just what are you going to do about it, Mr. Hume?"

There was a brief silence, and then Brett answered. "Guess that depends on you, Ms. Winslow."

Now flustered, Lee was done with the little game of cat and mouse. "I have no idea what you're talking about, Mr. Hume, and don't call back." She didn't wait for his reply and put down the phone. She wanted to cry but looked up to see Jase smiling at her.

"He isn't a worry," Jase assured.

"He knows something, Jase, or thinks he does anyway. I wish he'd just quit snooping around."

"All isn't what it appears to be at the moment, but trust me, he isn't a problem," Jase reassured.

Jase's words commanded more than just notice. In the blink of an eye, Lee trusted his assessment, and calm settled over her. "I'm so glad you're here."

"Me too. Now let's get this bird in the oven."

Brett stood staring at the payphone receiver in his hand. He put it to his ear once more to confirm that the call had been ended and haphazardly hung it back in its cradle. Jake's Tap would be closing early tonight, and on his sobering walk home, he would have time to consider the huge mistake he'd just made. Beer was not the best lubricant when one wanted to appear smooth, and Brett just had that point handed to him.

"I'm such an idiot, "he said aloud, chastising himself. He was only interested in the truth. Or was he? It was a question he'd avoided like the plague, but as long as he was beating himself up, he figured he may as well focus that truth detector inwardly. He bundled his unzipped coat around him as he turned the corner and headed into the cold night wind. Yes, it did cause him to be angry and suspicious when he encountered another man at Lee's place. But it wasn't as if she'd told him she lived alone and then lied. No.

So why was he suspicious at all? Maybe it was something else, something he didn't want to admit because it would mean he was weak and easily distracted. Brett figured he'd slain the green-eyed monster years ago, but here it was, rearing its ugly head. Was it that he was truly interested in this woman personally, or was she just an opportunity for a story that, at this point, didn't really exist? The conclusion was a bitter pill, but he swallowed hard. It wasn't the woman who was the path to a story. It was the story that created the pathway to the woman. And he just sent an M1 Abrams in to obliterate that path.

Only a block or so from home, he stopped. Whether it was the lessening effects of alcohol in his system or the mental self-abuse, a thought occurred to him. Not just a thought, it was an epiphany. "How could I have been so blind?" he questioned out loud. It was a shame Barbara wasn't there to make a joke at his expense, he mused. He checked his watch and realized Barbara would be home in about twenty minutes from a Giving of Thanks concert she helped organize with a local church youth group. It would give him just enough time to make a pot of coffee, shake off the beer buzz, and get her take on his newly enlightened thoughts.

Good Noose

ROM THE OFFICE OF STURMISCH'S Montana home, constructed in one of the rather spacious stopes of an abandoned mining property, he studied with pleasure all that went on in the world, sent to him via satellite. Picking out headlines and tracing the action back to his initial hand gave him not only pleasure but yet another example of his godlike stature. As for the god of the human chattel, he believed in no such creature. Sturmisch considered himself to be a far better indicator of true power, and neither he nor his hands were invisible to those he chose. His influence, in the form of capital, was used as a lure, a weapon, a punishment, a reward, and a disguise. Its placement earned compliance, and its withdrawal could topple empires. Both were considered positive actions to Sturmisch because he caused them. Causing action, action that would bring about perfection, was the driving force of his enlightened being.

Looking for patterns that included the words *victim, gunshot, riot, disaster*, and more of the same, Sturmisch could see his plan coming together nicely without having to lift a finger. Of course, after every event of human recklessness that caused death or violence and the inevitable fallout of starvation, social unrest, or the coming to power of a sociopathic dictator, no fingers were ever pointed at Sturmisch. He created pathways for events to flow smoothly, but never had to push the events down those paths. He was a force not unlike gravity. And he was untouchable. He was without blame. His Teflon coating of innocence let nothing stick, but *that* was what made it beyond great. It was godlike. Sturmisch often mused that at some point in history, accomplishments like his would be referred to as Sturmisch-like.

Sturmisch Swann considered himself to be the happiest man on earth when confronted with bad news. Bad news was good noose, he often joked. Bad news was an opportunity for him to do what he did best: guide, promote, invest, divest, and cajole. This was best illustrated when he was denied the purchase of a tract of reforested land that was between one of his abandoned mine acquisitions and a water resource he required. The land was under a long-term logging contract with a company that planned harvest two years in the future. They refused to give up their contract and prevented the owner from selling to Sturmisch.

In less than a month, a suspicious lightning strike caused a fire that threatened ecologically sensitive lands adjacent to that property. It was more than quick thinking on Sturmisch's part to dispatch an agent to the fire marshal to suggest a backfire be set on the reforested tract to mitigate fire damage in a delicate old growth ecosystem and prevent water pollution. It was also made clear that White Swann would see to the replanting of the backfire area while engaged in the reclamation of the abandoned mining site he owned. With the promise of a timber harvest gone, the land was sold to White Swann, the logging contractor received a gratuity in compensation for his loss, the fire marshal's daughter received a full college scholarship from one of Sturmisch's many philanthropic enterprises, and the green community promoted the sacrifice of White Swann to their cause. With an act of arson, Sturmisch corrected an act of God, which made him a hero, a benevolent savior, and a humanitarian. In Sturmisch's estimation, when one is clever enough, this is how the world really works.

At the age of eighty-six, Sturmisch knew his time was limited, but it mattered little to him. He'd spent a lifetime setting the stage for what he saw as mankind's ultimate perfection. Of course, he knew this transformation would not be through his efforts alone. He was simply a catalyst. Nor did it matter to him if mankind appreciated his sacrifice. After all, he was just doing what needed to be done. And it was going to be done *his* way.

The business breakdown was well within providing the necessary dividends to reorganize things. After all, the world was just a business like any other, and when things are outdated and fail to produce the desired outcome, you take them over, deconstruct, salvage anything left, and rebuild. Sturmisch wanted the business of the world to run seamlessly.

Of course, this exactitude would come at a price, but not one Sturmisch would have to pay personally. He would let the opposing forces provide that payment for him. In the meantime, he had busied himself reclaiming abandoned mines and turning them into, among other things, helpful farming ventures. The well-schooled minions at his disposal had done his bidding, jumping through bureaucratic hoops to obtain property and then the funds to further his goals. Surely the divine hand of circumstance was ushering him forward. At what other time or place in history could a man of his means exact a toll from the pocket of every pedestrian to build the never-ending maze of turnstiles they would gladly pay him to go through? It was undeniable proof of their need for his genius. Any population ignorant enough to allow itself to be put in this situation needed guidance, and Sturmisch Swann would guide it toward flawlessness.

Sturmisch was keenly aware of all the forces acting on the ebb and flow of human behavior. Every activity of mankind generated a force that he would divert and manage to his advantage. Religion, politics, economics, science, and social ideologies were the fuel to his engine of perfection. He would harness the energies from the friction that existed on the polarized extremes of all these sources. What delighted him the most was the way these forces nearly formed a conga line under his invisible direction. He was choreographing the dance between matter and antimatter, a touchy union that when managed properly produced untold power. Some sparks might fly and some adjustments might have to be made, but Sturmisch was ready to flip the switch.

Tentatively, Sturmisch had picked a date to which he would assign the beginning of his perfect world—or rather, present history had picked it for him. Between the Mayans, the Hopi, Nostradamus, the I Ching, and a few other predictors, December 21, 2012, seemed wholly logical. At least if humanity was already expecting something on that date, it wouldn't be difficult to get their attention when Sturmisch gave them direction. Even the gods of technology had jumped on this bandwagon with Web Bot examinations of future happenings. They all knew *something* was going to happen, but none of these prognostications offered anything other than a wait-and-see option. There were plenty of "maybe this or maybe that" suppositions that did little more than gear up useless knee-jerk reactions in an ignorant populace. As it was in any good crisis, why let all that energy go to waste? Sturmisch would rescue them, and the world would eventually thank him, or at least the ingrates should.

Scanning the news reports from all forms of media, deciding where and when to intervene with his subtle influence or just let events play into his hands on their own, always gave him a thrill without comparison. There was no drug available to equal the high induced by knowing all that he knew and all that was about to occur. What gave it the ultimate kick, that exquisite rush of pleasure unequaled by anything else on earth, was that it was only known to him. The truth was his to determine, and reality would be what he decided it would be.

The Season of Giving

IN LESS THAN TWO MONTHS' time, her world had changed so dramatically that Lee was faced with a situation she had never known before. Sure, when her children were small there was a particular delight with the coming of Christmas. The Santa Claus tradition brought smiles and cherished memories of small earthly dreams wrapped in shiny paper on that precious morning. She had to laugh at the fact that she was now overrun with happiness. At times it was more than she could contain. Like rain that fell through sunshine, her tears would flow past the smile on her face. She wondered at times if she had the capacity to accept with proper gratitude all the love that surrounded her. And it did cross her mind, briefly, that the joy she was experiencing was simply the contrast to so much longing in her past. She was reminded of something Aunt Jan once told her. Love is the one thing that when it is divided, it is multiplied. What Lee was experiencing was on the exponential level.

December brought with it a frosty white landscape befitting the season, and a month's worth of preparation was evident throughout the house. Jase and Nick had seen to tree procurement, as well as several armloads of cedar and pine that scented the house beautifully. With the help of Emily's girls, the tree was heaped with every ornament, string of beads, errant cat toy, and shaped confection available until it resembled a Gabor sister bag lady. An angelic kitty with wings and halo topped it off, much to Semi's delight. As this was obviously a monument erected in his honor, Mr. S claimed a spot beneath it in the plush green skirt.

It was shortly past two in the afternoon of Christmas Eve. The bulk of the celebration would begin with dinner around six and end with exhaustion around ten. It was customary for Lee to let

Emily's children open their gifts from her this evening, but she had one special gift for Jase that couldn't wait until then. Having finished outside chores, Jase entered the kitchen with a coffee can full of eggs.

"I thought Nick was with you," Lee remarked.

"He said he had a few last-minute things to do in town. Said he'd be back before the girls arrive."

"Good. As long as we have a moment to ourselves, I want to give you something."

"I had the same thought. I have something to give you as well," Jase replied, removing his boots.

"You didn't have to do that," Lee protested. "I can't think of a single thing I need."

Jase smiled. "It's something you asked for a long time ago."

"And *you* have a memory of this?" Lee responded, incredulous.

"Well, maybe I don't have a direct memory of it, but you do."

"Whatever it is, I'll love it, but me first." Lee disappeared to the bedroom and returned seconds later with her hands behind her back. "This is so you'll always know where you belong." She handed Jase a small black box tied with a gold ribbon.

He pulled off the ribbon, opened the box, and removed what it contained. "Oh, wow," he muttered with understatement that let her know it was just right. He held in his hand a gold dog tag on a chain with a simple JAG engraved on the side now face up. "Jase Albert Garrett," he said, reinforcing the obvious.

"Turn it over," Lee instructed.

On the back was the message in tiny script, "*You are never lost when you are loved.*" Jase stared at it for a moment and then closed his hand around it and hugged his sister. "It's perfect." He looped it over his head and tucked it inside his shirt with the words, "I'll never take it off."

"That was what I was thinking too," Lee agreed. "I've got egg-nog. Let's make a toast," Lee announced, walking to the counter and picked up two pewter Jefferson cups.

"Wait, before we do that, I need to give you my gift."

"Okay. I'll pour while you get it."

Jase didn't move. Instead, he continued, "First, I need another hug."

Lee laughed. "Well, if you insist." Lee placed the cups on the table and crossed the kitchen to grant him his wish.

Jase enveloped Lee in both arms and snuggled his face into her shoulder. Before releasing her from his embrace, he said two words: "Thank you."

Not quite understanding the need for this ceremony but enjoying it nonetheless, Lee replied, "Thank you too." Jase's hands were still on her shoulders as she began to back away, and she looked up. What she was seeing made her freeze for a moment. She blinked her eyes. Jase was smiling broadly.

"Merry Christmas, my wonderful sister."

Lee stood transfixed, not understanding what she was witnessing. She rubbed her eyes and looked at her brother again. For lack of any rational description, Jase appeared to glow. His entire being was outlined by a soft white light. She didn't know what to ask, so the only thing that escaped her lips was, "Jase?"

"It's okay. I'll explain."

"You can explain this? What's happening to you, Jase?"

"Nothing is happening to me, actually. It's your gift."

"*My* gift?"

"Have a seat, and I'll explain what you're seeing."

Not taking her eyes from Jase, Lee located one of the kitchen chairs with her hand and sat slowly. Semi, aware of his mistress's distress, left the comfort of his rocker and hopped into her lap. He purred deeply to indicate all was well.

Jase sat next to Lee at the table, smiled, and shook his head, deciding where to begin. "I want you to think back to the summer when you were eleven years old. You were in the backyard at Aunt Jan's helping her hang clothes on the line. You were lamenting the cruelty of one of the kids you had contact with in town. Do you remember?"

"I often did that, help hang clothes, I mean. And ask questions." Lee stroked Semi and tried to remember, never taking her eyes off Jase.

"Well, on this particular day, you wished that there was a way to see if someone was good or bad just by looking at them." Jase met Lee's stare as she thought back. Her eyes brightened as she recalled the conversation.

"I remember Sasha Parks calling me the crazy girl. She was a spoiled brat and so hateful. It was her MO to wait until she had an audience and then pick a target. But the worst part was, before she attacked, she would pretend to be your best friend. Anything you shared was used as a weapon in her game of personal assault. She was sneaky and devious, and she seemed to enjoy it. And yes, it was because of her that I wished it was possible to see if someone was going to be mean."

"That was it. And you got your wish."

"I'm not sure I understand. What does you becoming Mr. Glowworm have to do with me?"

"Well, your gift was the ability to perceive what already exists, not that you didn't have it all along, but it just got switched on."

Lee smiled wide and shook her head. "I just can't get over what I'm seeing. Can I touch it?"

"Sure you can."

Lee lowered Semi to the floor and stepped closer to Jase. She ran her hands through the aura surrounding him, marveling at how it moved in an almost fluid fashion, rippling and showing glints of gold.

"It's beautiful," she said, slowly moving her hands about four inches from Jase's body. Lee stepped behind him to get another view and asked, "Why does it only appear two dimensionally, like an outline?"

"You pay attention, don't you," Jase approved. "Have a seat, and I'll give you all the particulars." Lee sat and Jase began. "This glow, as you call it, is simply the light of the soul. When you get a broader perspective, you'll be able to tell by intensity, subtle changes, and color exactly what it tells you about a person. You'll be surprised how familiar these indicators are. As for your question about this appearing as an outline, this is not a measurable light of this world and, as such, is not something you are actually seeing with your eyes, as in it's not making the rods and cones in the retina react."

Taking in all she was being told, Lee brightened. "The eyes are the windows to the soul," she said wistfully.

"Exactly," Jase agreed. "And because of this, it doesn't reflect, it can't be photographed, and the only thing it illuminates is the character of the individual emitting it."

Lee looked down at her own body and realized she wasn't seeing any glow. "Uh, Jase? Is there a reason I can't see anything around me?"

"Good question. Each soul already knows its true nature. Others with the ability can see you, but there is no need for a soul to view itself. The only way an individual will know how they appear to others is to ask. And if they are lied to, it will show in the glow of the liar."

"*Others?* You mean there are folks running around now who can already see this?"

"Well, not the way you do now. The others I'm talking about are all the other people presently here on earth."

Lee looked puzzled. "All what other people?"

"Oh, they don't have it yet. You're going to give the ability to perceive to them."

Lee stood abruptly. "What? Okay, now I'm thoroughly confused. How can I give something when I'm not even sure how I got it?"

"Relax, Lee." Jase laughed. "You'll give it the same way I gave it to you, by touch." Lee calmed and went to the counter.

"I need coffee," she said with a hint of exhaustion. Trying to deal with what she was seeing and what she was being told was more than she had planned for this afternoon. She finished filling the coffeepot and returned to her chair. Jase was sampling a sugar cookie as he waited for her next question.

"You mean I have to hug everybody?"

Jase stifled a laugh with a mouthful of cookie. "No, no. Anyone with the perception can pass it on. For lack of a better descriptive term, it spreads like a virus, except that washing your hands won't prevent its distribution. All that's needed is touch."

Lee was reminded of a movie where Denzel Washington was chasing an evil spirit that leapt from person to person in much the same way and realized how quickly this could spread. "Let me get this straight. You mean when I touch someone, I pass this glow to them?"

"Not the glow. They already have that. What you pass will be the ability to perceive it. And those you touch will turn it on in others as well. You're going to turn on the world."

The weight of this thought was growing as Lee considered the effect she was about to unleash. "I'm not sure the world is ready for this."

"Not ready? Are you kidding? The world needs this now more than ever." Jase saw the look on his sister's face as she contemplated and acknowledged the enormity of her wish. "Lee, are you responsible for all the lies and evil in this world?"

"Of course not," she answered quietly.

"Then you don't have to worry about exposing the truth either. You aren't building anyone a house here. You're just handing them a hammer they've had all along. It's up to them what they do with it, if anything."

"Some hammer! And I can just imagine the twists and turns the press will give this one."

"No doubt, it will be interesting. But when the excitement dies down and they figure out that it isn't harmful, we can let the truth of it be known."

"We? What's this 'we' stuff? Just who do you think is going to believe Grandma Nobody from Farmville, Minnesota?"

"We'll cross that bridge later, but for right now, merry Christmas."

"You're right, and merry Christmas to you too. I should worry about the rest of the world when I'm going to be faced with explaining this to Emily tonight!" They both cracked up at that prospect. A little more calm but still fascinated with the novelty Jase sported, Lee got curious. "Jase, what do I look like? My glow, I mean."

"You're as beautiful on the outside as you are on the inside."

"No. I mean thanks, but can you describe it to me?"

Jase squinted a bit, feigning critical observation. "Mostly white light with streaks and sparks of orange and gold when you get excited that fades to a soft pink when you smile."

"Wow. I wish I could see it."

"Goes nice with your hair," Jase teased.

The sound of a truck crunching through the snow in the drive lane let them know Nick was back from town.

"Here comes your first victim," Jase said sarcastically.

"Oh geez. I hope I don't scare him."

"You won't. He'll get a kick out of it, I think."

Nick came in, a bag in each hand, and stomped his feet before stepping into the kitchen to place his purchases on the table. "Man, it's getting nasty out there, the roads I mean. Glad I left for town when I did because the snow is picking up." He noticed that both his mother and uncle were listening to him, but they weren't jabbering like they usually did, just smiling at him, and Nick suspected he was about to become the victim of some practical joke. "What? Why are you both looking at me funny?"

"No reason. Just wondering what's in the bags," Lee mentioned casually.

"Oh, I managed to find oysters and picked up a few goodies for the girls. I've been craving scalloped oysters for six months," Nick answered, still wary of an impending joke.

Lee stood without speaking and watched Nick empty a quart of oysters, a pound of butter, and a box of saltine crackers from the bag. "That's all the right stuff, isn't it?" Lee nodded yes but still just stood there grinning. "Okay, okay. What's up that you're not telling me? It has to be something."

Lee was anxious about passing the perception on to her son, but what captured her attention was the astounding halo surrounding his person. It was blue-white with spikes of lavender that would extend and withdraw as he spoke and tiny flashes that looked like rubies would appear, course a short distance, and disappear. It was breathtaking.

Nick looked all around. "What is it, you guys? Is there mistletoe hanging somewhere?"

Lee glanced at Jase, and he nodded toward Nick, letting her know it would be okay. "Nick, I have a gift for you," she addressed her son.

"Is that all? Cool."

Lee walked around the table and threw her arms around Nick. She had no idea what his reaction was going to be, but she knew there would be a reaction. She released him and backed up. For a few seconds he was a statue, only his eyes darting back and forth from Lee to Jase. He saw them both still smiling. And glowing. He shut his eyes tight and reopened them. "Okay, what gives? Is this some new Christmas gizmo, or have I just had a stroke?"

Lee and Jase both breathed a sigh of relief that was barely noticed due to the laughter. "No, sweetie. It's not a stroke. I'll let Jase explain."

"Oh, good. There is an explanation for this. Beyond the fact that I am now having a Matrix moment, I can't wait to hear this!"

Lee and Jase together shared both what this perception allowed and its limitations. For the most part, Nick was receptive, which wasn't a big surprise considering some of the situations he'd had to face as a marine. Still, Nick asked the definitive question. "Why is this happening now?"

Jase thought for a moment and then did his best to answer. "Look at the world around us. It's a mess. For as far as we've come as a civilization—technological advances in science, communication, agriculture, medicine, and travel—we are still struggling with what all that experience can't provide. Portions, and they are powerful portions of humanity, have let their accumulated knowledge and power to control, blind them to the fact that their self-awareness has made them less aware. They discount what they have no knowledge of by declaring that you can't weigh a unicorn with a yard stick, which is true, but rather than discover the proper tool of measure, it is far easier to declare the nonexistence of such a creature."

"As strange as that analogy was, I think I managed to follow you. This is revealing the unicorn," Nick declared.

"In a sense, yes," Jase replied.

Lee got the evening meal underway while listening and adding to this exchange. "And I guarantee the first thing the powers that be will do is attempt to measure, and when they discover they have no tools, then what? Do you think the arrogant know-it-alls are going to jump on the acceptance bandwagon? I don't think so," she chimed in.

"We shall see, but what's really going to set them on their heels is when it's revealed what this all means. Every individual will be able to see for themselves the truth of another individual without distortion. Seeing the unaltered truth is a powerful weapon."

"A weapon against what?" Nick asked.

"Evil," was Jase's one-word answer.

The conversation came to a halt as the outside door opened noisily, and the kitchen walkway was filled with little-girl voices. "Nana, it's snowing sheeps and bunnies out there!" Lorelei reported from the midst of a throng of tiny Eskimos trying to disrobe in the space of a phone booth. Emily and Matt picked their way through the confusion, each carrying a snowsuit that presumably contained a child. The entire Benson family was aglow.

"Hey, Mom, we're going to lay these napping ones on the sofa, and then I need to go get my pies. I'm glad we went to the early service at church. The place was packed due to the weather."

"I'll help you, Em," Nick offered.

"Thanks, Nick. I need to get my purse and two diaper bags too."

As Nick stood to help his sister, Lee took his arm and quietly admonished, "Careful not to touch her."

"No worries, Ma. I'm with the program."

Lee was hoping that Matt and Emily would be as instantly accepting of the amazing "stocking stuffer" they were about to receive. Matt returned from the living room after successfully depositing his sleeping son on the couch and sat at the far head of the table. Nick and Emily returned from the van, Nick placing the pies on the counter and Emily dropping her cargo in the living room. The three girls hovered over the plate of reindeer sugar cookies like sugarplum vultures, heeding previous instruction that dinner must be eaten first.

"Girls, would any of you like to open a little gift before dinner?" Lee asked. Emily nodded a reluctant okay, and the trio preceded Lee into the living room. Before she could hand out the third gift, Pam touched Lee's arm. Pam's eyes got huge, her mouth opened wide with surprise, and she pointed to her grandmother. Lee hadn't counted on this, but she had the presence of mind to head Pam off at the pass. "Shh." She put a finger to her lips. "It's Nana's Christmas light surprise. You can show Mom and Dad after you open your presents, okay?"

"Sure, Nana."

Lee left them to their fervor of paper tearing and returned to the kitchen, knowing her time to make a proper presentation to Em and Matt was limited now that the proverbial cat was out of the bag. Keeping an ear tuned to the direction of the living room,

Lee looked at Jase, made a strained toothy grin, and made it clear that the girls had been turned on. Nick, engaged in a weather discussion with his sister, caught the message passed from his mother to Jase.

To his mother Nick directed, "I see we are going to plan B?"

"Yep, a little sooner than I planned, but some things are unavoidable."

"I'll take Em, you get Matt."

Jase sat and watched the mother-son tag team go to work.

Nick stood and walked over to his sister with an open-armed gesture inviting a hug. "Merry Christmas, Em, and don't freak out."

Emily hugged him, and her response was, "Merry Christmas, Nick. Huh? Freak out over what?"

At the same time, Lee walked over to Matt and gave him a motherly shoulder hug as he sat in his chair.

Nick couldn't resist. "Over this!" He backed away and threw his hands in the air accompanied by a "Ta-da!"

Emily and Matt, both speechless, watched and tried to comprehend the scene before them. Lee, Jase, and Nick were laughing and watching them. At nearly the same instant, Emily and Matt looked at each other, and their jaws dropped open, which caused more laughter. Not two seconds had elapsed when Lorelei entered the kitchen with a complaint. "Pam says I'm pink, and I don't want to be pink. I want to be blue!"

Now addressing his mother through fits of amusement, Nick managed, "Oh yeah, Mom. What happened to 'careful not to touch her'?"

In much the same state, Lee replied, "What did you want me to do? Pelt the girls with boxes from across the room?"

In a commanding voice, Emily chimed in, "Excuse me! Would someone please let *us* in on what's going on here?"

Pam ran into the kitchen. "I see someone"—she said, pointing a finger over Lorelei's head—"wrecked Nana's Christmas light surprise!"

Renewed laughter followed but settled quickly as Lee understood the importance of bringing her daughter and son-in-law up to speed. Over dinner, the narrative of the mystery was quickly imparted, and all parties were made aware of what steps were next. It was expected that there would be quite an initial uproar, confusion, and a host of expert opinions, but the knock at the door was not expected.

Knock, Knock

WHILE MAKING HIS WAY THROUGH near-blizzard conditions to Lee's place, Brett questioned his judgment about the weather conditions, but not his intent. The plows had been through, but the wind pushed drifts back across the road in short order. On the seat next to him was a package the size of a paperback book, which was meant as much as a peace offering and apology as it was a Christmas gift. His discussion with Barbara, after the evening of the disastrous alcohol-induced phone call, made it very clear that Lee was as protective of her family as he was of his. This he understood, but was too thick-headed to understand her reservations with him personally until he, figuratively speaking, stepped into her shoes. Of course she was going to protect family. He'd beaten himself up about such shortsightedness for nearly a month. And if Cousin Fred was who Brett suspected he was, no wonder Lee saw a newspaper reporter as the enemy. It wasn't going to be easy to regain trust, but Brett was going to try.

Coming over the last small rise before Lee's farm, he noticed a large white-lighted star mounted on the side of the corn crib, twinkling through the cascading snowflakes. Several cars were parked near the house, and he won a bet with himself that she was home. He noticed Lee's egg sign was nearly buried in a drift as he pulled into the lane and parked across from the lighted kitchen entrance. He picked up his small offering, waded through the snow to the icy doorstep, and knocked on the door.

All Heaven Breaks Loose

BEFORE ANYONE COULD STOP HER, Pam ran to answer the knock at the door. And before anyone could intervene, Pam returned, announcing that some man wanted to talk to Nana. Like lightning, Lee made her way around the table to Pam and tried to remain composed.

"Did he touch you, sweetie?"

"No, Nana, and he isn't Santa Claus either," Pam replied, rather disheartened.

Lee proceeded to the door, and there stood Brett Hume on the lower landing, kicking the snow from his boots. "Mr. Hume, I thought I made myself clear—"

"Wait. I'm sorry, just wait. I came to apologize."

Before Lee could reply, Jase appeared at her shoulder and took the bull by the horns. "Ah, Mr. Hume, merry Christmas. Tough night to be out on the roads."

"Yes, it is, and I'm sorry to barge in like this, but merry Christmas to you too, Fred, is it?"

"Maybe. Please come in, and we'll discuss it over coffee."

Lee could not believe what she just heard but instinctively took Jase's lead and went to make a fresh pot of coffee. On the way through the kitchen, she mouthed the words "newspaper dude" to Emily, and she quickly ushered her girls into the living room. Unaware of the visitor's identity or importance, Nick and Matt remained seated at the table. Without making physical contact, Jase managed to escort Brett into the kitchen and offered him a chair at the remote end of the table. Having finished her task, Lee introduced her unexpected guest.

"Everyone, this is Brett Hume from the local newspaper. Brett, this is my son, Nick, and my son-in-law, Matt."

Hellos were exchanged, and Brett was offered the floor. Lee thought he looked nervous, but that wasn't all she noticed. The glow surrounding him was pleasant. Nearly all white with sprites of yellow brilliance that retreated into spots of soft aqua, it wasn't at all what she expected.

"I came here tonight to apologize to Lee and to give her this." He slid the package to the middle of the table. "I should have given it to you sometime ago, but I screwed up, and I'm sorry."

Curiosity overcame suspicion, and Lee picked up the gift and began to unwrap it. In a small polished brass frame was a picture Lee had never seen before, except for the face of her brother. It was her family. Everyone was smiling cheerily, the wind putting motion in their hair. Her parents were so young, still young in Lee's mind. Taken at the lake shore the summer before the accident, it mustered few memories of that day, but did bring on a yearning for things that could have been. "Thank you," were the only words that got past the torrent of emotion she was holding in. She handed the photograph to Jase.

"Will Koch at the department dug it out of the file for me. Of course, this is a copy of the original, and I had it blown up a little, and it's on acid-free paper," Brett babbled unnecessarily. Lee carefully placed Brett's coffee within reach.

"Black, right?"

"Yes, thanks," he replied, searching her face for any signs of forgiveness.

"I think we should address the other reason you are here, Mr. Hume," Jase spoke, changing the direction of the conversation.

"Maybe we should, and I guess I owe you an apology too, Jase, is it?"

"Apology accepted, and I'll extend mine as well for being less than truthful about my identity. Also, we are both grateful for your discretion regarding our privacy." A brief silence filled the kitchen like a vacuum.

"That went well, I think," Lee added, breaking the formality of the moment.

Nick was trying to get a clear handle on what this was all about and finally asked, "What's this all about?"

"Well, you see," Jase began, "Mr. Hume here is a reporter, and when your mother clued him in on the fact that I disappeared fifty years ago, he took interest. But when he met me here a couple months ago and started putting two and two together, he thought he'd like to write a story about it. What brings him here tonight is something his job requires he put aside—human decency. He still wants to write the story, but he'd actually like our permission. Is that about it?" Jase said, directing it to Brett.

"In a nutshell, and on your terms, of course," Brett agreed.

"I think we can work something out, after the holidays, if you don't mind," Jase conceded.

"Sounds good to me. January is a slow news month anyway." Brett extended his hand to shake on the deal, and Lee spoke up. "Uh, Jase, could I have a word with you please? Privately."

Lee and Jase excused themselves to the hallway where Lee no longer had to maintain her composure. "Are you insane? Letting him do a story is one thing, but touching him? How on earth is he going to react to that?"

"Badly, is my guess, but trust me, he's on our side. And we need him."

"We have sides now?"

"Trust me on this. It will be fine," Jase assured her.

Halfheartedly, Lee agreed. "Okay, but every time you say that, something weird happens."

"Oh, we're way past weird," Jase teased.

The pair reentered the kitchen, and Jase remained standing. He turned to Brett and extended his hand. "A deal's a deal," he stated, waiting for Brett to react in kind.

Without hesitation, they shook hands. Brett looked up at a room full of glowing people and snatched his hand away like a snake had bitten him. "What the—?" He blinked his eyes several times, trying to erase what he was seeing and not comprehending. Jase was amused by Brett's sudden loss of poise and tried to dispel his fears by once again offering his hand.

"Don't touch me!" Brett shouted. He grabbed a dining chair and used it as a shield as he backed toward the kitchen exit. Jase took a single step toward him, now laughing openly. "Stay back! Get away from me! What the hell are you people?" Desperate words were his only weapons as he made his way backward down the steps, wedging the dining chair between the walls as an obstacle to his would-be pursuers. His hand hit the storm door latch, and he flew out into the icy night, tripping over a rock beneath the snow cover, ripping his pant leg, and injuring his left knee. Ignoring the pain and springing to his feet in a sudden move that practically defied gravity, he made it to his car in five bounding steps while locating his keys in a jacket pocket. After three pulls on a frozen door latch, he was behind the wheel. His key slid into the ignition just in time to see two glowing faces peering out at him from the doorway. In his future recounting of this event, it would never be mentioned that at this moment, he screamed like a terrified little girl and had to stifle wetting his pants. The still-warm engine came to life immediately, and he slammed the car into reverse, spinning only momentarily before flying rearward onto a blessedly empty highway. Locking all the doors as he shifted into drive, the full force of the adrenaline rush caused his heart to beat like it was trying to escape his rib cage.

Hands shaking, he drove as fast as he dared, glancing in the rearview mirror every ten seconds to be sure he wasn't being followed. When he could see the lights of town ahead, he calmed down enough to notice not only that "Silent Night" was playing on the radio, but the throbbing in his knee was keeping time to the music. Having no common frame of reference for what he'd just experienced, his thoughts were all over the place, trying to rationalize, categorize, or identify. He faced the fact that he was too scared to think. He wondered if he should tell Barbara about what had just transpired and then decided he wouldn't look good in a straitjacket. If she told him something similar, he knew he would have serious doubts about her thoughts being of a cogent nature. No, this little episode he would keep to himself until he was sure he wasn't losing his mind.

It was nearly nine o'clock, and the streets were vacant as everyone was celebrating inside and avoiding the snow outside. He pulled in the driveway of home sweet home and tried to fill his mind with normal concerns, like having to clear the driveway of snow the following morning. It was no use. He pulled the car into the garage and used the remote to lower the door. It wasn't until he tried to get out of car that his knee complained heavily enough to distract him. Reaching down, the tear in his chinos was sticky with blood, but he felt the damage was minimal. He limped his way up the two steps into the house and opened the door to a hallway dimly lit by a kitchen light beyond.

"It's me, Barb," he called to his sister, thinking his voice sounded strained.

"I'm in the kitchen washing up a few things," she replied. "How did the gift delivery go?"

"Fine," was his curt answer.

"Just fine?" she inquired further.

Brett was in the laundry room removing his torn pants. "She liked it a lot, I think. You soak blood in cold water, right?"

"Yes. What on earth did you do?"

"Slipped and scraped my knee. No big deal, but these are dirt-work pants now."

"I'll sew them up for you. The concert went great this evening. It's a shame you missed it. Very uplifting."

Brett examined his knee and decided his worst enemy would be the swelling; otherwise, no permanent damage was done. He pulled on a pair of sweatpants from the stack of clean things in the laundry and proceeded to the kitchen. The fluorescent light over the sink was the only thing that illuminated the kitchen, and Brett automatically walked up behind his sister and gave her shoulder a quick squeeze hello. He was busy sorting out his wallet, keys, and change from his abandoned pants and placed them on a shelf for later retrieval. Barbara turned, plate in hand, to address Brett.

"I'm serious, Brett. You would have really enjoyed—" Before she could finish her sentence, the plate crashed to the floor.

"Don't move, Barb. I'll get the broom," Brett advised. He went back to the laundry room to grab a broom and dustpan.

Barbara stood perfectly still, not because Brett told her to, but because she was trying to assess what was happening. She thought she *saw* something, though she really wasn't sure since she had been deprived of this sense at birth and had no idea what *seeing* was. Brett returned and began gathering the shards of what had been a porcelain cookie plate into a pile. "It's okay, Barb, no harm done."

"Brett?" It was happening again. Whatever this was, it returned when Brett entered the kitchen.

"I've almost got it all," Brett tried to assure her.

"Brett!" Barbara spoke in a voice loud enough to get his attention. He looked up.

"Are you okay? Are you hurt?" His sister's eyes looked as if they were focused on him, and there was something else. She was backlit by the light over the sink, but strangely, there was more light coming from an unknown source.

"I'm not hurt. But something is happening here, Brett." He moved a step toward her. "There it is again! I can *see* something!"

"It was just a plate, Barbara," he said, ignoring what he knew couldn't be true.

"You're not listening to me, Brett!" She fairly yelled to make her point.

"Okay, okay, what is it?"

"Back up. Move away from me."

Amazingly, Barbara's eyes stayed focused on him as he backed up a short distance. He parked the broom against the wall.

"Okay, now what?"

"Brett, I can see you!"

"No, you can't, Barb. We both know that's impossible." It crossed his mind that his sister might be having some kind of seizure.

"I know it's impossible, but I'm telling you I *can* see something. And I think it's you!"

"Do you want to sit down?"

"No, I don't want to sit down! Raise one of your arms."

Brett raised his right arm above his head like a school kid hoping to be called upon by the teacher.

"Right!" Barbara pointed to the arm he held up. He put it down and raised the other arm. "Left!" she said and pointed to the appropriate side. He put the left arm down.

"Okay, now which side?" Brett raised both arms over his head.

Barbara placed her hands on her hips. "Both are up. And you, trying to trick a blind girl!" She nearly laughed.

This was impossible, Brett thought, but he had already drawn a direct connection to the other impossible things he witnessed earlier this evening.

Barbara crossed the kitchen and threw both arms around her brother. It was then that he noticed a light that seemed to emanate from within her and completely surrounded her. There was definitely a connection here. With this one instance, having his sister as the bearer of the mystery, all his fears dissipated. He escorted Barbara to the dining table. "I have something to tell you. It's about what happened tonight at Lee's, and I think it's directly related to what's going on here." He made tea and told her the whole story, minus the screaming part. Barbara listened intently and took it all in as a matter of course. When he was finished, she added some things he hadn't considered.

"Maybe I'm wrong, but consider this," she began. "When was it ever mentioned that someone granted sight to the blind?"

"I know what you're saying, Barb. But that's not my area of expertise. Miracles are a matter for the Vatican, not me."

"And I can't speak for anyone but myself," she continued, "but when you look down at yourself, what do you see?"

"Well, nothing, or at least not what I'm seeing around you anyway."

"Same here. I can only see what appears around you. It would stand to reason that if this was not of a spiritual nature but of a worldly nature, we would be able to view ourselves as we do others."

"You may be right. But as for what this all means, I have no clue."

"Go to the source," Barbara answered flatly.

"I'm not going to the Vatican, silly," Brett responded.

"No. Not the Vatican. Ask Lee's brother, Jase."

A Buzz

LEE AND JASE BOTH LOUNGED with their feet propped on the ottoman, each with a glass of wine in hand as they waited. Emily and Matt began their trek home nearly an hour earlier, and Lee received a text that they made it home unscathed. Nick retired for the evening, leaving his mother and uncle to wait for Santa's arrival, and the swooshing sounds of the dishwasher were music to Lee's ears.

"Quite an evening," Lee said with obvious understatement.

Finishing his sip of wine, Jase answered, "I thought it went well."

Both expressed amusement when the look on Brett's face was recalled. "Poor guy, he had no idea what he was in for when he walked through that door."

"Him? *I* had no idea either!" Lee thought about his rapid departure from the kitchen and began to imagine what was going to happen when this event became worldwide.

"It will all be okay. You'll see. After everyone discovers that not only is it harmless, but is also beneficial, they will appreciate its promotion of insight." Lee's phone began ringing, and Jase picked it up, adding, "This call will be for me."

Flipping it open and putting it to his ear, Jase answered the call. "I wondered how long it would take you to call. How's the knee?"

A brief silence followed, and finally Brett spoke. "The knee is fine. You knew I would call?"

"We're talking, aren't we?"

"Yes, I guess we are." Brett had a few hundred questions, but the first one to emerge was, "And I'm assuming you are the one I should address about tonight's events."

"Yes, I am. But before we get into any detail, I'd like to have this discussion in person, to preserve our privacy, if you catch my drift."

"Understood. When and where?"

"I'd like to invite you and your sister to Christmas dinner here, tomorrow at three. Does that work for you?"

"Yes, that works, but how did you know about my sister?"

"I'm not a spook, but I do have my sources. Trust me."

For reasons completely beyond logic, Brett did trust him. "We'll be there."

"Do me one small favor. Don't have physical contact with anyone before you arrive tomorrow. I think you know why."

"Yes, I do. My sister explained that one for me."

"You're an important part of this, Brett, and I want to thank you ahead of time."

Brett didn't know how to respond. "I'm not sure what you're thanking me for, but I guess I'll find out tomorrow."

"Yes, you will. See you at three. Bye."

Brett responded with a good-bye, and Jase closed the phone. Taking another sip of his wine, he addressed Lee. "Two more chairs for dinner. Is that okay?"

Chuckling to herself and shaking her head, Lee acquiesced. "Sure. The more, the merrier!"

⁕

Sturmisch was now less than a year away from his triumph. While many households of the world were waiting for a phantom fat man dressed in red to deliver undeserved gifts in celebration of the birth of a nonexistent man/god, he was tallying his gains, both monetary and political. His thought, after perusing another night's news, was that people were making this far too easy for him. There was no challenge in ease. Like a cat with a newly captured mouse, as long as it zips about, the cat's interest is keen, but when it becomes listless and won't move with the bat of a paw, it is no longer a challenge and becomes mere food.

And these *humans*, he thought after assessing his gains in technological stocks, so bent on having the newest and most effective ways to communicate and less and less of what they exchanged could be called information because it failed to inform. It was the exchange of words for the sake of exchanging words. He did, she did, they did. It was all after-the-fact drivel. They did so little with what they gained from these communications. Clearly, imagination and ideas had taken a backseat to useless gossip. Sturmisch had to blame himself for part of that because it was part of the process. Heap more and more praise upon less and less actual accomplishment until they are convinced they are geniuses for learning to tie their shoes properly. Eventually, he mused, they would all be reduced to the wonderment of Velcro.

One of the more complex processes Sturmisch had to formulate was how to domesticate humans. The first part of that process was to stop thinking of them as human. With animal bodies, they had the same requirements of other domesticated species. Horses, swine, cattle—all of these independent and useful animals had been successfully domesticated. When fenced in, provided sustenance, and taught the punishing sting of the electric fence, they eventually lost the quest for independence. They became more docile and used to the fetters of their existence. Those born into captivity would take even less effort to tame. They knew nothing of the freedom of the wild.

So it would be with these humans, Sturmisch had planned. The freedom they had come to enjoy was an impediment that would be removed by persuasion and eventually from memory. He would fence them in with rules and regulations in the guise of protection and necessary limitations to promote their well-being. They would be lured with unearned bounty until they depended upon it so heavily that their ability to be self-sustaining would disappear. Sturmisch would be *the* primary provider, especially to those praised as victims of their own intentionally created ineptitude. He would cater to those of succeeding generations not aware of the deprivation they've been born into and convince them that the previous generations were *saved* by the limitations placed upon them.

The generations of WWII and the Korean War were nearly extinct, and the majority of aging veterans of the Vietnam conflict would soon be too old to be taken seriously. Accusations of dementia and forgetfulness wouldn't quiet the truth they would impart, but it would cause hysterical deafness in the younger generations. Those children currently reaching the age of influence were perhaps Sturmisch's most perfect example of utter control.

Needless to say, there would be dissension occasionally from within the rank and file, but the dissenters would be culled carefully, as would the most violent and criminal sorts when their usefulness became unnecessary. For the moment, cultivating and preserving the criminal element was essential. They provided fear that demanded the protection of more laws.

And when the machinery was in place, every human would do as it was trained to do and become part of the machine. As the parts wore out, including humans, they would be replaced. Praise them when they jumped through the hoops, and withhold the necessities of life when they fell short. Sturmisch failed, or perhaps refused, to see that this formula was his own. His enormous ego was enough to obscure the fact that he was a product of just such a controlled and dismal environment. Prior to becoming Sturmisch Swann, multibillionaire and businessman, he was Twiford Schwartz.

Twiford Schwartz was born. The details of his birth were sketchy estimates, but that mattered not to him. In the brief search of his heritage, he went so far as to discover that his mother was most likely a prostitute, and he was one of the lucky few dumpster babies to be discovered before the elements claimed him as a statistic. The year of his birth was 1925, he was sure of that. Newly opened Holy Name Hospital was the address placed on his birth certificate because it sounded better than "the alley between Fifth Street and Dunn." The month could have been either October or November, but it was left up to the hospital to determine that his date of birth was the thirty-first of October.

At the time, the newspapers dubbed him the "All Hallows' Eve" baby, which gave him enough notoriety to be adopted almost instantly by a wealthy but childless couple from Teaneck, New Jersey. He had no real memory of his adoptive parents, the Schwartzes. His father was a casualty of the stock market crash, losing everything shortly before taking his own life. His mother, a delicate sort, unable to bear the burdens of loss, both personal and financial, relinquished her parental role to a second cousin of her mother. This gentleman was neither married, nor did he care to be, and saw the child as an indentured servant that came with a monthly stipend that would be wisely invested for his own personal benefit rather than wasted on this refuse of humanity. In this emotionless setting, Twiford learned to be self-sufficient and developed well-honed survival skills.

The mister, as his guardian was called, taught him the value of power. Rewards for sufficiently completing his duties came in the form of necessities such as food and water. Noncompliance brought about the withdrawal of these necessities. Thirst and hunger, young Twiford learned, were powerful incentives for learning. He took advantage of Mister's library full of books on economics and history. His children's literary fare was fed to the coal stove upon his arrival, but that introduction to the written word was a skill not wasted. At the age of seven, he'd devoured *Indian Currency and Finance* by John Maynard Keynes as well as Adam Smith's *Wealth of Nations*. He read about business and accounting, about banking and financial markets, and about governments of the world. This was his Mother Goose.

At the age of sixteen, he was more than ready to wear Mister's shoes. In an environment devoid of caring, Twiford never developed a thirst for the milk of human kindness. He'd managed quite well without it and now determined that it was truly a waste of time and effort. His effort was placed in not only learning about all the governing rules and laws, but in how to successfully circumvent them. This was not a difficult task because in nearly every dictate of man's power over men, there was a secret provision, a clause, always exempting those with the power. And it wasn't enough to discover those secrets. Twiford sought a position of power to influence the writers of rules. To obtain such a position meant becoming an artist of deceit, or in other words, a proficient liar. Direct lies, lies of omission, and lies to misdirect and deflect were the common course of every entity wielding power, and Twiford was the Leonardo da Vinci of falsehoods. He discovered the ease with which a soul could be purchased to do his bidding. As a skilled prevaricator, his blackmail, bribery, and even murder were all carried out by proxy, carefully separating him from all responsibility and granting him all privilege.

It was in college that a German language professor gave life to Sturmisch Swann. Taking note of Twiford's dispassionate demeanor, the professor inquired about the cause of such a stormy attitude. The description soon became a nickname that Twiford thought fitting as it spoke of something powerful, dark, mysterious, and beyond control. As much as anyone could, Sturmisch would live up to his new name and become the perfect storm.

Passing of the Torch

IT WAS BARELY SIX THIRTY in the morning when Lee got her wake-up call. "Nana! Nana! Santa brought us a pony!" It took Lee a few seconds to wrest enthusiasm from the grip of sleep and respond to Pam.

"Oh my! Isn't that wonderful!"

"We named her Beanie 'cause she's a red-and-white paint with a big spot that looks like a kidney bean," Pam informed her grandmother.

"That's terrific, sweetie. Sounds like a suitable name for a Shetland."

"How did you know she was a Shetland?"

Lee chastised herself for having her mouth in gear before her brain was fully engaged. "You did say she was a pony. Nana just guessed."

"Oh," Pam answered, satisfied with the response. "She's really cute, and we have a saddle and everything."

"Well, I know she'll be happy to have you girls loving and caring for her. Merry Christmas, sweetie. Is Mommy close by?"

"Sure, Nana. Merry Christmas to you too. Here she is." Pam handed the phone to her mother.

"Merry Christmas, Mom. Did we wake you?"

"Merry Christmas, Em, and it will be a better morning as soon as I get coffee. What time did they get you up?"

"Around five." Emily laughed. "And they couldn't understand why they had to put on coats and boots to see what Santa left in the shed."

"I can imagine. But I bet it was a nice surprise."

"Yes, Beanie is a definite hit. Thanks again, Mom."

"You're more than welcome. I'm glad I could help."

Things in the Benson household were as precarious as millions of other families dealing with the current financial upheaval. Upset in the world and regulation in the states caused a spike in fuel prices that pushed a jump in the cost of everything. Fewer people had the extra income to make new cabinets an option, so Matt's business was slower and more competitive. But as fuel and misplaced subsidies made corn prices go up and regulations prevented the culling of horse herds for meat, horses were suddenly cheap. Lee bought Beanie at a local stock auction for the princely sum of twenty-five dollars. She would be boarded in Lee's barn and pastured with the rest of her critters during the summer months. It made the best of a bad situation, but most of all, it made three little girls and one little pony very happy.

"What time should we arrive today, Mom? We have the use of the Schmidts' horse trailer all day, but I know the girls want to help get her room ready in the barn. Is noon too early?"

"Nope, noon sounds fine. You may even catch brunch leftovers. Dinner is at three. Oh, by the way," her mother continued, "we will be having two more guests at dinner."

"Really? Anybody I know or am possibly related too?"

Lee laughed, but the way things had been popping up lately, she couldn't blame her daughter for the sarcasm. "Uncle Jase extended the invitation. It will be Mr. Hume, whom you've already met, and his sister. I don't know her name, so I guess you'll be introduced when I am."

"Ha! After last night, I can't imagine him wanting to come anywhere near your place. I guess someone being terrified isn't supposed to be comical, but I swear his eyes were bugged out so far he looked like a cartoon."

"He was a sight," Lee agreed, "but considering what he saw, he probably thought we were a bunch of aliens."

"I guess since he's agreed to come to dinner, he's seen the light. Hardy har har."

"I'll let Jase make the explanations," Lee declared, amused by her daughter's remark.

"Okay, Mom. We'll see you all in a bit. Bye."

"Bye." Lee stood staring at the coffeemaker as it struggled through its brewing process. Semi, sitting on his rocker, meowed a demand for food, which was delivered by his mistress in her "semiconscious" state. No pun intended, she thought, but she kept it to herself. She grabbed a mug from the cupboard and stood ready to capture the first cup of fresh coffee. She had about five hours to get too much done, and the first thing on the list was a shower.

By eleven o'clock, Jase and Nick were both up, fed, and out doing chores when Emily, the three girls, and Beanie the pony arrived. There was much ado in the barn preparing her stall and finding a place for her saddle and bridle in the tack room. A pink bow was tied to her gate as a temporary marker until a proper nameplate could be added. Lee had managed to throw together the customary Christmas dinner fare in record time and, by one o'clock, had little more to do than enjoy the day and wait for the guests to arrive.

She watched the activity in the barnyard from the kitchen window and marveled at how quickly the novelty of inner light became just another feature of each individual. For the most part, the soft white light that surrounded each was the same, like a skin simply containing the spirit being within. But like the features of any face, subtle variations in color and intensity made each unique to the wearer. Emotions, desires, and intentions were expressed fleetingly on the canvas of light in patterns and designs characteristic to an individual in a wide palette of color; some Lee had no name for as they were not of the visible spectrum. She did notice that the girls wore uneven halos of light that reacted in a more chaotic manner than that of adults. It seemed to make sense that as we age and gain self-discipline, it would be displayed in such a fashion.

What she saw when Emily gathered her brood in moments of affection was more beautiful than she had words to describe. In the arms of their mother, each child seemed to glow brighter, and streaks of pink and gold glistened throughout. As well, Emily's aura seemed to envelop the children with swirls of magenta and a shade of violet Lee had no name for. There was an obvious give and take within the fusion of light. Similarly, when Matt arrived with the boys and he greeted Emily, the light between them merged before any physical contact was made, as if each was drawn to the other magnetically. Where the two came together, they knit together instantly, each adopting subtleties of the other until they were surrounded by a single uniform radiance. And when they parted, each resumed their singularity with flashes of the union fading into the individuality of each. Lee knew she was witnessing love.

The oven timer brought Lee out of her dreamy thoughts, and at the same time, her kitchen was flooded with rosy-cheeked munchkins with straw in their hair and smiles on their faces. As Lee donned oven mitts and pulled the rare roast "beast" from the oven, Lorelei began a discourse on her Nana's new responsibilities regarding Beanie.

"We put hay and sweet feed in her bunk, and her water pan is in the corner near the door. Mom says *we* have to deal with the poops. You can brush her and give her food."

"I would be delighted to feed and brush her. Thank you, Lorelei. Would you like to put the napkins on the table for Nana?"

Lee got the napkins and instructed Lorelei on how to fold and place each under a fork. Pam already knew her duty and busily filled glasses with ice. As she counted places at the table, Pam asked, "Why do we have two extra places, Nana?"

"Uncle Jase invited guests."

"Oh, good," she replied. "At least it's not talking dogs."

Lee thought that was an odd comment and decided to inquire further. "Now why on earth would Nana invite dogs to dinner?"

"Mom says it's a good thing dogs can't talk, otherwise they'd all talk you into bringing them home for dinner."

"Oh, really?" Lee couldn't help but laugh to herself. In a very real way, she did gladly take in anyone who needed a place to stay because she needed them far more than they needed her. What she received from them was a blessing in her life: the blessing of being necessary to people she cared about. At that moment, she recalled a conversation with her uncle Peter, Lisa's dad. When she was old enough to ask questions about being a part of her new family, Uncle Peter explained that this is what families do when they care about people, and it's been this way from the time we lived in caves. He said he could imagine his ancestors inviting friends and family into the safety of Cave 59. Over the years, Lee had the privilege of sharing her home with a range of good souls finding a refuge with her from a rocky point in their lives and moving on to a smoother future.

Shortly after two o'clock, the potatoes were put on to boil, and Lee opened a large bottle of Layton's Chance Joe's Cool Red, one of Emily's favorites, and the color was a perfect adjunct to the table setting. The men reclined in the living room enjoying the Western channel, and the girls were nesting on Lee's bed with Semi watching a movie. As it neared three, serving dishes and glasses were filled in preparation for the feast. At ten minutes till, the guests arrived.

Hearing the crunch of snow beneath tires and the cessation of a car engine, Lee turned to Emily. "The talking dogs are here."

A perplexed look was followed by a giggle of awareness. "I see the girls have been imparting my wisdom!" The giggle produced a ripple of yellow and orange throughout her daughter's glow that emitted tiny golden sparkles at the edges. It was exactly how Lee imagined a giggle would look.

Lee watched as Brett exited the driver's side of the car and promptly zipped around to the passenger side and opened the door. *Wow*, she thought, *somebody's momma taught him right*. It wasn't that she thought ill of the man; it was simply that she barely knew him at all. Their interactions to this point had been far less than intimate, but maybe there was hope for this one. Common courtesy was rarely displayed these days, and it was much missed in Lee's estimation. The sun had made a late but welcome appearance in the day, and the lady who stepped from the vehicle wearing sunglasses and a hooded ski jacket was glowing with colors Lee had never seen before. As she took Brett's arm to navigate the frozen ground, their devotion to one another was clear.

Made aware that his invited guests had arrived, Jase met the pair at the door with a sincere greeting. "You're just in time, and merry Christmas. Please come in."

Brett hesitated for the briefest of moments, recalling his departure from this doorstep less than twenty-four hours prior, then relaxed and escorted his sister over the threshold. "Merry Christmas to you too," he replied as they made their way inside.

Lee joined them at the doorway to the kitchen, offering to take their coats, and introduced herself to Brett's sister. "Hi, I'm Lee, and we're glad you could come on such short notice." Lee extended her hand, and Barbara accepted it immediately.

"Hi, I'm Barbara, and Brett has told me so much about you. All good, I assure you, with the exception perhaps of his little scare last night."

"I can imagine," Lee agreed. "But I will say it is a bit of a surprise when you don't know it's coming."

Both women felt an instant ease with the other. "And I'll thank you ahead of time for a wonderful meal. It smells fantastic," Barbara added. Lee noticed that Barbara did not remove her glasses, and it wasn't until Brett helped her to her seat next to Lee's that she realized Barbara was visually impaired.

The last thing to be placed on the table was a basket of hot rolls, and Lee called everyone to the kitchen to be seated for dinner. She introduced Brett and Barbara to her family and vice versa. With that formality complete, Jase was the last to be seated at the far head of the table, and Emily's girls gave the blessing. The "amens" were said all around, and Jase stood to make a toast to the day and to an event that would possibly change the world.

The Plan

DURING DINNER, EMILY NOTICED HER girls watching Barbara like a hawk, and finally one of them, Pam, spoke up.

"Miss Barbara, why are you wearing sunglasses inside?"

Calmly, Barbara rested her fork and dabbed her mouth with her napkin. "That's a good question, Pam." She went on to tell the girls, and everyone else listening, that her eyes don't work the way most people's eyes do. She was born with something the medical community call Leber's congenital amaurosis or LCA.

"Does it hurt you?" Pam asked with concern.

"Oh no, it doesn't hurt at all, unless I run into a table or something." Barbara smiled, getting a chuckle out of the girls, and with the discussion lightened, she went on to tell them that until last night, she'd never been able to see anything.

"Now you can see?" Pam asked.

"I can see the beautiful light around each of you."

"So why do you still need sunglasses?" Pam persisted.

Understanding that the mystery was yet unsolved for the child, Barbara continued, "Ah, so it's the glasses that are the issue. I wear these more for everyone else than for myself. Since my eyes don't focus on things, they tend to wiggle, and wiggly eyes make it hard for little girls not to laugh."

"Can I see?" Pam asked, unabashed.

Emily cringed when her daughter asked such a direct and possibly rude question that she hoped would not make Barbara feel embarrassed or self-conscious. It was no surprise to Brett at all when his sister responded with complete grace and composure.

"Sure," Barbara agreed and removed her glasses, revealing her stunning golden-topaz eyes.

"Cool!" Pam said instantly. "But they're not wiggling."

Brett got his sister's attention, and she turned toward him. "She's right. The nystagmus is gone, or nearly gone, and they are binocularly symmetrical too."

"What does that mean?" Pam asked, once again demanding to know.

Barbara redirected her gaze to Pam and gladly answered the child. "It must mean that now I have something to look at, so my eyes aren't lost anymore."

"So you don't need the glasses now either." Pam brightened.

"I guess you're right. I'm glad you asked about my glasses, Pam," Barbara praised and tucked the glasses in Brett's shirt pocket.

The conversation had captured the attention of everyone at the table, and as Lee put on another pot of coffee and Emily enticed the girls back into Lee's room with another movie, Jase decided it was time to unveil his simple plan.

To Brett and Barbara, Jase clarified what this light signified and what its limitations were. He went on to let them know that this was something that was going to be given to all of humanity.

"Not to derail your train of thought here, but where did this come from?" Brett interjected.

"You'll have to ask Lee that one," Jase replied.

All eyes turned to Lee. Well aware that they were looking to her for answers, her first instinct was to say, "What?" She stood there for a moment with the "deer in the headlights" look and finally came up with something to say. "All I can say is, be careful what you wish for."

"So you did this?" Brett asked, sounding somewhat dumbfounded.

"If I did, I certainly don't know how, but I'll admit that the wish was mine."

"The point is," Jase tried to clarify, "no matter what the cause, it's here, and it's at our disposal. Is everyone in?"

Everyone around the table—Matt, Emily, Lee, Nick, Brett, and Barbara—indicated in the affirmative. "Okay. Just to let everyone know, we're going to ruffle more than a few feathers once this goes viral. We have two stops to make tomorrow. The first is the Mall of America. Our second stop is just across the road at the airport, where we're picking up Lisa. Her flight arrives just after two in the afternoon, and the trick is going to be making the Mall the focus of any attention while we connect with travelers at the airport."

"Won't they shut down the airport if they think there's a problem?" Brett asked.

"I'm sure they will, but a few will slip through. Pandemonium will be our cover, but we have to be sure to be clear of the area if they shut down the roads."

"If my reaction from last night is any indication, you'll get plenty of cover," Brett asserted.

"We're going to take two vehicles," Jase continued, "in case one gets snarled in traffic. Make sure you have your press credentials with you, Brett. Lee, you'll be in charge of wrangling Lisa. If there are any questions, she'll trust you more than anyone else."

"I told her to pack light and not include identification in her bags due to identity thieves, so if we need to abandon her luggage, we can, but I think she's just going to bring a carry-on."

"There are identity thieves at the airport?" Brett asked.

"There might be, but I just made that up for her sake. She knows nothing about Jase or my little gift."

"*This* is going to be more than a little interesting!" Brett declared, shaking his head.

Jase added some last instructions. "Security cameras aren't going to be able to pick anything up, but it wouldn't hurt to pick up on the reactions once it begins and try to mimic the crowd. It doesn't have to be an Academy Award performance, but just enough so that none of us look *too* calm or out of place."

"Uh-hum," Barbara interrupted, holding a finger in the air. "I know you aren't going to be dragging a blind woman with you through this little ordeal, so how can I contribute?"

Jase turned to Barbara. "Glad you asked. We can't leave Emily and Matt's kids behind with an uninformed babysitter. We also need someone to monitor the local news and keep us informed by phone in case they start blocking the roadways. We need you to be our remote eyes and ears. Are you up to that?"

"I think I'm perfect for the job," Barbara replied, delighted to be handed so much responsibility.

"Assuming we succeed with this little venture, what happens after we get out and come back here?" Brett asked, looking for the bigger picture.

"We lay low until the event is local. Of course, I'm assuming there will be an initial knee-jerk reaction of isolation, but the naysayers will be the assets we can count on to spread it. I'm guessing in three or four days, we'll just be another part of public that's been affected." Jase knew that the experts were going to be somewhat of a problem. Too often their educated theories were taken as gospel, and they never had to prove anything, not even the basis of their theories, to have suspicions take hold and incite reaction. In the beginning, the greatest thing in their favor would be that no one would know for certain what this phenomenon indicated, but that wouldn't stop the experts from expressing their opinions as fact.

The remainder of the evening was spent downloading maps and planning specific routes to get in and out, including plan B routes in case of problems. For the most part, traffic should be light until they got near the Cities, and clear roads would stay that way, according to local weather forecasts. And even though it was a Monday, the after-Christmas shoppers would be out in force because of sales and returns. Jase knew that all of their steps were traceable, so he hoped picking up Lisa from a flight booked months in advance would keep the dogs off their scent. He counted on the legitimacy of their excursion, coupled with simple coincidence, being enough to mask their efforts and maintain the anonymity of ground zero.

With everyone aware of the significance and tentative logistics awaiting them the following day, Matt and Emily returned home with the kids and planned to meet everyone back at Lee's shortly before noon. Nick decided to retire as well, knowing his primary job tomorrow was to be a wheel man. Before Brett and Barbara headed for home, Lee insisted they stay and have coffee before going. It was a chance to discuss their lives before and after tomorrow.

Lee and Barbara discussed chickens and children. Jase took Brett aside to discuss exactly how important his role as a reporter was going to be. "I mentioned earlier that I wanted to thank you for what you're about to do, and as per our deal, I want you to document as best you can everything, exactly the way it's happening. I know this must sound a bit cloak-and-dagger, but you're going to come up against a torrent of opposition. They're going to attack you personally and professionally because the truth as it stands means absolutely nothing to them. You will be the enemy because as far as they are concerned, the truth is what they say it is, and they own it, and they will do literally *anything* to keep it that way—including murder."

"I understand the danger, but who are 'they'?" Brett acknowledged quickly and solemnly.

"The answer to that one, you will see for yourself. And it won't be just you in jeopardy. All of us here tonight will suffer the same scrutiny and possible peril except one. Me."

"What? Why not you? Obviously you know things I don't."

"True, but my destiny in this has a set conclusion. I was given a choice, and it's what I agreed to do. Knowing what you know now, I'm offering you a choice without a set conclusion. In or out?"

Brett didn't hesitate. "I'm in, definitely."

"You're a man of faith, Brett," Jase offered.

"Ordinarily, I'd say you're wrong about that, but after what I've seen lately, who knows?"

"I do. The truth of it surrounds you."

"Truth of what? And faith in what? Are you talking about God?"

"I'm talking about the truth of reality. You can call it whatever you like, but God is as good a name as any."

"God is the truth of reality? I thought religion—" Brett was cut short.

"Every religion is the history of the relationship between certain populations and the concept of God," Jase began. "God didn't physically write the books of that history either. Men did. Even if they are said to be God's own words, they went through man's hand to be delivered to us, and each man did his level best to deliver those words. God isn't an institution or a certain practice. God is God. It can be debated a thousand different ways from an infinite number of perspectives, and it remains the same. It can't be changed by belief or disbelief, and it can't be co-opted. It is what is." Jase could tell he was getting a bit ahead of himself.

"So if it is what it is, what is it?" Brett laughed. "I feel like I'm in one of those 'who's on first' conversations."

Jase shook his head and smiled. "I know, it's one of the most complex simple things to describe, but I'll try." He thought for a moment and asked Brett, "Do we exist?"

"Yes, I'd say there's plenty of evidence that we do exist."

"So knowing that we do exist, would you say nonexistence is a valid conditional state?"

"As the absence of existence, I'd say yes."

"Like darkness is the absence of light, true? It may very well be a condition in unto itself, but without light, we wouldn't know what darkness is, but we do. Light can be measured, but you can't measure darkness as anything other than an absence of light. Following me?"

"Yes, because of light, we recognize the concept of darkness."

"Okay, we've already concluded that we exist, and nonexistence is therefore a valid concept, correct?"

"Yes."

"Describe nonexistence for me," Jase challenged.

Brett thought. "Wow. This is hard. I keep coming up with a picture in my mind of a big black nothing, but that's still something."

"Yes," Jase agreed. "It isn't something you can describe in terms of the physical universe, even as we can describe darkness because we can imagine light, but absolute nonexistence is a concept only and therefore can be consciously recognized even if it can't be described. And a concept must be conceptualized in order to exist. Cosmologists and mathematicians wrestle with this question even now, and bringing together Einstein's gravitational physics and quantum mechanics is a difficult union."

"If you say so," Brett accepted, not quite knowing what to question. "But, okay, I got it. It's a concept. I know it's there even though I can't describe it. Is that about right?"

"I think that's close enough," Jase allowed. "So before the Big Bang, as they call it, took place, before our universe existed in its current state, there were two things balancing one another perfectly: nonexistence and the nonphysical conscious entity that recognized it as a concept. After all, if there wasn't anything to consciously recognize nonexistence, then we'd be stuck with the paradox that nonexistence doesn't exist. So that's how this universe started."

"All of this?"

"Put yourself in those shoes. Your entire job for eternity is to recognize nonexistence and imagine. When time isn't a constraint, you can imagine quite a bit. In very simplistic terms, everything is a product of specific imagination and the power of initial will. Energy in the form of light theoretically can become matter. The real question is, where did that energy originate?"

"I'm afraid I missed out on the quantum physics for dummies, but when you think about it, it's a pattern that occurs with more than a little frequency. On and off, positive and negative, electrons and protons, and even the binary switches of machine language, ones and zeros. Makes logical sense, I guess," Brett concurred.

"Yes, it does. I quote the German physicist, Max Planck. He said, 'All matter originates and exists only by virtue of a force which brings the particles of an atom to vibration which holds the atom together. We must assume behind this force is the existence of a conscious and intelligent mind. The mind is the matrix of all matter.' Physicists have since proven that human observation changes the way matter responds in test results. Of course, Max wasn't bound by the beliefs of anyone handing him grant money either. There will be a hundred or so detractors ready to poke holes in this nonscientific argument, but it doesn't change a thing. Science will dance around the singularity with string theory, M-theory, and parallel universes where their rippling edges meet as they travel through the eleventh dimension, producing matter, and that search is a good one. But even they will have to admit that some pretty heavy mysteries still exist. Something and nothing go hand in hand, and whatever you want to call it, God does exist because nonexistence is a conditional fact."

"Good. Now that we've sorted out the mystery of the universe, what time do you want us here tomorrow?" Brett replied, slapping his hands on his thighs and grimacing, forgetting his bruised knee.

"Noon should give us plenty of time." Jase chuckled.

Brett and Jase rejoined the women in the kitchen. Semi was curled in Barbara's lap, purring contentedly. "Are you ready to go, Barb?"

"Sure. I'll drive," she joked.

"Careful there, crazy lady. I just might let you," Brett replied as he gathered her coat. Tonight's good-byes were in stark comparison to those of the previous evening, and on the drive home, Barbara wondered aloud, "Kind of gives a whole new meaning to the phrase 'Let there be light,' don't you think?"

"Yes, it does, Barb. It certainly does."

The Mall

JENNY ALSAKER ALWAYS VIEWED THIS trip to the Mall as fun but necessary evil. She and the kids—baby Ron in the stroller and four-year-old Alyssa, encircling the mother-son pair like a moon with an erratic elliptical orbit—got a rare afternoon at the Mall of America. Yesterday being Christmas, otherwise referred to as "ugly sweater day," made this trip necessary. Going to the aquarium with gift passes made it fun.

Jenny's husband, Big Ron, was a thoughtful man with little or no taste when it came to something woolen worn above the waist unless you were a sheep. Never wanting to discourage her hubby's good intentions, she would ooh and aah over whatever monstrosity she pulled from the box on Christmas morning and would gladly try it on. She would then compliment him again by declaring that his eye always told him she was the trim woman he married, and she just *had* to get this in a larger size so it fit properly. Of course, whatever sweater she returned was always "very popular," and no larger size was available. Sales afforded her the luxury of another more sedate sweater and a blouse to match. Big Ron was happy, Jenny was happy, and the ugly sweater would receive new life as a throw rug of recycled material.

With her sweater return completed, Jenny and the children ventured into the underground world of glass tunnels through an aquarium of everything from jellyfish and seahorses to sharks, rays, and a myriad of colorful smaller fishes. The scenery was always changing, and even Alyssa's attention was captured by a hammerhead swimming above as they walked slowly through the exhibit. It's one of the few times when excited outbursts and frantic pointing were acceptable behaviors, even for the children.

As they wrapped up their underground aquarium tour and began the trek back to the SUV in the east parking area, Jenny had no idea that the excited outbursts and frantic pointing were just about to begin.

Lee, Emily, and Matt were surprised by relative lack of overcrowding in the parking area when they arrived at the Mall. They managed to find a spot on the second level near the front stairway to the east mall entrance. As they crossed East Broadway and made their way inside, none of them could have foreseen the events unfolding as they did. They stood near an ice cream vendor, anxiously waiting for Jase's call. Brett, Nick, and Jase were entering the Mall from the west end, on the opposite side of Nickelodeon Universe. The plan was to get the call, casually touch someone, and walk calmly back outside. Simple. No one counted on a whirling dervish named Alyssa to start things off on her schedule.

While perusing the hundred or so ice cream flavors available from the vendor, Lee felt a bump. She turned quickly and at first saw no one, until she looked down. This tiny human in a pink hooded jacket had been walking backward toward the ice cream shop, beckoning her mother to follow. When her progress was thwarted, the tot turned to see what had obstructed her path toward the ice cream. She looked up, and her eyes met Lee's. A look of utter surprise sent her fleeing to the safety of her mother, and she grabbed tight to the stroller. Then the child looked at her mother, and the bewilderment faded and was replaced by awe and then a huge smile.

"Pretty!" she exclaimed while her glowing mother pushed the stroller toward Lee to offer an apology.

"I'm so sorry," Jenny told Lee.

"It's quite all right. We have three of her at home," Lee said nervously. She was trying to find her phone in her purse, and Emily reminded her that it was in her pocket. Quickly, she called Nick's phone, and Jase answered.

"Hi. Just wanted to let you know Lisa's flight might be early. Maybe we should shop later."

"I see. Well, we just got inside, so we'll save our returns for later and meet you at the airport. Thanks for the heads-up."

"You're welcome. Bye."

Jase understood exactly what Lee had just told him, and it had nothing to do with Lisa's flight. They needed to make a quick and inconspicuous contact and set things in motion on their end. An elderly couple parted company as the lady headed to the restroom. Jase approached the gentleman bystander who was dutifully holding his wife's purse. As another woman approached, Jase stepped aside to allow her passage and, ever so slightly, brushed the man's arm. Quickly, he returned to Nick and Brett.

"Time to go, gang." No one asked Jase any questions and followed him back across West Market to where they had parked.

As the driver of Lee's truck, Matt had the doors unlocked before they reached it. They got inside and breathed a collective sigh of relief. They were to meet Jase and the others in short-term parking, and Jase would call to tell them where they were parked. Without incident, both vehicles left the parking facilities and made their way across I-494 to the airport.

Inside the Mall, little Alyssa was not at all disturbed by the sudden appearance of "pretty" light surrounding members of the Mall crowd. She was particularly drawn to baby Ron napping in his stroller. She stroked the white and lavender corona that encircled his blanketed form, delighting at the issuance of golden sparkles throughout. Then a female figure standing before a darkened storefront caught her eye. She made her way over to the lady engrossed in a cell phone conversation. As Alyssa approached, the woman ignored the child other than taking note of her reflected image in the glass window. The child reached up and touched the woman's arm with a single tiny finger, glancing over her shoulder to see if her mother was watching. Alyssa stood there, waiting for a reaction from the woman who was glowing a tangerine color.

Looking into the mirrorlike window, the woman acknowledged Alyssa with a smile. Alyssa smiled back and skipped back to her mother, who was demanding her return.

Jenny pushed the stroller toward the exit with Alyssa in tow as the tangerine lady finished her call. She closed her phone, faced the open promenade of the Mall, took three steps, and stopped. Surveying the crowd, she blinked feverishly, closed her eyes tightly, and then reopened them. Trying to maintain the professional composure her business suit and heels demanded, she walked over to a kiosk and asked the gentleman behind the counter if he noticed anything odd about her eyes. With a quick glance, the man replied that he saw nothing. As he spoke, a funny light around him changed; blue spikes of irritation flashed as this nonpaying customer demanded his time. Tangerine lady begged his indulgence and asked for the use of a mirror that was behind the counter. Handing it to her, he touched her hand. That's when things went from unusual to frantic.

Eyes riveted on tangerine lady, the man uttered an unintelligible curse and snatched his mirror away. "What you do, lady? You on fire?" the excited proprietor boomed.

"No, no, I'm sorry. Something is wrong with my eyes." Tangerine lady's distress brought her to the edge of tears.

"You eyes is fine. But you need to stop, drop, and roll. You on fire, lady!"

Her tears were put on hold for the few seconds it took her to assure him she was not on fire. "Sir, do you see any smoke? I am not, I repeat, *not* on fire! Put that fire extinguisher down, sir!"

Backing up in spiked heels is something that should be relegated to circus performers and well-trained exotic dancers, not ladies on highly polished marble floors being pursued by extinguisher-wielding salesmen. The first blast turned the floor into a skating rink, and tangerine lady skittered in place like a cartoon and went down in a crumpled pile. A small crowd, keeping their distance until they knew what sort of assistance they could offer, stared with group incomprehension at the events unfolding before them. Extinguisher man then noticed the crowd, and what he saw caused an immediate retreat, flinging the small red cylinder to the floor and fleeing through the nearest exit.

A woman and gentleman from the crowd went to assist tangerine lady, identifying themselves as first responders.

"Are you hurt?" the gentleman asked.

"No, I'm okay. Bruised maybe, but nothing broken. I'm just having a problem with my eyes."

In about as much time as it took to ask about her injuries, the man touched her arm, nudged the lady rescuer at his side, who then backed into an onlooker, who sent the gift through the small crowd with the precision of a Rube Goldberg contraption. Mall security arrived, thinking it was a simple accidental fall, until he tapped the shoulder of the gentleman attending to the tangerine lady. Alerting the dispatch center by handheld radio, Officer 714 wanted to be sure that what he was seeing was being documented by surveillance cameras. The voice on the other end of the radio said they had the area covered.

"Control, this is 714. I'm at the east entrance, street level. A situation needs coverage here. Are you getting this, over?"

"We have an eye on you. All appears normal," his radio replied.

"What do you mean all appears normal? Are you saying you can't see this?"

"See what, sir?" the radio voice answered.

"*This!*" The officer was pointing to individuals in the crowd, most standing stock-still due to the shock of what had just been revealed to them.

"Sir," the voice continued, "all we see is you pointing at people."

"Something must be wrong with the cameras." The officer was becoming annoyed.

"Can you describe what it is you think we're not seeing, sir? The cameras are working just fine."

"Everyone down here is glowing. Are you sure you can't see this?"

"We have nothing on this end, sir. Have you been affected?"

The officer looked down at himself and declared, "No, I don't seem to be affected."

Tangerine lady and a few of the others decided it was time to make themselves scarce and headed toward the Mall exit. In a less than official capacity, the security officer tried to persuade everyone to remain as they were until whatever was affecting them could be cleared. "People, we all need to remain calm and find out exactly what is wrong with you. Please remain where you are."

"Dude, what do you mean what's wrong with *us*? I suggest you look in the mirror, glow boy. I'm leavin'," declared a young man dressed in a camo jacket that matched his glow perfectly.

The officer dismissed the remark and tried to make sense of what he was seeing. At that point, he radioed his command. "Maybe it's just the lighting down here, guys. I'm coming to you. Get someone from plainclothes ops to cover this for me. And call maintenance. Someone discharged a fire extinguisher down here."

On the other end of the Mall, a similar but less dramatic scenario was playing out as Mrs. Bystander finished in the ladies' room and appeared at her husband's side to reclaim her purse. Mr. Bystander relinquished the bag without making direct physical contact and complained that his glasses must be dirty. She studied the glasses, declared them suitable, and reminded her husband that he'd probably forgotten to take his pills again and was on the verge of a ministroke. "Serves ya right, Marvin. I'm not your mother, and if you need her to remind you to take your pills, you're well on your way to getting where she went twenty years ago." Marvin noticed waves of bright red and green light subsiding to white around his beloved and decided not to mention it as they toddled toward the exit doors where a polite young gentleman held the door open and patted Marvin's shoulder as he passed through.

Officer 714 made his way to the dispatch center noting that whatever this was, it seemed to be affecting every mall patron, but curiously, no one seemed the least bit aware. Again checking himself by both personal visual exam and checking his reflection in mirrored surfaces as he passed by, he noticed he was not yet affected, but there was something else. In the reflection, neither he nor any of the passersby were glowing, but in viewing them directly, the mysterious glow was there. Was this some sort of contamination screwing up his vision? The more questions that came to mind, the more his step quickened. He reached the center and punched in his code to allow access.

"I don't know what this is, but it's spreading fast," he said to the two officers monitoring a bank of computer screens. When they turned to look at him, he added, "Hate to tell you this, guys, but you are affected already."

"What the devil are you talking about? Take a look at the screens. Nothing is happening. And how can we be affected? We've been here the whole time. And you aren't glowing. Explain that!"

"I know I'm not affected, but you two are. Maybe it's airborne."

Officer 714 approached the screens for a closer look, demanding that the tech officer vacate his chair to prevent possible contamination.

"You're out of your mind! There's nothing wrong with us. I think you're seein' things, man."

To prove his point, the tech gave Officer 714's shoulder a quick nudge. What could now be viewed around Officer 714 made the tech back up and run into the other officer in the room. Now they were all equally affected.

"Oh man! Now look what you've done!" exclaimed the tech. "You brought it in here!"

Several minutes of argument ensued until they replayed the events since Officer 714 entered the room. Each had to convince the other two of what they were seeing. They came to the conclusion that proximity was a factor, but that didn't explain why Officer 714 could see the glow around the other two prior to the tech touching him. Nor did it explain why none of this was showing up on the cameras or why each could not see it in themselves. The next question was what agency should they notify? Almost in unison, the answer came. "All of them."

In the meantime, a total of 122 affected mall patrons had left the premises. Every ophthalmologist in the area was deluged with requests for appointments. The local media was being called by concerned citizens, but the event had yet to register as anything more than unusual crank calls. Officer 714 and his two companion tech operators had put a call in to their senior officer for advice. The senior officer, on vacation in Hawaii at the moment, had all the right questions, but they had no answers that made any sense, so it was suggested they contact the region 5 office of the EPA for initial advice. They were also warned that the Mall owners were not going to be pleased to hear this because of the possibility that it would put a damper on post-holiday shopping.

Officer 714 scanned the index of the "ca-ca hits the fan" manual and located the number for the EPA office in Chicago. He dialed the number and was sent on a wild-goose chase through a series of menus that didn't fit the situation exactly, but he hung on until he was offered a chance to speak with an actual human being. Finally, a human voice replaced the elevator music.

"Environmental Protection Agency. How can I direct your call?"

Officer 714 gave them his name and location but wasn't sure what the nature of this problem was. "We're not really sure what we've got here, but it's spreading rather quickly." He went on to describe what he had observed.

"Have you determined a point of origin?"

"Not specifically. Like I said, we don't know what this is. If we knew what it was, we'd know where to look."

"Based on your description, sir, there could be a variety of potential causes."

"None of our detection devices have indicated any known contaminant."

"Have there been any injuries or fatalities?"

"A lady fell down, but we think that was due to the discharge of a fire extinguisher. No fatalities that we know of."

"There was a fire?"

"No. No fire. We're not sure why the extinguisher was used."

"Could the contents of the extinguisher have been compromised?"

Officer 714 hadn't considered that possibility. What if it had been tampered with? Nerve gas maybe? He checked the monitor to view the area where the lady fell. It was clear. The tech noted that maintenance had been called, as per his request, and the area had been cleaned.

"It's a possibility, sir. We'll contact maintenance and get them to quarantine the equipment used for cleanup. But I don't think the extinguisher was the cause. This problem was, based on my observation, already affecting the general population that had no contact with the incident site."

"Did surveillance pick up anything?"

"We wish it did, sir. That would answer a lot of questions, but this doesn't register on video."

"And your cameras have been checked?"

"They are 100 percent, sir."

"Okay. Based on what you've told me and the ICS directives, I'll pass this information along and get an OSC up there. They can set up an ACP and determine the PRP. I'll notify CSB and NIMS as well."

In Officer 714's mind, the song "Initials" from the musical *Hair* came sharply into focus. "When will this OSC arrive, sir?"

"The on-scene coordinator will be in contact with you as soon as I notify them. They can give you a more accurate ETA."

"Thank you, sir. We'll be standing by for the call." Ending the call and turning to the two tech officers, Officer 714 lamented, "Now, we wait." They called maintenance and had the suspect mop cart and tools segregated and secured.

The Airport

JASE, BRETT, AND NICK FOUND a parking spot in the gold section of short-term parking at the Lindbergh Terminal and called Lee to let her know exactly where they were. In a few short moments, Lee's truck pulled into the empty spot beside them. They still had a fifteen-minute wait until Lisa's flight arrived, and in the relative privacy of the parking structure, they lowered their windows to converse.

"I'm really sorry I had to speed things up," Lee reported to Jase, "but a little girl ran into me."

"No harm done. We accomplished what was needed. And little ones are actually some of the best targets. They just figure it's something else they aren't familiar with." Lee remembered how Emily's girls just accepted this new light as something fun.

"Guess you're right. I'll keep that in mind."

Brett, busily writing things down on a notepad and checking his watch, mentioned that he would get her to recount their mall escapade in full when they returned home. She agreed, and after a short discussion about cash for parking and where to meet Lisa, Lee and Emily prepared to enter the airport for the second half of their mission. Lee sent a quick text message to Lisa's phone that would be turned on when her plane landed. It read simply, "Meet you in baggage claim 3."

While the men remained in the vehicles, Lee and Emily stepped out of the truck and started walking toward the entrance to the airport. Emily took a pen from her pocket and jotted something down on her palm.

"What did you write?" Lee asked.

"Our parking spot number and aisle, for a quick getaway if we need to."

"Good thinking, hon."

They took the elevator to the skyway level, and Lee let Emily take the lead. A sense of direction was not Lee's forte, and airports in particular were somewhat maze-like to her. They traversed the skyway, taking advantage of the moving sidewalks, and entered the spacious ticketing level that was not nearly as crowded as Lee thought it might be. Making a left, they headed for the escalator down to the baggage claim level, all the while keeping a safe distance from all other airport patrons. The arrivals board indicated that Lisa's plane had landed safely but was not yet at the gate. They found a vacant spot to stand away from the baggage conveyor to wait for her to disembark.

As she often did, Lee took this opportunity to engage in one of her favorite pastimes: people watching. Family members here to pick up long-separated loved ones smiled in anticipation of that meeting. There were hurried businessmen walking with long strides to get wherever they were going in the shortest amount of time possible. There were the vacationing pairs and groups, always dressed in some sort of attire to advertise where they were going or where they had been. Occasionally an individual, late for their flight, would scoot by in a half run, dragging a suitcase wobbling from wheel to wheel. There were also the quiet, solitary types trying to read, but always looking distracted by the possible funeral they must attend or loved one at their destination point who needed their care. Her favorites were, of course, the families. And at this moment, it was her privilege to witness a young man in digi-camo approach a young woman surrounded by four stair-step children that she guessed ranged in ages from nine to three. The full family embrace produced such a complex range of colors that the group had formed what appeared to be a single entity. It was an awesome sight.

Her people watching came to a halt when Emily tugged her jacket and said, "There's Aunt Lisa" and pointed toward the escalator.

"Okay, let me do the talking."

Lisa spotted the pair waiting to greet her and closed her phone. As she got within speaking distance, she mentioned, "I was just about to text you! All I have is this duffel, so we can skip the carousel." Delighted to see them both, she was about to bestow upon them her normal hug of greeting. Lee stopped her in her tracks.

"Lisa, stop!" Lee instructed by extending her hand with the palm facing Lisa. "Don't touch us."

"What do you mean? Are you sick?"

"Lisa, you know me very well, and for right now, do exactly as I ask. I'll let you know what's going on as soon as we get to the parking garage."

A bit put out by the less-than-enthusiastic welcome, she did know Lee very well and did as she was asked. "Okay, I'll play along, but this had better be good."

"It is," Emily responded.

"So you're in on this little secret too, Em?" Lisa remarked as she tried to keep up with the pair.

"Yes, but give us a few minutes, and you'll be in on it too."

Spotting a restroom, Lee announced that she had to use it and asked the two if they would wait while she took care of business. Lisa added that she had to go also but was summarily told that Lee had to go alone.

"Are you telling me that this secret has some bearing on me using the facilities?"

"Yes!" they both responded.

Lisa relented and said nothing more.

Lee walked through the offset opening to the restroom and spotted two of the stair-step children at the sink dutifully washing their hands. Keeping in mind what Jase mentioned earlier about children accepting this, she took the sink next to the smallest child, washed her hands, and let her elbow graze the child's arm as she left. Hurriedly, she rejoined Lisa and Emily, and they headed for the escalator to take them up to the skyway level. Lisa was silent as they approached the elevator. The doors opened, and they stepped into an empty elevator cab to take them to the proper garage level. When the doors closed, Lisa was about to throw some rain on this parade when both Lee and Emily burst out laughing and threw their arms around Lisa.

"Holy shmokes!" Lisa shrieked. "No wonder you didn't want me touch you! What the heck is this?"

Lee kissed her cousin's cheek and backed up, laughing. "I wish you could have seen your face when I told you not to use the bathroom. It was priceless!"

Lisa was studying the dance of light that surrounded Lee and Emily. "Priceless, eh? Do the two of you want to tell me what on earth, or *not* on earth, is going on here?"

The elevator doors opened to an empty waiting area, and Lee grabbed Lisa's bag. "Of course we will fill you in completely. Let's get to the truck, and all, or almost all, will be revealed."

"This is going to be one of those visits I remember very well, isn't it?"

"Undoubtedly," Lee answered.

In record time, Lisa's bag was stowed in the back of the truck, and they were on their way. Lisa didn't at first notice that the vehicle next to them in the parking garage was following them. She greeted Matt as he chauffeured them through the ticket gate and mentioned, "I guess you're in on this as well?"

"Yes, but you'll get used to it," he replied.

"Everyone will," Lee added.

On the way home, Lee did her best to describe what this new-found insight was all about. The only thing she left out was who gave her the gift. When they were nearly halfway home, Lee's phone rang. It was Jase.

"Still with us? Okay. You did? And? Uh-oh. I guess it begins. Okay. Bye."

By this time, Lisa was used to having things not make sense, but she decided to inquire anyway. "Who was that?"

"It was Nick," Lee fibbed. To Matt and Emily, she relayed that all was good at home with the kids, and according to the news, "something" has happened at the airport, but it was smooth sailing as far as the roads were concerned. Emily took note of the reddish needles that flashed and disappeared above her mother's head as she spoke this partial truth.

"Good, "Matt responded." I was looking forward to the leftovers when we get back," he joked.

Still somewhat in the dark but not shy about advancing her point, Lisa chimed in. "Yes, that does sound good, and a bathroom would be nice too."

"Good grief!" Lee apologized. "I completely forgot about that. I'm so sorry, Lisa."

"No worries. I can hold it."

"You get first dibs on the bathroom when we get home," Lee promised.

Matt turned on the radio and tuned to a talk station in the Cities. An AD for ice dam removal was followed by a breaking news report on the temporary shutdown at the airport. The show host repeated that security investigators had called for a lockdown for an, as yet, undisclosed event unfolding at the present time. It was reported that there were no injuries associated with this event, but for security purposes, the TSA called for the heightened security measures to assess any possible threat. VIPR team members were investigating reports coming in from at least four locations in both secure and nonsecure sections of the airport complex. The host vowed to keep his audience informed on any changing information as it came in to him. Matt then muted the radio.

"How many people did you touch, Lee?"

"Just one."

"Spreads fast," was Matt's observation.

For the last twenty minutes of their journey, they discussed gardening, children, and animals, all topics rooted in domestic tranquility and light-years away from the bizarre incident they'd just set in motion. The sun was setting as they pulled into the yard.

The Meeting

IN THE GRAND MARAIS CONFERENCE room on level 4 east at the Mall, a board meeting for White Swann Company was just coming to its conclusion. Sturmisch was satisfied that in the midst of a nationwide recession, his bottom line was well into the black. He would have preferred this be done via computer video conferencing, but for the sake of absolute privacy, this was a biannual necessity. White Swann's dealings were the smallest measure of the discussions at hand. The bulk of the discussion involved the status of various points of pressure Sturmisch had brought to bear on people and institutions around the world. Based on the results of that pressure, new steps were taken to further his goals by either providing incentive, withdrawing support, or eliminating impediments entirely. It was determined what politicians needed to be purchased, what business tycoons needed to be threatened, and which nonconforming vestige of underworld power needed to be influenced to bring about the destruction necessary to make room for Sturmisch's new world.

Though he met with the eighteen professionals in attendance in groups of six, he knew that at least some would not adhere to the strict secrecy clauses of their employment contracts with him. Truly, he could not blame them because of the shocking nature of some of their duties. For those prone to the weaknesses of human caring, devastating whole populations and causing untold deaths for profit made a few of them grow a conscience. Knowing this, bonuses were bestowed preemptively in amounts large enough to eradicate all sentimentality. Any proving themselves to be beyond purchase had "accidents," or members of their families had tragedies occur. Children were the best pawns. This is why Sturmisch always ended his meetings with these words of advice: "Take care of me, and I'll take care of you." There was no doubt in anyone's mind that what he really said was, "Take care of me, *or* I'll take care of you."

So with his generals given their marching orders, the eighteen were sent forth to do their jobs, and it was time for Sturmisch to get back to the sanctity of his private Montana lair and watch events unfold. His travel assistant, Daoud, had dispatched his things to the waiting limo now parked at the east entrance awaiting his departure. In an overcoat, dark glasses, and a black Stetson, he would not be recognized as the smiling farmer on every label of White Swann product, so as he exited the elevator and headed for the open door of the limo, the brush of a young man's arm entering the elevator rang no bells of alarm.

Carefully seating himself on the rear bench seat of the limo, Sturmisch motioned for Daoud to close the door and take his place with the driver. The slide was closed, and they began the short drive to the airport. After a few moments, Sturmisch heard the intercom come to life.

"Sir?"

"Yes, Daoud, what is it?"

"There seems to be a delay at the airport, sir."

"I'll take care of it. Proceed."

Selecting from his phone contact list one of the people he "owned" in airport security, the problem was quickly resolved. He buzzed Daoud.

"Humphrey instead of Lindbergh. Call the pilot when we arrive for the pickup."

"Yes, sir."

When they arrived at the Humphrey terminal, a large steel gate parted, and they drove directly onto the runway to meet Sturmisch's Learjet 31A/35. The pilot had the steps down and approached the limo to open the rear passenger door. Daoud saw to the luggage, and the limo driver stayed seated, awaiting instruction. Sturmisch exited the vehicle, carefully reseating his Stetson as he emerged, and walked the short distance to the plane. The pilot greeted him with the minimal politeness Sturmisch required.

"This way, sir." As he was ushering his passenger onto the plane, Sturmisch's forearm brushed the pilot's hand. The pilot turned to see Daoud approaching, having finished extending a gratuity to the limo driver. Daoud was glowing. The pilot said nothing, now understanding firsthand that the rumors circulating throughout the airport were more than rumors. Their employer had entered the plane. The pilot grabbed Daoud's arm. His face bore an expression of alarm that was suppressed by the pilot's words.

"Don't say anything. This is the problem shutting down the airport."

Daoud nodded his understanding. As they climbed aboard the plane, Sturmisch was already seated, reading a magazine. Both men headed for the cockpit section, Daoud doubling as the copilot, and each glanced at their boss, who showed no indication whatsoever that he was aware of anything amiss. They seated themselves and took care of preflight checks. As the jet engines were brought to life, the pilot keyed the intercom to inform their employer.

"Preparing to taxi, sir."

Still engrossed in his reading, Sturmisch nodded his acknowledgment. As they taxied toward the runway and prepared to take off, the two men in the cockpit studied the strange light that illuminated the other. As it did not appear to be of an immediately lethal nature, they put aside their slight distress and got on with the business at hand. They were cleared for takeoff and proceeded to do so. As soon as they reached the prescribed altitude dictated by their flight plan, Daoud caught the pilot's attention and asked the question they'd both been hesitant to ask until now.

"Did you see?" Daoud asked and moved his eyes toward the rear of the plane.

"Yes," the pilot responded.

It Begins

THE KMIN MOBILE REPORTING VAN parked a block away from the Mall, and Lydia Corvuso and her cameraman prepared to get a background shot of the entrance from across Killibrew Avenue. Her station had called the PR department, and their press badges were waiting at the east guest service desk, but Lydia was more interested in the shoppers leaving the Mall than the Mall itself. After receiving a rash of calls from concerned but anonymous sources about something strange taking place there, her station manager then got word that the airport had been locked down for an undisclosed security threat. Considering the proximity of one to the other, her manager sent Lydia to the Mall to see if the two events might be related. From the look of calm she observed outside the Mall, this was probably a wild-goose chase.

Quickly they set up for an intro shot, and Lydia began her impromptu spiel to preface a possible on-scene report for the evening news. "We're standing across the road from the entrance to the MOA where, earlier today, we received calls that something of an undetermined nature was taking place. At the moment, as you can see, all looks normal. We will attempt to interview some shoppers and find out what this is all about." Satisfied that the intro was presentable, they moved on to get some interviews. As they approached the east entrance, Lydia noticed a white unmarked step van parked in one of the Mall service parking areas. Maybe there was something to this after all, she thought.

"Wait here," she instructed her camera partner, "and I'll go get our press badges." She went inside and approached the service desk. A middle-aged gentleman in a dark suit stood behind the desk. Lydia could see no identification on his person as she asked for his assistance.

"I'm sorry, ma'am. We're not issuing press passes at this time."

"But my station manager called ahead, and they said we could pick them up here."

"They will be issued at a later time, but at the moment, I'm following my instructions. We're sorry for the inconvenience."

Lydia could tell he was not the least bit sorry, and she could also tell that there definitely was a story here. If that guy was a mall employee, she was the Easter Bunny. "Okay, thanks for your help," she replied as she turned to reunite with her partner outside.

Waiting patiently, the cameraman approached as she came through the doors. "No passes today," she informed him.

"Odd," was his single-word response.

"Let's wait. We'll pull someone across the street for an interview. I'm not leaving here empty-handed, and if you can get a quick shot of that van, do it." While the cameraman nonchalantly crossed the road to the parking garage side, Lydia spotted a trio of young girls coming through the Mall doors to leave. Immediately three names came to mind: Mizaru, Kikazaru, and Iwazaru of the "See no evil, hear no evil, speak no evil" fame. Lydia was hoping Shizaru was somewhere in this picture.

"Excuse me, girls, I was wondering if I could ask you about what's happening in the Mall."

The three giggled and looked at each other and giggled again. Finally one of them said, "Sure, but I don't think we're going to know any more than you do."

The girls agreed to conduct the interview off mall property to avoid any legal entanglements. As they crossed Killibrew Avenue, the cameraman caught up with the group. Before arranging for the question-and-answer session, he said one word to Lydia that gave her chills: "Hazmat." Putting her personal worries aside, she put her thoughts together about what questions to ask the girls.

Quickly, they set up, and the interview began. "We're standing here across the street from MOA with three shoppers. Can you tell us what's happening inside the Mall?" She directed her question to the young woman who seemed to be the spokesperson for them all.

"Well, like, we really don't know how this happened."

"Could you tell our viewers exactly what *this* is?" Lydia asked.

The young woman stared at Lydia with what could only be described as incredulity. "This!" she replied. "The same thing that's happened to you, duh."

Startled and confused, Lydia tried to stay on task. The cameraman expressed his own confusion with a look that told Lydia his camera wasn't capturing what "this" was either.

"Can you describe how this happened?" Lydia was desperate to get anything that made sense.

The girls giggled again. "We have no idea. Just one minute we were looking at jeans, and the next thing we know, it was like, we were all lit up."

"Lit up?" Lydia now wondered more about her subjects than the subject matter.

"Yeah. Like glowing."

Lydia signaled to cut the video. She figured they weren't going to use the footage, so releases weren't necessary. As she thanked the girls for their time, she politely extended her hand. The speaker of the three touched Lydia's hand, and the mystery was revealed. "Holy moly!" The girls laughed at her surprise. Lydia asked the camera guy if he could see what had just appeared to her. He said he saw nothing even though to her eyes he was glowing just like the girls, so it occurred to Lydia that touch seemed to be the mechanism for transfer. She touched his arm.

"Wow. Now we've got something," he told Lydia.

"Try filming me again," Lydia requested. A quick bit of video was captured and replayed, and as before, the camera recorded none of it. "Weird. Okay, we don't know what this is, but we do have something to report." Lydia knew it wouldn't be difficult to convince the station manager about the validity of what they failed to film. All she had to do was touch him.

On the way back to the studio, Lydia asked her coworker if he thought this was going to be significant. "Monumental, I predict," was his succinct response.

"Do you think this could be harmful?" she asked.

"No. I feel fine. Don't you?"

"Yes, other than excited, I feel fine too."

With only their personal observations and experience to go on, both concluded that whatever this was, it wasn't dangerous. Lydia had no idea why, but the steady white glow surrounding her coworker was reassuring of that fact. "What about the van? You mentioned Hazmat."

"I don't think they're going to find a thing because I don't think there is anything to find."

Lydia chuckled. "I guess Shizaru is here."

"Who is that?" her companion asked.

She mentioned her thoughts when she first saw the three girls. "He's the fourth monkey you don't hear about too often. Do no evil."

Meanwhile, Back at the Farm

After everyone was settled in and Lisa's necessities were seen to, introductions were made and children greeted. Lee mentioned to Lisa that she had one more surprise in store for her.

"Another surprise? Well, don't expect my reaction to be anything more than anticlimactic after the one you already sprang on me." Lisa laughed. She sat down next to Barbara, who had baby Albert sleeping soundly in her lap.

Lee's phone rang, and it was Nick this time. "We just stopped in town to fuel up and thought I'd call to see if we needed anything."

"We always need milk. Thanks, hon," Lee answered.

"Welcome. Be home in a few. Bye."

"I was wondering where Nick was," Lisa commented. "Need to hug that kid."

"You'll get your chance. He's on his way here now with Barbara's brother, Brett, and your other surprise."

Lee barely managed to get the leftovers on the table when Nick and his passengers came in the door. Before Aunt Lisa could attack, he managed to ask his mother if she'd been watching the news.

"No, we haven't," she answered just before Lisa had Nick smothered in a full-body expression of hello.

"So glad you're home safe and sound," Lisa extolled and planted a kiss on his cheek.

Lee introduced Brett, who was greeted with a more staid welcome, and before she could even remark on Jase's presence, Lisa looked at him and gasped.

"Oh, this can't be. You said…but I had no idea. Is this possible?" Lisa had run out of words to mark her surprise. She just hugged Jase furiously.

"Don't you just love those anticlimactic expressions," Lee teased.

Brushing away happy tears, Lisa admitted that she was a bit shocked.

"How did you know it was me?" Jase asked, more impressed than astonished.

"Who could forget those eyes! I got to stare into them more than once giving you a bottle when you were a baby."

"Not to break up this reunion, but you all need to see this," Nick said, directing their attention to a special news report. Lee picked up the remote and turned on the wall-mounted television in the kitchen.

As they all listened, it was clear that the trip today had been a success. Still wary of the phenomenon, local officials from a variety of government agencies, including the CDC and MNOSHA, were in the process of trying to determine exactly what sort of agent was causing these, as yet, undocumented lights. Listeners were told that at a local level only, thus far, water and air contamination had been eliminated, but testing would continue. "Whatever this is, it is spreading rapidly. Hospitals in the Minneapolis area have received no fewer than five hundred calls regarding the spread, and emergency rooms are currently at capacity. Viewers are urged that unless there is a coinciding medical emergency to please refrain from seeking emergency room treatment. At this time, no significant ill effects can be tied directly to this," reported a hospital spokesperson. At the national level, this unusual light was now being reported on the East Coast in Philadelphia and Baltimore, and it could not be confirmed, but reports from London and Canadian flights were now surfacing. The news agencies picked up on the social media chatter and had already given this spectacle its own name. From the words *beautiful glow* it was dubbed the Gleau.

Rumor and hysteria were rampant. Suppositions about its origin ranged from nuclear fallout from compromised reactors to extraterrestrial sources at Area 51. Some of the strongest opinions were from those not yet affected. One less-than-notable psychologist suggested that this was nothing more than mass hysteria coupled with a dash of Stockholm syndrome and peer pressure. He explained that adopting the symptoms of a favored group made one feel more a part of that group, and in this case, it was perfect, as no real physical proof was required to be a member. He stuck to that hypothesis until the interviewer touched him. The interview ended abruptly when the doctor was asked to explain his own personal experience. The interviewer closed the segment with, "Well, folks, there you have it. We're all a bit 'touched' in the head, until we're touched."

As the occupants of Lee's kitchen watched the news of her gift's journey, they were amazed at the speed it traveled.

"It travels quickly because affected or not, no one can tell who has or has not had the ability turned on. To anyone who hasn't received the gift, it appears no one has it, and to someone who has been affected, it appears that everyone already has it," Jase explained. "What will really blow their minds is when they find out that this is nothing new. The Gleau, as they have so named it, has been with every human being from day one. All Lee did was switch on the ability everyone already had to perceive it."

"And what will really get them scratching their collective heads is when they find out you don't need functioning eyes to perceive it, like me," Barbara added.

Lisa looked at Barbara in utter amazement. "You're blind? Really?"

Barbara laughed. "Now that was a first for me!" Barbara was seated in the kitchen giving the baby his bottle when the group returned, and from casual observance, nothing about her interactions indicated a lack of anything.

"Seriously?" Lisa inquired again.

"Truly," Barbara reiterated. "I've come to the conclusion this has more to do with an open mind than it does with open eyes."

"Well," Lisa joked, "hand me a bowl, Lee, because as much as my mind has been opened today, I'm going to need something to catch my brain when it falls out!"

"*Ew!*" Pam exclaimed, expressing her disgust.

Lee assured Pam that Aunt Lisa's brain was not going to fall out, and though she laughed as well, it was one of the few things she was absolutely sure about presently. Still in its infancy, Lee worried about the indirect consequences of the unveiling of this event. It was her earnest hope that no harm would come to anyone.

⟪❦⟫

Sturmisch's plane landed safely on his private airstrip, and they taxied to his Hummer parked at the end of the road leading to the security of his hidden abode. Without any fanfare, Daoud unbuckled his safety restraints and lowered the steps for their exit. The pilot stayed seated in preparation to continue his flight to Gardner Airport where the jet was kept for Sturmisch's disposal in a private hangar. Daoud hit the remote starter on his keychain, and the Hummer came to life. The passenger door was opened, and as Sturmisch seated himself, he remarked, "I assume you were affected at the airport."

"Yes, sir," Daoud responded. He closed the passenger door and retrieved the luggage from the plane. Nothing more was said as they drove the two and one half miles past Daoud's hunting cabin home to the secured adit to Sturmisch's bunker-like accommodation. Daoud placed the bags in the rear of the golf cart at the entrance and bid his employer a good evening. Sturmisch responded by closing the door. Daoud wasn't the least bit surprised or insulted by his boss's lack of proper etiquette. Moreover, he was grateful that no more questions were asked of him. He supposed at a later date, he may be asked to describe what he saw, but he would do so with intuitive caution.

The short drive back to his cabin was without incident, and he parked the Hummer in the small outbuilding next to it. The cabin was dark and empty, but he thought it was a better place to be than in the warm well-appointed lodgings with the man who employed him. He wasn't sure why, but what he viewed around the man did not bode well. It was in such contrast to the light that surrounded the pilot, a man he knew not by name but by job alone. That was how Sturmisch insisted it remain.

A few people knew Daoud, but his first name was all they knew about him personally. He was simply Sturmisch's assistant, nothing more. He supposed there were those who speculated about why he agreed to live in the lonely and austere conditions of the hunting cabin and have limited contact with family and none with the outside world, except Sturmisch. Daoud was filling a niche, not for Sturmisch, but for his family in Afghanistan. His separation from them was a small price to pay as his generous compensation from this effort supported his family back home. His only regret was the time missed with his grandchildren, but he knew that one day, maybe not soon, he would be with them.

Loyalty to his family was something engrained in his being when in his youth he fought with Mujahideen forces against the invading Soviet army. He had lost many friends and witnessed horrors he wished upon no one, which was why what he saw around Sturmisch Swann gave him pause. Daoud was no stranger to evil.

·⸱⸱⸱⸱⸱·

As the twenty-sixth of December was coming to a close, the eyes of the world were being opened. News of this event spread almost as quickly as the event itself, but the truth of the Gleau was not yet apparent. Science experts were scrambling to determine the nature of the light being emitted and whether or not it posed any physical threat. In the short time it had been available for study, they could only say what it was not, and so far, it was not deemed harmful. Armed with that information, government spokesmen asked the public to remain patient and calm, which to most meant "We don't the faintest idea what's going on and we don't want you overreacting and upsetting our apple cart."

Like anything else the government decided to take control of, it was beginning to be sucked into the vast pit of bureaucracy where blue ribbon committees, endless studies, nonproductive analysis, meaningless evaluations, and award-winning panels of opinion were the only things generated with efficiency at extreme cost. Eventually, it would be determined what each person would be charged to give them answers that didn't exist. Be that as it may, this was actually a benefit to the free flow of the Gleau. While government issuances creeped forth at a snail's pace, the Gleau coursed through humanity at lightning speed. Though there would be a few isolated pockets of population that would receive the Gleau well after news of it reached them, it would eventually become universal.

With their mission of the day accomplished, Lee's guests celebrated cautiously. And while they weren't glued to the television watching the evolving news alerts, they were recounting the day's events and becoming better acquainted. For the most part, Brett listened and recorded in his private shorthand the firsthand perspectives shared with all. As excited as he was about being able to share this scoop with the print media world, it was beginning to dawn on him the historic importance of what he was recording. Something Jase told him was weighing heavily on his mind as well. Jase had accepted his role in this endeavor with a set conclusion. Brett wondered what that conclusion was.

Barbara took great pride in describing her first ever experience in babysitting, and Emily was quite proud of her girls for helping in the process. While Barbara could see the children in her charge without difficulty, things like diapers, bottles, and socks were still invisible to her. The girls were pleased with the fact they were not just helpers but necessary elements in the smooth completion of the daily tasks. Emily cracked up when it came to Pam's comments about changing diapers.

"I told Miss Barbara she could do it if it was only wet, but if it was muddy, she would need my help. Poops are invisible," Pam explained, rolling her eyes, and at the same time a wedge of bright orange tipped with magenta flashed from ear to ear around her head.

"She's right." Barbara laughed. "And Lorelei was my seeing-eye child. I even managed to get a clean shirt on Mathew and was quite pleased with my effort until one of them mentioned it was on backward."

It was then that a report came in that the Gleau had been established in several prisons, and if the event wasn't perplexing enough, what was being relayed by guards and medical personnel took it a step beyond this new norm. Tales of some inmates being surrounded by what appeared to be a swirling darkness began to surface. Rather than exuding light, the descriptions were that they seemed to dispel and absorb it at the same time. One guard, rather shaken by the sight of a particularly renowned resident of death row, described it as a writhing of black snakes made of smoke, and he really didn't care much for snakes.

"I knew we would begin to see this," Jase commented.

"See what exactly?" Lisa asked with more than casual interest.

"The shadow dwellers," Jase replied.

"I got that much, but what does that mean?" she asked again.

"It means they're evil," Nick spoke up.

"Wow, that should make things a whole lot easier for the courts, I'd say," Lisa supposed.

"Not really," Jase countered. "Being a dark soul doesn't make you any more guilty of a particular crime than being a light soul makes you automatically innocent. Intent doesn't prove guilt. The courts are still going to have their work cut out for them."

"Then what does being a shadow dweller tell us about someone?" Lisa persisted.

"It tells us there is a profound absence of good in someone," Jase answered.

"Ah, it depends on what light things are viewed in as to whether or not this is a shady character," Lisa added, rather proud of her play on words.

"Exactly," Jase agreed. "But there are a few too many who have managed to appear to be what they are not."

"Yes. And for exactly that reason, the true meaning of this won't be revealed until they have unwittingly exposed themselves, right?" Brett sought.

"I knew you were the right man for this job," Jase said, indicating his confidence in Brett's appraisal. "After all, if we announced that anyone wearing a green hat was evil, I can almost guarantee that not a single green hat would be worn. Right now, the truly evil, those who have managed to disguise themselves, hide behind seemingly good deeds while leaving destruction in their wakes. They are unmasked. They have only the word of others to indicate how they appear. Their appearance, as it did for that corrections officer, will instill just suspicion for now. And the evil who currently wield power have always surrounded themselves with yes-men so they will be told what they wish to hear. Their own liars will keep them unmasked."

"What other things can be determined from the Gleau?" Matt asked.

"Most of it is already pretty familiar. Some things you'll recognize automatically, and some will be more subtle, gauged by pattern and movement," Jase informed. "For instance, deception is displayed in red above the shoulders, as in raising a red flag. When a deliberate lie is issued, usually a cone of red will appear, like a dunce cap. Anger will be in waves of vermillion about the chest. Contentment, something easily displayed by children, is demonstrated by a pinkish hue, hence being 'in the pink.' Remarks aimed to cause emotional hurt will be displayed in flashes around the sender: yellow for jealousy, green for envy, blue for sadness and arrogance. Then there are the combinations that run in ripples, waves, speckles, sprites. It's very individual, like a smile or a frown. One of my favorites is the one Pam demonstrated beautifully a few minutes ago, the eye roll."

Lee considered all that was being discussed and came to the conclusion that even before her gift had been presented, it had always been recognized subconsciously. This just gave people an obvious heads-up about what and who to avoid and who to engage and hold dear, she hoped. And something else came to mind. "This can't be faked, can it," she said more than asked.

"No. This has no poker face. That's why you could say it is literally the light of truth," Jase agreed. "And lying about what you've seen in others will show as well."

"Wow," Lisa added, "every one of us will be a walking lie detector."

"I'm not sure if anyone else noticed or not, but on our way home today when Jase called and Mom said it was Nick, I did notice little red spikes flare up around her head. She told a fib because Aunt Lisa didn't know Jase was with us yet, and until now, I wasn't sure what it meant," Emily declared.

"Yes," Jase laughed. "And that's one of the little drawbacks we'll face. Anyone asking someone's opinion will have to face the fact that sometimes when we wish to avoid hurting someone's feelings, we will stray from the complete truth."

"Maybe that will end those 'does this make my butt look big' questions," Matt joked.

"Not in a million years, Matt!" Emily chided her husband.

"There will be no doubt about the truly evil ones though," Jase said, bringing a serious quality back to the conversation. "The monsters are the ones that will be the least happy with this event."

"Monsters?" Emily asked.

"It's an appropriate moniker for them, but much worse than any Frankenstein or creature from the Black Lagoon. The monsters I'm talking about are the ones we've seen every day but have never been able to truly see what lies within. Until now, they have walked among us having their darkness hidden by lies and deceptions. They wear corruption like a halo, and they've learned the weaknesses of otherwise good people to have their dirty work done." Jase let his comments rest. It was far worse than he'd told his small audience thus far, but enough was said to make them wary.

"I think I know some of those monsters," Lisa disclosed. "I can't say I've seen them firsthand, but I've seen the results of their actions." She described situations where some preyed on the desperate, the weak, and the hopeful, offering help that never truly manifested. Others would devour their own kind, counting on greed, depravity, and apathy to gain them a rope of trust used to strangle those they ensnared. "Maybe they're only small monsters, but they are monsters just the same. They do purposely cater to the worst in people."

"I think we've all seen them, Lisa," Brett said in agreement. "We see the results of what they do on the news every day."

"You're both right. But the other thing we're going to see is how many more good people there are," Jase tempered.

"I'm glad to hear you say that, Jase. From what I saw today, everyone looked good to me, but then again, I wasn't looking for any shadowy folks either," Lee added.

"That is you, Mom, the eternal optimist. I'm not saying I'm a complete pessimist or a total cynic, but you offer a whole lot more trust than I do," Nick said to his mother.

Brett laughed at Nick's characterization. "You obviously haven't come up against her when she's protecting one of her own tribe! She's a mamma grizzly if I've ever seen one."

Lee blushed and realized how much her opinion of Mr. Brett Hume had changed over the past couple months. At first, he was simply a customer, then by mere chance a business acquaintance, then an enemy who threatened her family privacy, and now one of a trusted team involved in the inception of an event with untold possibilities. She reflected on that chain of thought and realized something else about him that truly impressed her. It wasn't the telltale light that framed his being, but his dedication to his sister that made her drop her guard entirely. This man was safe.

As the evening wore on, it was obvious that everyone was suffering from adrenaline rush exhaustion. Matt and Emily packed up their tribe, all giving Barbara hugs of thanks and affection, and headed for home. Brett decided he and Barbara should call it a night as well, but he let Jase know that he would contact him in the morning to discuss how events transpired overnight. Lisa stowed her things in Lee's room and readied herself for bed. Lee finished tidying the kitchen and decided to make a quick check of things outside before bed.

She pulled on her barn boots and coat, grabbed an egg basket and half a loaf of stale bread, and headed for the chicken house. The central pole light lit the main barnyard area while leaving most of the buildings in the shadows. Lee could see the soft glow of the heat lamp through the single window of the henhouse.

Usually Semi would be with her on these ventures, but he sat this one out from the comfort of his rocker next to the pellet stove in the kitchen. Not that she could blame him because it was in the minus of degrees, and he had no hat or boots.

Unlatching the door, she quickly entered the henhouse. Most of the occupants were roosting, but a few feathered inhabitants greeted her with enthusiasm—or greeted the bag of bread anyway. The egg basket was hung on a nail, and a five-gallon pail served as a seat as she scattered the bread for her flock. It was here, doing the simplest of tasks, that Lee felt closest to her world. Then Lee turned her head to listen, thinking she heard something. The chickens were clucking sleepily. It must have been them. As she handed out the last of the bread, she heard it again. *Voices*, she thought. It was a calm conversation, but low and muffled. Then it stopped. She stood and went out into the night and heard nothing more. She latched the henhouse door and headed for bed.

A Small Distraction

STURMISCH WAS GLAD TO BE back in his oasis of privacy. Confident that his instructions were being carried out to the letter, he quickly calculated the results and began formulating the next steps in his multileveled manipulation of the rise and fall and rise again of humanity. Occasionally, a domino failed to fall as precisely as it should, so the nudge of a pink slip or the extreme of a planned suicide was employed to get things back on track.

After a bowl of oatmeal and a cup of tea, he made himself comfortable in his custom recliner and swiveled the stand supporting his laptop to a suitable position. The screen came to life with the issuance of a verbal command, and he set about verifying his trusts. His first interest was the activity of his political puppets, but his attention was redirected by the media frenzy aimed at whatever nonsense had taken place at the airport earlier in the day. It came as no surprise that these servants of drama could be so easily distracted by something of no consequence. From his firsthand observation, he wasn't affected and neither his driver nor his pilot, who were affected, had dropped dead, so this preoccupation with some silly lights was beneath his concern. So what if some bioluminescent bug was at large? As long as it didn't interfere with his plans, the world needed to take a shower and get over it. He did though keep in mind that if it was a malady for which there was an antidote, he would be the first in line to support an expensive long-term study while developing a very expensive cure. Guilt, fear, and lies were making it so easy to capitalize on people that Sturmisch nearly felt sorry for them at one point, until he came to his senses and remembered that they asked for it. He, for one, would see to it that they got what they deserved.

Sturmisch scrubbed his mind of this irrelevant fluff and set about determining whether or not his dominoes were being set up as per his instructions. The CEO of the conglomerate who failed to grant him access to certain commodities had politely resigned so that Sturmisch's handpicked designate could be installed by the board. The two banking executives interfering with his wishes had coincidentally been eliminated by a tragic skiing accident and a private plane mishap. His propping of certain currencies was having the desired effect in preparation for his threatened withdrawal to force a particularly ruthless dictator to commit to Sturmisch's staged uprising. Old terrorists were taken out, and new terrorists were established where necessary. Everything was moving along like clockwork.

In less than two months, his candidate for the upcoming election would be center stage. It wasn't that there weren't suitable individuals to choose from the current public pool, but Sturmisch didn't have time to hold auditions, and he wanted total control. It was far quicker and easier to invent a stage-worthy candidate from within the ranks of White Swann, and Sturmisch knew he had the perfect man for the job. This gentleman's checkered past was a hand of which Sturmisch held all the cards. With the technologies available, his pocketed judicial puppets, his media influence, and his access to public records, Sturmisch set about creating his own Adam. The promise of scrutiny had forced the fabrication of a short but complex and verifiable past to be compiled, complete with photographs, documentation, personal testimonials, and the insertion of all such information in searchable databases with the dates of insertion falsified. No sense taking any chances when one had to adhere to a time line.

Aided by genuine natural disasters, his fist was closing on economies of the world at every level. He made sure the right kind of news was available to keep every side of an issue focused solidly on the chosen opposition. As demands for oil increased and decreased due to fluctuating economies, the price per barrel had to go up for a variety of unassailable reasons. Blame could not be aimed at the workers of foreign nations just trying to heat the mud hut and put goat on the table. It could not be aimed at the ridiculously rich families of those lands who so generously chose us a preferred customer; after all, the upkeep on a palace was expensive. It had to be blamed on an entity close at hand that would cause division, jealously, and hate. Those divisions were relatively easy to create and bring to a usable boil, but they needed constant pot stirring to maintain the proper simmer while not boiling over—not yet anyway.

When it came to creating vulnerability in a population under the impression that they were self-sufficient, Sturmisch was a pro. It was all in how something was presented, and it was never mentioned that, in general, everyone wanted the same good things. It was the tried-and-true method of pointing out a flaw and exaggerating it to the point of division. The division was created not by the problem itself, but by a solution that would benefit one segment and punish another while telling both to pay no attention to the man behind the curtain. It was an unsavory parallel to draw, but Sturmisch never put his own dog or cockerel into the fighting ring, but as merely the organizer of said entertainment, he felt his profits, unlike the bloodied animals, were clean.

Perish the thought, but if the schooled morons on either side of the divide ever figured out who the real enemy was, Sturmisch knew they would be a formidable force. But history was on his side, and current reality was in his total control, leaving him nothing to fear. The peons were kept in a frenzy of name-calling and hateful reprisal while Sturmisch worked his magic unmolested. Divide and conquer was a tried-and-true method that the know-it-alls thought couldn't possibly work now with all the communications access available, and Sturmisch would agree wholeheartedly with them as he watched them tear each other apart.

Time for the News

L YDIA CORVUSO WAS QUITE PROUD of the fact that her little blip of a story about the Gleau was the first registered with the Associated Press. The AP office in Minneapolis had been contacted shortly after they returned from their scouting mission at the Mall and walked into the KMIN station manager's office and touched him. Stricken with a measure of initial shock, he cautiously accepted that it wasn't deadly and registered the story at 2:27 p.m. central time. In addition to the unrevealing interview, Lydia wrote a short piece of copy to summarize their firsthand observations.

Every major news outlet and more than a few regional markets had the Gleau headlining their morning newscasts with more experts crawling out of the woodwork than you could shake a stick at, or so that was Nick's take on the situation. They had all seen Lydia's report, she being a local gal of note, and they were reasonably impressed with her accurate accounting and sound judgments about the benign nature of the phenomenon. In less than twenty-four hours, nearly every major city in the United States was reporting the influence of the Gleau. Schools, mercifully, were still on holiday break, so that complication was avoided for the time being.

Scientists, hoping opinion and conjecture would take a proper backseat to what they saw as their domain, were having a difficult time convincing anyone they were any closer to an accurate evaluation than the man on the street. So far, they could not quantify, qualify, measure, sample, or reproduce it. All they had was observation and the ability to remind everyone that they were trained observers. Lee decided that made them slightly less inept than Peeping Toms.

One of the few interviews dissecting this happening that Lee found insightful was with a member of the clergy who declared that he was a definite nonexpert. As he explained it, modern man has been taught that anything he cannot immediately explain or put to gainful use must be either dangerous or not worth notice. Our quest for knowledge, though admirable, has occasionally made us close the doors on learning based on what we have already learned. We judge unknowns by whether or not they fit existing criteria. This unknown, this Gleau, did not fit in any of the categories of hard modern science. Obviously, we were "seeing" it, but cameras could not. If modern science had exhausted their means of telling us what it is, the next question should be, what is its purpose? The interviewer then asked if this might have anything to do with God, to which this young clergyman, being true to his chosen mission in life, responded, "What doesn't?"

Others in various nontraditional theological sects were setting forth more unambiguous predictions, like the coming of the rapture or the opening of the fifth seal of Revelations. Though there was a warning involved in her gift, Lee did not think it was spawned by specific historical reference. Those less-established groups, viewed as cults, were having all sorts of conniption fits. Before anything concrete had been put forth regarding the substance, or lack of substance of the Gleau, the finger-pointing and blame began. If the event coincided with anything in a cult's particular doctrine, they claimed it as a sign of their validity. If it failed to support their doctrine, they claimed a government conspiracy. It was either co-opt or blame, but there was no discernible proof on any side. Rationalization, speculation, and assumption were the firm foundations they chose to stand upon. Regardless of the stance, each cult declared that this was an indication for even greater control over their devotees.

There was one peculiarity, as yet unrecognized and unreported, that seemed to be universal. Those who exercised or desired power over the lives of others were presenting themselves as shadowed figures. That was not to say that every person in a position of power was shadowy. The leaders—those who stood for principles others willingly followed individually, without coercion or obligation, without promise of gain or punishment—did not stand out. They were just like any other plain old Joe Nobody. There was no worldly status that guaranteed how an individual would appear to others. It was, however, a promising indicator that those glowing brightly outnumbered shadowed ones by approximately a thousand to one. Across every boundary of human distinction, there was not a single physical or societal attribute that dictated how someone gleaued, nor did it distort how they saw others. All of these things would remain a mystery until it was time to know. For now, humanity was being forced to think.

New Year

IN LESS THAN TWO WEEKS, Nick would be gone again. Lee was having a selfish moment wishing he could stay, but she knew that wasn't a possibility. At least he would be taking with him an ability that might offer some protection. Having completed a four-year obligation with the corps with three tours of combat duty under his belt, he would be returning to the theater as a civilian contractor. This didn't lessen Lee's concern for his safety. His Mdewakanton Sioux heritage did make it easier for him to blend in with the indigenous population, so, as he put it, he "didn't stand out as the white boy in the land of the brown people." Not carrying a weapon made him less of a target, but it also left him vulnerable. Nick understood his mother's worries and downplayed the danger, assuring her that he would be in the company of competent Marines. It was a partial truth she let him get away with. She knew mitigating danger did not eliminate it, and it was a part of life no matter where you were.

Lee's gift galloped around the globe, and in less than a single week, it was an international topic of curiosity and opinion, and as it had no measured ill effect on the physical body, it was no longer treated as a threat. It was just an anomaly with no known cause. Still, study of it persisted as did erroneous claims to its origins. In the meantime, Lee was planning a New Year's Eve celebration, and Nick was in charge of their personal fireworks display. Matt and Emily had invited a couple from their church, the Habermans, and their three children, so Nick knew he would have an appreciative audience. On the eve of the last day of the year, snow fell gently during the day with the promise of a starry evening ahead. Lee had a ham baking in the oven that would serve as sandwiches prior to midnight and breakfast the following morning. On his tabletop perch, Semi stared intently at Jase making his way across the barnyard from the barn to the house. As Jase disappeared around the corner, Semi hopped down to greet him as he entered the kitchen.

"Smells good in here," Jase declared as the aroma of baked ham and a hint of clove engulfed him.

"Thanks for feeding the girls," Lee opened. "And for tending to Beanie," she finished.

"Glad to be of service. I think the chickens know who I am now," Jase said proudly.

"I bet they do," Lee agreed.

"I was wondering if I could ask a favor," Jase said out of the blue.

"Anything," Lee answered automatically.

"I'd like to invite someone to the party tonight."

"Sure thing," Lee answered, having no clue who else he could be inviting because Brett and Barbara were already on the list. "Obviously this is someone I've not yet met," Lee stated, expecting a response.

"Not yet, but he'll be here in a minute, and I'll introduce you."

Jase had no cell phone of his own. Lee wondered when these plans were made. Who else could he know to invite? And how could word have gotten to Jase that his guest was only minutes away? Lee decided the answers were of no real consequence and let the questions evaporate. "Okay, sounds great. Hope they like ham."

Before Jase could respond, a tap on the door signaled the new partier's arrival. Jase welcomed the towering gentleman into the kitchen, and Semi immediately ran to him, vigorously arched and rubbed against his pant legs, meowing in what could only be described as a greeting to a long-lost friend.

"Well, Semi, maybe you should introduce me!" Lee looked into a face with an absolutely gorgeous smile. His likeness was one so familiar, and yet she knew they had never met. Suddenly it dawned on her.

"Hi, I'm Ben. Nice to meet you." He held out a hand that looked like a catcher's mitt.

"Hi, I'm Lee. And I'm glad you're on our side." Lee's hand disappeared in the grip as they greeted one another.

Ben let out a baritone laugh that rumbled like a landslide. His build was not disproportionate, but he was huge. His black hair, though quite long, was pulled back in a braid that extended nearly two feet down his back. Judging by the fact that he stooped a bit coming through the doorway, Lee guessed he was over six and a half feet tall, but he was one of the least menacing giants she had ever had the pleasure of meeting.

"Care for some coffee? I just made some," Lee offered.

"Sounds wonderful," Ben replied.

"Have a seat, or maybe two. They're small, and I'll have it coming right up," Lee joked.

Ben pulled out a chair and emitted a low thunderous chuckle. "Thanks," he responded.

Lee served his coffee in a large mug that looked like a dainty teacup in his hand. Aside from the fact that he glowed like the aurora borealis, everything about him was goodness. His smile never left his face, and his bold but refined bronze features revealed an egalitarian soul. His eyes, so dark they appeared black, smiled as well and brought to light a kindness of bottomless depth. No wonder Semi was immediately smitten. This man, for lack of a better description, was angelic.

"So, Ben, how long have you and my brother known one another?"

"Seems like forever," Ben responded, looking to Jase for confirmation.

"We met quite a while ago. Ben's in security," Jase added.

"No doubt," Lee responded, making no attempt to disguise her sarcasm. "I'd say he's the entire force."

Ben let go another deep laugh and looked at Jase. "You didn't tell me she was funny."

Jase smiled at Lee and asked, "What time is everyone arriving?"

"I told them the food would be ready at five, and Nick says the fireworks show will begin at seven. What time is it now?"

"A little after four," Jase answered, glancing at the clock behind Lee. Lee was staring at Ben with a puzzled look. Finally she spoke.

"Now I know who it is!" Neither Ben nor Jase had the slightest idea what she was talking about. Noticing their confusion, she explained. "I'm sorry. When you came in, you reminded me of someone, and I was having difficulty putting a name with the face I recalled. The man's name was Taoyateduta. You could be his brother. It's the eyes, I think."

"I see," Ben acknowledged.

"What's your last name, Ben?"

Ben gave Jase a quick look asking if it was okay to reveal the information. "Crow," he answered.

"Ben Crow. Has a nice ring." Lee grabbed a tray from the refrigerator, purposely ignoring what had to be more than a coincidence. "You guys can relax in the living room, if you'd like. I think there's a game on." She took the tray of vegetables, cheeses, and dips to the sideboard and told them to help themselves.

Lee crowded the kitchen table with bowls and platters of savory foods to be eaten on the run, along with the last vestiges of the Christmas sweets. A cooler of drinks was parked in the corner, and Lee declared her mission complete. Nick and Lisa returned from town with fireworks and a bottle of champagne to toast the New Year, and as it neared five o'clock, Brett and Barbara arrived. Lee sent Brett and Nick into the room with the men, and after a quick introduction to Ben, she escorted Barbara to a comfortable seat in the kitchen to engage in girl talk. The Benson clan and their guests arrived shortly thereafter, and while Nick readied his fireworks display, Lee was thankful that everyone brought good cheer and appetites. There was nothing better than the chaos of a good time, and of course, the topic of conversation got around to the Gleau.

The Habermans were the only attendees outside the loop of confidentiality, so discussion was guided accordingly. Mrs. Haberman let it be known that it was the general consensus of church parishioners that if this wasn't something generated by earthly means and it wasn't dangerous, then it must be something of a spiritual nature. Barbara agreed but wouldn't jump to any conclusions. If this was something of a secular nature, it would make sense that its origins and purpose would have been revealed by now, but until its significance was disclosed, she would have it remain an enigma, thus putting an end to the speculations. There was a great deal of interest in the verity that Barbara was able to perceive this spectacle despite her loss of vision. It was a factoid thus far the general media had either overlooked or avoided.

When the fireworks were complete, the Habermans thanked their hosts and headed for home, followed shortly by Matt and Em, eager to get children to bed. Nearly every television station was running its own program with highlights of the past year and predictions for the next, so the remaining revelers flipped through the offered fare with an ear trained on any new information on the Gleau.

Lee, Lisa, and Barbara gathered in the kitchen and watched as the people of Australia were the first to enter the new year. It took three days for the Gleau to reach the island continent, but when it did, the friendly Aussies took it in stride. The aboriginal people accepted it as a force of nature and didn't much worry about its origins, but immediately came up with a name for it that was as difficult to pronounce as it was easy to understand. The rough translation was "the light that does not cast shadows but reveals them." At a loss to capture anything on film, the media was beside itself trying to describe for their audience what could only be depicted by an artist's interpretation. Courtroom sketch artists and animation experts were working overtime providing the only depictions possible.

Having been brought up to speed about the meaning of all this, Lisa wanted more details. "When is everyone going to learn what this means?"

"I'm not sure," Lee answered.

"It will be after they stop searching for what it is and begin asking why it is, or that's my guess anyway," Barbara added.

"You're probably right. You know, at least a few are going to take advantage of the unknowns and claim responsibility," Lisa chimed in.

"That's what we want them to do," Jase spoke as he entered the room. He opened the refrigerator and grabbed three beers and a pop. "We want all the snakes feeling safe in the daylight, figuratively speaking."

"Most of them feel that way anyway. They are so much smarter than the rest of us, you know," Lisa added with definite sarcasm.

"In this case, they will be smart enough to outwit themselves." Jase laughed.

"Who's the lightweight?" Lee asked, nodding toward the cans in Jase's hands and knowing full well it was Nick. "Hey, Nick?" Lee called in a voice loud enough to be heard in the adjacent room. "You're my designated driver. Okay?"

"Sure, Mom. Where are we driving?"

"To the rock," she answered without explanation. Before anyone could ask, Lee went to the bedroom and quickly returned clutching a cigar in her teeth. "My annual tribute has to be made!"

"Will all seven of us fit in our car?" Barbara asked.

"We'll squish in. It's not that far. And we've got just enough time to get there and back before the new year is official," Lee explained as she pulled on her coat. Brett handed Nick the keys to warm up the engine, and everyone bundled up and squeezed into the sedan.

When Ben had successfully folded himself into a pretzel and the last door on the vehicle was closed, Lisa asked, "I'm game here, but where the heck are we going?"

"You'll see. It isn't far," Lee managed with the cigar still held in her teeth.

They turned left out of the drive and drove the four miles to a spot where Lee asked Nick to pull over. Not knowing what to expect, the group abandoned the relative warmth of the car to a spot in the middle of sleeping farmland covered with snow. Lee headed into the field, and they all followed her tracks across the ditch to a snow-covered rock that seemed out of place. Pulling a flashlight from her pocket, Lee carefully cleared the snow from the face of the rock, revealing a plaque.

"I think I know what this is," Barbara stated, holding fast to her brother's arm.

"I'm glad somebody does," Lisa said. "I'm still clueless."

Lee took the cigar and placed it at the foot of the rock. In nearly a whisper, she said, "Thank you."

"That's it?" Lisa asked.

"Yes," Lee replied.

"Well, would you care to share the significance?"

"Sure. I was thanking the people who made my children a possibility. That's all."

Lisa knew Lee's ex-husband was descended from Dakota Sioux but still wondered what this marker was all about. They all walked back to the car and piled in. Shaking off the chill of the night air, Lee embellished. "That stone is a tribute to Taoyateduta. In July of 1863, it was here while he was picking raspberries that he was killed. It was actually farther out in the field where there used to be a big oak tree. He was an interesting man, also known as Little Crow," Lee added, glancing over at Ben. So much of what was one of the bloodiest wars between indigenous and immigrating people was born of the same misunderstandings and government corruption that continued to this day. Reading the history of just this small area led Lee to believe that for all of man's progress, they were still blind to their own mistakes.

Light snow began falling as they arrived back at Lee's, and they had a little less than an hour left of 2011. As everyone shook the chill from the outing, the champagne was chilling for the toasts, and strains of "Auld Lang Syne" could be heard on the television from the Times Square venue. From the festive moods of the crowds gathered at the different locations around the country, it didn't seem that too many people were stricken with fear of the still unknown. In fact, word of mouth indicated that most found the Gleau to be an enjoyable new feature. Phrases like, "I always knew he was bright" and "She has that certain glow" were tossed about like punch lines to some great inside joke. Seeing the reactions of the crowds did much to lessen Lee's angst about releasing this ability, and she was feeling little less like Pandora or Typhoid Mary and maybe a little more like Johnny Appleseed.

Five minutes was left until midnight, and Lisa struggled to open the champagne until Jase came to her rescue. With a crisp *pop!*, the bubbly was divided among seven flutes, and all were summoned to the kitchen to make the moment official. In the three-minute-and-fifty-second wait until the countdown for the next journey around the sun began, Lee contemplated all that had changed in the past four months. She looked at each glowing figure in her kitchen and acknowledged her embarrassment of riches. It was a private wow moment.

"Ten, nine, eight," Lisa began, and everyone chimed in.

"Three, two, one, happy New Year!" they resounded in unison.

All the cheering got Semi's attention, and he watched wide eyed from the safety of his rocker as the room full of humans hugged and patted and kissed one another for reasons that escaped his curious little cat mind.

A spoon tapping crystal directed everyone's attention to Jase. "A toast," he began. "To our hostess, my sister Lee," he declared. "Thank you for your strength, patience, trust, and bravery."

Glasses were raised in agreement. "Thank you, but I think that applies to us all," Lee added.

"You forgot insanity," Lisa mentioned with a grin.

"You should know," Lee responded to Lisa, nudging her with a hip.

"Okay, everyone," Jase said, regaining everyone's attention. "We've succeeded planting this seed, and we're going to sit tight and watch it grow, but believe me, the opposition isn't going to ignore this. As it becomes more obvious what this indicates, the forces that it exposes are going to retaliate. Right now those forces are busy doing what they have laid the groundwork for, turning everything upside down, and capitalizing on every disaster, small and large, to further the fervor and incite otherwise good people to do bad things. It's not going to be pretty. The Gleau is going to make people aware after the fact at first, but it has to be that way. We have to let the shadow dwellers expose themselves."

"So for the time being, we should respond to solicitations for opinion in a manner not of disinterest but of seeking the same truth," Brett added. "Or at least that's how I'm going to present it in the paper."

"Good show," Jase agreed.

Ben had been noticeably reserved all evening, so when he spoke, his voice stood out. "For all of you here, should you feel you have need for protection from anything, that's why I'm here," his sonorous words assured.

"You've got my business," Lee answered. "Like I said before, glad you're on our side."

"What's your number so I can program it in my phone?" Brett asked flatly.

"No number. I'll be where I'm needed," Ben answered.

"Seriously," Jase concurred, "the man's been doing this for a long time. He'll be there."

Once again, Ben raised his glass. "Here's to an interesting year and the safety of all."

"Hear, hear," they all responded.

Weather Change

THIS WOULD BE *his* YEAR. Sturmisch celebrated the coming of the new year the way he always did: asleep and alone. He slept soundly secure in the notion that as he slept, every detail and task was being seen to with precision in mind. When he awoke at precisely quarter past five on January 1, 2012, the dawn brought with it not a sense of urgency, but a sense of calm. His life's work would soon be unveiled, and humanity would be on their knees seeking his will, his advice, and his wisdom.

The one thing that made Sturmisch sure beyond all doubt that humanity would submit was the fact that they were flawed. They had weaknesses and made honest mistakes that he was quick to capitalize upon. For all the bad press capitalism had gotten lately, to the point that one should apologize for making an honest living, they missed the largest capitalized-upon commodity in history: human beings. Slavery, being such an ugly word and frowned upon in civilized society, had to appear voluntary, and Sturmisch was a clever slave master. It mattered little to him what form of shackle was used, but it had to appear that the slave willingly applied the fetter as a matter of free choice, thus avoiding any claims of unfairness. One of Sturmisch's favorite quotes was by the renowned poet Robert Frost: "The strongest and most effective force in guaranteeing the long-term maintenance of power is not violence in all forms deployed by the dominant to control the dominated, but consent in all forms in which the dominated acquiesce in their own domination."

He took his morning tea with him as he opened his private e-mail account to check on his progress with his planet of pawns. Unless there was a failure or an emergency, each of his eighteen directors communicated on a weekly basis the status of directives set forth. He required no grand detail. A simple one-word entry in the subject line was often the entire update. He looked at the list of eighteen e-mails, and the word *done* appeared in the subject line of each, which set the mood of the day. While the rest of the world dealt with hangovers or church services or both, Sturmisch spent this first day of the new year calculating the strength of every string of influence and control that had been attached to vital businesses and organizations around the world.

The responses from his government connections, both high and low, were all the same, with the exception of one. A single sentence marked the concern. What of this Gleau?

Though satisfied that his wishes were being carried out and his new instructions were well on their way to becoming reality, Sturmisch decided that it was in the best interest of his plan to educate himself on all there was to know about this current anomaly. He requested all the scientific data available from a retired CDC biophysicist he kept on retainer for just such inquiries. Within the hour, he received a response that gave him all the particulars gathered to date, and though it was seemingly benevolent in its presentation, there was the one question that remained. How did he appear to others? It was a mere curiosity because surely what cloaked his being would make him unique. He summoned Daoud to meet him at the security door in an hour.

After readying himself for the day, he took the golf cart to the adit entrance to meet Daoud, who was standing beyond the door when it opened. Walking out into the frigid morning air, he greeted Daoud in his normal fashion, which was not at all, and began his questioning.

"I'm assuming you are familiar with the news of this Gleau that's being reported on."

Daoud was prepared for this line of questioning after what he and the pilot had observed on their return trip from the last meeting. He wasn't exactly sure why, but he knew he must be careful. "Yes, sir, I am familiar."

"I want you to describe to me how I am affected," Sturmisch insisted.

"I am sure you are affected as I am, sir, but as the individual you are."

Sturmisch viewed the corona of light that surrounded Daoud. "I see, but mine would necessarily be more pronounced than yours, wouldn't you say?"

"I cannot view what is around me, but I would instinctively agree with you, sir." Enduring his employer's silent appraisal, Daoud did not move. He wasn't sure if it was force of habit or what he saw writhing around Sturmisch's form that caused him to remain transfixed and absolutely still. It was as if he had come upon a saw-scaled viper and could hear the warning as it rubbed its scales together, creating a *shhhh* sound. He heeded that warning and did not move until Sturmisch slithered back into his cave, which he did without a word.

Sturmisch was satisfied that this light show would not affect his plans. Daoud's appraisal fulfilled his expectations and put the issue to rest personally. He would indicate in his next communication to his generals that this event was a non sequitur to the mission at hand.

The Wait

JANUARY WAS USUALLY A FRIGID month in Minnesota, and this one was no exception despite the fact that snowfall was less than normal. Sunny days were most beautiful after a night of hoary frost that set itself upon every surface, branch, and twig, and the world was dusted with opalescent fur. Ice-fishing houses crowded certain spots on the lakes nearby, and the northerns and walleyes were remarkably plentiful. As soon as the ice measured about a foot thick, small cities of fish houses would spring up on this winter-only real estate.

Lee knew her time with Nick was limited as January was also when he must return to the other side of the world. She was going to spend every moment he would spare until then sharing life with him. As the day approached in mid-January, they ventured out on to Cedar Lake pulling the portable fish house, auger, lines, and cooler behind the snowmobile. Very little wind made the setup a quick operation, and once inside with their lines set, they waited for a bite. The radio was tuned in to a country station, and the sonar fish finder was doing its job. Lee got comfortable in her low folding chair, and Nick was perched on a five-gallon bucket with a padded lid that served as their catch bucket. They enjoyed each other's company in silence, waiting to see who would get the first fish.

As much as Lee worried about Nick, it never ceased to surprise her when he worried about her. "Still have the mini in the pull down?" he asked.

"Yes, I do."

"With a full clip?"

"Of course," she replied. "And a full box to boot."

"Good."

"Don't worry about me. I'm not the one getting ready to go halfway around the world and get dropped into a war zone."

"I'll be fine. Even there it's hard to figure out who the enemy is."

"Maybe. And the Gleau might help remove some of the camouflage."

"I doubt it. When distrust is automatic and lying is the normal course for survival, it might get more people beaten and killed, but having people beaten and killed is normal there too. I'm not sure how it will affect that society unless it outs the evil of the ruling class. Even then, they will make up their own reasons for the Gleau, and a significant portion of the population will believe them. Over there, it is accepted that the truth is what the most powerful says it is. And you can't miss what you've never had—freedom."

"Very sad but true," Lee commented.

"That's why I'm glad it's happening here. Thanks to you. We know freedom or at least the concept of it. Too many take it for granted, but if we know who is actually threatening it, maybe that will be our saving grace."

Lee was dumbfounded for a moment. As much as she was aware of what the Gleau meant, it had never occurred to her that this would actually save anything. But insight and foresight do affect the choices people make and do so without affecting free will. Maybe he was her son, but Nick was the very first person to thank her for what this may accomplish. A wave of humility crashed over her, and it was an honor she would shrink from publicly because she knew she was not the one to thank. The wish may have been hers, but the creation of this event was not of her doing.

"Thanks, hon, but you do understand that I really don't have anything to do with this. I don't have nor will I ever have the kind of power necessary to manifest this."

Nick smiled at his mother. "Mom, that kind of thinking is exactly why you were chosen as a conduit, or at least that's how

I see it. You've always understood the value of contentment, and too many of the shortsighted think that always means settling for less than what you want. Ask just about anyone what it would take to make them happy, and I guarantee they would say that it is more than what they have now. They've been convinced that if they aren't happy, someone owes them something, and they believe the silver-tongued devils who say they can provide that happiness to them by extracting it from others. I always thought happiness was a choice made by a person rather than a commodity that could be given and taken away. That's what you taught me anyway."

Lee was quiet for a moment, absorbing all she had just heard. "Wow. I taught you that?"

"Maybe not in so many words, but certainly by example. I've watched you help people in times of need. You just did it."

"I did it because it was the right thing to do. And as far as I can tell, doing the right thing is an equal-opportunity endeavor."

Nick's line bowed down, and he quickly pulled back. "So is catching the first fish!" he exclaimed.

PART III

Illumination

Linda and Bonnie
(January 26, 2012)

AT THE REHOBOTH WING OF the Julyanna Care Facility and Rest Home, ninety-two-year-old Bonnie was finishing up some stitching on a quilt for her great-granddaughter. She looked up and saw that her sewing companion, Linda, had fallen asleep midstitch. Ordinarily, she was content to let her rest, but not when she threatened to drool on the quilt. With slight effort, she pushed back her chair and went to the aid of her companion. Not wishing to wake Linda but sure it was a certainty, she carefully removed the needle from her hand and affixed it to the quilt. Arranging the lap blanket over legs that once danced the polka, Bonnie released the brake on Trigger, Linda's trusty chrome-and-vinyl conveyance, and backed her away from the table. As the stirring failed to awaken her friend, Bonnie checked to be sure Linda was the victim of exhaustion rather than rigor mortis. Satisfied by the suppleness of her hands and the slight rise in her chest, Bonnie slowly escorted her friend back to her room.

From Trigger's saddlebag, Bonnie retrieved the room key and wheeled Linda into the dining area of the tiny two-roomed apartment. Linda's husband, Alvin, was stretched out on the sofa in much the same condition as his wife. He must have left his hearing aid on because when Bonnie approached to reduce the volume on the television, Alvin came to life.

"She poop out on ya again, Bonnie?" Alvin inquired.

"Must be you keeping her up at night, Alvin," Bonnie teased.

Alvin rose to a sitting position on the sofa and picked up his glasses. "I'd like to think so," Alvin responded in jest. Mustering the strength to display the modicum of agility his male pride demanded, he stood rather quickly. "Excuse me, Bonnie. Could you stay with her for a minute? Nature calls."

"Certainly," she answered.

He sidestepped the coffee table and began the short shuffle toward the facilities. Halfway across the room, it happened. He broke wind. Without missing a beat and foregoing the usual bother of embarrassment, he said, "Well, glad *that* still works."

Bonnie chuckled, and before Alvin reached his destination, Linda awoke. "Did we finish the quilt?"

"Not yet. We can work on it some more tomorrow, dear," Bonnie told her, patting her shoulder. Hoping that was true, Bonnie thought she noticed a decline in Linda lately. And this new light they had all begun seeing seemed to reflect those thoughts. In less than a week, the very even halo surrounding Linda from head to toe had grown less intense everywhere except above her shoulders. It improved slightly when the subject of her children and grandchildren was discussed, but diminished when the conversation faded. Maybe it meant nothing, but Bonnie hadn't spent ninety-two years here on earth being unobservant. When the event began, this Gleau, as the papers called it, nearly half the residents of the home recalled seeing it before at rather specific times. For Bonnie, it was during her recovery from bypass surgery. The details were rather confusing, but she had never died before and wasn't exactly prepared to take notes, but the one thing she did recall vividly was this light. She didn't question it at the time and wasn't about to start questioning it now. Whatever it was, for whatever reason it was, she felt all would be explained when it was necessary. Right now her concern was her dear friend Linda.

Butch (February 25, 2012)

BUTCH HAD TWO HOURS LEFT on his late shift at the Schmidt Schtop at the corner of Route 12 and Bennings Way. He was hoping his replacement wouldn't be late as his wife was in the third trimester of pregnancy with their first child, who could arrive at any time. As his second job, working at a place that advertised "Eat here *and* get gas" was a necessity of survival as well as a source of amusement.

He had been employed there long enough to recognize the regulars, and as they were not totally off the beaten path, they had more than their share of folks just passing through. On this February night, Butch received his first insight about the value of this Gleau that was, as yet, unexplained. At quarter till eleven, he busied himself filling things that needed filling, sweeping the floor, and preparing for the register reading before he cashed out his drawer. Two customers were at the pumps and a young woman had stopped for coffee when he noticed a young man standing to the left of the entrance door. The temperature outside was in the midteens, and he wore a bulky jacket over a hooded sweatshirt with the hood pulled over a full-face mask. Only the lady's car was parked where he could see it, but this guy could have arrived on a snowmobile, and he was certainly dressed for it, except for one thing: no gloves. Maybe he purposely left them with the snowmobile, but he had Butch's attention.

The lady paid for her coffee and left. She was surrounded by an even white glow with alternating yellow and bright-pink streaks. One of the customers at the pumps was a credit pay, and the other was cash, so Butch knew he would be in shortly to pay for his fuel. They both glowed with what he had come to recognize as a standard Joe Gleau. As he watched the pumps, he caught movement in his peripheral vision. The snowmobile guy approached the door and hesitated. Butch saw around him a broken light that flashed a dim yellow to red with gaps of darkness. Butch had no idea what prompted him to push the panic button under the counter, but before he could think, he had locked the doors, and the police were being automatically summoned. The young man at the door grabbed the handle and pulled. When the door failed to open, he yelled at Butch to unlock the door.

Butch was a good-sized fellow and could easily have overpowered this wisp of a man trying to gain entry, and for a second, Butch thought he had overreacted. How was he going to explain this to the cops? The kid outside rapped on the door with a bareknuckled hand, and Butch shook his head no in response. In a flash, the other hand was revealed, holding a small automatic pistol. A muffled demand to open the door made its way to Butch's ears just before three shots rang out and put Butch on the floor behind the cashier's counter, unscathed. In a state of both shock and grace, Butch peeked over the counter. The kid was gone. The floor was covered with bits of broken glass, but the door had not disintegrated. The cash customer was running toward the building, pointing out the direction the shooter had fled. Butch came around the counter and physically unlocked the door. In the distance, sirens indicated that the police were approaching.

The pump customer, as flustered as Butch was, asked, "Wow, man, are you okay?"

"I'm okay, thanks," Butch responded.

The police arrived seconds later while Butch was on the phone calling the owner of the Schmidt Schtop. His shift replacement drove up and started asking the police questions they had no answers for. Butch gave the police his statement. In determining the sequence of events, Butch could not explain why he had pushed the button before he saw that the man had a weapon. His only reason was that the man didn't look right. His Gleau was "off." The policeman taking his statement admitted that they had heard this before from other would-be victims who reacted similarly. It was nearly half past eleven when it struck him that he hadn't called home to explain why he was late. His wife answered sleepily, and Butch broke down in silent tears.

Victor Crenshaw
(March 12, 2012)

VICTOR CRENSHAW WAS AN UPSTANDING businessman with friends in high places and ladies begging to be on his arm, or at least that's how he saw himself. In reality, he was scum, and the Gleau displayed that fact to everyone but him. It mattered not that he swindled vulnerable and lonely women of means because his focus was always the money. The ladies he targeted were treated like queens, lavished with attention, and smothered with well-received compliments. He gave them what they needed and took from them what he needed. In his mind, it was a fair exchange. Then he met Sheila Prentiss.

Sheila was not the target of his latest investment of time and empty words of praise. She was the obstacle he faced getting the better of her employer, Ms. Rachel DuBois. Ms. DuBois was the beneficiary of her father's fortune, well kept and improved upon by her late husband. She was not a beautiful woman by standards past or present, and it would have been overstated to say that she even approached handsome. It was an issue that plagued her as a younger woman until she met Henry Dubois. Henry was a jeweler and recognized a diamond in the rough. What he saw in her transcended her coarse features, and she never doubted that her inner beauty was what Henry saw. It was her kindness and ready acceptance of the flaws and imperfections of the world that drew him to her, for Henry was as ugly as she was. Each held a beauty that only the other could see, and they shared a love unrivaled. So when Henry left this plane of existence for the next, Rachel lost more than her husband. She lost the reflection of beauty that only he saw in her. If it was not for the friendship and pure devotion of her personal assistant, Sheila, she would have lost considerably more than that. Sheila was twenty years Rachel's junior and had spent the same amount of time in her employ, so at the age of forty-eight, Sheila was nobody's fool and could see trouble coming.

As it often happens, Rachel and Henry had two children that were near-perfect specimens of physical beauty, but for this advantage they had fallen prey to the failure to develop it inwardly. The bond of family instilled in them was sufficient, and they lacked for nothing financially, so the choice to distance themselves from ugly parents was overlooked by everyone except Sheila. It broke her heart when invitations went unaccepted, or worse, ignored. Requests to visit her children were always forestalled by the excuse of previous engagements. It was at that period in Rachel's life that Victor Crenshaw made his troubling appearance.

What had been simply a family project on the DuBois estate grew into a hobby for Henry late in his life. Arabian show horses had become a passion born of his children's equestrian pursuits. Long after their interest in showing waned, Henry's interest in breeding and selling these majestic creatures grew. He had acquired four mares of excellent lineage and was quite successful when it came to selecting stallions that produced highly desired offspring. After Henry's death, Rachel turned the responsibility of the stables over to the competent hands of her late husband's trainer and manager. He proceeded with Henry's plans to sell two of the yearling offspring. So seven months after her husband's death and two and a half months after the appearance of the Gleau, Victor Crenshaw found his way to the DuBois Arabian stables. He had come to buy.

His game was the buying and selling of expensive show horses. Once a mark was established—properly wined, dined, and brought into his confidence—he would offer her the opportunity to become a partner or short-term financier in a fantastic deal. In this instance, he convinced his current mark that he would put up half the cost and would give his half of the ownership to her as a gift. Fairly impressed by such a generous gift, the mark jumped at the chance.

This would be a legitimate purchase from DuBois Stables with the agreed purchase price of twenty-five thousand dollars for an untrained year-old Arabian colt of proven lineage. Victor's mark was told that the price was one hundred thousand dollars and that he only had half the money because his capital at the moment was tied up in other ventures. Seeing that Victor was willing to risk fifty thousand of his own money, the mark figured this was a safe risk. Each party wrote out a check for their half of the one hundred thousand dollars, and Victor took it upon himself to finish the deal. Victor's check was destroyed, the mark's check was cashed, the seller got the twenty-five-thousand-dollar asking price, the mark got the horse, and Victor walked away with twenty-five thousand dollars in his pocket. In the course of completing his latest "job," he was made aware in casual conversation of the situation and the lady of the manor at Dubois stables. In typical Crenshaw style, he appeared on Rachel's doorstep with a bottle of 2002 Louis Roederer Cristal Brut Rose Champagne to offer his sincere thanks with the completion of their joint business. Sheila answered his summons.

The door opened, and Victor was prepared. He could muster a counterfeit smile as easily as most people could put on a hat. To the lady who opened the door, he offered, "Hello, madam. I am Victor Crenshaw, and I am so pleased to make your acquaintance."

"One moment please, sir. I will let Ms. Rachel know of your arrival." Immediately, Sheila took into account the muddy green light that clung to him like a purge of algae on the surface of a pond.

Victor removed the wasted smile and waited for the sturdy woman with tightly permed hair to return and deliver him to his lady in waiting.

Sheila went to the sitting room where she and Ms. Rachel had been enjoying a rerun of *Pawn Stars* and announced that the gentleman who purchased colt, a Mr. Crenshaw, had come bearing a gift. Rachel was neither accustomed nor comfortable receiving strangers, but made an exception as long as Sheila was with her. She primped her hair and asked if there were any bits of fruit in her teeth and instructed Sheila to deliver the gentleman to the study.

Patience was not one of Victor's virtues, and the three-and-a-half minutes he'd been kept waiting was added to the price he would exact. Sheila ushered him in with an undue apology. "Sorry to keep you waiting, Mr. Crenshaw. Right this way please."

Feeling the need to express his displeasure, he commented, "I was beginning to think you may have gotten lost."

Sheila smiled at his attempt to elevate himself. "As it will be with your gracious intentions, sir, nothing will be lost on me." Before he could reply, they were at the door to the study, and Rachel stood as Sheila presented the guest.

"Mr. Crenshaw," Rachel began, extending her hand. "How nice to meet you. To what do I owe this pleasure?"

For a split second, Victor was at the mercy of a pure reaction to the sight before him. This woman was by far the homeliest creature he'd ever placed eyes upon. With every bit of self-determination in his being, he forced himself to stick to his well-rehearsed script. "The pleasure is mine, Ms. DuBois. I wished merely to offer this token of my thanks."

"How thoughtful, Mr. Crenshaw." Directing her attention to Sheila, she asked, "If you would please, Sheila. And the fruit tray as well, if you would." Sheila accepted the bottle from Victor on Rachel's behalf and took it to the kitchen to prepare it for consumption.

With his hands now empty, Victor proceeded to accept Rachel's hand and deliver the only kiss possible while he was sober. She then invited him to sit in an upholstered pink silk bergère while she took a seat across from him in its twin. Victor began the exchange with his pleasure on acquiring such a magnificent animal from her stable. Rachel admitted knowing very little about the horses but was grateful when others shared her late husband's enthusiasm. Victor made it a point to offer his condolences on that matter.

Sheila returned just as the conversation had come to a standstill, wheeling a tea cart with the wrapped champagne nestled in ice and two flutes as well as the restocked fruit tray and sweetened crème fraîche. She seated the trays on the antique rice table centered between them and left the honor of pouring the champagne to Mr. Crenshaw. Sheila then disappeared beyond the archway leading to the kitchen and stood as instructed where Rachel could see her. In the niche just beyond the arch was a desk that held Sheila's personal laptop. Silently, her fingers raced across the keyboard to get a more in-depth reckoning of the man seated in the other room exchanging pleasantries with Rachel.

Satisfied that he was all alone with Medusa—or, uh, rather Rachel—he began his effort to sweep her off her feet. He found himself curiously at a loss when it came to complimenting her physically because surely this woman owned a mirror and had seen the pitiful countenance before him now. He would sound like an insincere fool to extol upon a beauty that she, herself, had to admit was nonexistent. Switching gears with the smoothness of slime, he gazed about the room for a moment. "What a gorgeous and comfortable room this is. So finely appointed. I take it you decorated it yourself?"

"That I did, Mr. Crenshaw. Thank you. My Henry said I had an eye for beauty," Rachel responded sincerely.

That remark found his ear midswallow of his champagne, and he nearly blew it through his nose. Using every ounce of strength he had left to maintain his composure, he swallowed hard. As he did, he could not help but notice her bloodhound eyes sagging down in search of nonexistent cheekbones. She smiled at him with desiccated lips stretched across a row of gleaming white near-perfect teeth, much like a handmaiden accompanying Tutankhamen in his tomb. Her earlobes, though certainly weighed down by what had to be four carats of gleaming diamonds, wobbled with the cadence of her speech like a pair of withered tongues lapping at her bony shoulders. He noticed all of that but failed to register the glorious light emanating from her being with the softness of cashmere and the luster of mother of pearl.

Victor was but one of many gifted with the ability to see what he also chose to ignore. Sheila, on the other hand, had her suspicions confirmed. A record of shifty dealings and his involvement with insurance claims on deceased animals under dubious circumstances made it crystal clear to Sheila that Victor Crenshaw would become less than a memory in the life of Ms. Rachel. She reentered the study with a small tray of shortbread carried in such a manner as to disguise the slight protuberance beneath her apron.

Feeling his veneer of sincerity thinning, Victor checked his watch. "Oh my," he issued falsely, placing his unfinished glass on the table. "Time has gotten away from me. I have a meeting scheduled within the hour and must see to it." Two red spikes shot up through the murkiness above Victor's head, giving him a look most suiting in Sheila's opinion.

Rachel stood as he did. "Well, I certainly do thank you for stopping and allowing the pleasure of making your acquaintance. I wish you the best with the colt," Rachel finished.

"It was my pleasure," Victor lied, maintaining his devilish spikes.

"I will see Mr. Crenshaw to the door, Miss Rachel," Sheila volunteered, nearly having to sprint to keep up with Victor as he made his escape. When they reached the entry, Sheila took hold of the door latch and turned to Victor, staying his departure momentarily. In defense of her employer and friend, she chose to impart wisdom she was sure would go unnoticed and a warning he could not possibly ignore.

"Mr. Crenshaw, you have been given both sight and insight, and yet you are blind to the beauty of the world before you, and given the driving forces in your so-called line of work, I am not surprised. You have set about destroying things of value for a gain that will never improve your pitiful state." As she opened the door to release him back into the wild, she made him turn once more and meet her gaze. When she was sure she had his attention, she withdrew from beneath her apron a lovely stainless .454 Casull. "And, Mr. Crenshaw, should you choose to pay no heed to my words, my good friend Henry here will geld you with lead."

The last Sheila saw of Mr. Victor Crenshaw was a flash of yellow, which she attributed to cowardice. As she reentered the study to remove the trays and glasses back to the kitchen, Rachel was there with a tray in hand. Wistfully, she stated, "It was a shame my Henry couldn't be here to share in the thanks for work he so dearly loved."

"Oh, Miss Rachel," Sheila assured. "Don't you worry. Henry was here."

April: Forcing the Hand

AS THE WORLD GREW COMFORTABLE with the Gleau, almost to the point of taking it for granted, Sturmisch took note of everything that was going right for him by going wrong with the world. Every ill turn of fortune and calamity inched him invisibly toward his goal of total destabilization. He was pleased that the privileged were attentive to every loud-mouthed sideshow barker that diverted their attention. He wanted them squabbling among themselves over trivial matters born of ego, attacking the messenger, and ignoring any prognostication of impending danger. Suitably distracted by this Gleau and convinced of their own entitlement, they would pooh-pooh any notion of doom proposed by some insane worst-possible-case scenario spinner. Sometimes Sturmisch thought it had to be too good to be true. Teaching people what to think and all the while neglecting to teach them how to think was truly an art. He scanned the many online news outlets and delighted at the proof before him.

Thinking out loud, he expressed his pleasure. "That's it. Just keep worrying about your shiny hair and your bright smiles. I do want you all looking your best." He chortled. "And don't worry about those few extra pounds you need to shed. I'm going to put you all on a diet shortly." Sturmisch had a handle on how to manipulate specific individuals, but his real target was broad based. The individuals in positions to wield power had researchable flaws he used as leverage to get them—with plausible reason but no genuine insight—to forward his broader agenda. Thanks to the normalcy bias, they had no idea what his true motives and desires were. In spite of all that was happening before their very eyes, he could hear the mantra "That can't happen here."

Because he was a businessman, they thought he wanted money, but Sturmisch had more than enough of that, and it was merely a tool.

His universal weapon was connected to everything. To many it would not appear to be a weapon at all, and Sturmisch counted on that. Instilling apathy was all it took to disarm a populace that would soon be his unwitting foot soldiers. Most had no conceivable notion that they had enlisted. It was a force that would diminish the last obstacle to his total control. Once fought and won here in the land of the free, the rest of the world would be easily put on notice. It saddened him a bit that because of the general breakdown, surely there would be clashes and moments of glory that the dismantled press would fail to capture, but the aftermath would surely be recorded for his entertainment.

Each time in the past that Sturmisch imagined the great battle, a variable or two would present itself that required some new regulation or subsidy to eliminate it as a concern. Rome may not have been built in a day, but Sturmisch had managed to amass his invisible army of millions in less than three decades. Sure, shots would be fired, but by sheer numbers alone, his army would vanquish the few that stood between him and his prize. In a little over eight months, the war to end all wars would begin.

He went to his e-mail expecting to see eighteen subject lines with the word *done* as the sole communication. He opened the single message with the word *problem* in its heading. The short note stated only that there was a problem with Adam. Furthermore, it was one that must be dealt with in person. Sturmisch was not pleased, but he hadn't come this far to let a single glitch thwart his purpose. Daoud was instructed to make arrangements for a trip, which he did with seamless efficiency, including his own liberation.

Loosening the Grip

NICK HAD BEEN GONE FOR nearly three months, which made Jase's presence all the more precious to Lee. An earlier-than-usual thaw had turned the dirty-white landscape back to just plain dirt for nearly two weeks, and then a wicked turn in the jet stream dumped another fourteen inches of whiteness on the ground that Lee would just as soon have avoided. Her gardening plans went on as scheduled with the exception of trays of tiny seedlings being rescued from the cold frame and scattered about the house. With Jase's help this year, her garden would be twice its normal size, and something told her that it was a good idea.

The news lately was not pleasant. The novelty of the Gleau had worn off, and though its causes were still being speculated upon, the media decided it was at best a nonevent. Even the finding that the Gleau was detectable by the blind failed to impress them as anything more than freakish. After all, they were at a loss to do anything but describe what they were told to describe, which meant it wasn't really news, just someone's opinion tempered by personal depth of vocabulary. It was much the same with every other topic they brought to the attention of the public; too often they reported what they were told to report. And too often it ran in direct contradiction to what people were experiencing firsthand, but the blissfully ignorant repeated the official news like trained parrots on steroids.

Unemployment, rising prices, foreclosures, businesses collapsing, and a looming financial burden placed upon taxpayers by irresponsible tax collectors were the realities everyone faced. But proper responsibility was rarely practiced by those who dictated responsibility to the general public. Like the cowardly captain of a sinking luxury liner, Lee imagined those at the helm of the USS *Government*, after disregarding proper advice and protocol and running the ship aground, blamed the demands of the passengers for their inattention and disregard as they shamelessly set to sea in the only lifeboat loaded with the remaining ship's stores. As the passengers and their families were forced into the shark-infested waters, the occupants of the lifeboat could be heard congratulating themselves on having saved lives. Lee didn't have answers or solutions for problems of such a magnitude, but she had her garden and her chickens and ultimately would do the right thing.

Jase had fallen right in to the rhythm of farm chores and seemed content getting his hands dirty. He had fixed a small hole in the barn roof, helped Lee complete a second lean-to for the horses and steers, and run the fences around the pasture clearing dead falls and repairing breaks. There was even a small circle blade-saw mill in a building behind the barn that Lee had never restored to working order, and Jase made it his project to get it up and running again. The overgrowth along the drainage ditch that ran north and south through the property yielded quite a bit of good lumber for all the repairs they were making. He didn't exactly have a farm boy background that Lee was aware of, but he seemed to fit in like he'd been doing it all his life.

Brett had become a regular visitor to the farm, and on random occasions Ben would show up, from who knows where, and join the discussion sessions. Brett kept his notes in hard copy at Lee's place and would bring new additions to Jase for review. He had written several opinion pieces for the *Review*, prompted by reader comment, but tempered his input based on general knowledge of the Gleau. He had even interviewed Lydia Corvuso and congratulated her on her excellent reporting of the initial event. Nearly every human soul on the planet was "turned on" to the Gleau at this point, but its impact on humanity was still negligible. People went about their daily routines, lived their lives, celebrated successes, suffered tragedies, and struggled to make ends meet. It was not unlike what mankind had managed throughout history, but the struggle was getting worse.

The sandwich-board wearers of the past, foretelling the end of the world, were now standing not on the street corner, but in front of audiences of millions via television and the Internet. And so were the snake-oil salesmen. The difficulty was in determining where the truth resided. It was obvious to Lee that humanity had been devolving. What was once the lowest common denominator of human interaction was now just common. No one could solve problems anymore without resorting to infantile name-calling and playground-bully thug tactics. Courts of justice were being misused as weapons by the unethical that brought frivolous suits to bear upon the innocent, using costs of delay and mounting legal fees to defeat their targets. Meaningful dialogue disintegrated before it began because everyone already had answers that didn't solve problems, and those answers were always "who to blame." Lee often remembered something Uncle Peter had expressed years ago. He said, "Sometimes you are never so wrong as when you are right. And an argument that fails to promote positive action upon its conclusion is no more than a breeze of flapping lips producing spittle."

The absurd was becoming the common practice. There were even college courses now touting the value of violence and lawlessness in labor disputes, in direct contradiction to calls for decency, respect, and civility. Too often, the honor of being a civil servant in our society had digressed into something that was neither civil nor honorable and ostensibly self-serving. The system was standing firm, but those who occupied the seats of responsibility were, too often, no longer behaving responsibly. They had become sullen children caught with their hands in the cookie jar, holding fast to denials while issuing transparent lies from crumb-laden lips. Lee often wondered if they knew how they appeared. There was no shame in stealing anymore if you sat in a position of authority or receipt and called it by a polite name.

Lee had no quick fix in mind for these societal shortcomings, nor did she think she was alone in her thoughts, but she did know that humanity would reap what it had sown, and the harvest would be measured in human misery. Her hope was that this could be avoided, and maybe the Gleau would play a part in that reality. While certainly aware of things beyond her control, she threw herself into those things within her control.

Despite the shorter growing season at this latitude, once summer did arrive, her garden dwellers thrived like kudzu in a well-turned garden of heavy black loam fortified with enough organic matter to keep it light and maintain moisture even in the hottest days of August. Her animals provided abundant composted manure, so she had no need for chemical fertilizers. Lisa teased her about her method of companion planting, insisting that plants should be able to all just get along.

Strange elixirs of marigold petals and nicotiana tea discouraged most pests, and diluted naptha soap made the slugs recoil in horror. Lee had formed an unusual alliance with braconid wasps when it came to the great tomato hornworm caterpillar battle. Because of the hornworm's ability to camouflage itself in the tomato foliage, the white eggs of the parasitic wasp on its back made it easier to spot. Otherwise, Lee spent a great deal of time inspecting the ground beneath the stripped vines for caterpillar excrement to locate the voracious devils. Her friend *Bacillus thuringiensis* gave the cabbage looper population terminal constipation, thus insuring the health of her *brassicaeae cruciferae*. Lee wasn't driven by any holier-than-thou gardening guru when it came to her practices with food she grew for human consumption. It was the way her aunt and uncle had done it, and it worked. For that matter, it was the way it had been done for thousands of years, and humanity thrived. The age of having result speak for itself was gone, however. The truth of a product was now indicated by a label rather than the product itself, and the only real guarantee to the consumer via a label was that the cost of the intrusion would be passed on to them. Lee had more faith in compost than she did in labels.

April would soon be May, and as soon as the ground shed enough moisture from the snow melt, the plow would be hooked up behind Lee's trusty DC Case, and the manure she spread last fall would become worm and plant food. It was a time she looked forward to each year. It was a renewal of life that would sustain her through the following winter until the next spring season of rebirth. Unbeknownst to Lee, powers beyond reason were seeking to change that sequence of events.

PART IV

New Eden

Adam

THE FLIGHT FROM MONTANA TO Denver was uneventful due to Daoud's meticulous attention to all details, including the weather. Back in the midnineties, Sturmisch had an indirect hand in the construction of the new airport both monetarily and because of reins strategically placed on prominent and influential individuals, thus securing a place if needed in a facility that didn't officially exist. It was another example of where conspiracy theorists made things easier by making them laughable. You can get away with so much more when there are fingers of ridicule pointed at your detractors. And by feeding the frenzy with in-your-face hints, you can fuel doubt and distract from the truth while thumbing your nose at the public.

Upon landing, Sturmisch made his way to his well-guarded and private section of tunnel pathways that led to the business offices of one of his White Swann facilities. It was one of the first of his underground mushroom farms to be retrofitted with grow lights to sustain aboveground crops if necessary. As well as his private abode in Montana, several other installations had been equipped similarly with artificial sunlight and hydroponic technology. In several test facilities, tanks of water hyacinth were being used to clean contaminated water and then use the plants themselves as biomass fuels and a substrate for mushroom beds. It was in the infancy of these developments in the latter half of the nineties that Sturmisch met Adam for the first time. Adam, though that was not his real name, was a brilliant plant molecular and cellular biology student with keen instincts when it came to applying micro discoveries to macro applications. That fact alone would have made him an indispensable asset to Sturmisch's team, but his expertise with the plant sciences was not what made him so valuable. Before completing his PhD, he had applied for a much sought position at White Swann and was the first of five applicants that Sturmisch would interview personally.

The interview went quite well for Adam. So well in fact that Sturmisch dismissed all subsequent applicants in favor of this young man who displayed social characteristics that attracted Sturmisch immediately. A marked disdain for the bulk of humanity coupled with a certain charm that made that derision an all but invisible fact made this man almost enviable, which was why Sturmisch *had* to have him. Not only did he have Gregory Peck good looks, an educated mind, and a suave manner, but he was a chameleon, adapting with no gaps in behavioral editing, and he could AD-lib his way in to any situation. He was an actor. And he was a manipulator. He probably would have gone on to do great things without Sturmisch's help, but Sturmisch wanted control of those great things. Wasting no time with research about Adam's past to find an existing hook, Sturmisch determined it would be far more to his advantage to create his own hook. So in the spring of 1997, Sturmisch went fishing.

On the morning of his scheduled meeting at White Swann to solidify his employment agreement, Adam awoke in his apartment bedroom to a horrific sight. Barely awake from the grip of sleep and trying to ignore a throbbing headache, his mind tried desperately to account for the scene before him. Curiously, he had no conscious memory of the night before, past 4:30 p.m. when his last class ended. Yet here he was, naked in his own bed with the body of an unknown woman at his side. Her pallor left little question that he would never get to know her to a greater degree than he did at that moment. One of his belts was cinched tightly around her neck. He glanced at the clock. His meeting was scheduled for nine, and he would be late due to these circumstances that had his mind swirling. Trying to remain calm and before deciding what to do about his unfortunate guest, he thought it would be best to call White Swann and reschedule.

He dug the card out of his jacket pocket and dialed the office number he'd been given. Without quite knowing why but prodded by instinct, he pushed the record button on his answering machine as it began ringing.

A secretary answered Adam's call, and the moment he mentioned his name, his call was sent directly to Sturmisch's office.

"Hello, Adam. I'm assuming you're stuck in traffic on your way here, and I know that construction has things slowed, so not to worry." Sturmisch knew exactly where Adam was and knew that traffic had nothing to do with his delay.

"Thanks, Mr. Swann, but I may need to reschedule for this afternoon if that's possible."

"Of course it's possible. Is everything okay? You sound a bit under the weather," Sturmisch offered.

"Oh no, I'm fine. I just have a problem I need to take care of."

The hook was in, but not yet set. "A problem? Anything I can help you with? If any of the resources I have at my disposal would help, I'm certainly offering them to you now."

"Well, I have a bit of a situation here," Adam admitted, doing his best to sound understated.

"You're talking to the situation man here, Adam." Sturmisch laughed insincerely. "Just let me know what I can do. I certainly don't want to lose you to a competitor because of a simple problem." Sturmisch felt another tug at the line.

"Oh no, sir, Mr. Swann. I had every intention of becoming a White Swann employee this morning, except for this one unforeseen detail."

It was time to set the hook and reel him in. "Now, son," Sturmisch mustered in his best good ol' boy twang, "there is nothin' we can't fix. Tell me what's up."

Adam slowly revealed exactly what his situation was and the seriousness of his plight. Mimicking the interest of a concerned father, Sturmisch questioned Adam's memory of the apparent event and was pleased that the drug administered to him in a beer at around eight o'clock the previous evening had a retroactive effect. He didn't recall at all receiving a call that directed him to meet a White Swann associate at an out-of-the-way beer joint whose owner was indebted to Sturmisch.

"Now listen to me clearly here, son. Just do exactly as I tell you to do, and we'll make this a nonevent."

Adam did exactly as Sturmisch directed. He showered and got dressed, avoiding his bed and what he considered an uninvited complication. It never crossed his mind to think that this deceased young woman was somebody's daughter, maybe a sister, or that she might be missed. She was nothing to him—a thing, an it. He was the victim, and she was an encumbrance. He put the apartment key in his pocket to be left in the mailbox in the lobby and then did one thing Sturmisch had not asked him to do. He removed the tape from the answering machine and slid it into his pocket before heading out to meet with the man who was going to fix things.

When he arrived at the White Swann offices, the secretary ushered him into Sturmisch's office without a moment's wait. Sturmisch stood from behind his desk and walked across the small room, hand extended, greeting him like a longtime friend he was eager to see. He shook Adam's sweaty hand in both of his and invited him to take a seat. The secretary was sent for coffee, and Sturmisch handed him a bound folder of documents.

"This is just the usual stuff, company policies and OSHA compliance, insurance info, 401(k) info, stuff like that. Last page is the one we'll take care of first, the employment agreement. You can read through it all later. Pretty dry, but my lawyers are thorough."

"Thanks," Adam replied, retrieving a pen from his inside jacket pocket. He signed and dated the document and set it aside. They discussed Adam's placement in the company, the inception date of his employ, his advancement possibilities, and what sort of projects he was interested in tackling, but no mention was made of the little problem back at his apartment until he got ready to leave.

"Well, I think we're getting off on the right foot here, and I'm looking forward to seeing what we can accomplish together."

"Thank you, sir. So am I," Adam responded.

"Now you go on home and finish your studies or relax. The future looks bright for both us." Sturmisch shook Adam's hand and walked him to the door. The door opened, and Adam hesitated.

"I'm not too sure I should go back to my apartment, sir."

"Oh, that. Not to worry. It never happened. My people took care of it."

"But what about the, well, you know, the—"

"The girl?"

"Yes, sir."

"She's been taken care of, so don't give it another thought. I'll treat her with the same respect I would my own mother, and no one will ever find her unless it's necessary." Sturmisch stifled the impulse to smile at his own private joke.

"It won't be, sir, I assure you." Adam smiled a perfect chameleon smile of gratitude. Well aware now that this incident was an insurance policy guaranteeing his loyalty, he was more complimented by Sturmisch's recognition of his value than he was angry about being set up. He supposed that in Sturmisch's position, he may have done the same thing and was impressed, but not bested.

On his way back to his apartment, Adam stopped at an ATM and withdrew enough cash to make a necessary purchase at the local electronics emporium. He arrived home to a spotless apartment provided by Sturmisch's "cleaning service" and began making copies of the tape for future use.

Both the tapes and the body of the young woman remained lost to this day, but not forgotten. The association between Sturmisch and Adam was a fruitful one for both, and as Adam's career with White Swann grew, so did his involvement in the processes of local government. He had a flair for fence-sitting issues emotionally while always offering plausible solutions directed at those before him. His background in the business of

White Swann was one of using resources at hand that produced a desired product while cleaning up messes from the past, which were both admirable pursuits. While White Swann was a privately owned company with the vested interest of its employees, the details of monumental tax breaks and subsidies were never discussed publicly. Nonetheless, Adam's bid for county councilman was well received, and thus he got his feet wet in the political pool. He discovered as well his appetite for the limelight. While Sturmisch preferred the shadows, Adam worked well on the stage. After all, he was an actor at heart, and there wasn't a script he couldn't deliver without making women swoon and intelligent men bow to his intellectual prowess. As he was being groomed for his candidacy to the highest office in the land, this Gleau thing happened. Suddenly, doors weren't magically opening when he uttered his "open sesame." Something had changed.

In the Mirror

AS STURMISCH ENTERED THE CONFERENCE room of the facility followed closely by Daoud, he was greeted by an underling he recognized but never bothered to remember his name.

"Okay, Smith, I'm here. Where is Adam?"

Smith was wide-eyed staring at Sturmisch when his eyes met Daoud's. The intensity of expression on the assistant's face was a warning to say nothing.

"He's on his way, sir. May I see to anything on your behalf?" Smith tendered.

"Tea," Sturmisch replied curtly, questioning Smith's audacity to find the question necessary.

"I will see to it," Daoud offered instantly, motioning with his eyes for Smith to accompany him. The door to the conference room closed behind them, and at once, Daoud made his warning audible. "Do not admit to what you see, but do not offer a false response to his questions. It will save your life."

"Understood. But I know something you don't," Smith added.

At the far end of the corridor, Adam appeared, striding toward them on his way to the conference room. As he walked past the virtually invisible pair, both noticed the striking similarity of the gloominess cast about Adam to that which surrounded Sturmisch. Daoud replied, "Not anymore."

They reached the preparation room, and as Smith grabbed the door handle to enter the room, Daoud continued down the hallway. "Wait," Smith gently enlightened. "The kitchen is here."

Daoud slowed and turned for a moment. "I am leaving. Say nothing. I suggest you do the same." With that said, Daoud walked to the end of the hall and continued to his right, never to be seen again.

Flustered by these quickly changing events, Smith stayed on task and completed brewing the tea, all the while seriously considering Daoud's advice. He noted automatically that an order to Gilliards of Bath would need to be made to refill the supply of Darjeeling Broken Orange Pekoe, and then discarded the notion as he planned his own departure. He filled the tray with necessary condiments and the freshly brewed tea and headed for the conference room.

Smith backed through the double doors and crossed the room to the lounge area to the left of the conference table and placed the tray on the coffee table within Sturmisch's reach. He purposely avoided looking at the two men sharing the room, suspecting that at any moment, an alien may burst from the chest of either. A pause in the conversation allowed him to speak. "Will that be all, sir?"

Much to his dismay, it was not. "Smith," Sturmisch directed, "do you notice anything different about how either of us appear?"

Smith reluctantly glanced at the two men. "Certainly, sir." As he told the truth as Daoud instructed, no deception was indicated.

"And to what might you attribute these differences?" Sturmisch inquired further.

Smith, subduing the urge to cringe, carefully deliberated how to answer. "Well, sir, as I cannot see myself as I do the two of you, I would say you both appear as men of power."

Sturmisch digested the response and then bid Smith his release. "That will be all, Smith."

Grateful for Daoud's advice, he left the conference room and the two…whatever they were, to continue their discussion in privacy. More than intuition now guided his steps toward the exit to the facility.

Sturmisch quickly deduced Adam's problem alluded to in the e-mail. As Adam relayed it, too many of his closest associates and acquaintances were giving him the cold shoulder or seemed to distance themselves a bit. It truly bothered Adam when his audiences failed to receive his performances with proper applause.

In an effort to calm Adam's fears, Sturmisch spoke. "Now fear not, son. You're just a victim of something I don't have—vanity. Can't you see that what you perceive as coldness or disdain is just jealousy?"

"You really think that's it?" Adam asked, brightening a little.

"Of course it is. You heard Smith. You and I are powerful men, and that always provokes jealousy in the little people. Now go on out there and conjure up some display of humility, and that will warm things back up."

A tad embarrassed that his Achilles' heel had been on display in front of Sturmisch, he was equally complimented by the acknowledgment that he was a man of power. They left the conference room, and Adam walked with Sturmisch to the point where their paths diverged, discussing upcoming events that would be used to their advantage. They parted company, and Sturmisch was suddenly aware of Daoud's absence. Before he could consider punitive actions for the transgression, his pilot appeared.

"Sir, we must leave immediately. Daoud was accosted by two men bearing weapons." As he told it, it was the truth. Quickly, he ushered Sturmisch past security and directly to the waiting plane, feigning concern for his employer's safety. It was only after they were in the air heading back to Montana that the pilot thought kindly of his friend Daoud now traveling home to see his grandchildren in the company of his brother and son-in-law.

After the short flight back to Montana, the pilot's assistance was enlisted. Sturmisch bemoaned the fact that the keys to the Hummer were in Daoud's possession until the pilot produced a spare key for just such emergencies. Sturmisch congratulated him for his forward thinking. It was, of course, the key that Daoud left with the pilot prior to his vanishing. The pilot drove Sturmisch to the entrance, loaded the luggage on the back of the golf cart, and incorrectly assumed that Sturmisch would drive him back to the plane. With his standard lack of common courtesy, Sturmisch instructed the pilot to leave the Hummer at the cabin and walk the remaining mile back to the airstrip. He closed the door without another word.

With the same disregard he was offered, the pilot then drove directly to the airstrip, leaving the Hummer there, and breathed a sigh of relief knowing he would never return to this place again.

Revealing

THE MONTH OF MAY ARRIVED before spring became summer. The ground was almost dry enough to plow, and Lee did her best to find other positive pursuits to distract her from that fact. Sometimes the jokes about eight months of winter and four months of poor sledding in this area were too close to the truth. The weather made her doubly grateful for Jase's presence. When they weren't tending to chores, Jase enlisted her help dragging trees from the woods and running them through the mill. She had enough plank amassed to build another barn and enough scrap for firewood for the next two years. Those evenings when they still had enough energy to engage in more than sleep, they played backgammon, and Lee recounted tales of the children while they were growing up. To most people, it wasn't a very exciting existence, but sometimes excitement wasn't all it was cracked up to be. Lee wasn't completely sure, but something told her life was getting ready to be more exciting than she cared for it to be.

It was nearly seven on the Wednesday evening of May 2 when Lee answered the familiar knock at the door. Brett arrived just as Jase finished showering off the dust and dirt of the day. Jase retrieved the well-worn manila envelope containing handwritten copies of Brett's notes. The article, the first step in revealing to the world exactly what the Gleau indicated, was to be released the following Saturday. Though not specifically planned to share the spotlight with other festivities, Brett figured it would give people something interesting to read while they were enjoying their enchiladas, menudo, tortillas, and salsa and maybe a margarita or two. Brett opened his laptop, and with Jase's help, they composed the article. It was decided to include just enough information to provide a target to see what, if anything, might be aiming at them. In less than an hour, it was complete.

The Article

By Brett Hume
Chief News Editor
The Gleau?

As most of the world is now fully aware, an unusual
phenomenon has beset humanity. Most of the questions
regarding the physical properties of this light are
unanswered by a scientific community that has exhausted
every tool at their disposal. The fact that it is harmless is
the one determination that has been made based on the
benign interaction with human physiology.

Perhaps the best way to understand what this is
all about is to answer two more questions: where did it
come from, and what does it mean? The first of those
two questions will be answered here, and it was at the
request of my source that it is brought to light now. By
sheer coincidence, it was the privilege of this reporter to
be present at the time and place where this originated. As
many of the readers of this article experienced, I too was
surprised and a bit shocked when this was first introduced.
I have been assured by my source that not only is this
not harmful, but as the individual with whom this event
began has explained, this is a gift of monumental good.
Many of you, without specific knowledge, have intuitively
discovered the benefits of what this indicates. In the most
simplistic terms, this event was the result of a child's wish.

As science has indicated, this is not a light of the
visible spectrum, nor does it register on any other part of
the electromagnetic spectrum. It does not reflect, and it
cannot be photographed. As a few have already surmised,
it is not actually seen with our eyes. This is why the blind
have the same ability as the sighted. This Gleau, as it

referred to, is a gift of perception. What we are observing is technically not of this existence, and it has always been a part of each of us. What has changed is that our ability to perceive it has been turned on. For those of you wondering why an individual cannot see what others perceive in them, there is no need. As it was explained to this reporter, each of us is fully aware of what dwells within.

The second of the two aforementioned questions will be answered by my source before a live audience at a time and place that will be announced in the near future. Readers are invited to submit questions that will be addressed during that session. Submissions may be sent to the office address of this publication or to our e-mail address listed on our website.

"WELL, THIS SHOULD DO IT," Brett said in a positive but still hopeful voice. "If there are any snakes in the grass—and I guarantee you there are—this should flush them out into the open." Brett was confident that responses to his invitation would run about 40 percent serious inquiry to gain information, 40 percent opportunists offering opinion in the form of loaded questions, about 18 percent loonies and nuts, and a scary 2 percent on a fact-finding mission to do harm if they think this disclosure will discredit them.

"It's always the tiniest percentage who manages to do the most damage," Jase agreed. "Everyone needs to be on guard. This could get ugly."

By Saturday, Lee's mood had brightened considerably when she saw local farmers in several fields plowing on her way to town to pick up a commemorative copy of the *Review* and do some necessary errands. Brett's article appeared below the fold but garnered immediate attention from both the individual reader and some regional news outlets. Local talk radio that based many of its daily discussions on what appeared in the written press hopped on the topic to determine if this claim was the real deal or just another empty bid to increase the circulation of the paper.

As both Brett and Jase had suspected, it was the messenger that was attacked first.

Hundreds of e-mails were submitted in just the first hour after the Saturday edition was released, and they ran true to predictions. And in the short time Brett was in the paper office, he fielded at least fifty phone calls where he instructed the callers that questions had to be submitted in writing either by e-mail or snail mail. He would have muted the ringer on the phone except that calls for ads or subscription business might come in.

Upon opening the e-mail account for the paper, more than a few of the letters he sampled asked the same question: why did you wait so long? He guessed they all thought he could violate with impunity the confidences and wishes of a source. No crime had been committed, so the only compelling force for the delay involved exclusivity and respecting the wishes of his source. Ultimately, it was a question for Jase anyway. There were a few rather ugly letters issuing threats for reasons unknown, but for some, inner turmoil is enough to justify any form of violence these days. Many dismissed Brett's revelation as a lie, calling him just another seeker of his fifteen minutes of fame. Then there were kinder notes from people who had avoided catastrophe based on their intuitions enhanced by what they observed.

Brett categorized the e-mails and placed them in appropriate files labeled the good, the bad, and the ugly, knowing Mr. Eastwood would approve. At a quarter till three, he was closing up shop and prepared to engage the out-of-office message on the phone when it rang one last time. It was a local television affiliate offering their station as a candidate to air Jase's announcement. Politely, Brett informed the lady caller that no concrete commitments had been made yet, but their submission would be considered. He thanked her and finished closing the office.

Cloudy

STILL STEWING OVER DAOUD'S UNEXPECTED departure, Sturmisch contemplated checking his e-mail and decided to entertain himself with news of the turmoil in the world instead. Bringing up the online *Post* edition, his scan of the week's headlines made no mention of any known abduction at DIA. It was an issue he would pursue at a later date. The word *swarming* in a headline caught his attention and held his interest as he read about the ingenuity not of insects, but of thieves.

In groups of two dozen or so, these bold bandits would overwhelm retail establishments by entering quickly, brazenly stealing and making off with their booty, nearly daring anyone to stop them. This tactic was not new. Gangs of shoplifters had often made clothing stores a target, grabbing whole racks of jeans or coats and selling them in a secondary market of stolen merchandise. But this incident was different. The objective described in this article was food at a grocery store. These weren't starving individuals with babies to feed either. They were opportunists taking what they wanted, defying the law, and obtaining something that was in demand and getting more expensive by the day. It gave Sturmisch a heightened sense of pride knowing that this well-fed populace was not going to be denied the lifestyle to which they had become accustomed. After all, cutting out the middleman was a centuries-old business practice. Instead of waiting for someone to steal on their behalf, they took the initiative and just did it without the help of the master thief. He wondered how long it would take these new entrepreneurs of his coming chaos to figure out that they could go directly to the farm for things they desired.

Clicking back to his homepage, Sturmisch checked out closing stock numbers, deriving pleasure from the doubling and near tripling of select commodity prices and noticed in the Breakingnews.com section a blurb about the Gleau. "Review Editor to Reveal Gleau Source" it stated with a continuance that said it would be a televised event. A reprint of Brett's short article accompanied the secondary opinion piece, and Sturmisch made a note of the byline and the small town where the paper was published. If there was any substance whatsoever to this source, Sturmisch thought that information should be his for the taking, and he wouldn't be kept waiting on some dog-and-pony show to get it. If there was even a shred of proof that this source existed, the power to execute a worldwide phenomenon was a power Sturmisch wanted to control. He made a phone call and was assured that by the following Wednesday, he'd have his answers. It was probably nothing, but Sturmisch rarely left anything to chance. He finished the call with a final instruction: "No witnesses."

·ᴧ·Qᴧⁱᴧₐ·ᴧ·

Barbara stood doing dishes and breathed in the heavenly scent of roses wafting through the open window above the sink. Monday was traditionally a day off in the spring months as they had a less hectic rehearsal schedule for the upcoming summer concert series. Brett had gone to the paper office an hour early to check out the replies to the article printed two days earlier. She finished rinsing the last glass, and just as she placed it in the drying rack, she heard a rustle from outside. Thinking it was perhaps the neighbor's dog, she shooed it verbally. The sound of quick steps crunching dry leaves diminished as the suspected canine retreated to his own yard, and Barbara made her way to the pantry to feel labels.

Brett would be home in a couple hours, and it was always a treat to exercise her cooking muscles. As she felt her way across the tops of various cans, reading the Braille labels stuck on each can, she found what she needed. Backing out of the pantry, she heard the distinct click of the inner-garage doorknob. In silence she waited to hear Brett announce himself. There was not a sound, only that of her own exhalation. Finally she called out.

"Brett? Is that you?" There was no answer. With the can in her right hand, she closed the pantry door, giving her direct line of sight to the door in question. In the unlit windowless hallway came no sound, but *something* was there. In her gray-black world, she saw a broken outline of indigo. If this was a person, they exhibited a Gleau like none she'd seen before. Knots of what appeared to be shadow slithered along the edges, and specks of deep red emerged and then sank back into nothingness. This form didn't move, but Barbara was becoming terrified. Again she spoke, this time to whatever was standing in hallway. "Hello? I know you're there."

The figure advanced, and Barbara readied the only weapon she had—a can of beans. She began backing into the kitchen, and from seemingly nowhere, someone called her name. It wasn't from the figure coming toward her, and as she turned her head to see what might be behind her, she caught a glimpse of a satiny white Gleau that extended from the floor to the ceiling. The white figure wrapped two huge arms around Barbara, and she heard a snap. She struggled to gain release from grip of whomever this was that held her, and then she recognized a familiar voice. He was begging her forgiveness and trying to calm her. He set her down on uneven ground, and she smelled the strong odor of manure.

"You're okay, Barbara. I didn't mean to surprise you like that, but I needed to act fast." It was Ben.

"Ben! Now that I know it's you, I'm glad you did surprise me. Who else was here? And where did they go? Something smells funny."

"We're in the barn," Ben informed her.

"What? We don't have a barn."

"Lee's barn. I had to get you out of your house."

"What on earth are we doing in Lee's barn? And better yet, how on earth did we get here?" To say that the events of the last minute or so were confusing was a huge understatement, but Barbara felt ridiculous standing in Lee's barn holding a can of beans when only seconds earlier she was in her own kitchen.

"I'm a Traveler," Ben explained, or tried to.

"A Traveler? What does that have to do with me being in this barn?"

"I brought you here for your security. It's what I do." Ben led Barbara to the barn door, and as she stepped over the threshold, she could feel the delicate heat of the sun on her face, and the smell of manure gave way to that of fresh grass and earth. Slowly he escorted her across the barnyard to the house.

"I know Jase said you were in security, but *how* do you do what you do?"

"It's my talent," Ben answered matter-of-factly.

"Some talent. Are you an angel or something?"

Ben laughed in his low rumble. "You make beautiful music, and I can't. That's your talent. Does that make you an angel?"

"Well, no, but I'd say what I do is more a skill."

"The act of pressing on the keys is skill. The talent involves knowing the difference between making noise or a thing of auditory beauty."

Barbara was pleasantly stunned by that insight but still had questions. "You know, Ben, just now I decided I really do like you, but I still want to know what a Traveler is."

"I move people or things, or sometimes just myself, by thought. I don't really know how it works, and guess it wouldn't matter if I did know. I just know it comes in handy."

"Yes, it does, and thank you, by the way."

"You're welcome."

"You don't by chance know who that was at my house, do you? I think that was my first exposure to what Jase calls a shadow dweller."

"I don't know who that was, but I think you're right about the shadow dweller part." As they got to the door to Lee's house, Semi shot out the cat door to greet the pair. Ben alerted Lee to their presence by shouting to her through the screen door.

"I'm in here washing eggs. Come on in," Lee called back.

Lee turned from the sink full of eggs and was both surprised and delighted to see Barbara. Having Ben pop in and out had become routine, but now Lee figured she would get some answers to unasked questions.

"Good grief, where did you two come from? I didn't hear anyone drive up. Is Brett here too?"

"No," Ben replied. "I need to borrow your phone to call him and let him know we have Barbara here with us."

"Sure thing," Lee answered and dried her hands and went to retrieve the phone. She dialed Brett's cell number and handed the phone to Ben then turned her attention to Barbara. "I'm almost afraid to ask, but how did you get here?"

"I'm almost afraid to answer." Barbara laughed. "It's just one more thing to add to the growing list of weird things that have happened lately. Oh, and I brought you some beans." More than capturing Lee's attention with the description of what happened in her kitchen, Barb went on to tell her about Ben the Traveler. Not as shocked as she would have been a year ago, Lee's interest was piqued hearing about how they ended up in her barn. Confusion gave way to a good laugh for them both when Lee figured out why she had been handed a can of beans.

"What did it feel like, you know, the traveling part?" Lee asked.

"Other than hearing what sounded like the snap of electricity, it was like turning around and being somewhere else. It was instantaneous."

"Oh, that is so cool!" Lee responded. "I knew something was up with him appearing and disappearing without explanation, and now I have one."

Ben finished his call and handed the phone to Lee. "Brett will be here in about half an hour. Where's Jase?"

"He should be back any second. He went to the mill to get feed," Lee informed. "By the way, I hear you're a man with some extraordinary talents."

Ben widened his existing smile. "Not as extraordinary as they seem, but I'm glad I was able to employ them for Barbara's sake."

"Me too," Lee agreed.

Lee set about preparing sustenance for the impromptu gathering that was getting ready to take place while eliciting more details from Barbara about the intruder. Her description of the Gleau surrounding this bearer of ill will gave Lee gooseflesh. The dramatic differences Barbara described gave Lee the impression that the shadow dwellers, the hard-core evil ones anyway, wouldn't be hard to spot. Hoping that was the case, it would be easier to steer clear of potential danger.

In a matter of minutes, Jase returned from the mill, and Ben brought him up to speed on the situation at the Humes' place.

"I told Brett that we have Barb here with us, and he's on his way," Ben stated.

"What about at the house? I wonder what they were looking for," Jase said, knowing there wasn't anything there for them to find.

"Brett is going to have the police check it out. I told him not to mention that Barbara was there and just report a break-in."

"Good idea," Jase agreed.

Sounds of a braking vehicle and the familiar thud of a car door closing told the preoccupied group that Brett had arrived. Without his usual knock of courtesy, Brett entered Lee's kitchen and went straight to Barbara. He wrapped his arms around her, and waves of relief pulsed through his Gleau like iridescent butterflies, cloaking them both. Over and over, he apologized to Barbara for a situation he thought he should have foreseen.

"Brett, it's okay. I'm okay. You can't control what others do. I'm just thankful that Ben is who he is," Barbara said, doing her best to reassure her brother that she was fine.

Brett lessened his embrace but still held his sister's hand as he turned to Ben. "I don't know how to thank you, Ben. Just know that I do."

"It's my job, Brett. Your thanks and Barbara's safety are more than enough recompense." There was a brief silence. Thinking he may have left things with too formal an air, Ben added, "We're good, bro." With that said, everyone seemed to relax.

In her own effort to comfort her guests, Lee announced, "Okay, you hungry people, it's food!" Far from exotic cuisine, the platters of breads, meats, cheeses, and vegetable garnishes more than satisfied the appetites in Lee's kitchen.

This episode raised the level of caution that would be observed, and potential steps were discussed to maintain the secrecy of Jase as the source. It was Barbara's privilege to educate Brett about Ben's special talents. It was an unknown that Brett shoved aside due to his overwhelming concern for his sister until he calmed, and the question of how his sister was rescued became obvious.

"A Traveler, huh? And you transport people and things by thought," he repeated.

"That's about it," Ben replied.

"Are you human? I mean, you look human, and you Gleau like a human," Brett pressed.

"Then I guess I'm human," Ben said with a broad grin.

Brett understood Ben's reticence to elaborate. "Even when I don't understand it, I learn something new every day," Brett said, grinning back at the giant who packed half a hoagie in his mouth like it was a tea sandwich.

Not Knowing

STURMISCH WAS SITTING UPON HIS throne when the phone rang. With irritation, he answered. It was his little Chicago buddy, hopefully with some early and valuable information on the Gleau source from the cow-infested town in Central Minnesota.

Answering in his usual manner, he said, "What have you got for me?"

"More questions, Mr. Swann," his buddy answered.

"I'm paying you for answers, not questions. I ask the questions."

"Yes, sir, you do. But what the scavenger brought back from his hunt prompts answers there were no questions for."

"No games. What did he find?"

"Nothing. Not at the house anyway. But he did run into something unusual. This reporter, Hume, was at the paper office, he was sure of that. He went to the house for a laptop or anything else useful. There was a woman there."

"I trust he took care of it and got the name of the source."

"No, sir. To quote him exactly, sir, he said when he approached the woman to eliminate her, a giant Indian came out of nowhere, grabbed the woman, and the two of them vanished into thin air."

Sturmisch was silent for a moment, taking in the idiocy of what he'd just been told. "You have two days. Get me what I asked for." Before his Chicago buddy could reaffirm the instructions, Sturmisch hung up.

"Stupid," Sturmisch muttered. He stood and offered a fitting response to the tale of the disappearing Indian—he flushed. Incompetence was something not tolerated. It was unfortunate for this scavenger that he was now just as much a loose end as the woman, and once Sturmisch had the information he sought, a cleanup crew would take care of them both. *If* there actually was a giant Indian—and Sturmisch suspected this was an element of total fabrication—he was on the list as well.

Tuesday, May 8, 2012

L EE HAD BEEN ANTICIPATING THIS day for nearly five months, and a break in the rain finally allowed the ground to dry enough to put a plow to it. The garden would be more than just a necessity this year. Her surplus would provide much-needed income for her farm and a valuable source of fresh produce for those dependent on a not-so-dependable marketplace. Food prices rose sharply in the past year due to the cost of growing them and then getting them to market. It wasn't rocket science to figure out why, and the math didn't lie. The system was simply too burdened and failing. Cause and effect could not be avoided. It made Lee's head spin to think about it too much, so she decided to plant twice as many potatoes this year.

The little four-bottom Oliver plow made quick work of turning the garden, and the chickens enjoyed the bounty of earthworms the effort produced. After smoothing it all out with the disc, Lee could pick out unearthed rocks that the last ice age glaciers so generously deposited in this area. It was backbreaking, time-sensitive, weather-dependent, maintenance-intensive work that Lee loved. There was a true satisfaction in watching things grow and having the actual fruits of your labors in hand when the season concluded. Of course, she wasn't a big farmer, and her ways were deemed antiquated and too inefficient by today's market standards. Lee didn't worry much about that because she knew this thousands-of-years-old process was tried and true, and she didn't have to fix anything that wasn't broken. Farming this way wasn't going to make her a millionaire, but it made her life rich. Lee often wondered if the millionaire farmers felt the way she did.

Over a year ago, a noted professor had warned of a specific side effect of a well-known herbicide and the genetically altered crops created to withstand the effects of its lethal properties. At the time it was developed, this codependent match was a boon for agriculture. No one, including the millionaire farmers, could have foreseen the discovery of unknown microfungal organism that had the potential to destroy agricultural infrastructure, so for that reason, the warning had the same effect as Chicken Little declaring that the sky was falling.

It was a wonder that no great alarms were sounded, but no one really knew if this was just an undiscovered bug or a newly created one. No one knew if the active ingredient in the herbicide or the genetically engineered crops created a suitable environment for this bug to become a problem. What they did discover was that dairy cows, swine, and beef cattle were spontaneously aborting and having fertility difficulties, and this organism was found in the placentas of animals eating the treated food. Animals fed non-treated hay were not experiencing such difficulties at exaggerated rates. It was also affecting immune systems of corn and soy beans, making them in some cases susceptible to Goss's wilt and SDS. This virus-sized microfungal organism had the rare distinction of affecting both plant and animal species. Lee hoped humans wouldn't be one of them, but until people started spontaneously aborting at the same rate as animals or succumbing to Goss's wilt, it was profitable enough to be ignored—just like asbestos was once upon a time. Humanity was the one species that held the distinction of finding its strengths in its weaknesses; in other words, we learned from our mistakes if they didn't kill us first.

Though a wetter-than-normal spring may have delayed her garden planting, Lee was optimistic about the coming season that she would get to share with Jase. Dandelions had popped up, and that meant morels were about a week away if they hadn't drowned in the woods beyond the pasture. Just doing *anything* with Jase as company changed how life and the world looked. It wasn't something she expounded upon AD nauseam, but when they weren't involved in work, she just had to touch him, pat his shoulder, hold his hand, or wrap an arm around his waist. He responded in kind and seemed to understand these gestures of reassurance. He also knew she still had questions.

"I guess the first thing we should do before we start planting is set up the trellis for the cucumbers and pole beans," Lee instructed.

"Sounds like a plan." On their way to the corn crib where the fence poles and cattle panels were stored, Jase asked Lee a question. "Have you ever wondered why things happened the way they did?"

"You mean right now or in general?"

"I mean with you and me. Our family."

"Sure, but every family has things happen that they wish they could change. Not that I think life would have been perfect if things hadn't happened the way they did, but I wish our family could have had more time together here." Lee was quiet for a moment then added, "Funny how you can miss the potential of things you never had."

"I think the reason we miss them is because we had them at all," Jase added.

"True, and it's made me more grateful for what I do have: Nick and Em, Matt and the girls, and now you."

"Yes. And if it wasn't for what happened all those years ago, things might be different."

Lee hesitated for a moment. "Yes, they would. Mom and Dad could be here with us now planting the garden," she said wistfully.

"That's not what I meant, but I have the advantage of another perspective," Jase prompted.

"And what perspective might that be?" Lee asked.

"All those years ago, it wasn't that Mom and Dad were taken. What happened was that you and I were saved."

"What? Of course they were taken."

"I'm not making myself very clear," he said, shaking his head. "My point is that you and I were supposed to go with them, but we didn't. Our fate was changed, not theirs."

Lee thought for a moment. "Why?" was her single-word question.

"Because we were needed here."

"No. I meant why, if it was possible to save us, Mom and Dad weren't saved too."

Jase put an arm around Lee's shoulders and pulled her close. "I don't know the answer to that one. Like a wise man once said, not understanding the facts doesn't change them. Just know that they are fine, and when the time comes, we'll all be together again."

"And you know this for a fact?"

"Yes, I do."

"You've been there? You've seen them?" Lee was really hoping Jase would reveal this great mystery to her.

"No, I haven't seen them, not yet. What I do know is that the scope of reality is so much bigger than what we can fathom from this tiny, limited speck in the universe that I have no doubt that they are there."

"Is that a belief based on faith or knowledge based on fact?"

"Both. Stand here on a cloudless night and look up, and it is obvious ours is not the only speck."

"Okay, the odds are in favor of that, but where does faith fit in?"

"Who do you think is responsible for all the specks?"

"The optician?" Lee replied glibly.

Jase appreciated her lightening of the conversation. "One power created all we see and much more. It's beyond our comprehension in our limited existence. That same power gave us the ability to study all the sciences while being a part of them, gave us minds capable of acknowledging both the material and the intangible, gave us imaginations to take us beyond what is at hand, and gave us these physical bodies so that we could experience and understand what is most valuable in this existence and the next."

"And that would be?" Lee asked, knowing full well what the answer had to be.

Jase decided to follow her cryptic lead. "That which exists on all planes, throughout and beyond time, never diminishes and always grows."

"Hmm. A sense of humor?" Lee prodded.

"Love," he replied. "But you knew that."

"It still doesn't explain why things happened the way they did."

"Maybe not, but as much as you and I love our parents, do you think their love for us still exists?"

"Of course it does."

"*Amo ergo sum.* I love therefore I exist. I'm not sure who I'm quoting there," Jase added.

"I have a better one. 'It's strong and it's sudden and it's cruel sometimes, but it might just save your life. That's the power of love.' Huey Lewis." Lee crawled into the attic section of the corn crib and lowered three metal fence posts to Jase. "You know, I guess if I had to wear Mom and Dad's shoes, I would do the same thing."

"What thing is that?" Jase asked, helping Lee down the ladder.

"If I knew I and my children were in peril and they could be spared, I'd agree to that."

"There you have it. Understanding the value of love is what life here is all about."

Lee took one end of a cattle panel while Jase took the other, and they marched it out to the garden. On their way back to the corn crib for the remaining panel, Lee added, "And understanding the value of sacrifice is what love is all about too."

Jase was silent in his agreement. He hoped his sister would understand the value of his sacrifice.

PART V

Chaos Begins

New Reality

AS HUMANITY'S GENERAL DECLINE ESCALATED, Sturmisch prepared to send forth his beacon of light for all to follow. The fact that prices for necessities alone demanded more than 100 percent of most paychecks was ignored, and the decline was touted as a mere adjustment in the creation of fairness. For the most part, society bought the illusion. The checks may not have gone as far today as they did yesterday, but they were still coming. There were some isolated incidents of panic that produced documented shortages, but the spin was in, the necessary white lies were told, the witnesses were discredited as fear mongers, and all was set right.

Sturmisch had invested wisely in media, and it was his truth and his reality that people would believe rather than their own eyes and minds. He managed to pull off a reversal quite reminiscent of Orwell's sheep, and to his delight, his most dedicated supporters were those who fancied themselves educated free thinkers: low gas bad, high gas good. They were free to believe anything he told them to believe, and as long as their paychecks kept coming, his lies would be the only truth. When you controlled the height of genius and ridiculed any who admitted that they did not have all the answers, Sturmisch knew it was possible to flatter the intellectual to a point of stupidity. This had been illustrated but not publicly advertised when one of the great world powers collapsed, and graduates from their prestigious universities went out into the world and discovered that the college-level degree they earned and held in such high esteem was the equivalent of high school knowledge elsewhere in the world. They were embarrassed and angered by the fact that they had been fooled, but few would admit it. Most donned arrogance to avoid the shame. Sturmisch knew that when a well-worded lie made someone feel good and the truth hurt, most would stick to what felt good. Twain was right; the only thing more difficult than fooling someone was convincing them that they had been fooled.

Adam was busy making himself a household name, jumping on to the national stage with the flair of Mikhail Baryshnikov performing a grand jeté. He spouted the proper platitudes and sweeping anticipation of the betterment of all while adding a few specifics about the need to bolster our agricultural base to quell grumbling stomachs. He drew on his experience working for White Swann to demonstrate how reclamation and hard work could turn abandoned properties into productive ventures while omitting any mention of the cost to the taxpayer. His public hype was always directed at the hardworking base while his back-room negotiations were directed at undermining the competition. He learned the art of making the something-for-nothing promises while planning to take plenty and offer a tiny percentage back to a select few to make it technically legitimate. Anyone who dared point out the obvious was cast as a selfish capitalist who wanted to deprive the people of his generosity.

With the help of Sturmisch's network of sleuths and strong men, he presented himself as just a soul of the heartland with his Red Wings soiled by the precious life-giving earth while he hid the fact that his more important goal was to drag his opponents through the mud. It wasn't enough to be great upon your pedestal perch; you had to elevate yourself further by digging holes for detractors to stand in. Sturmisch made sure he had a big shovel, and when folks were a bit too direct and persistent, sometimes those holes turned into graves.

And then there was the issue of Adam's Gleau. Despite the efforts of his team of image crafters, personal appearances had to be staged perfectly. Without a formal explanation of what, if anything, his exceptional corona disclosed, his consultants ignored the gut reaction to the gloom and depravity it embodied and began touting it as intensity and passion for the cause of the people. One of Adam's favorite political posters featured him standing in a field backlit by a rising sun while planting a shovel into the earth whose handle doubled as a flagpole for the stars and stripes. The slogan was "Freedom Grows with Us!" Artistic license depicted spikes of red and blue that flowed from Adam's person to the respective colors on the flag. It became an instant collectible with those seeking political ephemera when Adam read an opinion piece that characterized the image as him sucking the very life out of liberty like a vampire. The printing and distribution of the poster was immediately canceled. With all of his knowledge and savvy, Adam could not rid himself of the vanity Sturmisch pointed out and was not adept at handling criticism of any kind.

When asked to explain a process he would employ for a specific promise made, Adam found that he could fashion a response from the flimsiest stock available, and it would take flight. He would always point to any past success and declare that the same method would yield similar results, thereby satisfying the question with no real answer at all.

Question: "Mr. Adam, with the inflationary trend we're in right now and the cost of business essentials driving up both commodity prices and unemployment figures, how do you propose we reverse this trend and get our economy running smoothly again, as you've suggested your policies will?"

Answer: "That is an excellent question with many tried-and-true answers. In much the same way we have maintained current solvency of Social Security, breathed new life into the automobile industry, tackled difficulties in the housing and banking markets, charted new horizons in alternative energy sources, we will continue to use what has obviously worked and saved many jobs."

Eyes would widen and heads would nod in approval, and the nonanswer would be treated as pearls of wisdom that only this genius before them could have grasped. It didn't matter what they thought about the answer. It only mattered that it made them feel good. It was as if these questioners were on crack. They would ask these same questions over and over again, treating the answer like their next fix. When the feel good wore off, they would ask the same worn-out questions again. Adam found it quite fitting to privately refer to them as dope addicts.

For the few not under the spell of Dr. Feelgood, any insistence that he embellish further was met with personal insult that labeled them ugly dissidents whose lack of intelligence caused an inability to grasp certain well known elementary concepts.

> Question: "Mr. Adam, could you elaborate further on the specifics of your plans A, B, and C?"

> Answer: "I believe those specifics have been made quite clear, but for you, sir, I have a fourth grader from Mrs. Jones's class sitting in the back taking notes who would be more than willing to explain it to you."

This sort of exchange always extended the life of a "fix" with laughter at the expense of the subject who invited public degradation.

As Adam's popularity and notoriety grew, so did Sturmisch's need to bridle and saddle this remarkable steed so that when this race was over, it would be Sturmisch with the winner's cup in one hand and the lead rope in the other. Adam didn't need to be reminded that his jockey, or more accurately the monkey on his back, was a certain young woman that Sturmisch had placed in protective custody many years ago.

It Is Time

I<small>T HAD TAKEN</small> B<small>RETT NEARLY</small> three weeks to glean through nearly fifteen hundred e-mails and blessedly fewer pieces of written correspondence to compile a list of twenty questions that the inquiring public decided needed answers. After Barbara's disturbing episode two days after the article appeared, Brett was necessarily more cautious and aware of everything around him. To the point of near paranoia, every unfamiliar vehicle, new face, and suspicious noise got his attention. Even the occasional Internet disturbance raised his hackles and put him in immediate defensive mode. He knew Ben was seeing to Barbara's safety, but it was paramount in his thoughts that his own safety was as much in jeopardy, and it was his duty to take care of her after this was over.

His visits to Lee's shouldn't have caused too much undue attention because he always made his exit carrying eggs. Twice, using Ben's specialized talents, Jase had come to his place to help select questions for the televised event that they would soon schedule. Nonetheless, when a dark-colored Escalade with tinted windows was parked on the opposite side of the street from the paper office, Brett paid a visit to the luncheonette one block down and caught sight of a figure sitting in the driver's seat. Not that it was unusual for a man to wait in a parked vehicle while his wife shopped, but few men had the patience to wait for over four hours on a street with metered parking while the wifey-poo tried on dresses. Ordering a Reuben to go, he walked past the Escalade on his return trip and noted that the driver watched him while he used his peripheral vision to watch the driver.

Upon entering the paper office, he was spooked enough by this entity to call Jase, but not panicked enough to call the police.

He lowered the blinds on the front office windows and the door and made his call. Lee answered on the second ring.

"Hey, Ms. Winslow, is your brother around?"

"Right here, Mr. Hume." She handed the phone to Jase without hesitation.

Before Jase could inquire about the reason for his call, Brett began, "Was wondering if you had any fresh eggs?" That was their signal for a possible problem.

"Yes, we do. Gathered some this morning. Anything wrong with the ones you last bought?"

"Got one bad one," Brett answered.

"Okay, thanks for the heads-up, and we'll take care of it."

"I'll be there in about half an hour to pick them up."

Both men ended the call, and Jase closed the phone and handed it to Lee. "Brett may have a problem. He's coming here."

"Maybe his unwanted visitor has returned," Lee suggested.

"That's what I'm thinking too. I'll get Ben to watch out for him."

It was five minutes before closing time at the paper, but Brett had already forwarded the office calls to his phone. He grabbed the thin folder containing the twenty questions for the interview and peeked through the blinds to see if the watcher in the Escalade was still there. He was. Hoping his suspicions were wrong and having no real reason to tempt fate, Brett left his parking spot in the alley behind the office and pulled up to red light on Main Street where he was sure to be seen if this guy was watching. He stopped at the light and put his left-turn signal on. The Escalade roared to life and pulled out into traffic. Brett got the green light and made his turn with the Escalade one car behind him, waiting for the light to turn. At the next intersection, Brett was first at the red light, and the Escalade caught up, still one car back. At the upcoming roundabout, he would take the third right and be on Route 12 headed for Lee's farm. This was no time to be wishing he had taken that defensive driving course recommended by his insurance company, so instead, what came to mind was every car chase he'd ever seen in movies.

When the light turned green, Brett gunned it, hoping the car behind him would slow the progress of his possible pursuer. Clear of oncoming traffic, the car behind him made a left, and the Escalade closed the distance between them at warp speed. His rearview mirror showed nothing but the dark windshield of the tailing SUV as they entered the roundabout. As they both made the right to Route 12, he was quite sure his crappy little beater sedan had no chance outrunning the Cadillac monster, now trying to crawl into his trunk at fifty miles per hour, so he thought maybe if he just played it cool, the beast would get bored and just pass him. It remained just a thought. Nearly a mile and a half out of town, his tail was a respectable six inches behind him, and Brett felt his steering wheel getting slippery as his hands started to sweat. Then he felt the nudge.

"That jerk hit me!" Brett said out loud. He stepped on the gas, taking note that they were the only two cars on this not-so-heavily-traveled county road. As Brett's car finally went into overdrive, he glanced in his rearview mirror and saw nothing but empty road. His relief lasted maybe a second and a half when he looked to his left, and the Escalade was pacing him in the oncoming lane. As it inched to the right, threatening to make contact, Brett could just make out the driver. He was bald and wore dark sunglasses and looked like he was surrounded by flames. Instinctively, Brett jammed on his brakes. The SUV sped ahead and did a perfect quarter-turn skidding stop and blocked the roadway. As the roads in this area were elevated with deep ditches on either side to aid in winter snow removal, they were now handling spring runoff and were full of water. He couldn't go around the guy, but he saw his escape. About half the distance between them was a gravel road to the left. Brett knew it went around Lake Isabelle and reconnected with Route 12. He stepped on the gas, made the turn, and the SUV gave chase.

Winter weather and farm equipment traffic made the packed earth road surface far from smooth, and as his speed increased, so did the punishment to his shocks. Incredibly, in this moment approaching sheer terror, it crossed his mind that he might be saved by flying gravel if his tires could kick up enough at the maniac behind him. That idiotic thought evaporated when the trailing behemoth slammed into him hard enough to make him bite his tongue. They approached a small grove of trees bisected by the gravel road, and before Brett could regain total control, he was hit again. This time his front wheels caught the soft edge of the barely existent shoulder, and he was headed for the ditch. Daring not to brake for fear of getting stuck, he put the gas to the floor and made it to the other side of the ditch. He welcomed the smoother ride until he realized he was airborne. Out of nowhere, he heard his name called, and the last thing he saw through his windshield was a cottonwood tree about half the width of his car.

The Debate

T O GET THE PUBLIC'S ATTENTION first and set the direction and tone for the upcoming national election, Sturmisch knew controlling both the venue and the rules for the debate was essential. He cared less about who would be debating and quite a bit more about what would be debated. The mouthpiece could be replaced, but controlling the topics for discussion was his goal. Filtering the funding through several layers of hands was necessary to barely conform to existing laws of campaign contributing, but it would not dilute his absolute control over the event. With only six months remaining before his Adam puppet would be elected, controlling what people were told they should be concerned about and what they should ignore was his greatest challenge. The entire process of controlling delighted him. Rarely did he get to experience the true thrill of the hunt.

The election event itself concerned him not at all. He knew there were going to be issues of voter fraud because he made them issues. He wanted the focus to be on the fabricated skirmishes outside voting stations. He wanted stacks of premarked ballots discovered in broom closets. He wanted the endless nitpicking and folderol to be the magnet because the fix was already in. He didn't care how close the numbers were; his paid ex-hackers now turned legitimate programmers knew where the higher number would always be applied. In the event of any outright accusations of fraud based on the counter of the numbers, Sturmisch had his team of analysts ready to confront the issue. In this age of advanced technology, a computer glitch was just part of the daily routine. Of course, this wasn't something Sturmisch shared with Adam. He would get a much better performance from Adam if he thought he had to actually earn the applause.

Like Adam, there were several candidates who had popped up seemingly out of the blue to toss their hats into the ring. No one in today's world, who did anything the least bit noteworthy, did so in total obscurity, but none of these Jane and Johnny-come-latelies appeared formidable to Sturmisch. If he couldn't poke holes in their ideas—accuse them of being selfish and cold-hearted, wishing ill upon the downtrodden and the elderly, stealing candy from babies, or whatever—he would go after any chink in their personal armor that existed. They may have had rocky marriages, children born out of wedlock, past dalliances with drugs or alcohol, or maybe even unpaid parking tickets. When their personal slate was clean, then immediate and extended family members became targets. Any little piece of inconsequential fluff that could be blown out of proportion was used to obfuscate any good that individual had to offer. And it was a method that hadn't failed because human beings fell for it. A hint of imperfection was worth a pile of manure. Not to mention, it also took every other issue worth discussion off the table.

No Accident

THE DRIVER OF THE ESCALADE watched in fascination as the reporter's jalopy took flight. In the blink of an eye, it struck a huge tree and crumpled like an accordion, its tail end dropping to the ground, leaving it in a semivertical pose like some injured creature attempting to climb the tree. Backing up the short distance to the scene of the demolished target, the flaming spook parked and crossed the ditch to inspect what he'd accomplished and gather anything of value that might be in the car.

Fully expecting to find the reporter vanquished behind the wheel, he was hoping death was instant and none of what he sought was soiled with blood. He donned a pair of rubber gloves to prevent, among other things, leaving any prints. A man in his business had to be aware of the dangers of bodily fluids in these times. The dying vehicle hissed and creaked and smelled of burning rubber and gasoline. He reached the driver's door, and what he didn't see prompted immediate inspection of the windshield. The driver was not behind the wheel, and the windshield was cracked like party ice, but still intact. The driver and the passenger airbags had discharged and deflated. He checked the backseat to see if perhaps the reporter had been thrown or somehow crawled there. There was nothing. It was then that he noticed that the driver's seat belt was still fastened. It was a mystery he could not dally about in case one of the local inhabitants of bovine central happened upon this spot. He could see no papers or laptop inside. The trunk lid had popped open upon impact and was angled like a kickstand, allowing him to view some spare tire tools and a few empty egg cartons.

He left the scene wondering exactly how he was going to report this to the man in charge. Removing his rubber gloves, he opened the back of the Escalade to retrieve a shop broom and eradicated his obvious tracks. He drove away knowing that the truth of this would have him watching his back.

In the Barn

"**T**HAT WAS A CLOSE ONE."

Brett was frozen in place, his hands still clutching a nonexistent steering wheel. Realizing it was Ben's voice he heard, his body went limp, and he lost his balance. Ben grabbed and steadied him.

"Is Barbara okay?" Brett asked instantly.

"She's fine. I think you're going to need a new car though." A man of few but very direct words, Ben let him know that Jase was waiting to speak with him.

"Where are we? Is this Lee's barn?" One of the steers answered that question, bellowing loudly.

"Yes," Ben confirmed. "We need to go to the house now."

When they entered Lee's kitchen, Jase was on the phone. He finished his call and turned his attention to Brett. Brett described the incident, the driver of the Escalade, and his miraculous transportation to Lee's barn.

"Here's the plan," Jase began. "That was Barbara on the phone. I told her what happened and that you are safe. She's on her way home now, but I told her to meet you at the paper office. Ben will get you back there. From your office, call the police and report that your car was stolen. An officer will give you both a ride to your place from there."

"Who do you think was driving that SUV?" Brett asked.

"Who knows, but we've obviously got someone's attention, and they are not happy. I'll be at your place later tonight, and we'll pick a date for that televised Q&A."

"Oh man!" Brett exclaimed. "I left the folder with the questions in my car!"

Ben spoke up. "No, I have the questions." Rolled into a tube that nearly disappeared in Ben's hand was the slim folder.

"Man, you are better than good."

"I try. Thanks," Ben replied, handing Brett the papers.

"Just a thank-you won't do it from my end this time. Just don't whisk me off to Timbuktu." Brett embraced the grinning giant to acknowledge his gratitude and felt a huge hand on his shoulder in return.

"No problem, Brett. All in a day's work."

Lee smiled at this spectacle and noticed Semi doing the same. "You guys better hurry. Barbara will beat you to the office."

"She's right," Jase agreed.

Brett turned to Lee, and in the emotional high of the moment, he hugged her too, something that ordinarily would have been off-putting for Lee. In this instance though, it felt right, and Lee returned the embrace in kind. "I'll be back for eggs," Brett added, trying to bring some normalcy back to the day's events.

"Tell Barb I have rhubarb too."

"Will do," Brett acknowledged. With that said, Ben placed a hand on Brett's arm, and the two of them vanished. There was no sound, no puff of smoke, no manifestation of light or sudden change in air pressure; they were just not there.

Lee looked at Jase, amazed at the instant departure, and said, "Beam me up, Scotty."

Loose Ends

STURMISCH ANSWERED HIS PHONE, EXPECTING good news. What he got was something he despised because it wasn't what he demanded.

Without addressing the spook by name, he was prepared to get what he wanted. "You have the name of the source," Sturmisch spoke, phrasing it less like a question and more like an assumption.

"Not yet. I'll have to go back to the paper office," the spook replied.

"Did you contact the reporter?"

"Yes and no, but he didn't have any information with him."

Sturmisch was never in the mood to mince words. "And am I to assume you could not persuade him to give you the information I've paid you handsomely to retrieve?"

"Persuasion wasn't an option."

"Get to the point," Sturmisch issued, his words seething.

"I followed him out of town, and there was an accident."

Before deciding what to do with this piece of human incompetence, Sturmisch needed to know where all his pieces stood on the board. "And?" he begged the spook to continue.

"His car veered off the road and hit a tree."

Sturmisch said nothing, which unnerved the spook more than any words could have. "I went back to the car. There was nothing in it that provided the information you wanted."

"And the driver?" Sturmisch asked with a calm that indicated anything but.

"The reporter was gone."

"When I said no witnesses, I assumed you understood that was *after* I got the information."

"No, no. He wasn't dead. He just wasn't there. The windshield was intact, and the seat belt was still buckled, and I got back to the car quick enough so that no one could have walked away from that without me seeing them."

Sturmisch had heard enough. "Where are you now?"

Grateful for the subject change and feeling that he'd dodged a bullet, the spook let Sturmisch know he was on a gravel back road heading back to his motel until things settled down.

"Did anyone see you?" Sturmisch asked, letting false concern invade his question.

"No, no one but the birds, sir."

"And is anyone around you now?" Sturmisch asked.

"No. Like I said, there's no traffic here except me." Thinking he was going to get a continuation of instruction, he listened intently. The last words he heard left him with the last question his mind would ever ponder.

"You didn't see any giant Indians lurking about, did you?" With that question asked, Sturmisch pressed a four-digit code on the keypad of his phone. He could only imagine the look of confusion on the face of the spook when his phone issued a slightly audible squeal just before his Escalade was transformed into a flaming explosion of recyclable steel.

Sturmisch closed his phone and ended the call as well as one irritating detail.

The tedium of dealing directly with details was something Sturmisch normally avoided, but there was a new blip on Sturmisch's radar that garnered his notice. So far, the media was treating him like a joke, but Sturmisch wasn't so sure. Little was known about him because of his rather peculiar and ingenious approach.

This gentleman was purported to be a farmer and astute businessman who came from humble beginnings, just like Sturmisch, but what made him an object of interest to Mr. Swann was something he denied ever had value: this man was seemingly adored by many. In Sturmisch's mind, that made him dangerous. The other odd bit about him was his reported Gleau. With little or no exception, portions of the press were extolling his brilliance, and too many were failing to enumerate his shortcomings, though none were quite sure if this was a genuine bid. Sturmisch had not seen this man in the flesh, but from what he read, this man was the antithesis of how a powerful man should Gleau. His message was equally irritating as it ran counter to the path Sturmisch had worked so hard to create. Sturmisch would not see his following duped by this flash in the pan that made a mockery of stately process and did it with near anonymity.

PART VI

A New Light

Punch Line

IT WAS MORE THAN THE press could assess accurately, but what wasn't when the press was told what to report and how. Sturmisch had his hands full shaping and preparing Adam to symbolically represent his new world order, and now this. As this problem presented itself publically, access to this person wasn't a problem, but undoing the damage that ran counter to Sturmisch's carefully crafted propaganda would take some quick and decisive action. What the reports sometimes classified as a stunt, Sturmisch saw as a potential problem, and it could be bigger than this Gleau if he didn't shut this ignoramus up. It wasn't the stunt per se, but the message that directed his ire.

It began in Iowa in the parking lot of an established mom-and-pop concern called Pantry O Plenty with the pomp and circumstance of a grocery store opening but blossomed into a fully fledged national campaign with little effort. With a bullhorn and a wooden crate, the upstart executed his pitch. He was dressed in an oversized blue jumpsuit dotted with big white stars, a red satin top hat that sat atop a profusion of white fun fur hair, and his face was diagonally bisected with red and blue face paint with white stars adorning one eye and the opposite cheek, and the visage was completed by a bulbous red ball nose. His shoes were the traditional oversized bright red floppers. He was a vision of patriotic splendor, and his words bent an ear or two.

"Howdy, folks! I'm looking for something here, and perhaps you could help me find it." A few people exiting the market took notice and listened.

"It's what we're all supposed to be born with, but I know way too many have lost it, and I'm making it my job to return it to the rightful owners." As he spoke, patrons on their way in to the market stopped too, captured as much by his radiant Gleau as his words. "As a matter of fact, there should be piles of the stuff lying all over the place because with all that's been happening lately, I'd say way too many have abandoned all of it they ever had." Having spiked their curiosity, the small crowd now waited for his next words. "I'm talking about common sense." A few giggled, some shook their heads in agreement, and there were even a couple "amens" uttered. Now that he had their attention, he wouldn't waste their time.

"I guess you're all wondering, who is this clown? That's the question every undeserving holder of power asks when he doesn't want to answer a question we ask with honesty. I can tell you, good people, that this is one clown who doesn't think what's going on in this fantastic country of ours is very funny. I can find no humor in the derision of our free markets, the regulation of our businesses into oblivion, the crippling taxation, and the erosion of our personal freedoms. You see before you a man wearing a mask, but this is a far more honest disguise than that worn by the liars and artists of deception now in power and seeking more. You need to know less about who I am and more about what I stand for on behalf of all citizens. We are unique in this world. We are a free people directed not by other men but by whatever power guides our individual souls. It is for us to choose. That is what our freedom gives us—choice for the individual. Too many have been fooled into thinking that choosing a collective, giving up the choice of the individual to that of the collective, allows them to maintain their freedom because they have exercised choice. They are wrong. Once in the collective, they have given up both choice and freedom. They are slaves by choice. Why would they do this? Because they have been lied to."

The small but growing throng was silenced for a moment as they absorbed what he said. "I will not lie to you, and I think this Gleau that has affected us all will bear me out. Tell your neighbors and friends that I will be carrying my message to all who will listen, and we will recover all that we have lost. To those of you who think that this is a joke, it is not. It is my contention that the real joke is being played on the trusting souls of our nation by those in power now. I am not a joke. I am the Punch Line!"

After half a dozen appearances in tiny impromptu venues, Punch Line was invited to speak at a rural civic organization meeting where his image and message were first captured and handed to the world via the most reliable news outfit on earth: YouTube.

The Questions

AFTER CALLING BRETT TO BE sure he and Barbara had made it home safely, Jase made plans to meet him at eight that evening. It would give them both an opportunity to pick a target date for the televised question-and-answer session. Ben delivered Jase to Brett's garage and rejoined Lee at her place. Barbara was pleased that she got to play hostess to their meeting and met Jase at the inside garage door.

"Come on in, Jase. Brett's changing, and I made blueberry muffins. Only burnt myself twice," she announced proudly. Jase wasn't sure which she was more proud of.

"Well, from the wonderful aroma in here, I guess it beats burning the muffins," he replied, getting a chuckle out of Barbara.

Brett appeared showered and in sweats with the slim folder in hand. "Ready to play twenty questions?"

"Let's get to it." Jase took a seat at the dining table and opened the folder.

"How soon do you want to schedule this interview? I imagine any station willing to televise this would like some notice," Brett added.

"Today is the ninth. Would a month be enough time?"

"I think so. I've had an offer from a local cable station, so they may be prepared for a schedule change on short notice."

"By the way, how did your stolen car report go?" Jase asked.

Brett laughed. "I'm not sure they bought it, but I attributed as much as I could to my own stupidity. This Gleau doesn't help matters. I had to tell them that I left the car running while I went back in to the office to get some paperwork I forgot. I know my insurance company is going to take issue with that, but it was the only way I could explain why my keys were in the ignition."

"Did they find your car?"

"Yes, they did," Brett answered emphatically. "And I had no explanation for why the seat belt was fastened with no driver behind the wheel."

Jase smiled. "Better to let that be a mystery than to have to explain Ben."

"I agree," Brett concurred. "I don't think they're going to be too concerned about my little mishap though. While they were there taking my report, they got a call about an explosion out on a gravel road off Route 12. An Escalade was found in about a million pieces, and so was the driver."

"Apparently, you aren't the only one angry about the loss of your vehicle," Jase replied with heavy sarcasm.

"Some rogue fanatic arborist perhaps?" Brett added with a chuckle.

Jase was reading over the questions in the folder while still engaged in the conversation. "Whoever it is that's interested in what you know wasn't driving that Escalade, I'm sure of that much."

"So I won't drop my guard just yet either," Brett answered. "What do you think?"

"You're right. None of us should," Jase responded.

"No, I mean about the questions," Brett said, motioning toward the folder in Jase's hands.

"The questions look fine. I'm just not too sure they're going to like the answers I give them because some of the answers aren't mine to give."

"Guess that will lead to more questions, huh?"

"It usually does."

The Questions

Question 1:   Who are you?
Answer: My name is Jase Garrett. I'm just a man.

Question 2:   Are you the "second coming"?
Answer: No, that job is not mine. See answer 1.

Question 3:   Where did this come from?
Answer: The phenomenon is generated within each of you, as well as the ability to perceive it and has always been there. It was merely switched on.

Question 4:   Is this a prelude to the end of the world?
Answer: Any day could be that prelude, but that's not for us to know. This is simply an opportunity to learn more and perhaps prevent one possible end.

Question 5:   What is this if it isn't light of the visible spectrum?
Answer: It is something we bring with us from our other existence. Technically, in the physics of this universe, it doesn't exist. It is one sense we've always had but haven't used until now.

Question 6:   What does this indicate?
Answer: It indicates the quality and condition of the being within.

Question 7:   Why do the colors change, and what does that mean?

Answer: The colors change with our emotions and intent. Even before this ability was switched on, we verbalized these indicators: being in the pink, green with envy, feeling blue, etc. I'm sure some of you have seen colors there are no names for as well. The meaning is as individual as a smile or a frown. A smile can indicate happiness, contentment, delight, serenity. A frown can indicate sadness, anger, disgust, or pondering. Some expressions are universal, and some are more subtle and mixed. It also depends upon how well an individual is known.

Question 8: Why can't we see ourselves?
Answer: There is no need. Each of us knows already what dwells within. It's sort of like the reason why other people can physically tickle us, but we can't tickle ourselves.

Question 9: Is this physically harmful at all?
Answer: No. It is as helpful to each of us as are our other five physical senses. It is, for lack of a better description, a perceptible manifestation that confirms intuition, just as sight confirms the chair beside us or touch confirms the coldness of ice.

Question 10: What gives you the right to affect us this way if in fact you are responsible?
Answer: Neither the right nor the decision to activate this ability were mine. I delivered what was asked.

Question 11: Who do you work for?
Answer: Right now, I work on a farm.

Question 12: If I don't believe in God and this Gleau supposedly comes from God, as many people say,
why can I see it?

Answer: (This one made me laugh). Whether or not you
believe in God doesn't change reality. Though
understanding the concept of the initial consciousness that you call God could change your
personal reality. Either way, if you are a human
being, this ability is yours.

Question 13: My neighbor is a terrible gossip, and when she
tells me things, these red triangles show up on
her head. What does this mean?

Answer: Red flashes are just what they appear to be: red
flags. Dishonesty or the telling of lies causes
this display. An outright lie appears like a red
warning cone or a dunce cap. Both indicating a
lack of truthfulness.

Question 14: What does this ability teach us?

Answer: This teaches a variety of things. Just as touch
teaches us not to put our hand in fire, most of us
have been burned at one time or another. For the
most part, this is going to show you how many
good people there are in this world. It will also
reveal the dark truth of some despite their words
to the contrary. It will teach us the power of our
words and actions as the impact of either will be
displayed by those at whom they are directed.

Question 15: Why don't animals display a Gleau?

Answer: For the same reason a radio doesn't display a
picture—different frequency, different equipment, and different perception. Animals have
their own abilities.

Question 16: Can we change how we Gleau, how we appear to others?

Answer: This is a manifestation of the reality of each of us. Thinking you're a good person doesn't change who you really are any more than putting on a tiara makes you a princess or donning a crown makes you a king.

Question 17: Why is this happening now?

Answer: Now is when it was necessary.

Question 18: I work in maternity at our local hospital. All the babies seem to be born with the same Gleau. What makes it change?

Answer: The change happens based on the circumstances presented in our lives and the choices made based on those circumstances.

Question 19: Will this ability be with us forever now?

Answer: Unfortunately, no. It will disappear exactly one year from the date it began, so humanity has about six months to learn as much as they can with it and document its existence.

Question 20: I know a couple people who Gleau differently than most. They are dark. One of these people I always liked and one I didn't. Now the one I liked repulses me a bit, and I'm not sure why. What does the dark Gleau mean?

Answer: From my explanation about what the various characteristic colors mean, a dark Gleau means just what you would think. I call them the shadow dwellers. The darkness indicates a lack of good at best and a predominance of evil at worst. Throughout history, they have been called dark hearted, black hearts, darkest evil, and the like. Evil does not care for the light and wishes to hide from the truth. Due to the Gleau, the truth of evil is on display, has been unmasked but will fail to admit to what others see, content to hide behind lies and deceit. Heed the warning.

Three hours and two blueberry muffins later, both men were satisfied that enough information had been disclosed to make the Gleau a useful tool for humanity to apply if they chose to do so. Tentatively, June the second, a Saturday, would be the day the televised interview would air, and Brett would set up all the particulars when he contacted the station. They chose to offer the opportunity to the tiny local cable station that first called Brett. At the time the call was received, Brett jotted down the phone number only, assuming he could fill in the blanks later if necessary.

"When the date is set and they agree to it, make sure they understand that this event cannot be advertised until twenty-four hours prior to airing," Jase insisted.

"I think they'll agree to that. Their advertisers will be scrambling, but I think it will be an obstacle they'll be willing to overcome. I'll call them in the morning and set up a face-to-face meeting," Brett informed.

"Good deal," Jase agreed, and there was quiet knock on the inner garage door. "My 'ride' is here." He smiled.

Brett quickly answered the knock, and Ben followed him through the kitchen to the dining table.

Spying the platter of muffins, Ben asked, "Did you bake?"

"Barbara did. Help yourself," Brett offered.

Ben popped a whole muffin in his mouth like it was an after-dinner mint. He swallowed and added, "Tell Barbara they were delicious and thanks."

"Will do," Brett promised.

Calling it an evening, Jase stated that he would wait for Brett's call the following day, and they would get all their ducks in a row. That said, Ben placed one of his huge arms around Jase's shoulders, and they were gone.

"That is so freakin' cool!" Brett remarked, knowing the novelty of that particular talent would never wear off.

Brett wasted no time the following morning finding the number and calling the station that offered to arrange for the televised interview. He was also surprised when the phone was answered by a secretary with the greeting, "KMIN, how may I direct your call?"

"May I please speak with your station manager? This is Brett Hume calling on behalf of an earlier request."

"Right away, Mr. Hume. Hold for a moment while I transfer you." With a couple clicks and half a ring, the phone was answered. "Mr. Hume," the gentleman answered, obviously pleased. "This is Blake Ryan, station manager here at KMIN. Needless to say, I was looking forward to your return call."

"Thanks, Mr. Ryan." Before Brett could get to the reason for his call, the man spoke up. "You can just call me Blake," he interjected.

"Ah, well, thanks, Blake. Brett here. I was just calling to find out if your offer still holds to host the live interview?"

"Indeed it does. We've got a scheduling opening we've held in reserve on the off chance you would accept. Now I don't know if there is a time table you need to adhere to, but how does the second Friday in July sound to you?"

Brett thought for a moment and couldn't see where that would be an issue and tentatively accepted the spot. "Of course, I do need to run this by my source and get them to confirm it, but I'm almost 100 percent certain that it will do. And there is one more thing, and I'm hoping it won't peeve your advertisers."

"They'll be lined up around the block, so anything we can do to make this happen won't be too much to ask," Blake responded confidently.

"My source has requested that the venue not be advertised until twenty-four hours prior to the event. Will that be a problem?"

Blake was silent and then answered with assurance. "I think that's doable. I can get sponsors to sign on without a specific date, and it will take a couple to weeks to line up a location. Does your source have any requirements about the size of the audience?"

"I'd say not too big. Make it manageable, say, three hundred tops," Brett estimated.

"Broad-based cozy is what we call that, and it gives us plenty of options. All we need is for you to come in sometime before the first of July and sign the contracts on behalf of your source. Go ahead and discuss the particulars with them and give me a call back. We'll get the ball rolling," Blake said, barely able to contain his enthusiasm.

"I'll get back with you within the next couple hours. Thanks, Blake." Before issuing his good-bye, Brett added, "Oh, and by the way, let Lydia Corvuso know we appreciated her report when this first broke."

"You know our Lydia?" Blake asked, rather surprised.

"Yes. And she's from our neck of the woods, and she did a great job with it."

"I'll be certain to let her know. She'll be quite pleased that you accepted her offer as well."

"Her offer?"

"Yes. She's the brave soul who called your office right after the article appeared."

"Well, imagine that," Brett said, obviously impressed. "Thanks, Mr. Ryan. We'll talk soon."

Still without new wheels, Brett decided to call Jase and fill him in on the call before deciding on the expedience of a rental or the hit and miss of locating a decent used vehicle. He dialed Lee's cell number, and she answered.

"Good morning, Ms. Winslow. Is your brother handy?"

"Good morning to you too, Brett. He's right here." Lee handed the phone to Jase.

Jase followed the toast he'd just finished with a gulp of juice and accepted the call. "Hey, Brett, you found something out already?"

"Yes. Called that first offer, and they are eager."

"That was easy enough. What station?"

"Remember the little gal that broke the story to the AP? Lydia Corvuso?"

"Have we got a date?"

"They have an open the second Friday in July. Does that work?"

"Does for me." Affecting his best Jean-Luc Picard imitation, he stated, "Make it so, Number One."

Brett could hear Lee laughing in the background. "I'll give the station a call back and confirm. Then I need to find some wheels."

"Speaking of that, Lee suggested you use the blue farm pickup she has here. It's nothing fancy, but beats walking."

Brett ruminated for a few seconds over the offer then answered, "That would work, as long it won't inconvenience her. Not sure when I'll be able to make it out there to get it, but—"

Jase interrupted. "Look behind you."

"What?" At the same moment Brett turned to look, he heard a baritone chuckle. The sight of Ben standing in his kitchen made him jump despite the fact that Jase had alerted him. "Geez! What are you grinning at?" Brett asked, addressing Ben.

Jase could hear Ben respond with a more intense expression of amusement. "What's he laughing at?"

Seated at the dining table in a pair of yellow duckie-print boxers, Brett responded, "Never mind. Let me throw some clothes on, and I'll be right there."

Clowning Around

WITH NO APPARENT BACKING, PUNCH Line was gaining national notoriety, and so was his significance. Hits on several of the uploads sent to YouTube had exceeded three million in less than a week. Transcripts of his speeches had already been translated into five languages, and word on the street was that perhaps this man had something to do with the manifestation of the Gleau. His message was nearly as powerful as his mystery, and that made Sturmisch care even less for this competition.

In a rural township in northern Iowa, Punch Line appeared at a local craft fair in the public park. "Don't wait for answers, people! The answers are right in front of you. Who demands something from you? Who wishes to divide us based on the slightest differences? Who tells you that you need them, when in fact, they depend solely on you for their existence? Think, people! *Think!*" Punch Line was getting their attention, making people think about the obfuscated obvious. Those sticking with the status quo tried to discredit him, but short of declaring that his act was not living up to Barnum and Bailey standards of humor, they were limited to poking holes in air. As their frustration grew, his detractors taunted and insulted, but Punch Line laughed at them.

After fielding a question phrased as an accusation that his lack of support for the bloated government institutions developed to help the poor made him a member of the callous, uncaring and greedy rich, he responded instantly and with fury.

"On what do you base your assumption, sir? Could it be that you wish my message to be clouded with your hate? You see before you one of the hardworking trying desperately to hang on to the investment of my life while providing necessities to my family and fellow man. I am one of the working poor! Those whose job it is to collect and redistribute on behalf of the poor pay themselves handsomely. Do you excoriate them? They take without asking from me and millions like me to live like comparative kings while handing out subsistence that keeps the poor in a continuing state of destitution. They spend millions on programs that employ their like kind with a pitiful return on the investment, and you praise them as devout benefactors of caring! If I expended four hundred dollars on the growing of a single carrot, would you then call me a genius or an idiot? Could you afford a four-hundred-and-fifty-dollar carrot, granting me a twelve and a half percent profit from which another 35 percent of that is confiscated? Just because I hired fifty of my friends and cohorts to aid in the growing of that carrot does not justify the ridiculous price. That is what is being sold to us in the guise of helping the poor, a carrot with a *k*, made more expensive by choice and corruption than necessity. The poor are being used! I can remember as a child watching the busses arrive at the corner of the field, offering ten dollars and a half pint in return for placing a marked ballot in the box on voting day. That was a far more honest and open deceit than the checks that arrive monthly to too many in a cheap exchange for the same. We've been sold the validity of the four-hundred-and-fifty-dollar carrot, and with it, our freedom!"

When the cheering and applause of the modest crowd subsided, another question was hurled at Punch Line like a Molotov cocktail.

"Well, if you're so poor, how can you afford to campaign?"

"Oh, so you want to know the identity of my backers?" Index finger on his temple, Punch Line struck an exaggerated pensive pose. "They are before you, sir!" The crowd cheered in agreement and quieted instantly as he began to speak again. "You have concerned yourself with a question of money when we all know you have already formed the answer you will report. But to preempt the dissemination of your fabrication, I will hand you the truth. I have no financial backing other than what I have earned myself. It is meager, but it will see me through because when you spend only what you earn, you spend it wisely and carefully. I dare say, before the advent of expensive modern communication, word of mouth took the words of great men far and wide, and it is those words I borrow and repeat because they are as true today as they were in times past. You see before you, sir, the body of my campaign and I thank each and every one of them for their support, not of me, but for the truth. The unadorned truth unites mankind while lies threaten to divide us. To quote Abraham Lincoln, 'A house divided against itself cannot stand,' and I am here to unite this house!"

Punch Line finished, and there were no more questions from the now-befuddled seeker of facts to twist. The questioner continued to scribble on his notepad and looked up only when Punch Line spoke to him directly. "I thank you, sir, for the work you do." Somewhat stunned by the expression of gratitude, he looked up at the comic face that was surrounded by an indescribable light that drew the eye to it despite its radiant intensity.

As the rally came to a close, Punch Line bid the crowd a good evening and safe journey. Though using a portable microphone supplied by a local civic organization to address the current gathering, he stepped down from his wooden crate and carried both his signature megaphone and his portable stage to a waiting older model GMC Jimmy. His gear was stowed in the hatch, and as he took his place in the rear passenger area, he waved good-bye. The Jimmy drove four blocks and parked. All four doors opened, and four Punch Lines exited. Each took a separate direction and walked to four different vehicles, high-fiving well-wishers as they walked. Each left and went their separate ways. Two stopped and entered clothing stores from which they never emerged. One entered a theater, and the fourth entered a grocery store, from which neither were detected exiting. The Jimmy left on the street was picked up by an unknown driver fifteen minutes after it was parked.

Punch Line's appearances were random and unannounced, often taking advantage of preexisting happenings taking place in small towns. For that reason, Sturmisch had cast a broad net of small-time private eye types within a hundred-mile radius of the bozo's last reported event. It was a frustration Sturmisch did not suffer well.

The Mutt and Jeff pair hired to investigate at this particular location couldn't believe their luck when the masked moron made an appearance. But as they were quickly outflanked by these amateurs, they decided not to report the results of the day's investigation. The two vehicles they did manage to record the tag numbers for were rentals. Proprietors of the car rental outfits did not file police reports for anything stolen, recovering them within an hour with the official word being that they were temporarily misplaced.

The groundswell created by Punch Line's original approach, continued anonymity, and distinct message, coupled by a reported Gleau that was as soothing to the soul as a cool swallow of the purest water from a desert oasis, had Sturmisch incensed to the point where action must be taken. It was time to turn up the heat and head the herd toward the edge of the plateau. It would not be a full-out stampede just yet, but those second in line on the precipice would let the rest know the fate of those first in line who failed to notice the cliff.

Early in the gold-buying trend, Sturmisch traded paper he would soon devalue into nothingness for precious metals. That investment was simply a hedge against his own actions as it was used as an exchange for necessities of life. His true intention was to corner the market on the necessities. Water might fall from the skies, but food, the land it was grown on, and the animals that grazed upon it, including the fuel to power the machinery to till it, would not be provided like manna. Knowing that land was a finite commodity being depended upon by an ever-growing population made it an excellent lever with which to tilt the playing field and direct the herd. Food would be the key to his control. Even the largest best-equipped standing army on the planet would fail to conquer starvation in the event of a dwindling supply, so food and every one of the mechanisms to produce it was the ultimate weapon Sturmisch had chosen to employ. Buying precious and industrial metals was just a step in that direction as they would be traded for the only thing ultimately more valuable: farmland.

Being a farmer already, his domestic acquisitions of foreclosed agricultural properties went unnoticed, but it paled in comparison to his land purchases around the world. There would be some forward-thinking individuals who would try to organize and maintain farming ventures to provide for the few, but they would be no match for the roving hoards of starving refugees. Sturmisch could count on the ignorant masses of ravenous refugees from the cities to overwhelm to a point of destruction any residual pockets of production. After all, it is what they were trained to do.

So while the world focused on the inflated dollar, growing national debt, higher taxes, high fuel prices, rising crime, unemployment, natural disasters, and any other contrived distraction Sturmisch could throw at it to assign blame and promote division, he was busy monopolizing the one thing that no human could survive without: food. In his view of the future, the 450-dollar carrot would become a reality, and privately, he would muse, "Let them eat gold and drink oil. Bon appétit!"

Exposing the Truth

DRESSED IN JEANS AND A red flannel shirt, Brett arrived in Lee's barn via Ben's magic carpet ride. As the two walked toward the house, Brett asked a question that had been pestering him recently. "Not that it matters much, Ben, but why the barn?"

"Why not? It works."

"Guess that answers that," he said, shaking his head and smiling.

In an uncharacteristically loquacious moment, Ben volunteered, "If there is one thing I've learned in my line of work, it is that not all questions need the answers they demand."

Brett considered Ben's words. "Unfortunately, in my line of work, they do."

About halfway across the barnyard, an engine came to life, and an ancient-looking blue pickup lumbered in reverse from behind the granary, backfired once in an unhealthy display of mechanical flatulence, and squealed to a slow stop across the path of the two walking toward the house. Lee leaned from the behind the steering wheel and cranked down the passenger window. Over the settling idle of the engine, she called to Brett, "Just blowin' out the bird nests and cobwebs. You can drive a four speed, right?"

Brett nodded in affirmation with a look of concern that made Lee laugh. As they met Jase at the door, Lee killed the engine and followed the three men inside. Brett made his call to Blake Ryan and confirmed the date for the interview with the repeated instruction that it not be advertised until twenty-four hours prior. Everything was agreed to verbally, and plans were made to sign contracts within the week. Lee went to the calendar to mark the date. "Whoa. You guys know what the second Friday in July is, right?"

"Full moon?" Brett piped up.

"I wish," Lee responded. "It's the thirteenth."

"You? You are superstitious?" Brett remarked, never supposing it was anything else.

"I never was until a few years ago. And it's more an anniversary than a superstition."

"Anniversary of what?"

Jase watched his sister carefully, knowing the significance of the date.

"I lost a very dear and close friend on that date. Everyone that knew her could see her reaction in the afterlife to this coincidence, and I know she rolls her eyes at it still. It's a pretty poignant reminder when that day rolls around, regardless of the month."

"Geez, I'm sorry to hear that. What happened?"

"She was a nurse for critically ill children and infants and did the scheduling for nursing care through an agency." Lee's mood was somber, then brightened. "She did love kids, especially her own two. I can recall a conversation when Em was pregnant with her first. Hers were still teenagers, but she said she couldn't wait to have grands of her own."

"Sounds like you really miss her," Brett added.

"Every day. An inattentive driver went through a stop sign, and she was gone in an instant. Funny thing, knowing her as well as I did, her heart was big enough to feel for the poor soul who had to live with that one huge mistake for the rest of his life. The only way I ever came to grips with that loss was imagining being in God's shoes. I'd want her too. And that's why Em named her first daughter Pam."

Brett was quiet for a moment and then asked, "Was that about nine years ago?"

"Yes. Yes, it was. Did you know her?"

"Was her husband a mechanic?"

"Still is."

"I do remember that incident. Her husband did some work for me."

For whatever reason, that remote connection was enough to allow Brett a closer place in Lee's life. "This world was a much better place when she was in it, and I have to believe her influence lives on." Lee sighed deeply, cleansing her thoughts of anything other than good memories.

Jase and Ben exchanged glances and both smiled.

The television in the kitchen was tuned to a local news station with the volume low when the face of a clown filled the screen. "Have you heard about this guy?" Lee asked while grabbing the remote and turning the volume up before going to the sink to wash her hands.

The reporter was just finishing a sound bite regarding Punch Line. "There you have it. No one knows the identity of this comic with apparent political aspirations, but he's certainly becoming a household name. His appearances, which, to this point, are never announced, will make it a wait-and-see game before we know if he will attend the scheduled debate on Saturday, the eleventh of August, sponsored by one of our competitor networks at the Moscone Center in San Francisco."

"He's been a big hit on YouTube, or so I've heard," Brett answered.

"He's smart," Jase added.

"He's a guy in a clown suit trying to make political hay. What's smart about that?"

"Granted, the gimmick is a bit distracting, but once you get past that, the truth he's dispensing can't be polluted or diluted with personal poison. Too many wear no mask and tell lies, and yet so many would find that less deceitful. See him in person, and then tell me he isn't smart."

"You've seen him in person?" Brett asked, honestly wondering.

"No, I haven't. But according to what's been reported about his Gleau, that's what I base my judgment on. Right now, there is no reason to distort the truth of what people are seeing because no one knows for sure what this means, but they will know a few weeks from now. The reports are consistent, and it seems this man dares to tell the truth while stifling those who would sully his message by attacking him personally. They can only attack the fact that he wears a clown suit, and they won't touch the truth. It's a pretty smart move."

"From that perspective, I guess you're right," Brett agreed. "But what happens when he takes off the mask?"

"I guess we'll all see that when it happens," Ben spoke up.

"You really think this guy is serious?" Brett uttered with skepticism. His Gleau displayed an emerald to cerulean beneath his corona of aqua and white, indicating his sincerity of thought.

With a wink and a smile, Jase replied, "Haven't you heard? This man is no joke. He's the Punch Line."

"Indeed," Lee added, drying her hands. "And the man who arrived in my barn less than half an hour ago via Ben the Traveler is having difficulty conceiving of the notion that a man of the truth in a clown suit could be a bona fide contender. Give me a break!"

"Okay, okay." Brett laughed self-consciously. "You do know how to make a contrasting point. I'll waive any further judgment until after the debate on August eleventh."

What Lee thought she heard Brett say was something about a debate on August eleventh. "What did you just say?"

"I said I won't judge the clown until after I see how he does in the debate against some serious competition."

"No, no. I mean the date," Lee asked him to clarify.

"It's on a Saturday, the big kick-off debate between the heavy hitters. I think I heard them say that the clown will be invited. It's the eleventh of August. I'm pretty sure that's what they just said."

"I missed that," Lee replied. Brett would not have understood the import of that specific date for Lee. He may have remembered helping her locate the news copy for that week, but he knew nothing of the Bad Day.

This has to be more than just simple coincidence, Lee thought.

Noticing Lee's apprehension, Jase moved to her side and placed his arm around her shoulders. "What do you think we'll see when his mask is removed?" Jase asked, addressing Brett.

"I don't have any real idea," Brett said honestly.

"Maybe his mask has already been removed," Jase suggested.

"How do you figure that?" Brett asked, not quite sure where Jase was going with this line of questioning.

"This clown isn't hiding behind any of the earthly trappings used to impress and divide. He doesn't wear a mask of supremacy over others to indicate that he is smarter or wiser or richer or more popular or the right age or right color or height, or even the right party. None of those things embody the message. He's handing out the truth, and the mere suggestion of such a thing can cause some to try to silence this endeavor, as you can attest to by personal experience. You have been my mask for the past six months or so. When the truth of the Gleau is revealed, do you or I, as the individuals we are, have any bearing whatsoever on that truth?"

"Putting it that way, I see your point. I just think people are so set in how they view things that change is going to be a struggle. It isn't going to be easy."

"Evil and every one of its lazy, miserable, and slipshod ways, counts on that. Evil always provides the easy way out while never mentioning the dire eventual consequences. Evil is the first to bear false witness, the first to tell lies, the first to cry foul, and the first to resort to oppression and violence in support of its cause for the simple reason that it is a coward. Evil is a seducer. Rife with insincere promises, it dispels with arrogance while secretly despising those it seduces for their ignorance at being seduced. Its perfection and its flaw are one in the same. You're right, it isn't going to be easy, but that is why the Gleau will give them a new way to view things."

"Okay. I think I get it. No matter who the messenger is, look past the clown suit, and see the truth."

"I couldn't have put it better."

Clown Indeed

STURMISCH WASN'T LAUGHING. THIS PUNCH Line was starting to gain a substantial following and had no problem
countering every bit of puffery handed to him by the ego-
bloated zombies that spouted Sturmisch's yards of rhetoric. He
hated to admit it, but this clown was good, and that made him
bad for Sturmisch's cause. This painted wonder had no problem
dismantling decades of circular logic and did it without shaming
those he enlightened. He gently pried open the minds of those
held prisoner by stating the obvious, and it was painfully clear to
Sturmisch that this thorn in his side had to go. If a threat to the
power of the powerful could not be tolerated or endured, it must
be eradicated.

Sturmisch was currently faced with the unprecedented and
less expedient task of attacking the only vulnerable flank offered:
Punch Line's message. Every syllable uttered by this fool would
be dissected and countered by Adam's speech writers, but it did
not prevent him from running his mouth in public and gaining
ground at every turn. His paid informants were already set upon
the task of discovering the true name of this foppish character
to pave the way for his personal destruction, but that took time.
Knowing the true identity of this joker in question would allow
Sturmisch's well-compensated accomplices in the media to make
short work of this not-so-funny man. But if all else failed and he
could not be discredited personally, threatened privately, or convinced to fold up his tent and disappear, he needed to be made
null and void.

Mr. Swann, and Adam more so, had difficulty with all the
glowing reports of this unknown's Gleau. Too many positive
adjectives were noted describing what crowds observed. *Brilliant,*

mesmerizing, radiant, and the favorite, *sparkling new star,* head-lined nearly every bit of copy generated by Punch Line's speaking engagements. It was enough to make Adam Gleau chartreuse with envy and scarlet with anger. While discussing their options regarding Punch Line and the upcoming invitational debate Sturmisch was surreptitiously sponsoring, Sturmisch grew weary of Adam's conspicuous narcissism and was forced to flick him from his tiny pedestal.

Via their latest phone discussion, Sturmisch did his utmost to encourage Adam while putting him in his place. "That clown can't upstage you if you don't let him. You're the pretty boy in this picture, hands down. Just stick to the script. You can woo the round heels with the smile and charm, but you need to stay sharp and stick it to this guy on the intellectual level to keep the testosterone thinkers on board. Now go polish your prose while I figure out how to bury this guy." Before Adam could respond, Sturmisch hung up.

Adam knew Sturmisch was right, and he would be as sharp as any tack could possibly be when it came to debating the clown. He did have to admit that he was smitten with all that was Hollywood about the campaign. The power stroking of the applauding audiences was euphoric. Secretly though, he begrudged the fact that he didn't have a gimmick like the clown. If he did, he would be a Utopian superhero, not because he had any faith in that fairy tale, but because he thought he'd look great in light-blue tights. As deep as Adam's dark side was, there was a very shallow end to his emotional pool as well.

The Squeeze

PUTTING THE SITUATION WITH ADAM aside, Sturmisch turned his attention to the daily news and determined that he needed more focus on shortages he was busily creating. The problem had to get large enough to overwhelm while falling short of all-out chaos. As several governments around the world had tried to alleviate the fuel price problem by releasing some of their emergency reserves, Sturmisch saw that as an opportunity to buy and increase his own reserves at a lowered cost. The artificial glut calmed fears as prices returned to a dollar and a half more than they were the previous year. Sturmisch counted on this reaction.

As fuel prices fluctuated back up to levels that caused inconvenience and objection, Sturmisch saw his armies forming. Food prices were still climbing, and as they did, wage earners demanded increases to offset the expense. Every product and service of necessity bumped its cost accordingly, and as that dog chased its tail, expenditures on nonessentials tanked. Those selling the knickknacks and luxuries of life found themselves with little or no market. The ranks of unemployed and truly needy swelled as expected, and the desperate began resorting to crime when even the givers of charity were near bankrupt.

Still, Sturmisch wanted the fear to creep up the leg of society like a gangrenous infection that only threatened the body with problems of mobility, not imminent death. Desperation needed to be exported to the suburbs. The ostrich flock awaited with their heads buried deep, still believing that all upheaval only happened elsewhere to other people but not to them. They had the guarantees of the biggest of the big that the piece of paper with numbers on it was worth something. That notion was destined to be disproved, and Sturmisch would see to it that they understood who was in charge.

Cattle rustling on a small scale had hit the news. It seemed though that thieves were unable to tell the difference between dairy cows and beef cattle, so one pair of would-be cattle barons got caught at a local livestock buyer wishing to sell for slaughter a very distraught Holstein cow with a distended udder and a missing ear tag. Dairy farmers, though fewer in number than in years past, started keeping their herds close, some even standing nightly vigils armed with shotguns.

Amid the reporting of all things negative was a small blurb that sought to put the silver lining ahead of an ominous cloud. Pawn shops were seeing an unprecedented increase in business as families sold and pawned whatever was necessary to make ends meet. Owners were greeted each morning by long lines of individuals with items for sale that had become less precious than a mortgage payment or an overdue electric bill.

Store shelves weren't bare yet, but there was a noticeable increase in the price of fresh and perishable fruits and vegetables as diesel costs were added to the price. Seafood haulers had been the preferred target of freight hijackers, netting thieves a quarter to a half a million dollars for a single truckload of shellfish delicacies. Now everything from sweet corn to strawberries was worth the gamble. Insurance companies began increasing policy rates for truckers to offset increasing and future losses due to the growing risk, and the percentage of independent truckers were forced to park or hand over their trucks to the banks.

The number of thefts, break-ins, and robberies had jumped to a level that threatened to overwhelm police departments who were forced to concentrate on those cases where personal injury or assault were a factor and put aside any incident involving strict property loss. The public was encouraged not to engage would-be robbers to avoid endangering themselves, which to too many meant becoming sitting ducks for thieves. After this trend was reported in the news, nonconfrontational pilfering tripled as thieves realized they would not be sought.

Lost in his depraved thoughts for a moment, a huge smile nearly cut Sturmisch's face in half as he read a statistic declaring that suicide deaths had surpassed in number those killed in automobile accidents. It was proof that the pressure brought to bear was having the effect he so desired. The only deaths more convenient to his cause were those created by war because he was certain that a life taken defending freedom was to his advantage.

As difficulties and costs of doing business increased, the ten-dollar-per-pound beef no longer shocked people. The gentleman in the overcoat who once hawked stolen or knock-off watches now surreptitiously allowed customers a peek at his vacuum-wrapped New York strip and Delmonico steaks that hung partially frozen in the lining of his wearable walk-in cooler. A group of older yuppies, still in pursuit of things natural and organic, were horrified to learn that their delicious grass-fed hormone-free beef was actually horse meat. The wild chickens, whose release was an unintended consequence of storms, used to be a problem in some states. They had all but disappeared, along with ducks from park ponds and pigeons bent on soiling public statuary. Feral pigs were a nuisance that became a much-sought-after resource as well. Deer poaching was still a crime, but considering the circumstances, it was being overlooked to a great degree. Pet store owners had become wary of repeat customers for cute little bunnies, especially when they referred to them as lapin. All of these semidrastic measures being taken to offset the burgeoning cost of feeding a family pleased Sturmisch. It meant his squeeze was being felt, but until the official panic began, the genuine riots and looting would wait for his command.

Next Stop

THE GENTLEMAN KNOWN TO THE public as Punch Line took advantage of his anonymity to scour local papers and pinup boards for events that would suit his purpose. He had no definite schedule or a planned route, so as he and his three buddies meandered west into Nebraska searching for the next venue, they stopped at a local campground to prepare and even take in a little fishing. It was a chance to converse with other vacationers and locals, getting wind of fairs and festivals and finding out what people thought about his unorthodox campaign without having to disclose his identity.

After the last appearance, it was well documented that someone had taken more than a casual curiosity in Punch Line's activities, so their security measures were well worth the effort. The car rental employee at their last stop described an outsider asking too many questions and packing heat. The description of the outsider's Gleau was a telltale sign that his intentions too were less than cordial. He would mention to the crowd at his next gathering that his message was powerful enough to draw powerful enemies, thereby enlisting the eyes and ears of his public supporters. This focused attention wasn't something unforeseen, nor was it a deterrent. To the contrary, it indicated that they were striking just the right chord and intended to play it even louder.

Punch Line and his three companions, like quite a few others, thought they had discovered what the Gleau truly meant. By trial and error, they tested their assumptions and discovered that deception was displayed rather vigorously. For the time being, it was an awareness they would keep to themselves. After a conversation with a golden-Gleau retired couple from Tennessee, they decided the next port of call would be the North Platte area for the NEBRASKAᴸᴬᴺᴰ DAYS festival. In their rented RV, they had no trouble blending in with the crowd.

The Spiral

B Y MID-JUNE, EVEN WITH THE delayed planting this year, Lee noticed the larger-than-usual crowds at the farmer's market. She had to increase the price of her eggs to keep up with increased feed and fuel prices but managed to have it stay where it was competitive and affordable. The talk among her customers was centered on the news of the continuing decline in densely populated areas near large cities. By the sheer number of reports, crimes had become so frequent that a large percentage weren't being attended to by anything more than a phone call. If there was no personal injury, victims were being told to document by photograph any damage, list stolen items, repair anything that compromised security, and keep their doors locked. Otherwise, there was little that the police could do. They were strained to the breaking point, and criminals knew it. "Crooks watch TV too," declared an elderly gal in a broad-brimmed sunhat. Many held a fear that before anything got better, it was going to get much worse.

Despite the less-than-joyful topic of conversation, Lee managed to compliment the weather and take note of the fact that not a single shadow dweller was in the park, at least not that she could see. She was surrounded by a bright spot of humanity and let that be her greater comfort. It confirmed her faith in people when so many still wanted to do the right thing even though the wrong things were being done to them. At any moment, a new law or regulation could make today's law-abiding citizen tomorrow's criminal, but it was maintained that truth and justice could never truly be corrupted, just the people delivering them.

The *Independence Review* and their now semifamous editor, Brett Hume, were topics of discussion that had many speculating about the identity of the source. Lee listened with interest as they bantered about which of the town notables might be the deliverer of the Gleau. Maxine Rowe, chairwoman of the Ladies in Bloom flower arranging club and self-proclaimed provider of worldly culture to this backward township, then directed a question to Lee. "Ms. Winslow, what do you think this is all about?"

Caught off guard a bit, she hesitated for a moment. "If you're asking me about the Gleau itself, I'd say it's telling us to pay attention."

Mrs. Rowe wasn't satisfied with that answer. "Pay attention to what exactly?"

"My best answer to that would be each other," Lee stated, noticing the pronounced deep violet to cherry red manifesting around Mrs. Rowe's generous midsection. Without revealing her personal insight with regard to the Gleau, Lee added, "Maybe it just fills in a blank."

Mrs. Rowe pursed her lips in dissatisfaction with Lee's answer. "What blank are you referring to, dearie?" she condescended.

"The one we see around ourselves, of course," Lee shot back with a tone expressing the fact that Maxine most certainly already knew this.

"Oh yes, of course," Maxine replied curtly.

Mrs. Rowe lightened up in both her Gleau and her disposition after being tossed a response that she could not dispute. Her original intention was to wow the small audience gathered in front of Lee's table with her wisdom about how the Gleau reflected true intelligence and use Lee's response as her point of disagreement until she realized she couldn't rate herself at the top of the heap without asking someone else how she appeared. In retrospect, Lee had to thank Sasha Parks for the lesson in dealing with the likes of Mrs. Rowe and let the matter drop. The bait ignored, she asked Maxine if she needed eggs. Two dozen eggs were dispensed, and Mrs. Rowe bid the bundle of ladies adieu.

"You handled that beautifully," Mrs. Davis piped up as she was next in line to purchase eggs. "But I was really hoping to hear yet another reason why Maxine is our better!" The group giggled at what they all had experienced at one time or another in Maxine's presence.

"I'm sure we'll all find out was this is about soon enough," Lee tempered the group.

Mrs. Davis couldn't resist commenting while counting out her coins. "For all the culture she's been exposed to, I find it amazing that the art of humility has escaped her entirely," she pronounced in her best Bostonian debutante speak.

Lee bagged Mrs. Davis's eggs and handed them to her with a smile generated by the last comment. As the market came to a close, she began to pack up and tended to her last customer of the day. Dressed in suit trousers and a tie, the gentleman purchased her last dozen eggs and hurried off, telling her to keep the change.

Of Hypocrites and Actors

ADAM HAD PUT A SPIT shine on the answers he would hand to his adoring public. For the most part, they would fit any question that came his way, and because they were *his* people, the subject matter always fell within predictable parameters. Specifics were answered with generalities, and broad-based questions were reduced to specific examples. It was all kept neat, tidy, and conformist so the same few ideas could be recycled without appearing to be repetitive. It took a great deal of organizational skill to plan and gather the correct audience, so Adam always did his best to show his gratitude for their attendance. It never looked as if he was at a loss for words; he never stuttered or broke his pattern of speech with "ums" or "uhs." His script was smooth and polished and oozed patriarchal symbolisms to calm the nervous children he addressed. He let them know that they would be taken care of, and all they rightfully deserved and needed would be provided via his capable means. When he was acting the role of "the candidate," there was such a feeling of confidence harvested during the execution that it overcame the fact that he knew none of it was true. He didn't care that it was pure baloney. He cared that it made him recognized to the point of worship, and that made the means justify the ends in his view.

Through it all though, Adam never lost sight of the fact that if it weren't for Sturmisch's bottomless coffers of support, none of this would be possible. The old man saw to it that everything was timed, funded, arranged, written, chauffeured, and catered to perfectly. It had to make Mr. Swann rather proud to see how well his actor performed, given so total an investment. But Adam knew one thing that Sturmisch never would. Adam knew what it felt like to be adored by the crowd.

Though it did test his mental agility, Sturmisch did some of his best organizational juggling with so many balls in the air that even Chris Bliss would be impressed. While managing the managers of Adam's campaign and tweaking the worldwide actions of his generals on the economic and political fronts based on current happenings, he was also directing the discovery of the source of the Gleau as well as determining the identity of this despicable clown, Punch Line. What would have other heads spinning with crushing detail caused Sturmisch to be further engaged and entertained. The world was his canvas, control was his medium, and his masterpiece would be a creation for the entire world to see.

When things didn't go quite as planned, Sturmisch always had a new plan, and things would eventually go his way. He knew this because of the depth of the roots of his psychological plantings that thrived in society. Some would say it would have been impossible to go against the grain of certain cultural structures set in place hundreds of years before, but prosperity provided Sturmisch with the perfect opportunity. He knew it was important that his children be heard and eventually listened to and obeyed. Sixty years ago, the parents of the baby boom generation had failed miserably at perfecting the world, but they did manage to forge an economy that grew and improved a robust middle class that spawned advancements in business and technology as well as a standard of living for the majority unequaled anywhere else on earth. In that fertile ground, Sturmisch planted his seeds of discontent.

What parent wouldn't want to give their offspring a happy childhood? After the realities and hardships the previous three generations had endured, it was with great zeal that they spared the innocent children from the horrors and deprivation that they had suffered, and they could afford to do so. These children were immunized, educated, entertained, catered to, and coddled to the point of withease. Much like a disease, a with ease infects when stresses and responsibilities are withheld. The unburdened ego, buoyed by praise and unencumbered by the likes of shame, humility, or introspection, grew to a point where it was allowed and encouraged to view the old order of things as substandard and in need not only of change, but deserving of disrespect and pointed criticism. Sturmisch knew that there were none as bold as those who have never met challenge. Imperfect people didn't deserve respect, and with new math came new history that hammered that point home at every level of education

As such, the discredited and obsolete generations of the past were admonished for their lack of fairness and perfection and were blind to the withease of this new generation. It spread like a plague. In no need of a vaccine, it was rather fostered with self-interest and broadcast with awareness of self-importance. These minions were taught what was necessary to foment dissent without apology because they would forever point to the failures of the past to justify their own wise and superior thinking. Sturmisch was pleased that his children were unafraid to display their brilliance, and the only admitted shame they shared with him was for the defective stock from which they sprang.

What this generation of Einsteins didn't need to know, Sturmisch wasn't going to tell them either. He would simply continue to remark about their never-before-reached level of knowledge and understanding. They were hip, with it, and in the groove. College educations were the hallmark of this generation, and many earned a certain level of arrogance right along with their degree. So it was in the infancy of Sturmisch's army, the highly educated with opinions and no real experience began setting their elder inferiors straight on how things should be done. If they had bothered to notice, history did not begin when they were born, and this same scenario had been played out many times before. It was an interesting juxtaposition that Sturmisch was pleased that this fact was monumentally overlooked, but at the same time he despised their proud ignorance.

Was it any wonder that they gave birth, somewhat begrudgingly, to a generation that they were quick to slap a derogatory label upon: the "me" generation. Of course, labeling people just like stereotyping or prejudice were the very things they criticized their predecessors for, but no matter. As the chosen ones, it was dismissed and denied as aggressively as it was practiced. As a matter of fact, every "ism" in the book that they decried as somehow subhuman was being practiced on a new enlightened level. As they insisted on new standards of tolerance and acceptance, name-calling had simply been renamed self-expression. The broad brush they had been so quick to censure was now back in fashion, and they denied any similarity in its usage even as they tossed about phrases like "dumb slut" or "*those* Christians." Hate was alive and well, living in the hearts and minds of practitioners as the correct application of fairness. Sturmisch had to admit, the mental and emotional contortions demanded to achieve this feat were near miraculous. His children possessed such devout wisdom in his cause that they didn't have to think anymore, but of course they denied it vehemently while failing to produce the logic that explained their derisiveness. They had been taught in the interest of fairness to covet while denying the theft. Sturmisch wished he was two people just so he could pat himself on the back, having successfully convinced so many that arbitrary application of intolerance and prejudice was justified when done correctly.

Above the Grain Belt

EW OF THE VENDORS HAD yet to open their booths as Punch Line took a leisurely morning stroll down the main thoroughfare of the NEBRASKALAND DAYS Fair. The aroma of chili and cinnamon rolls combined to produce something remarkably delicious. Half the distance back to the RV, a seller of Western garb was arranging his wares and a rack of cowboy hats caught Punch Line's eye. He picked up a 20X natural straw hat with a four-inch brim.

"That hat's been a-waitin' for you," said the salesman.

"You may be right," Punch Line answered as he smiled and placed the hat on his head. Checking his reflection in the mirror, it was to his liking. "Yep, this one had my name on it." Punch Line paid the vendor and made his way back to the RV with his new hat and the saunter it inspired. As he strode across the last twenty feet of parking lot, he saw something unexpected.

"Like the hat," mentioned the first of Punch Line's companions to address him as he entered the motor home.

"Thanks. You can wear it when we do our thing later. Guess who just pulled up in the back parking area," Punch line prodded, placing his hat on his friend's head. It was June 23, the last Saturday of the NEBRASKALAND DAYS Fair, so he knew attendance would be high, and at last he would have an opportunity to put the competition on notice face-to-face.

"Could it be Buffalo Bill Cody?"

"Good guess, but not even close. Mr. Adam and his entourage have blessed the good people of North Platte with their distinguished company."

All three of his fellow travelers took interest immediately. "I'm guessing we're going to crash his party," stated the burly gentleman now adorned with the hat.

"Crash? Nah. We're invited. We bought tickets just like everyone else."

The youngest of the group, a mere child of forty-two, pulled on his jeans and snap-front shirt and announced that he would go nose around and find out what the schedule was for the bestowing of Adam's speech to the country folk. It took less than an hour to gather the necessary reconnaissance. "They're setting up a portable stage inside the fence of the show parking area just north of the rodeo shack."

"Guess the pretty boy needs protection from his adoring public." The new wearer of Punch Line's hat laughed. "What time does the extravaganza begin?"

"Word from our new friend inside the pavilion is just before the arena events begin. It wasn't a scheduled event, but they paid handsomely for the privilege. The arena grandstand does need more repairs," he added.

"You think they have any clue we're here?" The third member of Punch Line's crew was pulling on his boots.

"If they don't already, we'll make it obvious," Punch Line answered as he applied his now well-known face paint. "Our friend has everything ready and knows what to do?"

"Readying as we speak. They'll all be waiting for the word," the youngest member reported.

"Good," Punch Line answered. "There will definitely be snakes in the crowd tonight."

Love Takes Action

HER BUSY MARKET DAY POSTPONED but did not negate the balance of chores waiting for Lee at home. Em and family were coming for dinner, so she hurried to feed up and gather eggs before starting the evening meal. Jase had gone to the mill to get the meager ration of feed they could afford. Grain prices had soared, and our daily bread was now our weekly bread at nearly four dollars a loaf.

Lee headed to the chicken house carrying a wire egg basket and her Mini-14 in anticipation of spotting one of the coyotes she'd seen the day before. It was rare to see one in daylight hours, but her free-range flock was a dinner bell they had difficulty ignoring. Semi continued his nap on the rocker in the kitchen, declining an invitation to venture into the afternoon heat. Lee surveyed the woods line closest to the barn and was satisfied that the predators, at least for now, weren't lurking within striking distance. She stood the Mini-14 next to the doorway and entered the henhouse. The girls outdid themselves with nearly three dozen eggs, and Lee grabbed the Mini-14 on her way to the house to wash and refrigerate the eggs before checking the garden.

As she reached the kitchen door, she noticed a car pulling up the drive. Just in time gathering the eggs, she thought as she placed them and the rifle inside the door on the step leading up to the kitchen. The gentleman driver slowed, stopped, and made his approach upon getting out of his car. Lee recognized him instantly as her last customer at the market, but now he looked even more uncomfortable wearing the suit jacket that coordinated with his shirt and tie.

"I was wondering if I could get a couple dozen more eggs," he asked, smiling pleasantly. "You left the market before I could get there and buy two more that my wife wanted."

Out of habit, Lee returned the smile until she saw a starburst of red spikes issue about his head and shoulders. Resisting the urge to react suddenly, she watched as the pale yellow light that led her to believe he was just a customer dulled and began to turn from yellow ochre to putrid brownish gray. His smile withdrew, and Lee spoke up quickly and casually in hopes it would give her time to retreat into the house. "I just gathered some. Let me grab a couple cartons." Trying not to appear nervous, she pulled open the screen door and ducked inside. Before she could close the door completely, a flash of fur slid like quicksilver through the narrowing gap and, like a guided missile, leapt upon the arm of the fake customer. Semi sunk his teeth into the man's hand that, moments before, had secured what looked like a toy from his rear waistband. The Glock 33 SIG proved not to be a toy as it discharged a .357 round into the wooden deck just outside the door. The man's efforts to shake loose the attacking feline failed as Semi repeatedly bit the hand that held the weapon.

When not even the sound of the gunshot could diminish the fury of this little cat, the man grabbed him from behind the neck and pulled. Semi's jaws closed tightly into the meaty part of the man's thumb and tore the flesh as the man forced his release and slammed him to the ground with a sickening and deadly thud. The man, dripping blood from the severe lacerations and puncture wounds, looked toward the screen door, expecting to gain entry and finish his work. In the matter of seconds it took Semi to defend Lee, it was enough time for her to chamber a round in the Mini-14 and squeeze the stock between her elbow and hip before sending a shot through the screen and into the intruder's neck. At this close range, the round went through the flesh, missing the spine and barely causing the man to show surprise. Before he could move out of her line of sight, she pulled the trigger again, hitting him just right in the center of the chest. Despite the small caliber, the soft-nosed bullet took its toll. With an upward jerk of his hands, he fell to his side just beyond the doorway.

Immediately but not without her weapon, she went to Semi. His lifeless little body lay broken, and Lee did her best to move him into a more natural posture. Still warm to her touch, his mouth was stained with the blood of her attacker. This tiny animal, her friend, had made the ultimate sacrifice in her defense. More than the attack itself, his loss was the bigger shock. She turned to be sure the intruder was permanently incapacitated, not sure if he was wearing body armor and merely stunned. With tears welling, she stood and walked the few steps to where he lay motionless. More than his lack of animation and despite the lack of blood loss, other than what surrounded the tiny entrance wound, she knew he was dead. The Gleau that had surrounded him was gone. She knew she would have to call the police, but at this moment, she sat her rifle aside and gathered Semi's body into her arms. In the kitchen she sat in his favorite chair and rocked him, tears streaming as she thanked him and mourned his loss. Not sure if it was seconds or minutes that had passed, Lee was aware that she was no longer alone in the room. "When did you get here?" she asked the presence.

"Not soon enough. I could not see this. I saw only that you were out of danger," Ben answered solemnly.

"It's okay. He understands even if I don't," Lee answered with halting speech.

"He's still with you."

"He'll always be with me, in my heart," Lee agreed.

"No. I mean now. He's at your feet wanting to know why you are so sad."

The full weight and meaning of Ben's words escaped her for the moment. Wondering and wishing she had the ability to see Semi alive again, it was very much his way to get as close as possible when Lee was saddened.

Jase pulled into the barnyard past the stranger's car and hit the brakes hard enough to slide on the gravel when he saw the body lying near the doorstep. Seeing the rifle discarded on the deck, he called Lee's name as he neared the door, and Ben answered. "We're in here."

Jase's face fell when he saw his sister's cheeks strewn with tears, waves of cobalt and white crashing about her like an angry sea, and a lifeless Semi curled carefully in her lap. "Oh, Lee, I'm so sorry." He went to her and knelt, placing his arm on hers.

"He saved my life, Jase."

"I'm grateful that he did, but I know how high this cost is to you."

"Immeasurable," was her one-word response. Lee told Jase and Ben what had transpired and how this stranger had not appeared to be a threat initially. She wished she had been more aware, more intuitive, and more distrustful. She wished for anything that could have changed the outcome of this afternoon.

"Did he say anything to you, Lee?" She was lost in the grief and didn't reply. "Lee," Jase repeated more emphatically.

Finally, she answered. "I saw him at the market today. He didn't look like a shadow dweller. He was my last customer. He said he was here to get a couple dozen more eggs. I have to call the police," Lee recounted, doing her best to suppress all emotion.

Jase stood and conferred with Ben then spoke to Lee again. "I know that would be the right thing to do ordinarily, but for your sake and ours, I think it would be safer if we postpone doing that for right now."

"Okay," Lee agreed, not caring what she was agreeing to at the moment. Her mind was busy gathering every memory she shared with Semi. Suddenly, her mind bounced back to the reality at hand. "The girls! Em and the girls are coming for dinner. What time is it?"

Jase looked at Ben and said nothing. To that Ben responded, "I'll take care of it." Ben vanished, and in a matter of seconds, he returned and handed Jase a wallet and cell phone.

"We'll be back in a few minutes, Lee," Jase assured his sister.

Alone in the kitchen, Lee heard two engines start. In less than an hour, she would have to break the news to her granddaughters that Semi had gone to heaven. She debated how and when she should tell the girls and decided she would say nothing unless they asked. It was delaying the inevitable, but at this juncture, it was the only option she could deal with. In her lap, Semi looked almost like he was asleep. She scratched his head one last time and held his paws, cooling as the warmth of life left his body, and whispered in his ear, "Good-bye, my dear friend. As always, I love you." She wrapped him in his favorite fleece throw from the sofa and carried him to the basement until she was afforded the opportunity to find a suitable spot for his eternal repose.

Lee forced herself to get on with the tasks at hand knowing that at any moment, Emily and the girls would arrive. Remembering that she had left the rifle outside, she was surprised to see it had been stowed safely in the pull down. Other than the bullet hole in the deck and a couple small holes in the screen door, everything outside looked as it did when she awoke this morning. Lee hoped the holes would go unnoticed, including the one in her heart.

The basket of eggs was carried to the sink for cleaning, and Jase and Ben returned when she was about half-finished. Other than an initial greeting to make Lee aware that they were back, both went to her in silence and expressed their condolences with an embrace that said more than words could convey. Finally Ben spoke, hoping to lighten her burden. "He's still here, Lee," Ben stated.

"I know," she responded in simple agreement.

"No, I don't think you do know. Semi is still here. His body may not have survived this life, but his life has survived his body's demise." Lee turned and stared at Ben, waiting for a more thorough explanation. "Animals make the transition far more fluidly than humans do. Those with a connection here tend to linger, not understanding that they can no longer be seen. To them, life simply goes on. He is here, asking to be noticed."

Lee trusted Ben, but what he was telling her gave rise to a new dilemma. "If he is still here, I don't want him to think I'm ignoring him. Tell me where he is," she implored, wishing to spare Semi any further undo anguish.

"He's at your feet." Lee knelt and held out her hands. Though she could not feel or see anything to indicate his presence, she offered her attention and spoke his name. Ben watched. Lee could not see it, but as the spiritual Semi accepted her gesture and wove between her hands, the Gleau surrounding them sparkled with glints of gold.

"Can't he move on? I mean, all life goes back to where it came from, doesn't it?"

Ben understood her concern. "Yes, it does, but his strongest connection was with you."

"What can I do? I don't want him here thinking I don't care about him anymore just because I can't see him."

"There is a woman here who says she knew him in this life. Tell him to go with her, and you will be there when you can."

Immediately, Lee knew exactly who this woman was. She did as Ben instructed, and though it was beyond her ability to actually see what was happening, her sorrow lifted and her thanks deepened as Pam carried Semi to a safe, loving place in the next realm of existence to wait for her.

"Thank you, Ben."

"You're welcome. If it had been within my power to do more—"

Lee stopped him. "I know you would, but I'm grateful beyond measure for all that you have already done." Her Gleau brightened slightly with a sigh.

Ben wondered if she would feel the same way a little over a month from now.

It wasn't until after the evening meal was consumed and the girls and Ben were in the barn tending to Beanie that the news was broken to Emily and Matt of what had happened earlier in the day. Emily agreed to tell the girls about Semi after they were back at home, assuring them that he was a very brave cat that was now in heaven. Why the man had come to Lee's place could only be speculated upon, but it was apparent that he found his way there by the address displayed on the egg carton found in the front seat of his car. Clearly the target must have been Brett's source, but it was unclear whether the intruder had seen Lee and Brett together and figured she was either a source of information or the source itself. It had also been deduced that this individual had probably been sent by the same organization that sent the goons to Barbara and Brett.

"No wonder you sent Ben to the barn with the girls," Emily noted.

"Obviously, this guy didn't get to make a report after your mother ended his mission, but we have no way of knowing what information he forwarded prior to his demise," Jase explained.

"What's that about?" Emily was pointing to a cell phone immersed in a glass of water on the counter.

"It's the guy's cell phone. We copied all the information we could find in it, pulled the battery and SIM card, and drowned it just to be sure," Lee answered.

"Where's the guy, or should I not want to know?"

Lee looked to Jase for the answer and then gave Em the only answer she had. "Ben stashed him somewhere until it's safe to report it to the police."

"His car is parked at the Best Western where his parking permit indicated he was registered. I'm hoping that will give us some time," Jase volunteered.

"Time for what?" Emily asked.

"Time before it's discovered that anything is amiss. I don't know whose attention we've gotten, but they have the resources to be persistent."

Gazing out the kitchen windows toward the barn, Lee watched her gaggle of granddaughters and one giant making their way toward the house. Sitting in the crook of one of Ben's substantial arms was Joy, looking very much like Fay Wray being carried by King Kong before ascending the Empire State Building. Unexpectedly, a pickup pulled into the yard and blocked her view of the group. A fraction of a second of panic dissipated when she recognized her own truck, and Brett opened the driver's door and ran around to the passenger side to escort Barbara. Catching up to the newly arrived pair, Ben offered his available arm to Barbara, and Brett hurried ahead into the house.

Immediately going to Lee to express his sorrow about Semi's untimely death, Brett stayed by her side while updating Jase. "I just got done talking to Blake Ryan at KMIN. He's agreed to reschedule the interview to next Wednesday, the twenty-seventh. I told him why we needed to speed things up, and he understood."

"That's good," Jase answered. "The sooner the focus is on what the Gleau means, the better for all."

"Except the shadow dwellers, of course," Brett added.

Lee spoke up. "I still don't understand why the Gleau did not reveal the danger of that guy until it was too late."

"Individuals like him," Jase attempted to explain, "are capable of telling a shallow truth that, to them, has no bearing or association with any intention that may follow. In his line of work, morality must be ignored. In his mind, he was telling the truth about wanting to purchase eggs because it was a logical step. That truth got him close to you, and it was a logical step in gaining your trust. As soon as he gained your trust, his intention was no longer to buy eggs because it was no longer necessary. When his intentions changed, only then was the danger revealed."

"They hide behind a simple truth because their ultimate goal is the creation of a willing victim," Ben added. "Not all venomous snakes shake a rattle."

"You are right. Where is St. Patrick when you need him?" Lee asked with half a smile.

"Figuratively speaking, he'll be here on Wednesday," Brett assured, giving Lee's shoulder a squeeze.

A Fight to Pick

IT WASN'T QUITE DARK YET, and Adam's crew knew that to
make the most of their light-and-video presentation, a setting
sun wasn't optimum, but it would have to do. They had twice
cycled through a collection of popular country and Western tunes
to draw and entertain a waiting audience. With only forty-five
minutes left before the arena events began, that left Adam only a
five-minute window for applause that should follow each utterance of his speech. He delivered his snake-oil salesman script
from a recessed point on the stage that offered barely a sixty-
degree front viewing area with large video screens flanking the
recession that gave all but the rail huggers a Gleau-less picture.
Behind him was a backdrop of dark forest that morphed through
a series of visually complex images of nature, and he was spot-
lighted heavily from the front. He assumed this was to enhance
his image, but it was more to camouflage the voluminous cloak
of repugnant luminosity that clung to him like desiccated flesh
on a rotting corpse.

As day was barely turning to night, an anonymous gentleman
walked to the center stage before a weighted blue nylon curtain
to perform a last-minute sound check. "Testing… Can everyone
out there hear me?" Muffled shouts of "yeah" were heard throughout the sparse but building crowd. "Volume okay?" he inquired.
Shouts to the affirmative led him to indicate that the presentation would begin in moments. The stage went dark. Light strains
of John Phillip Sousa's "Stars and Stripes Forever" fed through
the elaborate sound system, coordinating with video footage of
a flag waving in the wind. A dim light shown through the thin
stage curtain and the silhouette of a man with upstretched arms
seemed to magically appear.

As the curtain withdrew, white light carefully aimed center stage revealed the stunning figure of a man in evening cowboy attire. From the elegantly stitched full-quill ostrich Nebraska Husker cowboy boots, to the jeans with properly worn knees, to the pleat-front diamond snap white dress Western shirt and bolo tie, the ornate silver belt buckle, and the 4X Corral Buffalo fur-felt sand-colored Stetson, Adam was the picture of a pseudo cowboy. Actor that he was, he dropped his East Coast perfect diction and addressed his crowd.

"How y'all doin' this fine evenin'?" A less-than-powerful response prompted his next guilt-provoking line. "Come on now, folks! God has given us this perfect weather for a meet 'n' greet, and I am grateful for this here opportunity." A bit more enthusiastic but still tepid, he accepted the invitation that wasn't offered. He also thought perhaps that his use of colloquial speech was a bit heavy handed, so he decided to turn it down a notch. "This great nation of ours has been handed some heavy challenges of late, and I for one think we're up to these challenges. We're no strangers to hard work. And whatever it takes, I'm willin' to lead every citizen forward and meet these challenges. As it was in the days of Buffalo Bill Cody, we need to depend on each other, pull together, and put our collective minds and hearts together. We can beat anything standing in the way of making this, once again, the most looked-up-to nation on earth!" A smattering of applause rose just loud and long enough to drown out the crickets for ten seconds. "Now I know," he said, including a pause for dramatic effect, "I do truly know that the past few years have been hard on us all, and this is going to be a monumental task, but if we work together, there is no reason things can't turn around."

The crowd was still unimpressed, and Adam wondered exactly what it would take to elevate the enthusiasm of these hayseeds. From the back of the growing gathering there was some rumbling. The crowd was moving aside, and a figure was making its way forward aided by the parting crowd. Thinking it might be just the spark he needed to ignite the excitement in this box of damp kindling, he engaged the assemblage before him. "Let him through! Let this gentleman join the ranks of those willing to help the cause of our great nation!" The bright lights cast in his direction made it difficult for him to see, but Adam caught sight of a bright-red cowboy hat approaching the stage. Again, he encouraged this distraction to make it his own. "Come right on up here, son!"

With that phrase uttered, the figure stopped twenty yards shy of the stage and seemed to rise slightly above the people around him. A bull horn was raised, and Punch Line let Adam know he had just entered a stink contest with a skunk. "Sir, you and I may be many things, but related ain't one of 'em!"

Before the laughter subsided, Adam directed his lighting crew to spotlight this interloper so that when he took aim and shot him down, all would see and all would know who the most powerful, intelligent and persuasive speaker at this gathering was. As well, his security team was dispatched to intercept Punch Line at the conclusion of this event and detain him for questioning as a security precaution.

"Ah! Ladies and gentlemen, it appears that the comic relief is here. You are that YouTube fellow I presume, Punch Bag, isn't it?"

Punch Line let out a whoop of exaggerated laughter that came to an instant halt. He looked at the not-so-bewildered faces around him and smiled. The crowd smiled back, and Punch Line directed his attention to the lone figure on the stage. "Oh, come on, sir. Is that really the best you've got? Why is it that guys like you always resort to a potty mouth when confronted with something you don't want to deal with on a substantive level?"

Adam resisted the temptation to become defensive and decided that he would show the crowd who the bigger man was by taking the high road. "In order to deal with something on a substantive level, it must first be of substance. I refuse to waste the time of these good people debating matters of importance with someone who mocks the very people he claims to support by showing up in a Halloween costume!"

"Oh, I see," Punch Line replied. "It's my attire you take as offensive. I would have come dressed as the Rhinestone Cowboy, but as we can all see, that one was already taken!"

The crowd roared. The backdrop and bright spotlights could not hide the crimson corona of anger that was beginning to form around Adam from head to toe. Punch Line knew he was on the right track.

"Now that we've gotten the formalities out of the way, I have just a couple bones to pick with you, sir," said the clown in the red cowboy hat.

Seething inside and believing his manner and words could disguise that fact, Adam attempted to portray a calm and graceful demeanor, deferring to Punch Line's request. "By all means, sir, I will accommodate any question worthy of an answer," he responded with a slap of indignation.

"Thank you," Punch Line continued and bowed in acceptance of the opportunity that Adam would regret allowing him. "You have made a mistake, sir. You came here tonight dressed up thinking that all these rubes would adopt you as one of their own simply because your wardrobe coordinators spent too much on your Ken doll Western getup. Then you dipped in to your collection of grammatically challenged and patronizing vernaculars and thought that you could connect on a deeper level if you used single-syllable words, poor colloquial grammar, and spoke slowly. You invoked the names of God and Buffalo Bill Cody not to honor them, but to ingratiate yourself. You speak of burdens placed on our people like they magically appeared when not a soul here is unaware of the fact that nearly every detriment to our current society was cooked up in some back room by the powers that be to further their own goals and pad their wallets at the expense of every family here. But you are right about one thing. We are no strangers to hard work, but at every step and turn, our leaders turned masters have seen fit to increase our burden under the guise of protection that has become the same racket employed by the criminal mobsters of the past: pay up, or we will destroy you. You, and those like you, have made a grave error, sir. You underestimate the power of truth, the power of the individual, and the power of freedom. You talk of the collective mind like it is some utopia we should aspire to rather than the nightmare it is as presented by the fictional Borg. In this case, resistance is not futile. It is the response you will encounter when free men are told that this nation could become better by giving up the freedom that makes this nation still the greatest on earth. May I suggest," Punch Line said, directing his words to Adam, "that you rethink your educated notion that people, in general, are stupid and will march up your gangway to slaughter in the interest of compliance over their inalienable right to freedom!"

The crowd, in rapt silence until Punch Line finished his response, erupted with deafening applause. It was almost more than Adam could stand, and the jealousy he could not avoid presented itself as knives of the most emerald green slicing through the blood red of his resentment. Telling his biggest lie thus far, Adam refused to be seen as shrinking from this exchange. "I do not doubt the sincerity you've expressed, but I do think your shortsighted and shallow assessment of my intent is categorically false."

Punch Line was silent. The spectacle growing before the crowd viewing Adam directly was not expected. Blood-colored serpentine tendrils flowed from his entire being. His Stetson sported a spectacular set of what could be best described as flaming ibex horns, wavering and entwining, giving him alternately the appearance of a ram and a unicorn. Oblivious to the display he was presenting, Adam addressed Punch Line once more. "It would be my distinct pleasure at some point in the future to discuss in detail the workable solutions to problems at hand, that is, if you can be more forthcoming with actual knowledge and facts than you are about your true identity. How can we trust the truth of your words when you are not willing to reveal the truth of yourself?" Adam's security detail was poised to intercept Punch Line.

A reply to the challenge was immediate. "Based on the fact that the truth depends on no man, I wholeheartedly accept your offer, sir." With that said, Punch Line thanked his host and the crowd for their indulgence and stepped down from his crate. As he did, a group of ten individuals in Punch Line garb and makeup carrying flags entered the crowd. They made their way to where Punch Line stood, surrounded him, and surreptitiously handed him a flag. As a group, they paraded their way through the crowd and headed for the rodeo shack.

Once inside, all the Punch Lines disappeared. It was suspected that video surveillance of all who entered and left the shack was a given, so it was preplanned that a bearded gentleman entering the building left clean shaven, and the real Punch Line left the building wearing his whiskers and clothing. It was a more elaborate misdirection than the security professionals were prepared to encounter, and even a close scrutiny of the video tape failed to pinpoint the real Punch Line.

Folding his tent earlier than expected, Adam let his video presentation "America Reborn" play for what was left of the audience and went to his Marathon custom coach to fume. Feeling he had been ambushed, he would seek Sturmisch's council in what to do about this creepy, vile clown. Before his video presentation was complete, he instructed his driver to head for the next scheduled tour stop ahead of his stage truck and crew. The security van followed, but considering the total incompetence they had demonstrated, he wondered if they were worth the considerable expense and, now, aggravation.

In near-record time, the video of the NEBRASKALAND encounter between Punch Line and Adam was uploaded. The guarantors of all news and knowledge fit to view verbally stoned the messenger in a concerted effort to discredit the message and, in typical fashion, warned viewers to "pay no attention to the man behind the curtain." Of course, that warning drew viewers like moths to a flame. Making their usual baseless assertions, the opinion heads declared a mass conspiracy backed by deep pockets because, once again, Punch Line managed to escape with his anonymity intact aided by what had to be a huge well-oiled machine. Though no crime had been committed, no law broken, no regulation thwarted, it was deemed a necessity that a government investigation be directed against this clown to prevent any undermining of national tranquility. Before the uploaded video could be scrubbed from the public domain, it had been copied thousands of times, which set the witch hunt into full swing.

On Tuesday, the twenty-sixth of June, the noon news segment at KMIN was postscripted by an announcement that many had been waiting to hear. The "source" interview would be aired before a live audience at five o'clock Central time the following day. The taping would begin promptly at four with a follow-up discussion and audience interviews. Those with intentions marked by honest interest gathered quickly to get one of the limited tickets to the event for the nominal cost of five dollars. Those whose intentions were other and were first in line to grab the opportunity were sorely disappointed when the ticket sales were limited to one per customer to prevent scalping. Declarations of unfairness fell on deaf ears, and attempts to purchase a place in line to subvert the rule were not for sale at any price. A single attempt to intimidate a ticket purchaser with threats of bodily harm was quickly squelched when others in line came to his aid and, by sheer numbers, convinced the extortionist to cease and desist. The tickets, each bearing a specific barcode, were gone in less than an hour, and two of those tickets had been secured by "sanitation" employees of White Swann Mushroom Company.

Blake Ryan had been assured by Jase that he would supply his own security and would arrive at the studio fifteen minutes prior to airtime. Sturmisch's employees had camped out in the ticket line making small talk with three other enthusiasts eager to get front-row seats in this first-come-first-seated venue. Not yet having the details they sought, the five spent much time in speculation and appraisal of the Gleau that surrounded each and what this all may ultimately mean. Sturmisch's pair, a man and a woman, stuck more to asking questions than giving answers, so the true nature of their participation was tucked safely in the background, never displayed. The "secret squirrel" mentality overwhelmed their true personalities, which had been all but eradicated by the discipline of their job. When on the clock, they set aside their roles as human beings and became machinelike manipulators of trust in pursuit of information. For them, concealment took no effort; it was just part of the job.

Having so many irons in so many fires created such delight in Sturmisch's existence early that Tuesday evening that he almost smiled twice in one day. Word that his henchmen had secured tickets to the interview guaranteed the knowledge he sought concerning the source of the Gleau. Those dispatched in the endeavor connected to the newspaper editor were reassigned to shadow the clown. He wondered briefly about the AWOL investigator who failed to check in, but it mattered little now. He would be fired when heard from.

Like a smart-aleck child repeatedly offering and withdrawing a gift in an irritating tease, Sturmisch used a mere portion of his invested wealth to make markets around the world yo-yo, steadily spiraling downward and then recovering in what his paid analysts called predictable adjustments and what Sturmisch called warming the frog. Grand fortunes to most, his losses were a small price to pay for the entertainment he received listening to the fear and torment of those who trusted so-called safe investments as they watched their life's work disappear on paper. He often wondered what part of *risk* they failed to comprehend. When the world no longer believed in the promise of a printable piece of paper currency, they would still believe in land, food, fuel, and the protection of the former. And when the private producers were sufficiently crippled and the limited food stores dwindled, Sturmisch would own the golden goose. It was, indeed, something to smile about. His investments were tangible. He gobbled up farmland and other significant pieces of real estate that he tucked away in nontaxable frauds that they barely, but by legal description, satisfied. Too many trusting but misled souls missed the fact that the letter of the law was written by the letterers of the law, which should engender the notion that most of them were suspect. Making things purposely complicated and include a single exacting exclusion, Sturmisch could do anything he wanted when it was put in writing. His lawyers were paid well to write the regulations that bypassed the representatives of the people in his favor and disguised that fact.

The news—local, national, and international—had become a strange monotony of horror and the absurd. Wars, skirmishes, and armed rebellions had become headline staples with the death tolls being reported like sport scores. The poor were still being pointed out as a cause for concern, but their ranks had swelled to majority levels, making it more and more difficult to use their plight as a call to action when it was being created and fostered at the highest levels. National leaders were being assassinated when they couldn't be overthrown, and it seemed that nearly every civilian population had to contend with violence in some semi-organized form.

Sturmisch saw to it that any news unfavorable to his indirect actions was upstaged by a contrived event that took the focus of the public, and especially the media, to a focal point in the opposite direction. No one dared point out the glaring inconsistencies and coincidences. Anyone who correctly reported the facts or falsehoods suffered the consequences of ridicule, job loss, public humiliation, being ostracized, or worst of all, had an accident. Where designated warring factions weren't an official occurrence, the criminal element was expressing itself with drive by shootings, kidnappings, suicide bombings, and all manner of senseless murder and mayhem in an increasing frequency while thumbing their noses at both the law and common decency. Every natural disaster was measured and reported for maximum hand wringing and justification for the stripping of another ounce of flesh to aid the victims by paying those in control. True charity had to be eradicated. The only way to help victims was to victimize anyone who was not. In much the same way, the poor were being taken care of by making everyone poorer. Offsetting those dreadful happenings was the bombardment of frivolity that had the balance of humanity seeking perky boobs, chemically enhanced perfect bodies, medical procedures to remove the effects of aging, and a pill for every bad mood or bodily malfunction. To an outside observer, it would seem that by elimination or alteration, humans were trying to perfect themselves, but it wasn't working. The Gleau was no longer considered news worthy as it did nothing obvious to cure or prevent the ills of the body or society, nor was it something to fear. It had no power to sway action or opinion. It simply *was*. Save those few whose intuition it enhanced, it held the significance of flatulence; it was a fleeting reality that was noticed and tolerated with minimal concern. But that was all about to change.

The Interview

AT EXACTLY QUARTER TILL FOUR on the afternoon of Wednesday, June 27, a studio assistant answered the knock at the rear door of the temporary KMIN broadcast studio. Ben and Jase were promptly escorted to makeup. Ben laughed as Jase let himself be subjected to what was a necessary evil. Though he considered it a nonessential, Jase let the peacock-Gleauing young woman perform the duty to which she'd been assigned without complaint. When she was satisfied that her job was complete, Jase thanked her. At almost the same moment, Blake Ryan stuck his head in the door and told Jase he had five minutes before the taping would begin.

"Is there anything you'll need on stage?" Blake asked. "We have the mic ready, copies of the questions you answered are in each seat, the subtitle tech is prepared to insert copy for the secondary audience to identify what the video can't record, and the place is full. I'll introduce you after the countdown from the break."

"Thanks. If there's a chair available, I don't think I'll need anything else."

"Gotcha," Blake replied and disappeared into the hallway.

Jase's attire was uninspired. A white buttoned-down shirt and jeans went just fine with his Redwing work boots, or so he thought. Lee did insist upon ironing the shirt and nearly had to force him to get a haircut two days earlier. Escorted by Ben, the two ventured toward a pair of double doors that were opened quietly and magically in response to their knock by a young gentleman wearing an official-looking headset and carrying a clipboard. He ushered them silently to a spot behind a short wall and motioned with his free hand for them to wait there. A second young man appeared and attached a transmitter to Jase's waistband and clipped a lavalier mic to his shirt. Ben stood with one hand over the other, watching the activity before him and listening to all that wasn't within his view. Hearing Blake giving audience instructions, the headset guy reappeared and held up his free hand getting ready to give a silent countdown to Jase's launch in to the spotlight. Three, two, one; the assistant's fingers dropped, and Jase was ushered around the corner as Blake introduced him by name. A short but enthusiastic applause began to fade as Blake welcomed him with a handshake and wished him luck.

Jase looked out at the well-lit crowd, a rainbow of humanity in both body and Gleau. Immediately, he picked out the minority of shadow dwellers he expected would attend. All eyes were on him as quiet replaced the polite welcome of clapping hands. Before he sat, he raised one hand in a gesture of greeting and spoke a single word of hello.

"Hi." Feeling all eyes glued to him, he continued. "My name is Jase Garrett. I've come here today to answer any questions for which I have the answers about the Gleau. At each of your seats there should be a copy of twenty questions gleaned from submissions to the *Independence Review* and my answers to those questions. For the next half hour, I will try to answer any subsequent questions. If anyone has not yet had an opportunity to read through them, I'd be happy to give you a few moments to look them over, or I can accept questions now." Jase could tell immediately when someone got to question twenty. Without fail, they cast their eyes around the room and zeroed in on the shadow dwellers.

A woman in the third row, surrounded by a salmon hue tipped with green barbs, raised her hand and in seconds had a microphone at her disposal. "If you are just a man, as you've stated in the first question, what qualified you more than anyone else to deliver this?"

"Good question. I don't suppose there is anything that makes me, personally, any more special than anyone else. It just happened that the wish that made this possible belonged to my sister."

"And who is your sister?" the woman followed up immediately, tingeing her green barbs with magenta flares.

"Who she is really has no bearing on the phenomena itself, and I'm not at liberty to violate her privacy."

"So you won't tell us who she is?"

"For the sake of argument, she could be you." All eyes in the audience focused instantly on the questioner.

"I'm *not* your sister," the woman insisted. The pressure in the room changed for a moment, and the woman felt it.

"No, you aren't, but if you were, having you suffer all the scrutiny and badgering in the world would not change the reality or the meaning of what we all have been experiencing. The message is important. Destroying the messenger won't change that."

Dissatisfied with Jase's answer but reluctant to admit to anyone that attacking the messenger was her intention, she sat down. Two more enthusiastic hands had been raised. A gentleman appearing to be in his seventies with a Gleau of royal blue to the purest white stood unsteadily as the microphone was presented to him. His question was preceded by a brief statement.

"I want to thank you, Mr. Garrett, for having the courage to come forward and help us understand this mystery." Save a few, including the shadow dwellers, his remark generated applause of concurrence.

"You're welcome," Jase replied automatically.

"I say courage because the answer to my question may just put a bull's-eye on your chest," the old man apologized.

Jase smiled and made light of the remark. "I'm bulletproof. Shoot."

The old fellow got a charge out of Jase's confident humor and laughed. "What I need to know is exactly what the message is."

Jase took a deep breath. "That is the big question, isn't it? The short version is that the truth is important because without it, making real choices is impossible, and it's time to make a choice. This ability to perceive allows us to discern the truth of an individual without the distortion of media filters, propaganda, or hearsay. Humanity has some important decisions to make, and they need to be based on truth with an unfettered will, or there is no real freedom of choice."

The old man nodded. "Sounds about right to me, but what sort of decisions are we going to have to make?"

"Unfortunately, they are the same decisions humanity has had the opportunity to make many, many times before. Each time, less-than-optimum choices were made, and the setbacks suffered were catastrophic. That's not to say that all was lost. Mistakes are to be learned from. This human endeavor on this little planet is for the progression of the soul in this physical environment." The old man furrowed his brow in contemplation, and rumblings were heard throughout the room. Jase continued, "The choice is the same as it has always been: are human beings going to become intelligent spiritual beings that exist harmoniously in physical bodies, or are we going to remain smart animals that ignore the existence of the spirit and give in to vicious and vindictive behaviors that lead to our destruction once again? At this point in time, in this span of existence, we've come to a point where every advantage to achieve that greater goal is present, but the weakness of smart animals threatens to thwart that progress."

The old man shook his head in understanding, and another questioner was given the floor. "What do you mean by smart animals?"

"Excellent question. I'm not talking about trained seals. Smart animals are the people content with the notion that we are just animals, nothing more, giving some the right to act without conscience. We are in animal bodies, subject to the same survival instincts and frailties of other life forms, but we embody more. This cannot be proved or disproved by the science of this existence. For the smart animals, that inability is enough to discount the existence of 'more.' The Gleau is an indication of what they discount, and in scientific terms, it doesn't exist either, yet every person in this room can perceive it. Smart animals are those who refuse to see that we are more than what physical science can bear out. It doesn't make them bad, just stubbornly shortsighted because they are not willing to believe what hasn't been proven to them by means of this existence." Jase knew this was just scratching the surface of what he wished to impart, but he stopped there and acknowledged a man in the back row.

"You said a moment ago, 'Lead to our destruction again.' Do you mean another war?"

"That's possible. We certainly have the ability to destroy ourselves ten times over, but I'm no Edgar Cayce and have no way of knowing for sure. I just know that we have made this choice many times before."

"You mean in the course of human history," the man followed up.

"I mean in the history of existence. Just because scientists have been able to calculate the expansion of this universe and count backward to determine its approximate age doesn't mean that existence began at that point. I don't know how many times this universe has been conceived, but I know this was not the first."

A young woman in a tight pink mohair sweater that matched her purse, rhinestone-studded espadrilles, and Gleau stood ready to ask the next question. "I think animals are very smart. My bichon frise, Skylar, understands and listens better than my kids. Can't regular animals be smart?" By contrast, this question drew giggles and groans.

Jase raised his hand to diminish the reaction. "There are no invalid questions." He smiled at the well-meaning woman and answered her question seriously. "I used the term *animal* in a biological sense and wasn't referring to our furry or feathered companions. All animal species have the problem-solving capabilities to some degree to manipulate the environment for survival and propagation, but humans have been given the capacity to always improve, change, and increase our abilities and understanding. Because of our intelligence, we understand abstract concepts, we recognize our own mortality, we are aware of our emotions, and we distinguish between right and wrong based on moral principles. Biologically, we experience thirst, hunger, fear, and the instinct for procreation, just like any other animal, but we are more. Being clever, conniving, sly, or shrewd while ignoring the basics of right and wrong for advantage or purposeless gain is often, but not always, the folly of the smart animal until he is exposed. It would be pitiful if it wasn't more shameful." Jase thought of Semi when he offered his next insight. "I know people act like animals sometimes, even when they have not earned the privilege, but animals are blessed to exist without moral culpability for their instinct to survive. They are motivated by necessity, not greed or avarice. They defend themselves without directed hate, jealousy, or vengeance, but out of wariness of danger for the sake of self-preservation and a keen ability to detect ill intent. They have no need to be greater than exactly what they are, unburdened of being proud or humble because of their existence. Humanity doesn't have that luxury. With the privilege of knowledge beyond necessity goes a spiritual responsibility for the way we live our lives. Our existence is a gift, and so are the animals we share this existence with. By choice we ask our pets to share their lives with us, but it is truly the animal that accepts us as a member of their pack, herd, or flock. So you are right. Animals display ability for self-sufficiency and a nonjudgmental acceptance and loyalty to humans they deem valued members of their extended families."

Pleased by the vindication Jase offered, the woman smiled and produced a Gleau of satisfaction and settled back in her seat. A middle-aged woman two rows back was next. With her copy of the twenty questions in hand, she lowered her glasses and began. "In question seventeen, you say that this is happening now because it is necessary, but what, specifically, makes it necessary now?"

"That information, I don't have. I do know it's a choice that will have to be made. The Gleau is present to help us make that choice. That said, there could be natural disasters that coincide with the making of this choice, but this isn't predicting some cataclysmic event like an asteroid strike or a shift in tectonic plates. This has more to do with a direction we choose, and I don't have a specific time table either."

The woman looked up at Jase when he finished speaking and added, "I don't know what sort of choice could be all that important. And I don't buy that the sky is falling."

"It isn't. But think about this. Are you willing to believe every lie you are told? The truth of every individual is now on display, and it's up to you to choose what to believe."

"Now that just sounds a bit farfetched to me," she stated with satisfaction as she took her seat.

"Smart animals would agree with you, and they count on that very fact," Jase replied. Music began to play as a break was being introduced. Blake Ryan and the makeup gal appeared from the wings offering encouragement and shine removal respectively. Before making his exit, Blake asked if Jase needed anything, to which he got a negative response with a head shake. They both disappeared as the music was cued up and the count was issued for taping to resume. The young man with the clipboard did his finger thing and pointed to Jase.

Having received his cue, Jase continued, "Next question."

No fewer than six hands went up, and the two audience attendants coordinated their moves. One of Sturmisch's employees, a shadow dweller, handed Jase the next question.

"Why should we believe you? For all we know, you're a fraud."

"I'm telling the truth, and if I wasn't, every person in this room would know it."

"Maybe. But how do we know it works the way you say it does?" the shadow dweller challenged.

"Try me. Ask me something I could lie about."

"Are you a man or a woman?" When the laughter subsided, Jase answered.

"That's a good one, and I'm going to lie about it." The white flames surrounding Jase were steady and uniform until he spoke the untrue words. In a falsetto voice, he declared, "Underneath this gruff exterior, I am the female of our species." Immediately, sharp rockets of red appeared above his head. Positive murmurs and pointing issued from those seated before him. As the red faded to orange and then yellow, Jase asked, "What did you see?"

A twenty-something guy in a plaid shirt spoke up. "I saw that unless it's a kilt, you shouldn't wear a skirt." Those within earshot were amused, but the shadow dweller wasn't convinced.

"That was good, but how do we know you didn't just make it happen, like some magician's trick?" the shadow dweller persisted.

"Ask anyone else the same question and have them reply falsely," Jase challenged. A few people began blurting out declarations of belonging to the opposite sex, and what had appeared around Jase repeated around those individuals.

"Maybe that one was too easy," the shadowy questioner declared. He regrouped and asked another question. "Who sent you here to lie to all of us?"

"A friend sent me to reveal the truth," Jase replied instantly, maintaining his truthful expression of light and then demanded an answer from the shadow dweller. "What truths are you hiding with lies?"

Unaware of the cesspool of swirling darkness that was becoming more pronounced around him, a ruddy jagged-edged corona issued from his entire body before he spat out his response. "I have nothing to hide because I'm not the one here being interviewed." A smug expression wasn't concealing what lurked below the surface of this man with less-than-honorable intentions. Gasps were heard and shoulders were tapped as all eyes were directed at the proud menace in their midst. The woman seated to the left of the questioner instructed him to sit down while the little gray-haired lady to his right stared wide-eyed and tried to create a distance between her and the man now being encouraged to sit.

"I fully understand why people don't instantly accept the truth about the Gleau, but when they discover that the Gleau displays the truth and outs the liars, they won't need any proof from me or anyone else. Next question."

A microphone attendant went to a slightly balding gentleman wearing horn-rimmed glasses. "I'm a scientist, Mr. Garrett, and I'm quite interested in the nature of this phenomenon. Clearly it can be detected, but why does it defy scientific principles and means of study? Is this something new?"

"To answer your last question first, no, this is not new, nor is the ability to perceive it. It has merely been switched on, as I stated in the questionnaire."

The man begged Jase's pardon and interrupted. "How was it switched on?"

"It is beyond my knowledge exactly how it is switched on, but the mechanism for transfer is human touch."

"I think we're all aware of that, but why if I can see this or my brain perceives this as a visual phenomenon, what kind of light is it that we're seeing that behaves outside the laws of physics?"

"Because you are a scientist, I'm sure you are aware of the tests that revealed no reaction from the rods and cones in the retina of the human eye when studies were conducted in darkroom experiments." The gentleman nodded his head yes. "As well, they are now trying to discover which portions of the human brain are stimulated while observing the Gleau using subjects, some of whom have been blind since birth, with similar results."

"I've heard that, but I have yet to read any conclusions," the man added.

"And I doubt you will, for the same reason that I doubt during the entirety of your career you have ever accurately measured or scientifically reproduced results in experiments focused on love, faith, happiness, or sorrow. You can qualify the reality of the expression but can't quantify by physical measure the cause."

A bright glow of realization appeared above the spectacled questioner's head. "Ah. I see. No quantifiable empirical data puts this in the soft science category."

"You may put it in any category you wish. It simply is what it is." Music indicated another break. Blake Ryan approached with a look of satisfaction. "You're doing great. Shame our network audiences won't be able to see what's happening. There's no way our subtitle tech could adequately describe what was around that dark dude."

"What it provokes in response defies words sometimes, but I'm sure your tech will do a great job," Jase replied, expressing his confidence.

Before the break finished, raised voices could be heard from the audience right. A stage tech appeared and stated that someone had gone "Jerry Springer." A rather large man with an ominous Gleau was standing from his seat glaring down at man and woman beside him. Over the murmurs in the otherwise well-mannered crowd, the man could be heard demanding, "What are you lookin' at?"

The seated couple didn't reply, which prompted the man to repeat his question in an even louder voice. "I asked you what you were lookin' at!" he fairly yelled, demanding a response to justify his overreaction.

Jase asked that his microphone be turned on. "Sir, do you have a question?" Jase asked the darkening figure.

The man's escalating vexation was arrested temporarily. Waves of bluish-black pulsed more slowly and became intermittent with bands of red and yellow. Jase knew this wasn't a scarlet king snake; it was a venomous coral snake that would strike out for no apparent reason.

"They was starin' at me, and I asked em what they were lookin' at," he answered.

"Is there an answer to that question that would appease you?"

"What's that mean?"

"It means is there an answer to that question that would satisfy you?"

The man with his boorish manner and thin skin thought for a moment. Pulling in his fangs and deciding the odds weren't in his favor at this time, he decided not to admit that he knew full well what drew their stare. "I don't like people starin' at me, is all." He sat but maintained his threatening Gleau.

Having defused the situation for the moment, Jase was signaled that taping had begun. Again he addressed the now-seated antagonist. "No one enjoys being stared at for no reason, sir. I agree with you on that count. But if you know in your heart that those staring have *no* reason, it is your choice to ignore the rude intrusion and let the problem remain with them. Take no offense when you can leave it. Your choice is your power. Observe and learn from what the Gleau tells you, and imagined threats will disappear." Being generous to this oaf with a lifelong chip on his shoulder was enough to dim the anger toward his neighbors and put his focus in Jase's direction, but it did little to reduce the ball of indiscriminate rage he contained or the angst of the couple seated next to him.

Standing and ready to ask the next question was a gentleman who's Gleau depicted the solid soul of a dynamic and well-intentioned being. In stark contrast to the last unfortunate fellow, the two were night and day in how they appeared. With a smile on his face, he began. "Now that we know what this could tell us, how do we put it to effective use?"

Jase had been waiting for this question. "As you would any of your other senses, learn from it. Pay attention to what it reveals, and it will shed a whole new light on this world—no pun intended. This is not going to make all the bad go away any more than our sensitivity to heat has prevented all fires or the fact that we get burned. This will reveal the true meaning of any razzle-dazzle, flowery, or deceptive speech that might attempt to camouflage a lie. It will indicate when an emotional bid is insincere or when it is genuine. It will expose the flaw of the misrepresented statistic. It will help you to avoid danger and recognize the virtuous."

"That makes sense, except for one thing," the current questioner continued. "If this is supposed to help us see the truth of people, like those running for public office, and this can't be filmed, how will it help? Most of us only ever see important people on television. Do we have to see everyone in person? Not every single person will have the opportunity to make a firsthand judgment."

"Excellent point. Television and radio don't lie. People do. Of course, television, radio, and all other forms of communication carry the lies of people with the same ease as the truth. When a lie is told through either medium and then retold face-to-face, it is still a lie and will display itself as such. A lie will still be a lie, regardless of the sincerity or intent of the teller. Those denying the reality of what they observed will be outed as liars also. You cannot blame the means by which you received message. It is the initiator of the lie who bears all responsibility. For instance, I'm going to give you a million dollars. How do I appear?" Spears of reddish light flashed around Jase's head and shoulders.

"I'd say I'm not getting my million dollars," the gentleman acknowledged.

"Now, if you would help me illustrate my point, repeat my lie to the man next to you."

"Okay." The man turned to his right to address the young fellow seated next to him. "Jase is going to give me a million dollars," he repeated with conviction. A triangle of poppy red that started at his ears came to a point a foot above his head.

"To further my point, I'll demonstrate how carrying tales appears." Jase chose a young woman seated in the front row. "If you would please, ma'am, indicate with a lie how this gentleman just appeared."

Eager to participate, the woman stood and responded as Jase requested. "That guy told the truth." Again, the lie was obvious. There was a collective "ah" from the audience.

"Granted, these are simple questions in a contrived situation, but the results will be the same no matter how complex the language or the situation. You can trust what you see."

The young gentleman who posed the initial question asked another. "What if someone avoids a direct answer by saying they don't know?"

"If they don't know the answer, they will indicate the truth. If they do know the answer and they are attempting to hide facts, the Gleau will reveal that detail, but it won't force them to talk. Being evasive is an art, and there are some good artists out there, so learn how to ask the right questions."

Without the aid of a microphone, the woman who began the question-and-answer session called out, "Like you were a good artist, not telling us your sister's name."

"I responded that I'm not at liberty to reveal that information, and that is true. It is also true that throwing her to the wolves will have no bearing on the Gleau. I stated complete fact. What I find interesting about your insistence is why you need that bit of information. Would your intention be to question her in order to attack me because you refuse to believe what you see?"

"Of course not!" the woman stated emphatically. A fan of spiked flames shot out from about her short cropped hairdo, giving the impression that her hair had suddenly caught fire.

As the audience reacted to the woman's condition, Jase commented, "I rest my case."

Music began again, signaling the beginning of the last break before the conclusion of the interview. Many in the audience, having taken Jase's explanation on faith, were eager to put their new skill to work. The implications of what could be learned and discovered were making some giddy with excitement. Others looked worried. Among the worried were Sturmisch's sanitation employees. Having asked Jase to prove his validity, the shadowy male of the pair was determined to discredit and expose what was really going on. His boss demanded information that would put whatever power created this Gleau firmly in his pocket, and this loyal henchman was going to do whatever was necessary to obtain that information.

The break ended. Jase prepared to offer his conclusion, and if time permitted, he would accept a last-minute question or two.

"I know many of you here today have had what you suspected already confirmed. But you may still be asking what the ultimate goal is in this exercise. As it states in the questionnaire, this manifestation will cease to exist exactly one year after the date of its inception. Will you learn enough in this short period of time to recognize that controlling power over mankind belongs to no man? You may ask how to recognize such a controlling force. Ask yourself three questions: what am I asked to give, what am I promised to receive, and when has any one man's power resulted in all receiving more than they have given? I can think of only a single instance."

There was a noticeable quiet when Jase finished. A hand directly in front of Jase was hesitantly raised. Stealthily, a mic was presented, and a young woman stood.

"Mr. Garrett, my question is totally off the topic of the Gleau, but I was just wondering if you might be able to offer some insight—"

Before the woman could finish, several shouts of alarm were issued as the shadow dweller from White Swann pushed his way brutishly past several in his row and knocked one of the microphone handlers to the ground. Bearing no obvious weapon, he was cloaked in a Gleau that oozed a greenish-black abhorrence. Charging toward Jase, he warned an audience member who dared to stand in his way that he should "move it or lose it." When the man made an attempt to block the assailant, the wearer of escalating corruption grabbed him by the shirt collar and threw him to the floor. Barely ten feet separated him from Jase, who had stood from his chair, when Ben gave up the anonymity of the wings and crossed three times that distance in less than half a dozen steps. Like two freight trains barreling toward one another, they met. In an instant, they were both gone, leaving those watching the event awestruck. Several close to the action found themselves left in a duck-and-cover cringe for a clash of titans that never occurred. In a matter of seconds, Ben appeared from the wings once again, walking calmly this time, and whispered to Jase, "I left him on the sidewalk out front."

"Thanks," Jase directed to Ben. "Is everyone okay? Is any-one hurt?" Jase asked the crowd. The two whose misfortune it had been to come into contact with the beast had recovered and brushed themselves off, signaling that everything was okay. Jase watched closely as the female companion to the ejected trouble-maker excused herself to the aisleway and glared back at him with both fear and hatred displayed by her Gleau before disappearing through the double doors at the rear of the studio theatre area.

In an effort to calm frazzled nerves and finish the interview, Jase sat back in his chair and asked, "Now, where were we?" A few anxious laughs accompanied the reduction of yellow and deep mauve that had flashed through those affected during the latest interruption, and many eyes were now on Ben, who remained standing calm but ever watchful behind Jase. From the wings, even Blake Ryan stared at Ben, wondering if what he had just witnessed was an illusion, but praying his cameras were able to capture the miraculous occurrence. Jase redirected his attention to the young woman in the front row.

"I believe you were going to ask for my insight on something."

Still a bit unnerved but wanting an answer now more than ever, she began her question again. Her eyes darted from Jase to Ben and back again. "I just wanted to ask for your thoughts on whether or not life exists beyond this earth, but after what I just saw, I think I got part of the answer."

Jase smiled and glanced over his shoulder at Ben. "Yes." Directing his attention to Ben, he added, "What would you say to that, Ben? Is there any life beyond this planet?"

In typical Ben baritone brevity, he answered, "Teeming."

"I hope that has answered your question," Jase responded, knowing it opened a whole new can of worms instead.

Another hand five doors down from the lady questioner shot up. "May we ask about the gentleman standing behind you?"

"You may," Jase answered with a huge smile, pulling the first worm from the can.

"Who is he, and how did he do that?"

"This is my friend and personal security associate, Ben. I don't know how he does that. He's talented."

Blake Ryan held up two fingers, informing Jase of his minutes left. "I know there are hundreds of questions I've left unanswered, but as each of you learns from this new perception, many of those questions will be answered. I'd like to thank you all for coming today." Ben came to Jase's side, dwarfing him even as he rose from his chair. "I'd also like to thank KMIN station manager Blake Ryan for this opportunity, and with the truth as your guide, be prepared to make an informed choice. That's about it." Jase unclipped his mic and removed the transmitter from his belt and looked up at Ben. As the music was coming back up again, the cameras caught Jase shaking hands with several audience members. He thanked the well-wishers and gave a single wave of good-bye. He turned his attention to Ben once more and mouthed the words, "Let's go." Ben placed one of giant mitts on Jase's shoulder, and they were gone.

Fallout

O N THE SIDEWALK IN FRONT of makeshift studio venue, the lady Swann employee met her frazzled companion as he tried to convey the substance of the interview and his abrupt ejection from the event to an individual on the other end of his cell phone conversation. After relaying the gist of the interview, giving a physical description of Jase and the man responsible for his unorthodox departure, he was surprised by the dedicated interest in the mammoth gentleman of Native American descent.

"I don't know how he did it, but it was so fast there wasn't even time for my head to spin," he reported. His female companion said nothing as he absorbed the phone end of the discussion. "I have no idea who he was or where he came from," he answered the unheard question. The woman, who had waited beyond the double doors, trying to decide what her next move should be after her coworker disappeared, heard Jase declare that this man was his security detail. To her partner, she mouthed the word *security*. After a questioning look, he relayed that bit of information. "According to my partner, he was security. A bodyguard, I guess." With his last statement, the male voice on the other end of the phone spoke loudly enough for his accomplice to hear. "Find out who he is!" The call ended, leaving him staring at an open phone.

Inside the theater/studio, Blake Ryan was beside himself with anticipation regarding the airing of this special event less than thirty minutes away. "Tell me we got the departure," Blake asked his lead-camera operator.

"We got it from three angles," he assured an almost-giddy boss.

318

"Inform me when editing is complete. I've got some calls to make." Only one of the major networks had agreed to carry his broadcast prior to the taping. By the time he got done explaining what he had in the can, two more had signed on. All agreed to preface the airing with a message to the viewing audience explaining both the subtitles and the fact that what they were about to see was edited for time constraints only; the content was being aired as it happened. As much as he was amazed by what he had just seen, Mr. Ryan kept at the forefront that he was a businessman in a very competitive market. He knew his advertising sponsors would be pleased with the expected high percentage of the viewing market but decided as well to toot KMIN's horn and enlighten all about the fact that it was his news division to first break the Gleau story to the Associated Press.

When his calls were complete, Blake thought about how fortunate he was to be one of only 325 human beings to see Jase Garrett in person. It was a story he imagined telling his grandchildren with no need for embellishment. It never entered his thoughts that he would not live to see his grandchildren.

Noticeably alone in her kitchen, Lee was more than grateful when she saw through the windows facing the barnyard Jase and Ben walking toward the house from the barn. The oven timer buzzed, and she was pleased that they were arriving just in time for fresh zucchini bread with black walnuts. The two men entered the kitchen, both remarking about the wonderful aroma that filled the room.

"Well, how did it go?" Lee asked, placing the loaf pan on a folded sack towel embroidered with Semi's likeness.

"In general, I'd say most took it well," Jase answered.

"That's it? I want details," Lee added.

"You'll get to see the details in about twenty minutes," Ben stated.

"No dissenters?" Lee queried.

"Just a couple, but we handled them with only minor discord," Jase allowed, and a single pink-tinged spear head made a two-second appearance.

"That's good to know." Lee smiled. "Milk or coffee?" she asked the two. Both requested milk. Lee grabbed the remote and selected the proper station. In relative silence, all three enjoyed hot zucchini bread and cold milk and waited for the airing this afternoon's adventure.

⁕

Having received a firsthand report from the sanitation employee that offered little in the way of the advantage he sought, Sturmisch was awaiting a faxed copy of the questions and answers provided at the interview. As much as he was eager to acquire the secret of spreading a phenomenon throughout the entirety of humanity, he was more intrigued by the reappearance of the giant Indian he had previously written off as a figment of gross imagination. If this individual in fact possessed the ability to transport human beings at will, he would be extended an offer he could not refuse, and that power would belong to Sturmisch. Regardless of station or standing, anyone could be and, in this case, *would* be leveraged to hand over their will and accept the honor of being well compensated as an employee of White Swann. In Sturmisch's mind, this was a foregone conclusion. No one ever denied or disappointed him without understanding the unspoken consequences.

Much like his main fungal product, Sturmisch was reclining comfortably in the environmentally controlled confines of his cave home, awaiting the answers he had been actively seeking. Fifteen minutes before the airing of the interview with Jase Garrett, he was studying the submitted questions and Jase's answers. None of the information caused him any great concern because of the answer to question nineteen. This was going to be history, and history could be controlled. Even with personal witness and photographic evidence, portions of history had already been rewritten and labeled the fantasy of fanatics. With the successful rebirth of the Flat Earth Society came proof that people will believe anything when the belief is praised and rewarded with a T-shirt declaring membership. If it wasn't for all pesky museums dedicated to the historical horror, the Holocaust would be sharing a shelf with Lewis Carroll's *Alice in Wonderland* and the tales of the brothers Grimm. Compared to denying man's landing on the moon, making the existence of the Gleau disappear would be a piece of cake. By its own nature, no proof of it—physical, photographic, or otherwise—would ever exist. Those having witnessed the interview in person were limited to just a few hundred, and the elimination of just one well-known and vocal witness would shut them all up. Thanks to its own limited lifespan, this Gleau was but a temporary bump in the road on the highway to Sturmisch's perfect world.

With the Gleau becoming a nonissue due to its set demise, Sturmisch turned his attention to the other thorn in his paw. It was less than three days prior that Adam's call of complaint about being ambushed by the clownish contender, Punch Line, was received only moments before the YouTube video of the NEBRASKALAND Days fiasco finished posting. It was clear that Adam had the skills, smarts, and desire for the role he sought, but not the stomach for it. Sturmisch had paved the way, smoothed the rough terrain, and spent countless millions making this diamond sparkle, but it was clear that in the shade of his own narcissism, Adam was becoming lackluster. And Sturmisch detected something new while reassuring his candidate that all would be well: petulance. It was enough to express concern about the opposition, but Adam was becoming a whiny spoiled child, demanding that Sturmisch make the bad clown go away, and he as much as threatened Sturmisch by reminding him that long ago, he made a certain young lady disappear. At an undetermined moment in that conversation, plan B was put into effect, and the first step was to eliminate plan A.

Taking a short break from his incognito appearances, Punch Line and his three musketeers sat in a booth enjoying an early supper and waiting like the rest of the patrons of Dave's Dive for the interview with the Gleau source. After his encounter with Adam the previous weekend, he was more determined than ever to expose the rot that oozed from his competition and the system that supported him. The NEBRASKALAND video sparked some of the vilest rhetoric from Adam's orchestrated support to date. T-shirts emblazoned with Punch Line's likeness and the caption "Don't Be a Clownshirt Nazi!" and another with him perched in a dunking booth with the bull's eye on his chest were being advertised on Adam-favorable websites. So much for the call to civility.

As the time grew near for the program to air, the plump waitress behind the counter turned up the volume on the television at the request of two regulars seated at the far end of the bar. Punch Line and his trio ordered more coffee. At precisely five o'clock Central time, the local affiliate began the broadcast with the information advisory Blake Ryan requested briefly shown, and then a news anchor appeared to announce that the program airing would be extended to one hour with the second half being dedicated to the full set of twenty questions and answers. A quick "Special Report" title gave way to Blake Ryan announcing and welcoming Jase Garrett to a small studio stage furnished with a single chair and a faded blue curtained backdrop.

"Appears to be a decent sort," Punch Line remarked.

"Yep. Not a fancy Dan," added the gentleman to his right.

As they watched the interaction with the audience and listened to his responses, Punch Line noted Jase's ease and steadfast manner. It was made clear that this interview was to inform rather than defend. It was also clear that his hunch about what this Gleau revealed was right on the mark.

⁘⸳⸰⸰⸰⸳⁘

Seated at Lee's kitchen table, all three in attendance looked up at a close-up of Jase being welcomed by Blake. As Jase sat and introduced himself onscreen, the one in Lee's kitchen remarked, "Do I really sound like that?" Having never heard his voice recorded and played back, it was quite unfamiliar.

"You sound fine," Lee assured him. "And your hair looks great," she added with a wink.

Jase took note that the subtitle crawler did an adequate job of describing what could only be seen by those in attendance. Unfazed by the televised version of what he'd experienced a little more than an hour ago, Ben refilled his glass of milk and cut another thick slice of zucchini bread, only glancing at the screen when the questioners spoke.

Lee smiled with approval when Jase spoke to the woman about smart animals, elevating both animals and humans. It wasn't until after the second break and Jase was already engaged in a conversation with a large disgruntled-looking gentleman that Lee felt any need to express concern. "Wow. He doesn't look happy." When the man's face was on camera, she read the description printed at the bottom of the screen. "A shadow dweller?" she asked Jase.

"Yes, but just a sad soul full of undirected hostility. He's one of those who never learned how to properly process it, so he just carries it around with him, and it spills over onto the unsuspecting."

The two men shared glances, wondering what she would say when Jase encountered the more demonstrative shadow dweller.

Lee's phone rang, and it was Brett. She greeted him, asked him to relay the same to Barbara, and handed the phone to Jase. After listening to Brett's initial comments Jase replied, "Yeah, I'm glad it's done too." To an unheard remark, he responded, "Not too bad. Ben took care of it, and as you'll see, his talents are now well-known." Lee gave Ben a puzzled look to which he smiled with a mouth full of bread. The short call ended with Jase promising to see them the following day.

Sturmisch watched the interview with great interest, assessing the man and his words. What he saw failed to impress him. This source was nothing more than a bumpkin peddling another great illusion dependent on faith. What he gathered from this so-called explanation was that Jase had no real answers, offered no real guidance, and had no real power. As far as he could tell, this phony made his words fit the situation, took advantage of what science couldn't prove, and presented himself as someone unlocking the mind of mankind when all he really did was stumble upon the key.

Still, the Gleau did exist, and Sturmisch had no idea what sort of power produced it. Then again, admittedly, neither did this Jase Garrett. Even if it wasn't true that the Gleau would cease to exist on the appointed date, he could make Jase Garrett cease to exist with a single phone call. As he watched the portion of the telecast where his idiot employee tried to rush the stage, his real interest was in this security guard. If, as it had been reported to him by the now-deceased goon sent to Brett Hume, it was true that this giant could appear at will and make people disappear, now there was a power he could use.

He studied the action as the camera captured his agent knocking a man to the ground. From a broader angle, the camera captured Jase Garrett rising from his chair and a huge man gliding past him to intercept the oncoming threat. He had to admit, if this wasn't trick photography or fancy editing, what he saw was amazing. When he finished watching the entire program, he replayed that segment a dozen times, slowing it down to pinpoint the exact moment the two men left the image. His less-than-expert eye could find no flaw in the action, particularly in the motion of the audience members directly behind the two. When the men vanished, the motion revealed behind them was captured seamlessly, without a glitch or stutter. Sturmisch would have one of his experts examine this footage. If it had not been for the fact that he received a call from his agent in the image to confirm the timeline of when this took place, he would have assumed that this was strictly a ruse concocted at some earlier date. This "talented" security guard, Ben, would be a very useful tool. As for Jase Garrett and his revelation about the Gleau, Sturmisch could destroy him with two words: *prove it.*

⚬⃝⃝⃝⃝⃝⚬

When the show was over, including the following half hour of discussion involving Jase Garrett's answers to the twenty submitted questions, Punch Line was very quiet. The four finished the pot of coffee on the table, tipped their waitress, and headed for the RV in the parking lot.

"Well, you were right," said the youngest of the group. "I guess this does show us what's inside."

Deep in thought, Punch Line didn't immediately jump at the chance to claim victory. As the four entered the RV and took their respective favorite seats, he finally spoke. "It was a logical assessment based on what we've been seeing, but I have sincere concerns that the rationalizing and excuse-making experts are going to put a supreme effort into negating its meaning."

"That kinda goes without saying, doesn't it?" asserted the burly member of the threesome. "It's always been the role of the devil's advocate to undermine anything based on faith. We all know they aren't exactly neutral."

"Too true," Punch Line responded. "And with the explanation that's been given, the experts have the same proof or lack of it that every other individual has, but the individual has to be taught that their instinct, their opinion, and their informed judgment carries just as much weight as any self-professed expert.

How do we impress upon each and every soul that they *are* the experts when it comes to determining what affects their destiny?"

"Now there's a challenge," agreed the youngster. "People would be scared to death to unhook from their outside pool of opinion and trust their own thoughts."

"Yeah, I see trouble in River City all right," the burly man added. "Those with their minds shut are gonna be mighty skeptical when they're told they should open their eyes and see that they've been being led by the one-eyed king."

Punch Line brightened. "You are a genius!"

"I am?" responded the burly man.

"Yes, you are!" Punch Line couldn't send his train of thought down the track fast enough. "Maybe it was the 'king' reference, but when you said that, the liar's paradox popped into my head."

"What's the liar's paradox? Can't say I'm familiar with such a thing," the newly discovered genius admitted.

"It's a logic riddle of sorts, usually cast with knights and knaves, but it's the logic I think we can use. It even has a math-based example."

"Slow down, Punchy. Let me catch up," his burly buddy requested.

"Me too," both the others replied in unison.

"It's one of those complex simple things, like a Mobius strip. How do you explain a three-dimensional object that has only one side?"

He was met with three blank stares. "Okay, I'm getting ahead of myself and beside myself at the same time here. I'll demonstrate that one to you later, but the liar's paradox is based on this: the truth told about the truth is the truth, and a lie told about a lie is also the truth." His audience was still silent. "Think back, guys, and I know I'm asking more of some than others here." Punch Line smiled. "In grade school when we were introduced to negative numbers, when you multiplied a positive number times a positive number, you got a positive answer. Simple enough. But when you multiplied a negative number times a negative number, you got a *positive* answer too."

"Oh man, don't make me do math," the young guy complained in jest.

Punch Line laughed and then asked his crew to help him construct the questions to prove his point.

See to Shining See

WHETHER HUMANITY LEARNED IN PERSON, via the telecast or by word of mouth, the newfound skill embodied in the Gleau now had a purpose. Certain occupations benefitted a great deal and found it to be a real time saver. Lawyers weren't exactly delighted about expedited depositions since they charged by the hour, but the truth allowed them to be better prepared for cases. They too were bound by truth when asked questions like "Are all these questions necessary?" and "Does this have to take so long?" Police interrogators were having their hunches based on limited evidence confirmed but were still stymied when it came to getting a recordable admission of guilt if the perp decided to clam up. Detectives found they wasted less time following dead-end leads where witness information was a key to investigations. For obvious reasons, judges were aided in the determination of decisions and spent less time and endured fewer games with both lawyers and their clients. Social workers took note of their clients' revealing Gleau but were advised not to become eligibility agents because of severe caseload reduction possibility. Medical insurance and disability fraud were instantly curtailed as well as the filing of contrived frivolous lawsuits.

The most frequently asked questions with regard to what the Gleau would indicate dealt with infidelity. For the time being, the clandestine affair was nearly impossible. For sexual predators and pedophiles as well as con men, scammers, illegal drug peddlers, prostitutes, and other assorted deviants and ne'er-do-wells, opportunity and business had taken a sudden downturn. People were becoming aware. Even some panhandlers felt the pinch as would-be contributors questioned the validity of cardboard signs declaring indigence.

As many would suspect, the group feeling the most directed pressure were politicians. From the local municipalities to the three branches at the federal level, elected and appointed officials were being bombarded by both the public and their opposing brethren with questions that truly needed answers. Town meetings and open public press conferences were seen by many as a chance to see for themselves who deserved their trust. The Gleau was putting *candid* back in *candidate*.

For any shadow dweller or possessor of "what they don't know won't hurt them" secrets, the public limelight was being made an uncomfortable place to be if telling the truth was demanded. Personalities and titles aside, the Gleau provided a lighted path to follow the money, and too often that led to corruption. Like a kitchen-light switch, the Gleau sent the cockroaches on the floors of government houses scurrying for cover. They couldn't hide forever, but a few decided they could survive by avoiding public scrutiny for the next six months, but going into hiding made them targets for distrust as well. There were a few repentant souls who tearfully came clean, enduring the shame and making public the weakness that allowed their arms to be twisted. The public forgave them. The arm twisters did not. Less than half a dozen had made their misdoings public before the first of them had their car mysteriously go over a cliff, and the second was found hanging in the foyer of his home with a typewritten suicide note. The rot of society was not going to go quietly into the night. It was going to hang on tooth and nail to preserve the carefully woven web of deceit and sleaze that it depended upon for survival until this bothersome Gleau played itself out and was purposely erased from all memory.

On the flip side of all the wrong that was being discovered was the vast majority of glorious good that had never shown so brightly before. The exceptional in every facet of society were on display and no longer beyond notice. Framed in a brilliance that often ran counter to a situation, the young mother tending to her unruly flock with patience and firmness was not unlike a marine drill instructor, teaching skills of survival because life depended on it. Even in the act of admonishment, their loving radiance was evident. It meant more to deliver a lesson that would promote life than it did to worry about how the self-proclaimed experts would grade their efforts. Their stake in these young human beings, these beloved children, meant more to them than any paycheck or Pulitzer Prize–winning study. Devoted parents were easy to spot.

The kind souls had a characteristic Gleau that was usually accompanied by a smile, a positive word of greeting, or a sincere interest in the distress of a total stranger. The truly charitable were for the first time in their lives open to view and the first to deny they deserved recognition. Good deeds, in their eyes, were to be done and not diminished by words. Though not exactly secrets, the bestowing of good fortune upon the less fortunate was a privilege. They knew that taking anything so much as credit diminished the power of generosity. Any looking for self-aggran-dizement missed the whole point, and those doing so would Gleau accordingly while feverishly spouting a list of altruistic associations. To those actually engaged in acts of consideration, it was nearly impossible to offer a helping hand if you were busily patting yourself on the back. Now, without a word ever said, those with a giving heart were seen, but their deeds remained safely hidden in their hearts.

On the less grand scale, neighborhood disputes were put to rest with the miraculous reappearance of lost borrowed tools and relocated tasteless lawn ornaments. Arguments over errantly bro-ken windows ended with apology and restitution rather than "sue me" challenges. The four-in-the-morning doggy-doo land mine miscreant was identified, and both lawn patch and words of con-fession were forthcoming. The petty lies that promoted dishar-mony were losing their power. A swift "I'm sorry" negated esca-lation of overreaction and unproductive retaliation, which had become all too common in the devolution of civility.

Like the first biting sensation a swimmer feels when entering the water, being immersed in the truth took some getting used to, but most found that once they took the leap, it was refreshing. Some dove in headfirst, enjoying the plunge and experiencing a loss of heaviness. Across the generations affected, the elderly seemed to be the least fazed by all that was revealed. In their day, the web of political correctness had yet been spun, and dealing with harsh truths was something they took in stride on a daily basis. Sure, there were personal skeletons resting in closets even then, but often they were there to protect the innocent more so than to protect and promote the guilty.

Once upon a time, and now for a small percentage of those considered old-fashioned, being known as an honest and ethical individual was a goal with untold value. Today's goal had been reduced to getting as far ahead as possible with the only guidelines being those of legality. Never mind that something was unethical or even immoral, as long as it was legal, no other considerations had to be made. And who decided what was legal or illegal and why? As civilizations shed the basics of right and wrong and replaced them with laws written by immoral men, complete with exceptions and exclusions, a new warped common sense and logic dictated that two wrongs could indeed make one right. Fortunately, the Gleau knew nothing of the law.

Now What?

EE FELT A HUGE BURDEN had been lifted as the interview was finally over. It had taken place without a hitch, and she hoped a normal though imperfect life would ensue. Semi was missed daily, and though he could never be replaced, she was hoping another of God's creatures would choose her as a friend soon. And there was still that little problem with the intruder. She was waiting for her cue from Jase to proceed with a police report. The .357 bullet discharged from the man's gun was left in the dirt under the deck, and Lee had carefully swabbed a blood specimen from Semi's mouth and saved it in the freezer. Of course there was still the little problem of the delay in reporting the incident and explaining the actions of her accomplices after the fact. Jase said she worried too much, but Lee knew even with all the facts and evidence on her side, being innocent until proved guilty held little sway these days.

It weighed heavily on her about exactly who this man was. Did he have a family who was now looking for him? Did he have children who were now without a father? All of these worries she had voiced to Jase, and he understood her instinct to be responsible, but he had some questions of his own. He asked Lee what her intentions were on that day and what were his. She was selling eggs. He was there to kill her. Every living being has the right to self-defense when threatened, and Lee did not choose for that man his occupation. The man came to her home, killed Semi, and attempted to kill Lee and did not succeed. In the grand scheme of things, justice had already been served. The law was important, and it wasn't being ignored.

To further their previous agreement, Brett was given the task of recording and presenting in book form the entire history of the Gleau, including his own involvement. It was an undertaking he was more than happy to oblige. The fact that this event would cease to exist made recording witness testimony vital. By the third week of July, treating it much like a current event as well as history, Brett presented his incomplete first draft to Jase for his appraisal and approval. With Barbara as his sidekick, they arrived in Lee's kitchen and sat down to a banquet featuring nearly everything from the garden and barnyard. Ben finished setting the table, and Jase filled glasses with ice as Lee crowded the table with a luscious bounty. When the basic appetites were sated, the five lingered over pie and coffee and discussed observations and news of the Gleau.

"I need to ask your permission for one other thing, Jase," Brett requested.

"What's that?" Jase answered while still studying the copy.

"I want to publish a photograph of you, just to give a face to the source."

"No problem. But I'm not really the source of the Gleau, just the source of the story."

"I'll make that clear. And not to be counting my chickens before they're hatched, but if there are any promotions, I'd like to you to accompany me."

Jase laughed. "I'm honored, but I think I've had enough exposure. You'll have to go solo."

Brett wasn't expecting an immediate rejection and then remembered what Jase told him about a set conclusion he had agreed to. Something told him this whole ordeal may not yet be finished.

The reaction to the interview had diminished from a high-pitched fervor to a dull roar with many using the ability afforded them. Strained budgets and the high cost of travel made the Gleau experience something that was an affordable distraction. Social gatherings, large and small, had suddenly become popular, with everything from dinner parties to block parties. People were foregoing the draw of reality TV and engaging in what television could not recreate—their own realities aided by the insight of the Gleau.

There was less apprehension about meeting new people, learning more about those already called friends, and discovering new facets about those closest. Most of what was discovered was positive, but not all, which is where the power of forgiveness was put to good use. In a few cases, the social comic was revealed to be truly shy and used a sense of humor as both protection and to gain acceptance. The braggart displayed insecurity, the bully was often afraid, and the snob was less sure of their own standing than they were of others. The quiet and reserved were now betrayed by signs of intense interest and unspoken appreciation. People in face-to-face situations became interesting and entertaining. The depth of the individual was being showcased on the stage of life. The reruns, sequels, remakes, and rehashed characters of the two-dimensional world of television were tossed aside, and it was the premier performance of the literal man on the street, girl next door, and face in the crowd that captured a new devoted following.

These were consequences, intentional or subsequent, that Lee had hoped for. Revealing the truth was fine, but the Gleau proved to disclose much more. Everyone was now seeing what she saw when she watched her granddaughters lead Beanie around the yard or tend to a new litter of barn kittens. Happiness, caring, and love were as appealing to the eye as they were to the soul. As much as the Gleau exposed the dark side of a soul, it brought to light the scope of all that made humanity amazing and extraordinary. Above all, laughter was a sight to behold. Lee described the giggles, tee-hees, and belly laughs produced by the girls as an exploding melted kaleidoscope of crayon colors. Watching the three of them paint these masterpieces with a brush of amusement reminded Lee of something that was granted exclusively to humans—a sense of humor. Surprise and physical antics often make animals react with funny behavior, but they won't be repeating the incident to their animal buddies for weeks on end and laughing again the way people do.

As this group of five relayed tales of the Gleau, they noted the uncertainty and dismal prospects still present in socioeconomic structure. Unemployment was still climbing, and people had pared down their expenditures to the bare bones. It was amazingly clear to all on the front lines of the economy that the generals on the hill had little more to offer than posturing and finger-pointing while they encouraged the enemy to help themselves to the armory just to keep the battle going, and they could maintain their position of command. It was becoming all too obvious that many of our good souls were falling victim to the friendly fire of overzealous regulation applied with an uneven hand. In the pursuit of supposed fairness, unopposed pursuit of happiness was granted only to those who supported the grantors. All others were persuaded to change their loyalties or suffer the hidden consequences. One example of misuse of power didn't seem to register, but as hundreds of examples began to surface, the rose-colored glasses were no longer a valid excuse for failing to see the forest for the trees.

Lee had always taken note of the news because of Nick's situation, but most of what was presented felt distant and far removed from her world. It didn't feel that way anymore.

"Is the Gleau going to be enough to make a real difference?" she asked her brother.

"I wish I could just say yes, but I don't have that answer," Jase answered. "I know the benefit the Gleau provides, but people can still exercise free will. It's the old adage that you can lead a horse to water, but you can't make him drink."

Ben took the last bite of his third piece of pie. "There is plenty of thirst out there, but horses are smart. They know when the spring is full of poison. Now because of the Gleau, people will be as smart as horses," Ben stated.

"True," Jase corroborated, "at least for a while. Marking every poisoned watering hole won't help after the Gleau is gone though. In these few short months, people must learn, *again*, how to determine the safe haven for their trust without the aid of the Gleau."

"And how on earth do you propose to do that?" Brett asked. "If the Gleau itself isn't enough to point out evil, what is?"

"Confrontation," Ben asserted. "You can't just point to evil and expect it to evaporate. It must be confronted. It must be unmasked."

Barbara began to laugh. "Am I the only blind one here who can actually see this!" Brett stared at his sister. Jase smiled knowingly at Ben, and Lee declared her interest in what she was missing.

"I give, what did I miss?"

"Evil has masked the good. You have to unmask the good as well!" Barbara exclaimed.

Adam put the North Platte debacle behind him, confident that Sturmisch would remove the funny man from the picture when the time was right, but that is where his confidence ended. He would never make the mistake of underestimating how powerful his behind-the-scenes benefactor was, but he resented what he saw as a failure being allowed to take place at all. Surely Sturmisch could have foreseen and prevented that whole exchange, but instead, he allowed that ignorant little fool the opportunity to upstage him. If Sturmisch couldn't see just how important and irreplaceable Adam was to the cause, he would have to be shown. It may very well be that it was Sturmisch's deck the game was being played with, but Adam had an ace up his sleeve that Sturmisch knew nothing about. Without admitting to it but certainly alluding to it, Adam used the existence of certain knowledge to impress upon Sturmisch just how important it was to see to his wishes. And what Sturmisch didn't know wouldn't hurt him, unless he did something really stupid like try to change horses midstream. Adam had seen to it that he would drown in the attempt.

Having buttoned up his situation with Sturmisch, he took his cue from a half-page AD posted by Punch Line in a dozen Midwestern papers and replied in kind. The clown wanted to know when and where to meet, so Adam chose to meet in the park near the Presidio on the afternoon prior to the real debate. He felt it was better to squash the problem early and wipe his feet clean of any clown debris before meeting the real establishment candidates head-on.

And as for the quaint "little farmer John" character that had crawled out from under a rock to enlighten all about the Gleau, Adam had already forgotten his name, and this Gleau issue would be resolved on its own. If anyone asked anything about the phenomenon or why Adam appeared as he did, he would smile and deny, charm and evade, and misdirect as he had always done and inform them that this is how forceful men Gleau. People had more faith in what they were told than what was real, and Adam could turn reality into whatever he wanted with words. He knew what his loyal following wanted to hear, and they would turn a deaf ear to anything to the contrary. They would avoid what they were told to avoid, believe what they were told to believe, and parrot derogatory insinuation on his say so. To question anything would lead to shame, and Adam and his devotees were not subject to shame.

Having picked up a newspaper in Buffalo as they zigzagged their way across Wyoming, Punch Line was pleased to discover, via Adam's response to his *Buffalo Bulletin* query, that they had two weeks to reach their appointed destination. They would spend the next ten days or so sightseeing through Yellowstone Park and, when afforded the opportunity, listen and learn from anyone they came in contact with. Old Faithful was of particular interest to all four, so they set the GPS for Cody.

As the veteran was at the helm of their live-in conveyance, Punch Line and the youngster shared the newspaper while the burly man napped in preparation for his turn to drive.

"This doesn't sound promising," the youngster relayed, reading the national news section.

"What's that?" Punch Line asked, his attention wrested from the sports news.

"They sure are protesting everything. Seem to be havin' trouble thinking of a single name to describe all this protest action."

Punch Line chuckled. "No doubt they have trouble thinking, but the action part is sure right." What started less than a year ago in large cities around the world supposedly as a voice against the power brokers of mankind had been hijacked and fully infiltrated by those who sought complete-domination free people.

"What could be more embarrassing than to discover that you're being used as a tool?" Punch Line said, shaking his head. "Your only recourse is to deny being a part of the resulting chaos you've unwittingly allowed yourself to become. Peaceful protests are great for making a point that is otherwise unheard, but the big shadow dwellers feed on anger, and they will co-opt any picnic they can and turn it into a food fight."

"Yeah," agreed the youngster, "and nobody ever gets fed in a food fight."

"Except the ones peddling the food," Punch Line agreed.

The napping gent awoke. "Where are we?" he asked through a yawn.

"Coming up on Shell," the driver announced.

"Anyone else hungry? Thought I heard somebody mention food, or was I dreamin' that?" he asked, rubbing his substantial midsection.

They all agreed that it was long enough past lunchtime and not too soon for supper, so in the tiny town of Shell, they pulled into the parking lot of an equally tiny café about twice the size of their RV. The parking lot was empty except for their monstrosity on wheels, but the lights inside indicated that they were open for business. Punch Line held the door for his three companions to enter, and he could hear a buzzer go off in the recesses of the kitchen area beyond a counter that was barely large enough for the three barstools crowded at its edge. Four couples tables lined the front wall, and with a sigh of relief, they spotted the only round-corner booth in the place. A female voice from the behind the counter area told them to make themselves at home, and she would be right with them. Punch Line pointed out the specials board. Neatly printed in pink chalk was "T-bone Special, $15.95 (Hank Gentry butchered 2 steers!)."

A smiling redhead, still tying her apron and carrying her order book in her mouth, sailed around the end of the counter to take their order. From her apron pocket she handed them four single-page menus, mentioned the steak special, and remarked about the weather in less than ten seconds. "Can I start you gentlemen off with something to drink?" she asked without taking a breath. They ordered steak specials and iced tea all around, and the pleasant waitress Tinker Belled her way back behind the counter, complete with a trail of pixie dust emanating from her Gleau. She placed the slip in a pass through with the words "Order up," and it was snatched up by a cousin of the Addams' Family Thing. The waitress returned in moments with beverages and a basket of warm rolls and honey butter.

Small talk and anticipation of their steaks was put on hold briefly as another patron entered the café, and the kitchen buzzer announced their arrival. Always cautious of anyone who may be following them, Punch Line looked in the direction of the door to size up the lone individual who quickly closed the door to keep the July heat at bay. Before assessing this new customer, he glanced through the open blinds to scan the parking lot. No new vehicle was in sight, but that didn't mean the patron hadn't parked around the corner of the building or was within walking distance of this establishment. His eyes returned to the man now being attended to by Tink the waitress. With a mild shock that he kept carefully hidden, he suddenly recognized this man. He did not know him as they had never met, but there was no mistaking who this gentleman was or where Punch Line had seen him recently. That recognition sparked excitement and calmed any worries as the man approached the booth, grabbed a chair from one of the tables, and placed it at the open end of the round table. Before sitting down, he introduced himself.

"Gentlemen, if you will allow my intrusion, my name is Ben Crow." Punch Line's three buddies exchanged glances that revealed a shared recognition of their new tablemate. Handshakes were traded around the table. Not only was this intrusion allowed, it was welcomed with enthusiasm.

Astounded by Ben's size, the veteran remarked, "You're a lot bigger fella in person."

Ben smiled in amusement. "So I'm told," he answered in his resonating baritone.

What Punch Line had been deprived of seeing when he saw Ben on the television interview was now in full view and had him captivated. Ben exuded a Gleau unlike any Punch Line had seen. Not wishing to stare at the man, Punch Line was yet drawn to this display as much in awe as in curiosity. "Mr. Crow," Punch Line began.

"Please, call me Ben," the big man interrupted.

"Okay, Ben it is. And I am—"

Again Ben stopped him. "I know who you are, and it is fully my pleasure and honor to make your acquaintance," Ben stated.

Not quite understanding the entire significance of Ben's statement, Punch Line was immediately engulfed in a Gleau of humility. Without his makeup, he assumed that Ben was aware of his clown alter ego and admitted as much. "Okay, I guess my Bozo routine didn't fool you, but I can't say I'm surprised."

"Your secret is safe with me," Ben said with a wink.

Tinker Bell arrived with steaks that had been detected by olfactory senses ten minutes before their exit from the kitchen. The table was crowded with entrée and salad plates and a fresh basket of rolls. Punch Line asked a quick blessing of their meal, and conversation took an even quicker backseat to its consumption and enjoyment.

With precision timing, Tinker Bell arrived when the last bite was devoured and cleared bone-strewn plates while offering the pie selection that was just removed from the oven. It was too good to pass up. Adorned with whipped cream, five huge pieces of apple pie were delivered to the table.

"Now this is heaven," the veteran remarked, shoving his last bite of pie in to his mouth. Heads bobbed in agreement.

"Close," Ben added.

Swallowing his last bite, Punch Line looked at Ben and added, "And I'm guessing you might know something about that."

Eyes around the table focused on Ben. He never broke stride, and before his last forkful of pie made its way to his face, he smiled slyly and responded, "I know what I need to know."

Punch Line laughed. "I figured as much." That one question was among the millions that Punch Line thought Ben may be able to answer, if this man was really who and what he suspected he may be, but the biggest question was why he was here sharing a meal with them. So Punch Line asked. "As much as we are grateful for your company, Ben, meeting here with us couldn't have been purely by chance. May I ask why you're here?"

"Encouragement mostly. You're on the right track, and I'll do what needs to be done to see that you're able to continue."

"Thank you." Punch Line hesitated. "You may not be able to warn us of any specific threat, but is there anything we may have overlooked to be aware of?"

With nothing but crumbs left on his plate, Ben put his fork down and picked up a napkin. His words rolled out like gentle distant thunder. "I understand why you mask your identity, just as I mask mine. You wish for your ideas to stand alone, and they do. They always have. This battle of the heart, for mankind to understand that it is wrong to have one man parasitic upon another, will be hard fought. To a dog, the parasitic tick is small, but many ticks can cause the dog to become anemic and die. Too many have been convinced that when every drop of blood is drained and the dog dies, the ticks then *become* the dog. Few will dispute that the taking of *a life*, ending it in death, is wrong, but too few understand that any amount of life taken by force, against the living individual's will and used to benefit another, is just as wrong. No matter the name it is given, the taking of life for the ease of another is condemning the former to the misery of a living death—a slow death of the spirit. Unlike other species of life on this earth, each human being embodies both king and worker. To ever separate the two diminishes both. Your battle has been to reveal the value of the spirit." Punch Line shook his head, indicating yes. "The Gleau reveals the existence of this living spirit," he concluded.

"And the truth," Punch Line added.

"Or the lack of it," Ben remarked. "Your greatest obstacle will be those who, by ignorance or choice, deny the existence of the spirit, thereby allowing them the right to subjugate men with righteous-sounding excuses that boil down to the worst kind of insatiable appetites. And then there are the skin thinkers."

"Skin thinkers?" Punch Line was both puzzled and intrigued by that turn of phrase.

"They use the wrong organ for thought. Too many fail to acknowledge the spirit within when they use as a distraction what they can see on the surface. Those who profess to not judge a book by its cover are quick to misjudge men based on that shallow assessment, and it is a practice they encourage with their illiterate followers while praising them for being well read. Those deprived of a depth of thought beyond what is tangible and provable in this limited existence will continue to ignore what the Gleau indicates. To them it is a mirage, something seen but meaningless because of its lack of provable substance."

"Skin thinkers. That does hit the nail on the head, doesn't it," Punch Line agreed. "If you see only the body and ignore what the spirit embodies, you have failed to read the book, and you base your opinions on admitted ignorance."

"And men do so at their peril. This is not a mirage to be disregarded. A feigned smile and empty promises have toppled empires."

"What, if anything, can I do to help those who will not see?" Punch Line asked in earnest.

"Finish what you have started. The Gleau has unmasked the evil. It is now time to unmask the good." Ben stood to leave the company of his four new friends and let them continue their journey. As he walked toward the door, Punch Line followed, mentioning to his companions that he would return in a moment.

Once outside, surrounded by privacy, Punch Line stood in Ben's encompassing shadow and offered his hand once again in thanks and farewell. "Sometimes I wonder if any of this will work because no one wants everything to fall apart just to prove our foundations may need some shoring up. It's easy to point out the destruction of an earthquake or a volcano, but no one seems to notice the slow erosion that threatens our stability."

"It will not be easy. When a child learns to read a written language, their eyes are taught to hear. You are now teaching them to listen to what they see. They must see the truth, of both good and evil, to make valid choices."

Punch Line nodded in agreement. "Yeah, opportunity and freedom are a hard sell when desperate people are being sold the illusion of El Dorado and the pot of gold at the end of the rainbow."

Before departing, Ben offered one more insight that shook Punch Line to his core. Overcome by this bit of news, he bowed his head as his eyes welled with tears, provoked by the enormity of what he was told. The shade he stood in gave way to the sun, and he looked up to see Ben walk around the side of the building. The thought of following was cut short by the knowledge that Ben would not be there. He gathered himself and returned to his three friends in the café.

PART VII

Showdown

STURMISCH WASTED NO TIME IN arranging Adam's erasure. As the plans for the meeting in the park with Punch Line solidified, so did Sturmisch's plans to kill two birds with one stone. It would be another spectacular historical mystery that would cast doubt and blame in every direction except his. The script was written to include confusing variables that would have the conspiracy theorists and official investigators twiddling their thumbs and offering suppositions of phantom gunmen on a grassy knoll for decades while *he* took full advantage of the unfortunate and tragic distraction. Certainly with Adam's demise, Sturmisch would be looked upon as a victim suffering the loss of a devoted employee and friend. A haphazard note of condolence would be tossed in Punch Line's direction as simple collateral damage because surely the intended target would be the "important" one. The press releases would immediately point to Adam's opposition as the responsible party, ensuring the sympathy vote. And at Sturmisch's direction, it would appear that nothing but gratitude and honor for the message Adam had presented so boldly could be responsible for the immediate transfer of the baton to plan B.

Tracking Adam was no problem due to the RFID he received during a dental procedure at a White Swann clinic. Tracking Punch Line was a whole different matter, but when he arrived at the appointed place and time, that issue would be solved.

The two teams of snipers and spotters had acquired and tested a wireless automatic trigger device that accounted for and adjusted for the scant time difference of firing the two weapons at exactly the same time, thus making it sound that a single shot would be fired. Acoustics experts would cast doubt on the single-shot declaration, but after the dust settled and recordings were collected, few would pay attention to their findings. After all, it wouldn't bring anyone back to life. The angles were calculated for the greatest amount of confusion when the trajectory of the impossible shot would be studied. As Adam was so disappointed by the performance of his security detail in North Platte, they had all been replaced by a group whose competence and loyalty suited Sturmisch and his plans. It delighted Sturmisch that Adam approved of these changes and was impressed by the addition of private SWAT-trained members. By some miracle, should either man not succumb instantly to a head shot, security personnel would rush to their aid with deadly syringes to finish the job.

Sturmisch chuckled to himself about the fact that this circus he would create would be attended by not just one but two clowns. He could only imagine the fervor this event would produce, dividing the populace to an even greater degree. It was his goal to scald and inflame while preventing things from bursting into flames until the time was right. Much to his chagrin, the televised message from the alleged source had cooled things off a bit, but they would be warmed back up with a sideshow of marketplace bombings, more small bank failures, and evaporating stimulus loans, and maybe an unprovoked murder spree or two. This was no time for introspection or study of the facts by the masses. Their focus needed to be on what they didn't have and who they should despise to justify its taking. He had come too far to let common sense and decency interfere with his objectives.

His plan B needed little polish as he was a stalwart establishment regular with deep roots in old money and a keen interest in keeping in place all the complexities, confusion, and exclusions that kept their kind at the top of the heap and prevented but a scant few from sharing that sacred mount. Maybe he didn't have Adam's flash and bling, as the young crowd referred to it, but he did have a wife ten years his junior and a fledgling pop star daughter to attract the mindless young. He could hear her now, accompanied by an urgent dance beat and bit of rap thrown in for good measure, encouraging all to join the "part-ay, part-ay!" They would quickly forget the Gleau and the Adam and Clownie episode. Confident of the small changes he was about to make, his grand scheme had accounted for all variables except one: the giant Indian. His experts had studied at length the footage from the interview with Jase Garrett, and it was their expert opinion that it had neither been edited nor doctored. Based solely on what appeared to be the case, Sturmisch was now more determined than ever to own this man and his superhuman technology. If he couldn't have it, no one would have it, including the Indian.

Wednesday
(August 8, 2012)

"WHY SO QUIET?" LEE PRODDED Jase.

Standing side by side at the kitchen counter, they peeled scalded tomatoes, readying them for canning. Jase finished the last remaining roma and rinsed his hands.

"I was just thinking about that length of pasture fence that crosses the slough to the east. I should tighten that tomorrow."

"No need to be in a hurry," Lee reminded. "We won't move the steers and horses to that pasture for another month. And besides, it's muddy in there now. I saw a flock of teal take off from the cattails before dark last night."

"It just crossed my mind, is all," he told his sister with a smile. He would be leaving a multitude of chores and repairs undone, and he would miss doing them. Like a kid in a candy store with five dollars burning a hole in his pocket, his time had been spent far too quickly, and he would take with him the appetite for this sweet life unsated, but that was exactly as it should be. He knew the terms to which he had agreed and would willingly abide by them, but the same could not be said for Lee. He did not look forward to telling her.

"Do you want to fill jars or do the lids and rings?"

His sister's question thankfully drew his thoughts back to the task at hand. "I'll fill. Less precision involved," he admitted.

Lee laughed, and Jase watched the pinkish lace of illumination that grew and danced about her slight form. At this moment he could think of nothing more beautiful. Images of his sister flashed through his memory, and he was grateful to have them. The wordless task of filling, capping, and loading the jars into the canner was completed, and Jase maintained the smile that thoughts of Lee created. Setting the timer and wiping her hands, Lee continued her ballet around the kitchen, depositing bowls and utensils in the sink, arranging a cutting board and towel to receive the finished jars, hanging potholders, and grabbing two glasses of iced tea. With a final flourish, she turned and landed gracefully in a chair. Already seated, Jase faced her with his smile.

"What?" Lee asked. "What are you smiling at?"

"Just you," he answered, smiling even wider. His smile remained as he looked over her shoulder and saw Ben emerge from the barn and move toward the house with his typical giant strides. "We've got company," Jase alerted Lee.

"Ben?" she asked without bothering to look. Jase nodded his head, affirming her guess, and she jumped up to get another glass of tea and placed a loaf of banana bread on the table. "Glad he decided to make an appearance. I can put you both to work in the garden pulling things together for market."

"Sounds like a plan," Jase responded, planning a private discussion with Ben while they filled baskets.

"I've got eggs to gather and a couple roosters to catch for dinner tomorrow night. Extend the invitation to Ben, if you would," Lee requested.

"I'll tell him to clear his schedule," Jase joked.

A soft rap on the screen door was followed by Jase's immediate, "Come on in!"

Ben ducked as he came through the doorway to the kitchen and instantly found his place at the table before the banana bread. Lee greeted him as she sped past with a basket in hand to gather eggs and leave the two to their discussions.

"I take it all is falling into place," Jase stated, expecting confirmation.

Having just wadded a whole slice of banana bread into his mouth, Ben nodded his head yes. He swallowed and washed it down with tea. "I'm going to miss this," Ben admitted in a soft bellow. He picked up a second piece of bread, and Jase watched it disappear in a single bite.

"I think she's going to miss your appreciation of her cooking too," Jase agreed. He waited while Ben savored the second mouthful. "You found our target?"

"Yes. The timing must be precise, but the closer we get to it, the clearer it becomes."

"You're the talented one. I'm just along for the ride," Jase added.

Ben acknowledged his friend's assessment and finished his tea. "Let's go fill some baskets," he suggested, leaving all of the coming reality unspoken and safely tucked away in silence.

New Faithful

THE FOUR STOOD WITH A group of twenty or so other eager viewers to witness Old Faithful do what it was so famous for. The benches were occupied by a gaggle of middle-aged ladies and their charges, including a retired accountant bent on predicting the exact time of the next eruption based on the duration of the last. One of the ladies, obviously the matriarchal hen in charge, approached the men and engaged them in conversation.

"You boys fishermen?" she asked forwardly.

"Occasionally, ma'am," offered the burly gent.

"I thought so," she began. "You fellas look more like cowboys, judging by your boots. Where are you from?"

Punch Line liked this old bird with a Gleau of lilac satin sprinkled with multicolored cupcake nonpareils. "You're right. We're from cowboy country. And it's my guess you are a schoolteacher."

"Such perception!" declared the woman. "Were you one of my students?"

"Not unless you taught back east, ma'am. You just have the Gleau of it about you."

"Lots of people tell me that," she confirmed, smiling proudly. "So tell me, what do you gentlemen think of this Gleau business?"

"I think it speaks for itself, frankly, and doesn't much care what my opinion is." Punch Line laughed.

"You know, young man, I think that's one of the most insightful answers I've ever received, and judging by the Gleau around you, I'd say it's from the heart as well."

"Kinda lets you see what's in the heart would be my thoughts, but that's just a guess."

"I suspect that may be true,' she said wistfully. "I don't know you, but what I see around you tells me there's a lot worth knowing. And because I'm as old as dirt, I know that a mind without a good heart is already wasted, and a misdirected heart with no sense about it is little more than good intentions, and we know where that leads."

"Now there's wisdom sweet as honey!" declared the vet.

The accountant in the teacher's group announced that the eruption was imminent, and the gurgling and hissing from the vent backed up the prediction. Before excusing herself to rejoin her group, she added prophetically, "The world could use a man like you right now, my good-hearted cowboy. It's been a pleasure making your acquaintance." She extended a withered hand and placed her other upon Punch Line's hand as he accepted the gesture. It may have been the advice of just one elderly schoolteacher, but her words cemented what his thoughts until this moment had failed to gel.

Old Faithful didn't disappoint. As the small crowd watched in awe, the tower of steaming water rose from the earth, the first shot providing shoulders for the main event to stand on. Having only seen still photographs and snippets of moving footage, the duration of the event was surprising. For a few seconds, Punch Line considered the power it took to accomplish this feat, and then all such thoughts gave way to the sheer beauty of the crystalline arrow aiming toward the equally clear blue sky.

Having seen what they came to see, the four followed the path back to the RV, each with the notion of having stricken one more thing from their personal bucket lists. It was easy to set thoughts free while gazing at wide expanses and wilderness enough for any man to lose himself in, but as they traveled west toward their appointed stop, it was becoming clearer by the mile that both freedom and thought were slowly being caged in the zoo that had become civilization.

Thursday (August 9, 2012)

HER SMALL KITCHEN WAS SO crowded that one might expect it to be a holiday celebration rather than just a family and friends get-together. Emily's family and Barbara and Brett made it an event that brought back memories from only eight months prior that felt more like eight years, with one large and one small exception. Nick was once again on the other side of the planet doing whatever it was that he did, and his absence was noted daily. Maybe Semi's absence wouldn't have been so noticeable if his presence in Lee's life hadn't been so great, but even surrounded by familiar happy voices and the aroma of baked chicken and sage, his loss still weighed heavily.

Lee turned and glanced at the empty rocker under the window and filled the void with a memory of him while continuing to stir the gravy. At the same instant, Lorelei and Joy wrapped themselves around her legs with purrs of, "We love you, Nana." Lee smiled and, with her free hand, stroked each silken head and thanked them, reminding them that she loved them back. They flitted off like butterflies in search of another flower, but the love remained.

"We have a surprise for you, Mom," Emily announced as she grabbed napkins for the table.

"Oh, you do, do you?" Lee responded, wondering what to expect. She poured the gravy into a bowl and placed it on the table.

Matt was standing across the kitchen holding their youngest, and Em finished her task and directed her mother's attention. "Watch this," she stated rather proudly.

Matt lowered Albert to the floor, and he steadied himself on chubby little legs. Emily squatted and encouraged her newest toddler as he took two slow deliberate steps in her direction. A huge smile crossed his face, and his pace increased to cover the ten-foot distance between them. Lee crouched down beside her daughter to capture all this offered from the right perspective. The Gleau surrounding Albert's cherubic figure radiated excitement and delight as waves of golden yellow tinged with rose coursed from within, extending a path of deep rose toward his intended goal. A wobbly pause lasted less than a second as he centered his balance with a wide step, and at the last moment, he turned and threw himself in Lee's direction. As grandson and grandmother's eyes met, the exchange filled Lee's heart past brimming. His black-eyed Susan eyes were wide with glee, and he threw himself into Lee's waiting embrace. It was a magical moment imparting far more than just delight of a newfound skill. These little moments were what life was all about.

As much as it was the task of the current generations to teach the young, this gift Lee received from this tiny soul was more precious than all the gold in the world. This moment transcended the barriers of time and space as it became the bounty she would take with her to the next existence and the gift she would leave here as well. Lee smiled as she considered the fact that in this simple trade, she could have her cake, share it, and eat it too.

Standing with Albert in her arms, it was reaffirmed that she had a specific mission in life to fulfill. She missed all those who had gone on to the next existence before her, but now her goal must be to gather all the wonderful gifts she could to take with her while giving them here. To arrive at the next destination with nothing but a bucket of sorrow would be silly when there were so many worthwhile things here to share. Lee brightened inside and out. Albert, still in her arms, had turned his attention to the necklace bobble dangling before him. He carefully examined the shiny object of silver, amethyst, and opal and met her close-quartered gaze. Now, what happened next could have been just a reflex, but Lee doubted it. Albert's expression of contemplation gave way to a slight grin, and he winked at her. She winked back, and his grin widened to a smile of confirmation that exposed all five of his brand-new teeth. "Thank you," she whispered. He finished the private exchange with a definite nod and went back to examining the necklace.

Emily situated the maple highchair at a spot next to her own, and Jase was busy filling glasses with tea. Pam had gathered an assortment of chairs from the closet and about the house to seat each diner and thwarted Joy's attempt to include the kitchen rocker.

"No, that's Semi's seat," she declared and told Joy to get the desk chair instead.

Lee handed Albert to Em and finished loading the table with the soon-to-be-consumed fare. As all twelve took their places, Jase asked a fitting blessing to their feast to begin the whirlwind of serving dishes from one end of the table to the other.

Amid the clinking of forks and dishes, the conversation was light and dotted with giggles. Lee expressed an interest in Barbara's latest works and promised that she would attend a concert soon. According to Brett, things at the paper had gone back to normal with the occasional letter to the editor still questioning the validity of the source. Em encouraged the girls to try a bit of everything on the table, and Lorelei declared that pear-lime gelatin mold counted as something green.

Seated beside his oldest daughter, Matt felt a rather sharp tug on his shirtsleeve and postponed the next forkful of mashed potatoes heading toward his mouth. Pam was wide-eyed and speechless but had to bring something to her father's attention. She was pointing to something across the room, and as his eye followed the direction of her point, he was momentarily struck dumb himself. He cleared his throat and, in a loud whisper, made Emily take notice. When she saw what had been brought to her attention, both hands covered her mouth in an attempt to quiet the startled yelp of surprise that escaped. In a matter of seconds, everyone's attention was captivated by the curious event. Under the window and next to the cold pellet stove, the rocking chair was rocking. The movement was deliberate and halting, indicating weight rather than wind. For a few seconds it continued. Then it stopped.

Pam was the first to speak up about what had just occurred. "Nana, was that Semi?" she asked.

"That's as good an explanation as any," Lee answered, not knowing if it was Semi or not.

At the tender age of four, Joy deepened the mystery a bit by answering her sister's question and posing another. "Yes, that was Semi. But who was that man, Nana?"

"What man, sweetie?" Lee asked her granddaughter.

Without missing a beat, Joy answered, "The one holding Semi."

The adults exchanged puzzled glances with one notable abstainer. Ben was starting on his second helping of everything when he realized he was the center of everyone's silent attention. He knew exactly who the man was, but naming names wasn't necessary. "Probably was just a friend of mine," he admitted, hoping it was enough. It was. Relief gave way to laughter, and the meal was finished with just a furtive peek or two in the direction of the rocker.

Baker Beach

THE SUN ROSE ON THE morning of Friday, August 10, 2012. With each man taking his turn at the wheel, Punch Line and his gang of three made short work of the last twenty-four hours of their journey and arrived in the California city associated with a well-known rice-and-pasta dish. Their RV was exchanged at the rental facility for an unremarkable sedan, and after obtaining rooms at a local motel with an adjoining inner door, they decided to go inspect the location where the afternoon debate was scheduled to take place.

As they pulled into the public parking area of Baker Beach, they took note of Adam's motor coach in residence in the no-parking zone. *Already the rules did not apply to this self-determined elite,* Punch Line thought. The fog had not yet lifted completely as the four, appearing to be nothing more than beachcombers, took in this setting for the public exchange. The half-mile strip of sandy beach was flanked by serpentine rock cliffs and the anxious waters of South Bay. They walked a fair distance past the deserted stage setup, which was placed at such an angle as to be framed by the Golden Gate Bridge in the background. Atop the elevated cliffs were trees and ample scrub that Punch Line scoured with his eyes for any sign of human occupation. Nothing looked out of place at the moment, but it still caused some warranted worry.

Before reversing their course, well short of the clothing optional portion of the beach, they were each compelled to remove their shoes and wet their feet in the waters of the Pacific. The view from this vantage point was, to say the least, impressive, and the history of the Presidio was well preserved with the Battery Chamberlin still in place. The fog lifted further, and the land-defining Bonita Cove came into view. Again Punch Line surveyed the tree line above them as they walked back to the parking lot, keeping Ben's words of warning to himself.

From the window of his motor coach, Adam saw but failed to recognize the focus of today's revenge. Instead, he saw all that he secretly held in contempt parading before him. It was Friday. This path of ocean-washed sand was well traveled by individuals engaged in the nonproductive pursuit of physical well-being. Walking couples were overtaken by those jogging a vigorous pace, going nowhere fast. Families and groups of friends meandered without fruitful purpose. The pairs strolling hand in hand were entwined in a single Gleau indicating enjoyment of more than just their surroundings. What earthly good were these aimless wanderings anyway? Unless they were picking up trash, these shirkers should be at work, Adam thought. When their workday was complete and they had contributed to the public coffers, then and only then had they earned the right to enjoy what this haven provided. And today they would receive a rare treat: Adam.

Forcing himself away from the window, he accepted the espresso offered by one of his new multitalented security personnel that Sturmisch had so magnanimously supplied. Today was going to be a great day. Today the clown would be destroyed twice—first by his superior oratory, and then by whatever method Sturmisch had concocted.

Friday (August 10, 2012)

MORE THAN THE SUNLIGHT FILTERING through the wooden blinds of his bedroom window, the aroma of frying bacon ended Jase's sleep. He could hear Lee's footfalls approach and pass his door. Today would be spent entirely with her, doing whatever she wished, or at least that was his plan at the moment. He rounded the corner of the archway to the kitchen just as she was headed for the basement steps.

"Good morning. What set you on fire this early?" he greeted Lee.

"Laundry," she laughed. "Coffee is ready, and I'll be right back up."

Jase settled himself on a chair after retrieving his morning brew and noticed that a basket of eggs had already been collected. Lee returned from the basement with a frozen chicken in one hand and folded towels in the other. Like a froth of cotton candy floating on a cloud, Lee was wearing a cloak of contentment that he wished would never be disturbed.

"I need to check the weather forecast," she informed as she deposited the chicken on the counter and sped to the linen closet to deposit the towels. When she reappeared, she checked the sizzling pan before heading for the basement again. "I forgot the fabric softener. Can you tune to KMIN? Weather should be on in a sec. Be right back," she requested.

"Sure," Jase replied and located the remote. He hit power and selected KMIN's station number. Expecting a smiling face behind a desk to appear on the screen, he thought he had hit the wrong button when a Please Stand By message came into view. There was no mistake when he entered the station number again carefully. "Hey, Lee," he called as he heard her heading back up the steps. "What's this?"

Entering the room and checking the screen, she accepted the remote and checked the stations above and below. Both were fine. "Not a satellite issue," she stated, returning to KMIN. "Maybe someone tripped over an electrical cord or something."

"I don't think so," Jase said with sudden awareness. "Look."

Lee followed his gaze to the view of the barnyard beyond the window. Ben was walking quickly toward the house. In his arms was the body of a woman exhibiting a diminished Gleau. Jase met them at the door, and as Ben crossed the threshold of the kitchen, Lee thought she recognized this person.

"Put her in here," Lee indicated, pointing to the sofa. A cut above the woman's eye was oozing fresh blood, and the torn upper sleeve of her blouse revealed another wound as a small red stain grew. As Ben gently lowered the unconscious woman to the sofa, Lee asked the obvious question. "What on earth happened?"

"It looks worse than it is, and her wounds aren't serious," Ben stated, dodging a direct answer.

Lee ran to the bathroom and returned with clean towels and a first-aid kit. Ben left the pair with the woman in Lee's competent care and joined Jase in the kitchen. Lee could hear a serious discussion between the two of them, but at the moment her attention was focused on her unexpected patient.

As Lee carefully wiped away the film of dirt on the familiar face, her identity was recalled. There was a hint of distress still in the Gleau surrounding her body, and at the points of injury, bright golden founts of light were fading slowly. The cut above her eye had stopped bleeding, and slight swelling had all but closed the clean-edged wound. As Lee determined that it didn't require stitches and applied a mild antiseptic, her patient winced.

"Lydia?" Lee spoke calmly. "Lydia, you're okay," she reassured. "Do you understand me?"

Without opening her eyes completely, Lydia asked, "Where am I?"

"You're safe," Lee answered. "And you're going to be okay. Does anything hurt?"

"My head," she answered as she attempted to sit up and immediately gave up the effort, continuing, "I'm dizzy. Are you a nurse?"

"Right now, I wish I was, but no. My name is Lee." She grabbed a small pillow and carefully elevated Lydia's head to a more comfortable position after checking her neck for anything that didn't feel normal.

"Thank you," Lydia responded to her caregiver.

"Can you open your eyes for me, Lydia?" Lee requested. Lydia opened her eyes and stared at Lee. Shadowing her face with a hand, Lee used the sunlight entering through a window to check the reaction of her patient's pupils. As far as Lee could tell, they were equal and responsive.

"Do I know you?" Lydia asked, wincing again after furrowing her brow with interest.

"We've never met, but you know my brother, Jase." That information didn't register immediately. Sticking to the task at hand, Lee rolled up the bloodstained shirtsleeve to discover little more than a healthy scratch that was, in fact, the graze of a bullet. Content that she had completed her amateur triage skills and her patient seemed to be making a steady recovery, Lee asked if there was anything she could offer to make Lydia more comfortable.

"A glass of water, maybe. My mouth feels gritty," she replied.

Lee stood to go to the kitchen as Ben entered the room. Lydia stared up at him, and her eyes widened. "You're...*him*," she declared as she slowly attempted to sit up. Ben offered a humongous hand, and she accepted.

"My name is Ben, and I need to know what you can recall about this morning. Anything you saw or heard."

Lee returned with water and tissues. Lydia was silent for a moment as she tried to collect her thoughts. "I had just parked my car in the lot behind our complex, and I was walking around the block to the front of the building, then...I saw Blake, then I woke up here."

"Where was Blake?" Ben asked.

"He was at the door getting ready to go in," Lydia struggled. "He was picking something up and—" She stopped and looked up at Ben in horror. "What happened to Blake?"

Not wanting to seem callous but in need of information, Ben stated the reality as delicately as he could. "He left this existence instantly. I'm sorry."

A look of shock preceded her next question. "Who on earth would do—"

"I'm not sure yet, but I need to know anything you remember," Ben insisted gently.

For a moment, Lydia said nothing. She picked up a tissue and pressed it to her eyes. "This morning I got up early. I walked to the kitchen and noticed an envelope had been slid under my apartment door. I thought it was a joke or just an idle threat, nothing serious. It was one of those hokey anonymous notes with the letters and words cut and pasted from various publications."

"What did it say?" Ben asked flatly.

"It said to stop promoting the validity of the Gleau unless we wished to become invalid. I was going to show it to Blake. I tried calling him this morning before I left, and the call went right to voice mail. Then I called my mom just to be sure my phone was in service."

Ben was impressed by Lydia's composed effort but needed to know more. "Then what did you do?"

"I told my mom about the note. She took it a bit more seriously than I did. Then I drove to work. I parked in the municipal lot and walked around the block." She was quiet for a few seconds, dissecting the sequence of events. "When I came around the corner, Blake was on the steps getting ready to go inside. He picked something up. I can't remember if it was a package or an envelope, maybe. Traffic is usually noisy in the morning, but I heard an engine rev up and a squeal of tires. I think I heard a backfire at that point and then something really loud. I don't remember anything past that."

Having pieced together what she could of her morning, Lydia gave in to what was a luxury at the moment—anger. What agenda was important enough to target such a wonderful, giving man? Her thoughts went swiftly to Blake's wife and children. This situation was devastating and pointless. Her anger was accompanied by welling tears, and a chasm of indigo formed at her chest, pulling in the white light that surrounded her.

Ben thanked her for what was a painful recollection and excused himself to the kitchen to continue his discussion with Jase. Lee offered her condolences and another tissue. "Is there anything I can do for you? Anyone you need to call?" she asked.

"I need to call my mom," Lydia managed.

"Here, use my cell. It's better that she hears this news from you rather than the television." Lydia shook her head in agreement, and Lee went to the kitchen as much to find out what Ben and Jase were concocting as she did to offer Lydia some privacy.

"She's calling her mom. I think she's going to be okay," Lee offered.

"Yes, she will be fine physically, but Blake wasn't the only target this morning. Lydia was also on the list. The backfire she heard before I swooped in and grabbed her was gunfire. I got a look at the vehicle, but it was a quick one. I was outrunning bullets at the time. Dark SUV with blackout-tint windows. Sound familiar?"

"Hmmm, yes, it does," Jase answered grimly.

"Blake wasn't the only casualty either," Ben admitted. "Others were shot."

Lee grabbed the remote and tuned in another local affiliate. As expected, what happened on the street in front of KMIN was breaking news. The crawler informed them that three others had been killed by gunfire, and two were wounded and hospitalized in serious condition. Camera shots zoomed in on debris beyond crime scene tape, highlighting fragments of concrete, broken glass, and the mangled remains of a pair of khaki pants wearing a single Rockport men's shoe. The three were silent as they listened for any information on a suspect or suspects.

"Can someone tell me where I am?" Lydia asked, still holding Lee's phone and standing in the archway to the kitchen. "I need to give my mom an address."

Lee muted the television instantly and handed the remote to Jase. She escorted Lydia to a chair with her back to the TV and scribbled her address on the back of an envelope. The information was relayed, and Lydia finished her call, assuring her mother that she could be reached at this number if there was any problem. She handed the phone to Lee with an automatic thank-you.

Still in shock but gaining her bearings quickly, Lydia suddenly recognized Jase. "You're the source," she remarked. "And now this is starting to make sense."

"Jase Garrett, Ms. Corvuso," he introduced himself.

"Please, call me Lydia." She shook her head with new understanding. "Now I have an idea about how I got here," she continued, addressing Ben. "But how did you know I needed help?"

"Your mother told me," Ben answered.

"Believe it or not, that makes sense," Lydia replied while shaking her head. "She's always saying she's sending me angels. Guess I didn't really need them until this morning."

"Yes, you did," Lee added.

A brief silence ended with Ben indicating that he and Jase had work to do. Lee needed no explanation, and they parted company with a final comment from Jase. "I'll see you later."

"Be careful," she responded. "Both of you." Ben gave Lee a quick wink of confirmation, and they were gone.

"Wow," Lydia remarked when the two men made their instant exit. "Does that happen often?"

"Every now and then." Lee chuckled, still amazed by the feat but no longer nonplused.

"Where did they go?" Lydia asked with a reporter's interest.

"My guess would be to sort this out," Lee answered plainly.

"I'd never be able to leave it at that," Lydia remarked.

"That's understandable. It's a job requirement for you." She left the room and returned in seconds with a clean white blouse. "Here, this should do. No need to worry your mom."

Lydia was quiet for a brief time, formulating her next question. "So you are *the* sister? As in, the sister with the wish," Lydia prodded.

"That would be me. Had I known it would be granted, maybe I should have asked for something less complicated, like world peace," she added with sarcasm and the hint of a laugh. "The bathroom is to the left, first door on your left."

"Thanks." When she stood, Lydia glanced up at the silent TV screen. An earnest-looking reporter was standing in front of police tape surrounding what she recognized as her building. "Can you turn this up," she asked Lee, postponing her taking leave. Describing the scene, the reporter revealed that this tragedy was twofold. Information from witnesses described an explosion and gunfire, and at this time in the initial phase of the investigation, it was assumed they were connected. Then a piece of video collected from a security camera on the opposite block captured Lydia's escape from the scene as well as the dark SUV. The tape was replayed in slow motion, highlighting the blur of her exit and the effect of the blast and gravity on her purse and briefcase. "Well, now I know where my phone is. What on earth am I going to tell them about what happened to me? You know they're going to ask."

"Tell them the truth. You were on the sidewalk when the blast occurred and subsequently rendered you unconscious. You awoke in a place you'd never been before under the care of a complete stranger. You called your mom to pick you up. End of story."

"You make it sound so simple." Lydia laughed, knowing she was in for some serious police grilling.

"The truth usually is. And I think they'll be far more interested in the note you received than in how you were rescued.

They already have that on tape, and you can tell them it was your mother's wish that saved you. All true, and they will be able to discern your forthrightness by your Gleau."

"Are you always so calm about this sort of thing?" Lydia remarked on her way to the bathroom.

"It's been a learning experience," Lee replied with a smile.

Before Lydia returned from changing, a red dual-cab pickup truck pulled up the drive. "Does your mom drive a big red pickup?" Lee called to the other room.

"That would be her," Lydia replied definitively and returned to the kitchen with only a Band-Aid over one eye marking her experience.

"You look much better. Don't keep her waiting," Lee encouraged.

It surprised Lee when Lydia gave her a hug with a thank-you. "I'd like to hear your take on all this sometime, if that is possible. And strictly off the record, of course."

"Anytime," Lee allowed.

From the kitchen window she watched as Lydia entered the passenger side of the vehicle and closed the door. An immediate mother-daughter conversation ensued, and even though it was beyond her ability to hear, she knew just what they were saying.

Tires crunched on the dry gravel as the truck backed and disappeared down the drive. Lee picked up the remote and turned off the television. The silence, interrupted by a scrambling flock of hens clucking a discovery, was an unexpected burden. What began as a bright day had lost a bit of its brilliance, and she thought the reason was obvious. Jasc was gone helping Ben. She still missed Semi. Either of those situations could account for the loneliness she was experiencing, but the significance of what tomorrow would bring completely escaped her.

Filling her momentary existence with something productive, she picked up a gathering basket and headed to the garden, leaving the loneliness in the empty house.

The Debate

RETURNING TO THE PARKING LOT more than an hour early to survey the crowd as it gathered, Punch Line's group was surprised by the minimal but swelling crowd that had already gathered. As they walked toward the temporary venue, Punch Line parted company with his three companions. The vet, the youngster, and the burly guy made their way toward the back of the cordoned-off area to keep an eye on things both in the crowd and behind them.

There were placards, both pro and con of the two speakers, carried by various patrons of the event, but one in particular caught the vet's eye. An elderly couple had it stuck in the sand between their beach chairs, and on it was a picture of the Lone Ranger staring at a likeness of Punch Line and asking "Who is *this* Masked Man?" The sign also got the attention of a twenty-something wearing a digi-camo shirt and who's Gleau indicated anything but a friendly nature.

"What the hell is that supposed to mean, old man?" The young antagonist laughed and pointed at the sign. His remark instantly put him on the vet's radar. "Why should you care about this stuff, y'old fool? You're gonna be dead soon anyway!" the heckler derided.

The old man stood using the strength of his pride to urge octogenarian legs to meet this miscreant eye to eye. Age may have taken its toll on his body, but a lifetime of experience was evident in the forceful Gleau he emitted.

"Sit down, pops! You ain't no threat."

Like lightning, the vet appeared at the older man's shoulder that bore a long-faded military tattoo. "Be on your way, son," the vet spoke with guarded calm.

"You ain't my daddy, and what's it to you? It's a free country," the emboldened piece of work in progress spouted back.

"Yes, it is, and if you had half a brain to go with that mouth, you'd recognize this gentleman as one of the many who preserved that gift for your gratuitously challenged kind. I suggest you offer this man a gesture of thanks and an apology," the vet stated more as a threat than a suggestion.

"Well, maybe he's *your* daddy. As for an apology, I'll not and say I did," the smart aleck replied as he took a step forward to assert a false position of power. The vet laughed as a veil of chrome yellow cowardice engulfed this twit.

"Though it would be an honor if this man of courage was my father, he is much more. He's my brother, and I suggest you heed my advice," the vet informed with a clenched jaw. The now-gutless wonder sought a retreat but was outflanked by the vet's other two buddies.

"Look, I was just kiddin' around," he offered as justifiable explanation for his unwarranted disrespect.

"That's fine. Now prove it," the vet challenged.

To affect his escape, the lowlife proffered an insincere "I'm sorry," to which the elderly gentleman replied instantly, "No doubt you are." The festering splinter of humanity extracted, the two soldiers separated by decades but united by duty exchanged knowing smiles and a handshake that cemented their victory.

In the next instant, a smattering of applause drew the crowd's attention to the once-vacant stage. Microphones on either side of the stage stood unattended, but a third was in the hand of the apparent emcee of today's event. A middle-aged man of African descent addressed the crowd. As well as an unabashed Gleau of crystalline white light, a red bow tie and a broad gap-toothed smile made him instantly appealing.

"Good afternoon, ladies and gentlemen. On behalf of our participants and our great host city, it is my pleasure to get this blissfully informal meeting of the minds underway." Pressured applause from the now considerable gathering expressed the audience's agreement with that notion. "Without further ado, I present the first half of our battling duo, a man known to all as Adam!" The emcee turned and extended a welcoming hand as Adam shed his human shield of three bodyguards and bounded onto the stage with the practiced enthusiasm of a game show host.

To a less-than-expected polite applause, Adam acknowledged the audience. "I'm delighted that you could all be here on this gorgeous afternoon to see me set the record straight," Adam began addressing the crowd, and before he could continue his self-aggrandizement, he was cut off.

Turning his back to Adam, the emcee proceeded to finish his introductions. "And, folks, I'd like to also introduce the second half of today's equation, the mystery man himself, Punch Line!" The man in the red bow tie extended a hand toward the empty end of the stage platform. The welcome of clapping hands was interrupted as the space remained empty. Adam would have wondered as the audience did where the clown could be, but he was too busy thinking about how he was going to admonish this impudent little man who so rudely cut him short. After all, who was this local nobody presuming to gain popular ground and notoriety at Adam's generous expense? A murmur of question replaced the applause, and Adam saw that as an opportunity.

"It seems the clown was of as little substance as I thought," he chuckled, hoping that somewhere in the sea of faces before him was at least one individual with half a brain to comprehend his humor.

"Excuse me, folks," the emcee broke in, once again cutting Adam off. Daggers of pea green emerged from Adam's chest, rising from a pool of dried blood red that engulfed his upper body and pointed directly at the little man with a grin that begged the attention of an orthodontist. "My name is Redgie Lewis, and I am Punch Line."

"You, sir, are a liar!" Adam responded, spewing a venomous beam of antilight in Redgie's direction.

"What I say is true," Redgie responded, countering Adam's declaration. The crowd watched in silent awe, awaiting more distinction of that truth than the bright Gleau around Redgie.

"Then again, it's plain that the clown doesn't ever tell the truth, so maybe you are him!" Adam rattled with confidence.

Redgie had waited for this moment. "I see," he began. "You always tell the truth, and Punch Line always lies. Is that right?"

"I think I made that clear," Adam replied with patronizing disgust.

Ignoring Adam's attitude, Redgie asked, "If Punch Line only lies, would he tell me that you are a liar?"

Adam replied with impatience, "Yes, he would."

"Hmm…" Redgie said aloud. "Then by your own admission, he did not lie. If he only lies and lied about the fact that you are a liar, then he told the truth, which you say he does not do. And as the self-proclaimed teller of truth, that makes you the liar." A few giggles arose from the crowd.

"Your trick questions are not amusing. If it will satisfy this charade, I will change my answer to no."

Redgie smiled at the crowd and rolled his eyes. He turned to Adam to finish making his point. "If you say he will not tell me you are a liar, then he will tell me you speak the truth, and according to you, he always lies. If that is your truth, it is a lie. How can that be?"

"I don't think these good people came to hear your empty ramblings," Adam addressed the crowd, thinking they would support his direction.

"I think they came to hear the truth, and you've just demonstrated a poor grasp of that. My name is Redgie Lewis, and I am Punch Line," he restated to a welcoming applause and calls of, "Way to go, Redge!" and "You tell him!" from his friends at the back of the group.

Adam was not going to be upstaged by this…this *person*, whoever he was, and sought control of the discussion as a corona of dull reddish-orange pulsed about his torso. "I've met the *real* Punch Line, and you—"

Redgie held up a hand and interrupted, knowing full well what it would generate within Adam. "Yes, we did meet. In Nebraska, I believe." Now he would let Adam speak.

"That proves nothing," Adam insisted. "Any idiot could know that."

Redgie ignored his insult and continued. "But that is not the very first time we met."

"Oh well, why don't you educate us all, little man," Adam lashed.

"Though I'm not known to frequent such establishments, I believe the first time I ever saw your face was in a bar in the late nineties. You were with a certain young lady, but I never saw her again after that evening."

"I recall no such meeting, and perhaps the drink distorted your memory."

"My memory is quite clear. I was the bartender." As Adam's Gleau dimmed a bit due to the confrontation, Redgie's was beginning to expand; a brilliant blue swelled beneath his white halo.

"I don't know what you're talking about," Adam stated defiantly.

With a swiftness that made Adam flinch, Redgie closed the short distance between them on the stage. On Adam's face was a look of surprised panic, fearing that this gentleman of relative diminutive stature was going to attack him physically. Dropping his microphone to his side and placing his other hand over the one Adam held, Redgie spoke a single-charged sentence. "She was my friend," he spoke in a harsh whisper.

Adam's eyes widened as he did indeed recall the event, but he failed to recognize Redgie being part of that long-ago evening. Even so, Redgie knew *something*, and this was a loose end that Sturmisch had failed to take into account. Preparing to dismiss both the event and this pushy impostor, Adam managed only, "This is not the time or place!" Before he could finish, a sharp crack followed by a shrill scream in the crowd ended the debate. The audience reacted with alarm and began moving in every direction.

Redgie reacted without thinking and forced Adam to the ground, shielding him from a potential second shot, but none came.

"Get off of me!" Adam demanded as the two lay in a pile on the stage floor. Adam's bodyguards reacted instantly, creating a visual barrier between the pair and the dispersing crowd while another two from the security team prepared to "help" Adam and Redgie to their feet. To their surprise, when they reached for the deadly syringes to finish the job Sturmisch sent them to do, they found only empty pockets. Unable to carry out their mission and forbidden the option of AD-libbing, they did what would appear normal and secured the stage. They were not paid to think, and short of strangling the pair in front of an audience of onlookers, they would reluctantly report to Sturmisch exactly what happened and what didn't.

As was planned before the event, Redgie knew his friends would meet him at the car if anything went wrong, and this certainly qualified as something wrong, but it wasn't what he expected. Glancing out at the quickly thinning crowd, he saw what sent the spectators scattering. Midway in the sand lay a body. It looked like a man, and he wasn't moving. With sincere regret, he left and headed toward the parking area.

⚜

When all hell broke loose and the bulk of the panicked crowd began to run, Redgie's buddies took it upon themselves to see to the safety of the elderly Lone Ranger couple and escort them to the parking area. With that errand complete and secure in the knowledge that Redgie could handle things on his own, they made their way through the chaos of the parking area to their vehicle. Redgie was nowhere in sight.

"Hope he's okay," the youngster remarked.

"I'd say he is. Saw him stand up next to the dandy before we headed here," the vet replied.

"I guarantee ya he's somewhere wondering where the heck we are," the burly gent added.

"Prolly right. Shotgun!" the vet announced as he made his way to the front passenger side of their car. He rounded the front of the sedan, and there, with his back against the door, sat Redgie. "Geez, Redge!" Certainly glad to see they were all together, the vet was suddenly concerned. "You okay?" he asked.

"Yeah, I'm fine." He extended a hand, and the vet pulled him to his feet.

Relinquishing his shotgun position, the vet opened the rear door and took a seat. In the distance, sounds of sirens were growing closer.

"Let's get outta here before things get any more interesting," the burly guy suggested as he took a seat in the back next to the vet.

"Agreed," confirmed the youngster as he slid behind the wheel and started the engine. They left unimpeded as the police in attendance had secured the event area to preserve whatever evidence of the shooter there was without undue public interference or contamination. As they neared the roadway leading into the park, an ambulance made a right with their lights flashing but no siren.

Redgie was silent until the ambulance had passed. "Poor guy. It should have been me."

The driver did a double take and asked, "What do you mean supposed to be you? You knew this was going to happen?"

"Not exactly. I knew *something* was going to happen, but I thought I would be the target."

With a look and tenor of incredulity, the youngster addressed Redgie again. "You knew something, and you didn't tell us? How did you know?"

"Ben. He didn't tell me what would happen. He said only that this debate was important. So important that it would have a cost in human life. And I thought he meant me."

"You should have said something," the vet chimed in.

"I couldn't. If I had mentioned that I thought my life would be at risk going through with this, you guys would have talked me out of it. And no way would I have knowingly put you three at risk. I was so sure the risk was mine. But I was wrong."

"You didn't cause this, Redge. Someone did, but you didn't. Who's to say it wouldn't have happened even if you weren't there?" the burly man tried to alleviate Redgie's self-imposed guilt. "It's not your fault."

"Thanks. But I knew what I was getting into, or thought I did anyway. I just wish there was something I could have done to prevent what did happen."

"Hey, you did what you came here to do. You let everyone know that liar for who he really is, and you let everyone know you're just a guy with the truth on his side. Mission accomplished, I'd say," the driver encouraged.

"Hope that's enough," Redgie replied.

"What is that smell?" the vet asked.

"It wasn't me," the burly man was quick to answer.

"No," the vet laughed. "It smells like bad cologne."

"It's me," Redgie admitted. "I need a shower. When I grabbed pretty boy to get us both out of the line of fire, he reeked so badly it made my eyes water. Guess he figures he can cover up a stench he can't see."

"Couldn't cover that up in a sandbox with an army of cats," laughed the big man as they turned in to the motel parking lot.

The ambulance drove past Adam's motor coach as it prepared to leave. Turning off its emergency lights, it drove without haste, picking its way through discarded coolers and beach chairs to the spot cordoned off with police tape. The two paramedics exited the van with the tools and speed their profession required only to be met by a single police officer and a man identifying himself as a doctor.

After introducing himself and showing credentials, the doctor brought the emergency crew up to speed. "He bled out quick. No pulse or respirations when I got to him. I called TOD at 4:48 p.m. I can wait for the coroner if you need me to corroborate anything," the pediatrician volunteered.

The paramedics thanked him and, with the permission of the officer in attendance, did their own evaluation of the body to confirm his assessment. In a supine position, the victim looked like he was taking a comfortable nap. Not adhering to the dictates of GQ, he wore oversized khaki pants that were soiled to match his dirty wrinkled shirt. His tangle of dirty hair and scruffy beard topped off the ensemble, and his feet were fashionably bare. The absence of a Gleau was something noted unofficially by the paramedics, but it was a visual confirmation of what their instruments registered. The man was deceased, and a rough estimate put his age in the middle range. A quick pat down to determine the corpse's identity yielded nothing.

"Did you find a wallet? Any ID?" the paramedic asked the attending officer.

"No. Haven't had a chance to look. Was waiting for you guys to give the okay," the officer replied.

"Go for it. I couldn't find anything."

A more thorough search of the dead man's pockets produced nothing more than lint. His arms were checked for identifying tattoos. None were found. A single shirt button was undone to check his neck, and that's when the officer discovered what he thought would be a significant clue. A chain around the man's neck bore a dog tag. Unfortunately, it seemed to be nothing more than a scavenged bauble lost by some luxury car owner.

By the time the coroner arrived, it was determined that this hapless soul was one of the many invisible homeless, and they would have to resort to fingerprints or dental records to discover his identity. The body was bagged and tagged, and as the paramedics packed up their gear, they stopped the officer to ask a question.

"From your account of what happened, you said there was a single shot, right?"

"Yes," the officer answered.

"Weird," the paramedic replied.

"Why weird?"

"Because unless that single shot entered that guy and did a one-eighty, I counted two entrance wounds, side by side."

"I guess anything is possible, but ask anyone here. Only a single shot was heard," the officer reported.

"And did you see his face?" the paramedic asked.

"Yeah, but can't say I recognized him."

"That's not what I meant. His expression was, well, it was odd." The officer gave him a puzzled look. "Did you notice that he was smiling?"

Best-Laid Plans

AFTER RECEIVING NOTIFICATION THAT HIS directives had been carried out in San Francisco, Sturmisch placed a planned call to Adam's cell phone. Fully expecting it to be answered by one of his hit team, he grew impatient after the third ring and was about to hang up and call back when someone answered.

"Hello?" he spoke at first, trying to sound like this was just a friendly call.

"Ah, Mr. Swann, hello. Sorry, my phone was in my vest pocket on the back of the chair."

Not expecting to hear Adam's voice, he immediately let his anger be known. "Finally. Took you long enough to answer. I thought you were perhaps being evasive."

"Of course not. I suppose you've already heard about our little mishap here," Adam reported and turned to one of the bodyguards in his presence and whispered, "Somebody forgot their meds."

"No, I haven't heard. Enlighten me," Sturmisch demanded with instant irritation.

"Some idiot took a pot shot at the stage and missed. No injuries of consequence occurred, including the infernal clown, who by the way revealed himself to be one Mr. Redgie Lewis. And Mr. Lewis has some information he shouldn't have, but don't worry. I'm taking care of it." Adam wasn't quite sure why, but he knew that keeping this loose end to himself was a card up his sleeve, should he ever need it.

Feigning concern, Sturmisch made a suggestion. "If you are in danger, we can certainly cancel tomorrow night's participation in the formal debate. If someone is out to do you harm, I simply won't have it," he offered.

"Not to worry. Of course I'm going to participate tomorrow night. Security will be tightened, and it will be fine. Of course, I am grateful for your concern," Adam lied.

"If you literally dodged a bullet today, I just don't know about you assuming further risk," Sturmisch lied back.

"It's what we've been working for, sir, and I'll not be cowered into silence. Besides, I have this new security team you put in place for me, and they did a splendid job today. No worries." Adam winked at the security officer seated next to him in the coach, punctuating the fact that he had put in a good word for them. The security officer remained a statue.

"All right then," Sturmisch conceded. "If you feel secure, we will proceed with plan A as scheduled." Without the formality of a good-bye, Sturmisch ended the call. Had anyone been in his physical presence at that moment, the Gleau he exhibited could have melted human flesh. Immediately he called the security officer in charge. The statue answered on the first ring.

"I'm assuming the twit is within earshot," Sturmisch stated as calmly as possible. "Excuse yourself and tell me what happened."

The statue did as he was asked, covering the mouthpiece and explaining to Adam that it was a business call. His Gleau showed no deception, and the officer used the bathroom facilities as a makeshift phone booth. Without making Sturmisch ask again, the officer began his explanation without excuse. "The targets were acquired and the site picture was perfect, but following the shot, a target of interference took both rounds."

"Are you kidding me? Please tell me you are because such blatant incompetence will not be tolerated!" Sturmisch spoke with vehemence.

"You can watch it yourself, sir. Less than a millisecond after initiation of the timed shots and at the precise intersection of both, an unknown interrupted what should have been a clean result." The officer knew the reality of this screwup made little difference to Sturmisch.

"An unknown? Does this superman have an identity? Because I may have some openings soon in security detail!" Beyond livid, threats were always resorted to when things didn't go Sturmisch's way.

"At this time, the identity of the unintended victim is not known, and he appears to have been a homeless person, but you may be correct about the superman part."

Intrigued by this remark, Sturmisch resisted any further personal attacks and begged the officer to explain. "Oh? And what miraculous feat would cause you to mention that?"

"Because, sir, at the moment of the shot, he had to defy gravity and be ten feet in the air to intercept the rounds," the officer stated plainly.

Sturmisch ended the call. He was growing weary of dealing with "wee, the people."

The Lecture

AVING TASTED THE BITTERNESS OF the unexpected, Sturmisch thought a spot of tea might help him swallow the unappetizing news he was served. What was the world coming to when the supposed professionals could screw up a simple and well-planned inside assassination? Disgust didn't begin to touch his view of the situation. Far more irritating than the survival of his intended targets was all the work that must be done to rectify the failure. Just what were the odds of being undone by some inconsequential homeless derelict in the wrong place at precisely the right time? Probably staggering, Sturmisch thought. Now the General's debut must be postponed, and the perfect opportunity had been wasted. The demise of Adam and the Redgie clown could be arranged at a future date, but it would lack the drama and poignancy of a successful Presidio execution. In contrast, the operation to eradicate those responsible for the Jase Garrett interview was, at least, a partial success. Sturmisch could almost forgive the shortfall of that exercise due to the use of nonprofessional gang hires and the interference of that infernal Indian. But this failure by the experts, this was inexcusable. As loose ends, it was with forethought of regret that these paid professionals were going to be eradicated after the assumed success of their mission. Regret was now replaced with deserved disdain.

Seated at his desk and wresting his ruminations from what the past denied change, he focused his thoughts on what his next move should be. Steeped and artificially sweetened, his tea was finally cool enough to consume. He brought the cup to his lips and savored one of the few physical delights he allowed himself. His eyelids were half-closed as he drew in the tepid brew until a gross movement in his peripheral vision caused a shudder of surprise that allowed tea to dribble down his chin. A shaky hand placed the teacup on its saucer while the other shaky hand retrieved a napkin to dab his chin. This all took place with his eyes glued to the shadowed figure with a dazzling outline that loomed behind him half a room away. None of his sophisticated protection and surveillance equipment had warned him of this potential intruder. Still somewhat startled but feeling less naked and vulnerable when his hand located his tiny Bernardelli, he swiveled around and managed to speak.

"Who goes there?" To his own ears, his voice sounded weak and thin. He cleared his throat and continued. "This is private property, and *you* are trespassing," Sturmisch spoke louder, trying to give weighted authority to his words.

"Relax, sir. I'm here only for conversation," Ben's voice echoed.

"Come into the light," Sturmisch demanded.

"I might request the same of you," Ben answered and moved slowly toward the seated older man whose Gleau was unlike any he had ever seen. A turbulent mass of greenish black contained his form as shots of rusty brown roiled and were consumed like the surface of a septic tank badly in need of pumping. Cords of gray rope would appear and float to the surface, strangling portions of the dark mass and pulling them inward. His perfectly cut crop of silver-gray hair was slicked to perfection, not a strand out of place, but he was unaware of the bright-red spiny sea urchin perched atop his head like a beret. Hundreds of needlelike blades retreated and were replaced with choreographed precision. As Ben ascended the three wide platform steps to enter the well-lighted portion of the cavernous room, several tendrils of yellow ochre and black oozed forth from about the old man's shoulders, seeming to seek him out. Like a pack of snakelike muzzled Chihuahuas, they sniffed the air in Ben's direction and recoiled like cowards, silently hiding behind their protector.

Instant recognition of the giant Indian replaced initial fear with instant intrigue. "To what do I owe this intrusion?"

Sturmisch stated, trying to hide his surprise of the invasion with nonchalance.

"You owe me nothing," Ben stately plainly.

"Then why are you here!" the old man asked, raising his voice in arrogant anger. "How dare you come into my home uninvited and without cause?"

Ben had heard enough. In less than the blink of an eye, Ben was close enough to whisper in Sturmisch's ear, "Forgive me." In an instant beyond the ability of the decrepit man to react, Ben was standing again in the same spot he was prior to his apology.

Visibly startled but refusing to break bearing, Sturmisch decided engagement would be his distraction. "Nice trick. Am I supposed to be impressed or frightened?"

"Neither," Ben answered.

"Then I suggest you cut to the chase and say your piece," Sturmisch responded, giving himself precious moments to concoct an offer to gain the exquisite power this man possessed. Caught off guard or not, Sturmisch was a businessman. *This day of failure might be salvaged after all*, he thought. Having what he sought be presented in this fashion was pure serendipity, and it was an opportunity he would not waste.

"I am here simply to deliver a message," Ben began. "Your debt has been paid."

"And what debt might that be?" Sturmisch scoffed and once again picked up his tea. If this man was here to do him harm, he would have done it by now, so he felt safe in the assumption that his demise was not part of the plan. He withdrew his hand from the pocket of his cashmere cardigan, leaving the Bernardelli stowed from sight and used his now free hand to steady his teacup. "I am not aware of any debt I owe. Who do you work for?"

"That is immaterial. The point is that you no longer owe the debt. It has been paid," Ben reiterated.

"It is not immaterial to me, but if your business is complete, and I'm assuming you are done, you may show yourself out the same way you came in." His tea was now cold, and he abandoned it after half a sip.

"You are forgetting your manners," Ben said sternly.

"Oh? Am I?" Sturmisch replied with an expression that could have been prompted by a gas pain but was rooted more in loathing. "Would these be the same manners that allowed you to invade my privacy without invitation? You said it yourself, I owe you nothing. Now get out!" The old man turned his back on Ben. He knew the Indian wouldn't leave immediately. He may have completed his assigned duty, but Sturmisch could tell there was more on his mind. And that was fine because there was more on Sturmisch's mind as well.

Holding a single gnarled index finger in the air, Sturmisch turned around to address Ben. "One last thing," he began, but Ben was gone. He muttered a curse of regret for having misread the giant and perhaps missed his best opportunity to co-opt the power he sought. Returning to face his desk, a jolt of surprise rocked him where he sat. There was Ben, looming over him from the front of his desk.

"Enough!" Sturmisch shouted, angered by surprise, and slammed one of his bony fists on the desk hard enough to make the teacup rattle. "If you have further business with me, make it known."

"You are a creature of habit, if nothing else," Ben responded, shaking his head.

"Do not attempt to patronize me. You know nothing about me," Sturmisch shot back.

"I know *everything* about you!" Ben boomed, his roar echoing throughout the premises. For the first time, a flash of yellow appeared around Sturmisch, and the darkness that surrounded him seemed to shrink with fear. In a split second, the cowardice of yellow was swallowed up by a tidal wave of putrid darkness, steadily gaining mass in preparation for a rebuttal.

"You may think you know about me, but it can be nothing more than I have allowed to be known." A ripple of violet interrupted the monk's robe of gloom he wore, signaling a new tack being taken. "You, on the other hand, are a complete mystery. I can see by certain of your abilities how you have been able to remain below the radar, but still, it causes me to wonder what agency or organization is still beyond my grasp. Without betraying any secrecy agreements, you could at least give me a hint as to whom I should credit with this near miraculous technology you possess." Sturmisch sounded almost friendly as he feigned a bit of humility. "Surely you understand that eventually I will have what I seek."

Ben was quiet for a moment, not contemplating the ridiculous offer that was just made but rather the pitiful rag of a human being before him. As Sturmisch fancied himself a man of power, this barren soul was so infinitesimally small, so ravaged and consumed with the darkness of hatred, that Ben could barely recall the potential that once existed. "What you seek, old man, will forever be beyond your grasp until you no longer seek it."

"You may address me as Mr. Swann, and if that is too much to ask, 'sir' will do," Sturmisch directed, suddenly keen on the use of proper etiquette. "And kindly keep your riddles to yourself. They are a useless bore. Obviously, you are nothing more than an overgrown errand boy sent to make me aware that this powerful tool exists, and you may inform your employer that I'm prepared to make an offer. Now be gone. Do your job, and don't keep me waiting." With a flourish of his hand, Sturmisch dismissed Ben with the same lack of respect he had routinely shown Daoud.

As his own reality was the only one that existed, Sturmisch prepared to open his laptop to see what other catastrophes needed his attention or at the very least offered some entertainment. It never crossed his mind that his instructions would be ignored because to do so had severe and immediate consequences. When he raised his eyes to see Ben standing in the same spot with arms folded across his chest, he was beyond incensed. He stood and placed both hands upon the desk as to lean forward and deliver both admonishments and orders. "Now see here, you impudent shred of protoplasm! Does your station preclude you to idiocy, or are you being obstinate out of poor habit?" Daggers of crimson, their edges dipped in tar, sliced through the air in scissor-like fashion from Sturmisch's sternum. A more subtle, but all-encompassing light of the purest laser intensity red surrounded him from the waist up.

"Your anger is noted. Your offer has been rejected," Ben informed his angry host. As he spoke, his own Gleau grew with intensity to the point where Sturmisch squinted and shielded his eyes.

"Stop it! You are blinding me!" the old man complained.

"You have been blind your entire adult life, and it has nothing to do with your eyes," Ben remarked with neither humor nor contempt.

"You presume to know anything about my life!" Sturmisch rebuked.

"I told you I know *everything* about you," Ben insisted.

"Then by all means, inform me. Tell me something I do not know," Sturmisch challenged.

"Your mother loves you," Ben stated directly, and his Gleau returned to its normal brilliance.

"Ha!" the now emboldened old man shot back. "You are misinformed to the point of stupidity, but I would say that bit of knowledge was purely a poke in the dark. Try again." Sturmisch had better and more necessary things to do with his time, and no patience was indicated in his Gleau or his words.

"Your mother does love you," Ben said again, with a calm that was an added irritation.

"For your information, you dimwitted lump, the woman who does not deserve that title but who gave birth to me was a *whore* who cared so little for her child that she literally treated it like garbage!" Sturmisch had no idea why he felt compelled to reveal this information, but the shame of it was not his and nor were the consequences. His Gleau cloaked him in the righteous indigo of self-satisfaction.

The response "You are wrong," stung the aged tyrant like a splash of acid. Ben waited stoically to be asked for the truth.

Those were words Sturmisch rarely heard and never twice from the same source without deadly repercussions, but if this man had any valid information, for the sake of utility, he would hear it. "Tell me what you know," he demanded.

"Your mother loved you. She gave her own life to save yours."

Before Ben could say more, Sturmisch responded, "Oh, what fantastic news. Do, please, tell me more of this fairy tale." His words were thick with sarcasm, and Ben ignored him and continued.

"Your mother was the thirteen-year-old daughter of an Irish immigrant maid, beset upon by her mother's employer. Innocent of the impending consequence of surviving the assault, she revealed nothing to protect her own mother's station. News of your birth was not proud information broadcast to any ears other than the Lord of the Manor, who never admitted his crime. For the sake of disguising his deed and placing the blame totally upon your mother, he convinced the maid to smother her grandchild to maintain her employ. Your mother overheard this plan and hid you from danger. She refused to reveal your whereabouts when questioned, and she took that information with her to her death at the hands of the man who fathered you."

"Interesting story," Sturmisch commented. "But even if there is a shred of truth to it, it has no bearing on the here and now."

"Don't you want to know why your life was saved?" Ben asked, ignoring the lack of impact this information seemed to have.

"Enlighten me," he scoffed, but his engagement betrayed his total disinterest.

"Because your mother asked me to," Ben stated.

Sturmisch's mind was in the process of reconfiguring Adam's demise when those preposterous words interrupted his thoughts. He defiantly locked eyes with the Gleauing giant and, with his words, tried to dismiss what was clearly a ruse. "And you expect me to believe this? How should I react? Fall to my knees and offer repentance to some fanciful god farce?"

"That choice is yours," Ben answered straight out. "You were given life, and with it came free will."

"Then I choose now that you respect my wishes and give me what I seek before I put you out of your misery, you insolent ape!" Sturmisch reached into the pocket of his sweater only to find it empty.

"Is this what you were looking for?" Ben laughed.

Sturmisch looked up to see his Bernardelli dangling in the air like a toy captured in a mechanical claw. With near embarrassment, he sought the role of the defenseless victim once again. "First you break into my home, and now you deprive me of my means to defend myself," he accused.

"Defend yourself? From what threat?" Ben inquired with a recognized calm that Sturmisch often used to psychologically torture his prey before execution.

"I will concede that you have gained the upper hand in these negotiations, and I will offer once and only once more a suitable recompense for the technology you have so effectively demonstrated, but I insist that we conclude our business because I have more pressing issues that beckon my attention." Sturmisch sat down in his chair with the manner of a judge issuing his final verdict.

"You demand the power of something that you declare does not exist, therefore you demand nothing, and that is what you shall receive. Your debt is paid, and our business is done." Ben knew his words would fall upon ears that could most certainly hear, but Sturmisch's heart was deaf.

Already dismissing Ben's parting words as they had no bearing on the case, Sturmisch tossed out a final question as one would pat a child on the head for trying their best. "Before you go, might I ask what the payment of my debt purchased?"

"Yes," Ben granted. "The free will of another preserved free will based on the truth."

"Oh goody," the old man condescended. "So glad it wasn't wasted on something worthwhile." A surge of rancid putrescent light overtook him as the hint of a smile appeared on his face.

Before Ben traveled away from his hellish company, he left him with a thought to chew on. "I would expect no less from a man who spent a lifetime hating a mother he never knew while learning from the man who fathered and raised him."

Ben was gone, and the Bernardelli dropped to the floor.

Not-So-Fond Farewell

HAVING FINISHED HIS SHOWER, REDGIE offered the facilities to the vet, who wasted little time accepting. In the adjoining room of their suite, the remaining two of the group were tending to much the same. A knock at the outside door signaled what Redgie thought was their pizza delivery, but when he answered, he was greeted by a pleasantly Gleauing plainclothes police officer and a uniformed backup who, it appeared, did not share his partner's good intentions.

"How may I help you?" Redgie instinctively greeted the detective.

"I am Detective Barns," he introduced himself and flipped open his identification for Redgie's quick perusal as he stepped just inside the threshold of Redgie's room. "Are you Redgie Lewis?"

"Yes, sir, I am." Standing there in only a pair of jeans and holding a wet towel, Redgie excused his condition. "Sorry about my less-than-informal attire. I just got out of the shower and thought you were the pizza guy." Redgie left the door to the room open and grabbed a clean shirt from the bed. Pulling it over his head, he smiled and extended his hand.

Detective Barns awkwardly refused the friendly gesture, making it clear that this was strictly a business call. "Mr. Lewis, my department has some questions we'd like you to answer about events that took place earlier today at Baker Beach."

"That's fine by me. I'll help if I can. And I've got a few questions of my own too," Redgie replied, still smiling.

"If you would accompany us, Mr. Lewis, this should take less than an hour," the detective offered.

"If it's all the same to you, I'll answer anything right here. And I'll even share my pizza," Redgie added with a good-humored chuckle.

As the detective declined the invitation and again insisted they answer questions in an office setting, Redgie noticed a change in the Gleau around the uniformed officer standing just beyond the door to his room. The sour gray-green aura had intensified, and now blackish shards sprang from his chest.

Three doors down from Redgie's room, a woman and three small children were preparing to reenter their room. The woman fed the plastic key card into the slot several times before the door buzzed open. Before she had ushered the little ones through the door, the shouting officer got her attention.

"Put the gun down!" he shouted and looked toward the woman while pointing his service revolver in the open door of Redgie's room. "I said put the gun down!" he yelled again. Having established the woman as his witness to what would be declared a case of self-defense, he fired a shot.

Caught off guard and flabbergasted by the actions of his attending uniformed partner, Detective Barns was not prepared. "What the—" was all he managed to say before Redgie tackled him to the floor between the two beds as the first shot was fired. As swift as Redgie's reaction was, the bullet managed to find the detective's right shoulder. A second shot went through the mattress and grazed Redgie's hip before disappearing under the far bed. Fearing yet another shot, the detective managed to retrieve his Glock from under his jacket and prepared to defend against the insane officer. Instead of another shot, the pair on the floor heard a loud thud and yelling.

"Don't you move a muscle!" the burly man yelled at the attacker, now flat on his belly outside the doorway with a human refrigerator perched on his back. The vet exited the bathroom wearing only a towel and quickly attended to the two men in the room.

"I'm okay," Redgie insisted. "But you'd better take a look at our friend here." Redgie yelled to the burly man. "Have you got him?"

"He's not going anywhere, and his weapon is secured. Just get your friend there to call this in so response knows who the good guys are. Are you okay?" the burly man asked.

"I'll live for now. Got grazed where I sit."

"We're still gonna get ya looked at," the vet broke in. "And our friend here could definitely use a medic," he added while maintaining pressure on the detective's shoulder wound.

While all of this was happening, the witness woman had called the front desk to report what she had seen, and with that, the manager had called 911. A swell of patrons emerged from their rooms to assess the situation. A gentleman who identified himself as off-duty security for a local mini mall stepped forward to question the burly man in the act of detaining a law enforcement officer.

"What's going on here?" the security guard asked as his Gleau produced alternating indications of caution and authoritarian alert. "Officer, are you in need of assistance?" His glower was directed at the burly gent still straddling the uniformed body in the walkway.

With a wide smile and cool demeanor, the big guy redirected the do-gooder's attention. "You'll need to take your questions to his boss. He's the one this guy just shot, in the room there, the detective," he indicated with a jut of his chin.

"Oh?" the confused security guard responded.

Mustering his strength, Detective Barns did his best to rid the situation of a potential complication. "Sir, we have backup on the way and these men saved my life. If you would, please see to it that the parking area is clear for the ambulance." Out of breath and going into shock, Detective Barns hoped this designated responsibility was enough to turn this well-intentioned problem into a distant solution.

"Yes, sir," the man replied and instantly did as he was asked.

Per Detective Barn's phone in of the incident, no fewer than five state and local law enforcement vehicles arrived due to the 10-00 code, as well as two ambulances and a herd of reporter types. In the midst of this circus, a young man in a red cap appeared on the scene trying to be heard over the commotion. "Did somebody here order a pizza?"

Sturmisch wasted no time redirecting his thoughts the instant the interloper vanished. It was a detail he would deal with later. He did briefly concede that it was an interesting interlude, but nothing that was imparted would have any bearing whatsoever on the completion of his life's work. Decades of careful cultivation were about to bear ripe fruit, and little more than a gentle breeze would allow gravity to bring it down to earth. It wasn't the most effective way to harvest humanity, but it disguised exactly where blame for the bruises should be placed. Sturmisch contemplated the coming fall that would precede the final fall.

To be sure the winds were blowing in his favored direction, Sturmisch downloaded several of the national daily news journals he subscribed to. His market manipulations had things yo-yoing at high-enough levels to encourage buying on the staged upswing that made his sells profitable. He had bought and sold enough economically imprudent politicians that he had half the world in debt beyond two generations. His shell companies were busy buying up companies that produced any necessity, often moving them beyond borders without notice, including means of personal defense. Regulations in the name of clean everything had forced shutdown of a good bit of the coal industry and relocation of refineries as planned. It had taken less than forty years for his bogus department in charge of crude oil independence to cripple an industry that affected nearly every other. It pleased him beyond words that in the name of all things natural, to the exclusion of humanity, he had fooled so many into sabotaging themselves and financially bankrupting humanity. Of course, the cost on paper didn't matter to Sturmisch. He could print all of that he needed. The real payment would be made in lives, in service to him or in the ground beneath his feet.

A headline brought a sneer of a smile to his face. The occasional lunatic going berserk on his own was an unplanned bonus that camouflaged Sturmisch's staged aggressions, which aided greatly to dismiss the foolish notion that each man could govern himself. This was being done incrementally with a constant barrage of stories about man's inhumanity to man in every form imaginable. Individuals left to their own devices statistically lose control at some point in their lives; therefore, it had to make sense that self-control was not only impractical, but a form of devastation to society. The people must demand their own constraints, and they were beginning to do just that. Comparisons to days gone by when a measure of civil law, mutual respect, and strong community loyalty kept things in check had to be discredited. The burgeoning population had to lose its ability to form cohesive bonds of security and become disjointed and fragile. Most of all, there had to be a sense of helplessness and mistrust.

Mr. Swann had catered to the ignorance he had created by providing unmitigated distortions and fabrications that once denied or defended became solid repeatable reality. By first convincing a population that they were brilliant, he had also convinced them that they could not be lied to, so they were content to question nothing. His sneer nearly became a grin as he fantasized about printing all of his outright frauds in a new publication called the *Denial Times*. Do this or that, and life will be wonderful and fair, he taught them. But if you do this or another, your money will disappear, your children will die, and you will have to eat poison for breakfast. No convincing was necessary that he could bring his hoards to a foam-mouthed pitch by simply accusing someone of a particular intention. It had to be presented with tabloid expertise. Pure fact would never stir enough emotion. Things had to be exaggerated, contorted, and focused upon to create the emotional kindling for his ultimate conflagration between the numbed apathetic and the wholly irritated. All of this social engineering and polarization was done in the name of caring, of course, when in fact he cared for none. Every last being on this planet would be either his servant or dead. It was to be their only choice. Those who were unable to serve would be taken care of in a manner befitting their contribution to his society. If only *Soylent Green* was a reality, Sturmisch mused, it would be one way that Grandma and Grandpa could really "give back to society."

One segment of that society that nearly made Sturmisch swell with pride in what he had accomplished was the children. If it wasn't for them and their irresponsible tendencies and self-centered id, his entire plan would have been impossible. He knew that the weakness in any adult could be found through a child, any child, including the child the adult once was. The little brats had to first be put on a pedestal, made untouchable and revered. It isn't that children weren't already cherished, but their value had to be announced and made official by the experts. Then laws could be passed regarding all forms of state-dictated action that must be adhered to on behalf of a child. Isolated instances of genuine abuse were showcased as what could happen to any child or even *every* child. Not even the most diligent parent was capable of avoiding every pitfall that existed for themselves, let alone a child. The experts were quick to point out that parents were only people, and people make mistakes; therefore, since parents made mistakes, they needed guidelines.

So in the interest of doing everything right for a child, every advantage could be taken of the innocent parent if necessary. Children had become unpunishable. After all, if children don't lie and they have had that notion rather than consequences for their actions drilled into their little heads, they were then free to believe their own lies as well as those heaped upon them so-called caring adults. If there was such a thing as God—and Sturmisch knew there wasn't—he would thank him greatly for this weakness.

Sturmisch knew children weren't stupid; they had to be taught what to ignore all the while being praised for their acumen. And with that action, Sturmisch had never been more successful. The majority of the last four generations of children had been taught that the experts—not their parents—had their best interests at heart. Certain children with the proper leanings learned to work the system. Bearing false witness and being irresponsible afforded them revenge as well as a possible monetary gain. The child had the power to wave the magic social services wand and destroy a parent who denied them unearned privilege, have a teacher fired with false claims of sexual abuse for a deserved bad grade, punish and win prizes in custody battles, or just get paid outright for contrived outrageous behavior in the form of "crazy checks." Preparations for the senior prom were made a year in advance to give those with foresight enough time to bear a child and get the checks coming to afford a proper dress and limo. And there was absolutely no shame in taking any undeserved gain because, after all, they were told it was free. Well-intentioned plans, like good pharmaceuticals, often have bad side effects. The childhood social ills cure was in, but it was these side effects that Sturmisch counted on. These subtle lessons were the basic thought patterning Sturmisch needed for his army of today, and the result was nothing less than spectacular. The previous generations were at the mercy of their children, and the children belonged to Sturmisch.

An unintentional barometer of Sturmisch's success in capturing the minds of the young were movie ticket sales. Rehashed plots, even those hundreds of years old, were dolled up with special effects and maybe some sexual situation passed off as romance and sold to current generations as "new" entertainment that a rather high percentage mistook for actual historic fact. In the world of Sturmisch's new reality, distinguishing fact from fiction was no longer necessary. Associating any proper historical figure with a fictional bogeyman created a new history that adoring fans took as gospel and filled the pockets of well-heeled movie moguls who smiled all the way to the bank. And Sturmisch let them. They were so impressed with themselves that they too failed to see the handwriting on the wall, and Sturmisch was content with their blindness. They were such dedicated and useful tools that

Sturmisch didn't have the heart to tell them that they were gain-fully employed in the destruction of their own paying audience.

The transformation may not have been total, but enough of the loyalty to family had been destroyed that Sturmisch knew they would be loyal to that check in the mailbox. The check may have been intended for the basics of life, but what it really pur-chased was disharmony, irresponsibility, and willfulness. Money well wasted, in Sturmisch's view.

Much to his chagrin, a percentage of young adults did not immediately succumb to the hijacking of their parents' influence, but there were ways of punishing them in the interest fairness. Often, when very young, children learned by experience that there was safety in silence. Questioning a teacher, when what was taught as rational fact ran in opposition to what they were taught at home, made them targets. The unquestioning children followed the example of a teacher, and when a teacher publicly humiliated a target, that lesson was not lost on their observant peers who were quickly persuaded to follow suit. The yet dis-closed targets hid in silence while their opportunistic class-mates directed arrows unmolested and were subtly praised for their lock-step accuracy. Easily denied as the true situation, the new unfairness that forbade but one opinion was established. If you couldn't prove it by the favored teaching, it wasn't reality. Students were graded on their opinions, often receiving poor grades for not toeing the party line, often with the reasoning that they did not provide enough substantive support, but Sturmisch knew that enough support would never exist. So it was easy to conquer a differing opinion with the stroke of a teacher's red pen. Even if you couldn't change the mind, a subjective assessment could destroy the potential of a child who attempted to circum-vent reeducation.

The new fairness was instilled in those currently teaching by the first outspoken and dedicated generation of Sturmisch's army. His timing had to be perfect, and as usual, it was. Those prone to thoughts of loyalty and freedom were weeded out unceremoniously with an event dictated by cowards who could not brand it a *real* war. Sending our brave men and women into the path of a tsunami of death and destruction was deemed a police action. Sturmisch didn't care what they called it and knew they were just covering their political assets. His rabble rousers were busy stateside as well, gathering the safe and spoiled on every acre of higher learning to object to everything. Expandable minds were encouraged to expand farther with the aid of illicit drugs that did little more than render the user the victim of a temporary lobotomy. Moral dictates that had in the past saved humanity from its own animalistic folly were deemed unfair restrictions. The act of procreation lost its revered status and became nothing more than a carnival ride with free tickets and no height restriction.

Sturmisch knew his work had paid off when the same generation that claimed insufferable injustices from their parent generations came to power. The children of the near past who had once carried flowers and banners in support of peace and love claimed freedom by ignoring personal hygiene, sated themselves on brain-warping chemicals, and adopted the sexual mores of a dysfunctional troop of chimpanzees were in a position to give Sturmisch his prize. It was just as Sturmisch knew it would be because *he* engineered it.

Those women demanding that powers at large stay out of their womb had gladly handed over their entire bodies to the sanctioning of strangers. Where quality of life was once the decision of the individual, it was now determined by bean counters who determined quality of life based on economic feasibility. Defective chromosomes were expensive and therefore negated, and the definition of defective changed with necessity. If the conditions of your body outweighed your ability to contribute to the general coffers, too bad for you. As you are nothing but your body from an economic standpoint, you could be disposed of as a detriment to society with a simple trial by medical science. The moral conscience attributed to the disreputable loony bins of the past was given charge over all medical administration because no matter how caring and sincere you were, cost was the ultimate deciding factor. The most used phrase in medicine would now be "I'm sorry." The cuckoo now had a new nest. Sturmisch snickered silently.

Our medical professionals would still provide the best care to be found anywhere in the world, and their success percentages would skyrocket due to screening of the patients placed in their care. Of course, these statistics gave little credit to the skill of the medical community and much credit to the new system. To disprove any favoritism, the media quickly showcased its selected successes and hid the mountain of failures. If Grandma didn't vote a certain way, Grandma's hip replacement could be denied. The bean counters would never have to disprove their subjective hypocrisy because general welfare would always outweigh that of a single individual. Sturmisch knew his social welfare mind meld was complete when no one questioned the fact that heads of state and millionaire flunkies always jumped the line for timely medical care. Sturmisch's expert board was now the determining factor in which lives were important and which ones were not. Though this was nothing new, any complaints by the chickens were now sent directly to the fox.

His daydreaming moved forward in time as he approved the day's headlines that touted the proper distractions and ignored any facts that might warn the populace of their impending new lack of real freedom. The weather, sports happenings, illegal activities of the Hollywood crowd, anything distressing in Europe, and at least one senseless killing—preferably involving a small innocent child and an assault weapon—were the daily requirements. Political uprisings that evolved into civil wars and civilian protests of fixed election results were a mainstay of Sturmisch's "sidetrack them with chaos" formula. As always, there was a bit of "too good to be true" news on the green front. Sturmisch laughed inwardly about how his experts had convinced governments to invest billions of taxpayer dollars into the idea of biomass fuels that didn't exist in marketable amounts and mandated its use by the military who were now fined for not using what they couldn't buy at any price. When it came to the shell-and-pea game, Sturmisch was an expert, and the taxpayers were paying him for the production equipment for this phantom fuel.

At this point, the furrows had been cut, the channels fortified, and weaknesses created to let little more than emotional gravity pull the situation toward his desired goal. Adam would appear at the debate the following evening with the scripted details provided for him. It was an art to create a speech that guaranteed everything while seeming to demand nothing and secretly taking everything. If Adam stuck to the script, he would be remembered as the man who gave the ultimate sacrifice for the cause. His untimely death at the hands of the greedy, evil opposition would motivate Sturmisch's army to do battle.

Sturmisch did congratulate himself on being one of the rare patient thinkers in history. Unlike his predecessors in history who sought world domination with war, he would not take the world by force but rather let the world place itself delicately at his feet. Once freedom and liberty were put to death here, where else were they going to go? Mars maybe? Sturmisch chuckled to himself. This was the last territory to conquer, and none of these blind fools would anticipate its scope. There was still the existence of the Gleau and its supposed powers of revealing the truth to contend with, but Sturmisch knew a promise, even an empty one, accompanied by an unfunded check would be all the truth the weak-minded needed.

Satisfied that the news reflected his wishes, Sturmisch thought a nap was in order. He would have to be at his best tomorrow, so proper rest now would ensure a mind like a steel trap. And with that trap now being set and camouflaged properly, all he had to do was wait.

Alone

HOPING JASE AND BEN WOULD back sooner rather than later, Lee reached deep into a tangle of vines to retrieve a ripe green zebra tomato. The cows and steers had returned from the back pasture to escape the flies and mosquitoes and were drinking heavily at the stock tank. Just having them in the paddock near the barn gave her comfort. But comfort from what? she wondered. She placed the tomato in the basket and glanced over her shoulder toward the house. It now possessed something that she didn't find inviting. As it stood, it was an empty shell, and she wondered what on earth would lead her to view it in such a light.

When the phone in her pocket rang, she jumped and answered as quickly as she could, as if hearing another voice would make this anxious feeling go away. She answered, trying to sound more positive than desperate. "Hello there."

"Well, hello there yourself. How are you?" Brett asked.

She wasn't expecting a call from Brett, but with all that had happened today, it was logical. "Couldn't be better," she lied. "I'm in the garden with my hands in the dirt. What's up?"

Not knowing for sure if the news about Blake and Lydia had reached her yet, Brett took an indirect approach. "I was wondering if your brother is available. I need some questions answered, if he can."

"I imagine he's looking for those answers now. He and Ben left a while ago."

"So you've heard, I'm assuming, about what happened at KMIN."

"Yes, most definitely, we heard."

Reading more into her response than he cared to discuss over the phone, he suggested an alternative. "Are you up for some company? Barb wants eggs, and we could both use a change of scenery."

Trying not to sound too eager, company was exactly what she needed at the moment. "That would be great. I've got a basket of ripe tomatoes with your name on it, and I'll put on the coffee."

Brett ended the call with, "We'll be there in twenty. Bye."

Lee wished the call had been longer. Once again, her eyes were drawn to the darkened windows of the house, and it stared back blankly. She shook it off, took in the fact that Bomber was resting easily in front of the barn door, and returned to her task at hand.

The basket was near overflowing by the time Brett and Barbara drove up the lane. Lee met them at the door and made an instant apology. "Hope you'll excuse my mess. Things got put on hold when Ben arrived with Lydia this forenoon."

"Lydia was here?" Brett questioned as he escorted Barbara into the house.

"Yes. Ben brought her here. She was shaken up, but physically, she's okay."

"I knew it!" Brett exclaimed. "I knew when they showed the security tape of her vanishing into thin air that Ben had to be part of this. It wasn't just a glitch in the video feed."

"Definitely not a glitch," Lee added in agreement. "And now they've gone to do whatever it is they can do." Lee excused herself to wash her hands. "I'll be right back."

Knowing his way around Lee's kitchen, Brett started the coffee. Lee returned to the kitchen with Lydia's stained blouse in hand and sat in a chair next to Barbara. She tried to rationalize away the instant sadness that overcame her and was displayed in her Gleau as ripples of ocean blue.

"You've had a lot to deal with today, Lee," Barbara comforted.

"I know Jase and Ben can take care of themselves, but I just can't shake this worry," Lee volunteered.

Reversing traditional roles, Brett placed a newly brewed mug of coffee in front of Lee. "I wouldn't worry about the guys, Lee." That said, Lee placed her face in her hands and let go tears that could no longer be held at bay. And as many men are ill equipped when it comes to dealing with that mystery, he instantly apologized for upsetting her.

"No, no, it was nothing you said," Lee replied, wiping the tears aside, and without thinking, she resorted to dark humor to pull herself together. "It's just that I take cream in my coffee," she stated with exaggerated importance and promptly burst out laughing.

Taken by surprise for a second or two, Brett and Barbara both joined her in a laugh of relief. First flabbergasted and then amused, Brett let her know that she had him worried, albeit briefly, but worried just the same. "You had me going there for a sec, Lee."

"I'm sorry," she admitted, still laughing through tears. "I just can't put my finger on any one thing that has me so upset. Certainly Blake's death is worth tears, but it's more than that," she tried to explain.

Barbara reached over and put her hand on Lee's. "Considering what a full plate you've had lately, it doesn't come as a surprise that you should worry about the guys. For crying out loud, your missing brother reappears, then the Gleau is revealed, your son returned to a war zone, you've been shot at, you lost Semi, and all while worrying about everyone around you, and not to mention, having to deal with my brother!"

Her last comment brought a look of surprise to Brett's face and another full-bodied laugh from Lee. Regaining her composure, Lee managed to reply, "Well, when you put it that way," and the two of them laughed again. "Aside from that, Mrs. Lincoln, how was the play?" Lee continued. Brett was not laughing but couldn't help smiling.

"Okay, you two. If I may make a suggestion, it's Friday night, and that means prime rib at the Road Kill. Let me take us out to eat."

"I don't know," Lee hesitated.

"Oh, I think that's a great idea," Barbara encouraged.

"Yes it is," Brett agreed, "because you always cook for everyone. Let me do this."

"Yes, let him do this, Lee. It beats having him cook for us!"

Before Brett could scold Barbara, Lee spoke up. "What if the guys return while we're gone?"

"We'll leave them a note. We won't be gone long," Brett nearly begged.

"Okay," Lee finally agreed. "Give me a couple minutes to clean up."

While Lee changed into something fit for public view, Brett jotted their whereabouts and tentative return time on an envelope and placed it conspicuously on the kitchen table. As they all walked out to the truck, Lee could not help but take one last look toward the barn. Bomber still stood guard, and all was quiet.

The Road Kill

ITH HER WORRY STILL IN tow, Lee felt honored to escort Barbara inside the tiny restaurant as Brett held open the door for his ladies. Less than a dozen tables surrounded by mismatched chairs and a single U-shaped booth crowded the small dining area. Barely separated by a narrow walkway was the bar nearly full of patrons exchanging local news and washing away the dust of the day with a draft or two. A bulletin board just inside the door was completely covered with homemade notices of local goods for sale and services for hire. The trio occupied a suitable table for four, and Lee instinctively took the seat that let her face the door as well as the television above the bar.

Within seconds after they all took a seat, a smiling young waiter appeared to produce menus and ice water and recite the specials of the day. This may not have been the Four Seasons, but the kitchen staff knew their way around a wood-fed oven and grill, so the choice of fare was simple. The waiter took his leave, and before conversation began, Lee noted a pair of local dairy farmers exchanging the current and increasing woes of their business and a husband-and-wife pair of road construction drivers doing much the same. It was plain to see that a chaos of constantly changing and increasing details brought upon those attempting to produce goods and services was taking a toll. Those bringing the chaos were under the illusion that they would remain unaffected as they would simply increase their own income and dole as prices went up. The family farmer and independent truck drivers of the world knew this was madness. Those voting themselves an infinitely larger and larger portion from the finite platter were content to let the cooks grow hungry. And Lee knew stomachs were rumbling.

"A pleasant change, don't you think?" Brett commented, pulling Lee away from her heavy thoughts.

A genuine smile crossed her face as she told him, "Yes, it is. Thank you for insisting that we do this."

"Well, I'd say you were way overdue," Barbara added.

Having no segue other than an awkward one, Brett broached the subject of Lydia's appearance at the farm. "I don't suppose Lydia had any ideas about who could have done what happened today."

Lee knew he was fishing, but she trusted his judgment about what to put and what not to put in the public domain. "Nothing that would have warned her not to walk into that melee, but she did receive a note she was taking to show Blake."

"In the mail?" Brett prompted.

"No. Someone slipped it under her apartment door." Before Lee could elaborate, she noticed all-too-familiar scenes from the said event on the silenced television above the bar. The caption running beneath stated relief by the police that Lydia Corvuso was not abducted as previously feared when her purse and briefcase were found abandoned at the scene. Questioning by police about her departure from the sidewalk at the moment of the blast yielded no clues about who may have been responsible for the deaths of three people and two others in serious but stable condition. Then Lee noticed today's date. "Oh wow! No wonder," she said aloud, realizing that her angst might be generated by a cause she had completely overlooked: the Bad Day. But it was supposed to be gone—or so she thought.

"What's the matter?" Brett asked, noticing her distraction.

Lee shook her head. "I just noticed today's date," she explained openly but without elaboration.

Brett looked pensive for a moment, trying to recall the significance of this date. Then he remembered her first visit to the paper. "Ah, yes," he said with subdued triumph. "Tomorrow is the anniversary of your parent's accident."

"That would certainly explain this anxiety, Lee," Barbara diagnosed. Neither Barbara nor Brett had any knowledge of the Bad Day.

"That very well could be it," Lee agreed and forced a smile to avoid any further explanation, but she was thinking that her Gleau would betray her.

In the next moment, their meals arrived. Welcoming the new focus, Lee put contemplation of the Bad Day aside and found herself with a renewed appetite. In a practiced gesture, Brett switched plates with Barbara and unceremoniously prepared her meal for easy consumption. Without remarking openly, Lee was once again impressed by Brett's automatic dedication to his sister and postponed attacking her own plate. Everything he did for her, when the rare occasion of necessity arose, was treated as an honor and handled as a privilege. Barbara folded her napkin and her hands and said a quick blessing for their meal that included a thank-you for the task Brett now attended to. When the plates were once again exchanged, they all enjoyed a literal rare treat, and Lee made it a point to ignore the television above the bar.

Mention of the letter delivered to Lydia Corvuso wasn't revisited until they were on their way back to Lee's place. She paraphrased the content of the cut-and-paste threat Lydia received, and as they pulled into the drive, Lee thought something looked different. "Did we leave the kitchen light on?"

"No, I don't think we did. The guys must be back," Brett answered. "Now we can both find out what's going on." Lee entered the kitchen ahead of the other two with a, "Hey, we're back." There was no reply. On the table was the note they had left before going to dinner, and in a familiar scrawl was a short and rather cryptic note.

> More to do. Be back late. Don't wait up. See you then.
> Love, Jase.

Brett and Barbara came in as she finished reading. "Shoot, we missed them. He left me this country boy haiku," she added, handing the note to Brett. Unwilling to let her company leave immediately after this setback, Lee offered coffee and fresh-baked brownies.

"I never turn down chocolate in any form," Barbara accepted, noting Lee's disappointment. "At least now you know the guys are okay."

"Kinda," Lee agreed. As she gathered the ingredients for the upcoming brownies, Brett got her to recount the rest of Lydia's emergency visit. While remembering and relaying all the details she could, Barbara got the task of mixing, and Brett made the coffee. In twenty minutes, the story was told, and the brownies were cool enough to cut, though technically still molten.

As night was just hinting of its arrival, Lee gazed hopefully toward the barn. Bomber lay curled in front the door, and all was quiet. Sated on chocolate and caffeine, Brett reluctantly begged their leave.

"Can I help you with chores before we make our way back to town?" he offered.

"Thanks, but I can handle what little there is to do." After a moment of hesitation, she added, "I'll be fine. I'm going to curl up in bed and get some rest until the guys come home. And thanks again for dinner. It was almost as spectacular as the company."

"I agree. We'll have to do it again with the guys. I can imagine Ben finishing off a prime rib in two bites." Brett laughed.

Lee gave Barbara a farewell hug and promised to let them in on any news the following day. As Brett escorted his sister to their conveyance, Lee closed the ladies up for the night and decided to do the same for herself. A stressful day and a full stomach prompted the need for sleep, and in less than twenty minutes, she was in bed and down for the count.

August 11, 2012

SEATED ON A DUNE WITH her knees pulled to her chest, Lee lifted her head and opened her eyes to a beautiful sight. Already above the eastern horizon, she could feel the early warmth of the sun as it touched all not hidden in the low-angled shadows of sculpted sand. She closed her eyes and let the balmy dreamscape caress and penetrate her soul. Upon reopening her eyes, it occurred to her without the least bit of fear that she was back in the dream. She wondered why.

More with expectation than dread, she searched the stretch of glittering sand in both directions for what she was supposed to learn. For as far as her eyes could see, she was alone. Should she wait? Should she go in search? As she pondered what to do, she stood and walked toward the ocean. Each footfall felt the embrace of soft sanded quartz that grew denser as she approached the water. She turned and walked backward for a few steps, marveling at how the dents in dry sand gradually became discernible evidence of her travel as the moistened sand held the definition of her bare feet. Footprints were something new to this experience. So was the sun being above the horizon when she arrived. The hissing rush of the surf was nothing new, but when she turned to face it and held still, waiting for it to strike an unmoving pose, it did not. A tidal pool marked a sand bar revealed by the retreating tide. The clear coke-bottle green water in the inviting puddle disguised its depth as she tested its wonder and sank to her knees. Laughing, she sought the secure footing of the beach again. The rugged surf had retreated beyond the sandbar, and the breakers became mere ripples as they traversed the pool and limply threw themselves upon the sand in exhaustion. All of this was new.

The swirl of a moon shell half buried in the sand caught her eye, and so did something else. As she bent down to dig up her treasure, movement of both a person and their shadow drew her glance. At a walk that was nearly a run, Jase drew near enough for her to hear his voice over the surf.

"About time you got here!" he welcomed and greeted his sister with a hug she returned in kind.

Kissing Jase on the cheek, his scruffy face felt wonderful. "What do you mean 'about time'? I had no idea I was coming here again in the first place." Lee laughed and hugged him again.

"Beautiful though, isn't it?" Jase observed, taking in the landscape before them.

"Yes, and it's different this time. Better since you got here though," she added.

"Better? Really?" he mused aloud.

"Of course it's better. I have someone to share it with," she said and placed the moon shell in his hand. With an acceptance that was almost automatic, this dream became as real to her as any day spent with Jase on the farm. Checking him out more to admire than critique, she suddenly found herself doing the latter. "Where did you get that shirt? It looks like you pulled it out of a garbage can." She laughed.

"Oh, this old thing?" he joked. "Can't you tell? I'm making a statement!" he embellished.

"Yeah, you are. Garbage Men's Quarterly."

Jase looked down at his rumpled shirt, smiled, and shook his head in agreement. Taking his sister by the hand, he asked, "Want to take a walk?"

"Sure. Can we?" she answered, a bit surprised.

"It's here. May as well walk on it," he replied. Choosing a direction in much the same manner as Dorothy and her three companions at the crossroads on the yellow brick road, Jase pointed to the south, and they began their stroll.

"I've never walked down this way," Lee mentioned as she took in the mirror image of her usual path.

"Me neither," Jase added. For a few minutes they walked without speaking, just enjoying the view and the sensations it offered. Jase was not looking forward to giving his sister the news he must deliver, but she ended his worry.

Lee squeezed his hand and released it, turning toward him and giving him a big sisterly hug. She took both his hands in hers and faced him with a calm he knew all too well. "You're staying here, aren't you," she challenged.

"Not here, exactly," he admitted.

"You know what I meant. You aren't coming back with me, are you?" she rephrased.

"How did you know?"

"I'm your sister. I felt it somehow, I guess." She was quiet for a moment. "I knew it the same way I knew you were coming back. I knew it all along, I think, but never wanted to admit it. But today, when you and Ben left, I felt it."

"I wanted to tell you, but—"

"I know, and it's okay. It wouldn't have changed any-thing, would it?" It was less a question and more an indication of understanding.

"No, I don't think so." Jase took her hand and continued their walk.

"So what happens now?" she asked.

"Well, you'll wake up eventually, of course."

"No, no. I mean with what has been set in motion in the world. Is it going to make a difference?"

"This time, I hope it does."

"What do you mean this time? This has happened before?" Lee asked, hoping she would gain some helpful insight.

"Not exactly this same thing, but many times before. Mixing spirit and flesh has had some interesting consequences, and the battle to acknowledge both while not allowing one to overcome the other is the issue," Jase tried to explain.

"I think we've tried to do just that, haven't we?" Lee posed.

"Every time, but it's a balancing act on this high wire of life. It's hard enough to compensate for the high winds of the physical existence, but the real challenge is when we spiritually blindfold ourselves."

Lee watched her feet as they walked, placing one foot carefully ahead of the other on an imaginary tightrope, and listened intently. As what Jase said sank in, she remarked casually, "So is that what the Gleau is for? To remove the blindfold?"

Jase smiled broadly. "If it was that easy, our problems would be solved. The Gleau is to make people aware of the fact that they are blindfolded in the first place. It's up to the individual to remove it, and even then, they have to choose to see."

Lee stopped walking. "Is it that we're blind to all but this existence, and as we gain knowledge here we discount anything else?"

"That's pretty close. We get impressed with what our technology can prove, but technology isn't the problem. Humanity too often gets impressed with what it can prove. And with themselves. Mystery is renamed myth and discarded."

"I see. So what is the real problem?" Lee asked and began walking back to where they began.

"I guess the best way to put it would be our degenerative tendencies," Jase responded.

Lee thought for a moment, slowing her pace to a near stop, and then demonstrated what she thought he meant. "Sort of like one step forward"—she took an exaggerated step ahead—"and two steps back," she finished, falling slightly behind Jase.

"In a way. As we take a step forward in our understanding of the physical world, we take two steps backward in the reality of our spiritual existence."

"Because we have free will or because we are in animal bodies or both?" Lee asked with a possible answer.

"A bit of both," Jase confirmed. "As spiritual beings capable of extended thought, we try to control."

"I'm assuming you mean other people," Lee posed.

"You assume correctly," Jase answered.

Lee walked a few more steps and paused. "Wow. Talk about a catch-22."

"Precisely," her brother agreed. "The same free will that opens the doors to all the knowledge of all reality can also close the mind to the very spirit from which it is granted. The lion may be the king of beasts, but not a single lion has ever tried to dominate the entire animal world."

Lee listened but at the same time was lost in thought that sought a solution she thought *had* to be obvious. "So what is it exactly that prompts us to close our minds to the spirit?"

"Fear," Jase answered instantly. "The same thing necessary for our physical survival prevents our spiritual evolution when fear is used as a weapon."

"Fear," Lee said out loud, pondering the hundreds of ways fear is a part of human existence. "I guess we use it like any other animal, except…" She trailed off.

"Except what?" Jase prompted.

"We abuse free will. It isn't necessary. Why do we do that?" she let herself wonder.

"It's the dark side of our intelligence and free will when combined in animal form. We do it because we can, and what is really sad is that we think we can get away with it. And as long as recognition of the spirit remains a choice not proven by physical science, fear is a potent weapon."

"Then why not let us have definitive proof of what exists beyond here?" Lee asked earnestly.

Jase laughed heartily, not at her question but at the answer she led him to. "I'm sorry," he said as his laughter subsided. "This is a tough school. It's understood how difficult it can be. Can you imagine what would happen to human existence if everyone knew without doubt they could escape the challenges, the pain, the emotional torment, and the general horrors of humanity that we create and be welcomed into a realm of peace and love and security by simply jumping off a cliff? Why on earth would any of us stay here?"

"Now there's a lovely mental image: human lemmings." Lee laughed. "Okay, I think I see your point. That's why we can't see beyond death. We fear it, so we stay here."

"Well, we fear the pain of death, but you're right. And sometimes we fear the pain of life. Escaping that pain before we're done learning is a sacrifice that carries regret into the next existence."

"So why are we here? What are we supposed to learn, and what do we do with it after we learn it?"

"Now there's the big question. Why are we here?" While Jase gathered his thoughts to provide an answer, Lee noticed that they were nearly back to where they started. "Let me put it this way. We're here to get brighter. If all of existence is a university, this earth, this existence, is prekindergarten."

"Seriously, are we that primitive?" Lee asked, thinking that humanity had made such great strides going from the cave to the double-wide.

"Not primitive. Humanity is young and immature and just learning what there is to learn. But what we learn here has a huge impact on our ability to mature in the next existence."

"I still feel just a little insulted by that whole primitive measure thing." Lee smiled.

"From an earthly perspective, of course we feel all wise and superior. In some circles it's known as the Yertle the Turtle effect," Jase said, cracking them both up. "But seriously, look at us. Even as adults we act like preschoolers. We still steal each other's crayons, covet toys brought in for show-and-tell, say and do things we know are wrong because we think the teacher won't see, and knock each other down on the playground. In spite of all of our so-called advancements, we're a devolving mess who label ourselves as adults based on nothing but age while behaving like nincompoops!"

Lee found both humor and truth in his caricature of humanity. "But we do learn, right? I mean, we learn the difference between right and wrong and strive to live accordingly."

"Most do. But there are a few who never learn more by choosing lessons of brutal ease. The ultimate expression of power to them is to deprive others of free will while using their own as a weapon. They think they are smart enough to beat the system because they can't imagine past this one. They break the rules as they disrespect the teacher. They continue to steal and lie. They learn to instill fear and terror to control those around them. Some are bullies and others just manipulators who lie about their intent, but they are equally drawn to the shadows."

"Hmmm. They grow, but they never mature spiritually. They become shadow dwellers."

"Unfortunately, yes," Jase concurred. "They despise the free will of others. To believe in anything greater than themselves is to deny their own greatness. Admitting a mistake or misdeed means they weren't smart enough, or clever enough, or worst of all, powerful enough. They will exercise free will, cling to their dark ways, and seek control even as it means potential destruction of humanity. They will remain childish, soulless animals by choice, denying what faith cannot prove, and thinking they can become all powerful in this existence by denying the next. But the next will come for them as surely as it comes for every living thing. They can't deny that."

They reached the spot where their footfalls began. Lee wanted Jase to continue explaining, not because she thought he could make his point any clearer, but because she wanted to prolong her time with him. This parting would not be sweet, but she would deny her bitterness as she knew Jase would always be with her. "I guess it's time to wake up, huh?" she mustered the courage to say and hugged him furiously.

"It's Saturday. You can sleep in a while. Besides, I brought someone with me to see you," Jase whispered in her ear.

She released him and stared into his face and asked excitedly, "Who?" She looked left and right and saw only bare dunes and ocean. Then she felt something. A soft cool pressure grazed the calf of her right leg. She looked down and was met by a set of sparkling light-blue eyes. Semi purred loudly and meowed a greeting that was unmistakably him. Her legs felt weak with happiness as she bent down and took him in her arms. He was soft and warm and light as a feather as she pulled him to her chest. Customarily, he wrapped a paw on either side of her neck and nuzzled her chin with his face.

Jase smiled as each enjoyed the treasure of the other. Semi then put both paws on one side of her neck and slid his face under Lee's hair and rested on the back of her neck. He relaxed and purred, giving her a gift she truly missed. "Thank you," she mouthed to Jase.

"I pulled a few strings," he joked. "And you're welcome."

Knowing their time was short, Lee asked if there was anything she could do on Jase's behalf after she awoke. "Nah, I took care of everything before I left. But there is one thing I'd like you to remember."

"Sure, anything," she replied.

"I'm not exactly sure who I'm quoting here, but it says things in simple terms. 'There is a light within a man of light, and he lights up the whole world. If he does not shine, he is darkness.' Got it?"

He repeated it for Lee, having her say it with him so it was committed to memory. "Write it down when you wake up."

"I will," she promised. He gave her shoulder a squeeze, and as she hugged Semi, she closed her eyes and left the beach.

As sleep released its hold on her consciousness, she lay still, opening only her eyes and preserving the feeling of Semi nestled about her neck. It lasted as long as she needed it to, and she smiled, stretched, and kicked off the sheet. Contentment followed her into the kitchen to start coffee brewing, and as she stared out the double windows facing the barnyard, she realized why. She would never lose a connection fashioned from the most durable substance in this universe and beyond—love. She smiled at that thought and glanced over at Semi's rocker. The seat wasn't empty. On it was a piece of paper with a three-word message, and beside that was a waterworn moon shell. The message made her laugh. It said, "Write it down!"

The Letters

LEE'S MOOD OF EASE FOLLOWED her into the noon hours of the day, and it was no surprise at all when Brett and Barbara pulled in the lane unannounced. She knew Brett would figure out ahead of most who the vagrant killed at Baker Beach really was. The photo of the lifeless, unkempt face would have been a mystery to all save those closest to him, but the dog tag was unmistakable. With faces full of condolence that matched the Gleau of cerulean sadness that surrounded them both, they met Lee sitting on the bench next to the kitchen door.

"What can I say, Lee, other than I am truly sorry for your loss," Brett spoke with a heaviness Lee had never heard before. She stood, and he met her with an embrace that seconded his words.

"Thanks, Brett. I know he was fond of you too."

Barbara was next, hugging Lee gently and echoing her brother's sentiment. "If there is anything we can do for you, please know it would be an honor," Barbara added.

"You're doing that right now," Lee offered with a smile and asked them both inside. They were welcomed to a table, in traditional Lee fashion, loaded with farm fare fit for a king. Taking note of the look of amazement on Brett's face and Barbara's well-trained nose detecting the evidence of her efforts, Lee explained, "I couldn't help myself. Cooking is my therapy."

"And eating is my therapy," sounded a deep male voice in the kitchen entry.

"Ben!" Lee exclaimed with both surprise and gratitude. "I was hoping you would make an appearance today to shed some light on this for all of us," she said, dragging him to the table by both hands.

"I'm glad you are both here," Ben addressed the Hume siblings. "Jase wanted me to speak with all of you, but there is one more person who must be here to hear what I have to tell you."

"By all means, we'll be happy to have them," Lee encouraged.

"Save me a drumstick, Brett. I'll be right back," Ben acknowledged and was gone.

"Geez, that was a short stay," Brett commented, wide-eyed. "And why on earth would he single me out when it came to saving food for him," Brett said, picking up two fried chicken legs and attacking them furiously.

Humor may not have been the typically appropriate approach to this situation, but Lee thought it was just what this day needed and laughed at Brett's antics. Before the smile left her face, she looked outside. "Boy, he wasn't kidding when he said he'd be right back." Emerging from the barn was Ben and someone else, a dark-skinned man with a smile as broad and exceptional as his Gleau. "I suspect I know who that is," Lee guessed and went to welcome them both at the door.

"You must be Lee," Redgie spoke as she opened the door and ushered them in.

"Mr. Lewis, I presume," she responded and extended her hand. In his startlingly familiar grasp, his steadfast devotion to the truth enveloped her, and she was eager to have him join their gathering.

When the introductions had been made and the five had settled around Lee's kitchen table, Ben pulled a folded envelope from his shirt pocket. "When I had everyone here, Jase wanted me to read this." In his smooth baritone Ben began.

> Hello to you all,
>
> By now you all know that my mission here came to a close yesterday. And though it may not be apparent, it was a successful mission. I did not succeed on my own. Each of you had, and still has, an important role to fulfill. The mission is not complete. My life goes on just as it does for

each of you, though in another existence. I therefore ask one favor of each of you while in this one.

Brett, I ask that you make the following letter a matter of public record.

Redgie, I ask that you continue to do battle with logic as your sword.

Ben, I ask of you what you already know. Protect our friends.

Barbara, I ask that you open the eyes of the world with a heart that sees what cannot be seen.

And, Lee, I ask that you take care of our family.

What I ask of each of you is a request, not an order, but I ask it of each of you because the truth is coming.

The five sat in silence until Redgie spoke up. "I'm in."

"So am I," Brett responded.

"I think he knew he could count on all of us," Barbara stated with confidence. "But I'm not really sure what I'm being asked to do."

"It'll come to you," Ben reassured.

"I seem to be getting a lighter load than the rest of you, but I'm in as well," Lee agreed.

Then Ben handed a second envelope to Brett. "This is what he wants to be made public in his name."

"Can we read it now?" Brett asked, staring at the envelope like a kid with a wrapped present the day before his birthday.

"I don't see why not," Ben conceded.

With that said, Brett carefully and with just a bit of exaggerated fanfare took a knife to the short end and pulled out the folded handwritten pages.

To all who choose to listen,

I am no longer here, but the Gleau remains. It is my wish that each of you, every living soul, heeds and acknowledges the truth it reveals. As with any test of faith, you cannot be forced to believe what is yet a mystery, so I ask you merely to think.

I was asked why this is happening now, and I answered because now is when it is necessary. It is necessary because the earth is finite in both size and duration. You have reached a point in your civilization where there is no more room for second chances. You must now decide (again) which way humanity will go. One choice will lead to all truth. The other will lead to your self-destruction. Knowing this, how will you choose this time?

Over and over again in the past, humanity chose not to see the truth and instead chose destruction. Yes, you have been at this crossroads before, and yes, you have gained knowledge, but it must lead to wisdom, not proud arrogance. You toss about the noble ideals of tolerance and open-mindedness—both praise-worthy pursuits— but you fail to see that the door is supposed to remain open. You let yourselves be led by those very ideals into societies where the door slams shut. Be very aware of those who claim to be open-minded and tolerant in exchange for loyalty to them because that very request negates their claim. They will not be tolerant of or open-minded about differing views they deem disloyal. Dissenting opinion is important. It is by the existence of differing opinions that we learn from our past and are able to draw contrast and ascertain the truth.

Beware of those willing to share ill-gotten bounty for bartered silence. Beware of those who bait effective traps with borrowed kindness. Beware of those who demand trust and extend none. Beware of those who make rules and exempt themselves. Beware of any who claim to protect you by making you defenseless. Beware of those who give support by pressuring you. Beware of any who ask you to ignore personal differences while pointing them out. Beware of any who point to the guilty without first pointing to themselves. Beware of any who lead by dominating. And beware of any who make claims of free offerings. All things truly free already belong to each of you. The only thing any human can offer has a human cost. You have been given a temporary gift to discern for yourselves that what I warn you about is true. Use it.

In my last duty while in this existence, it was my choice to preserve the lie in order to save the truth. One without the other denies what belongs to every human being—the free will to choose. And it is at this time that humanity must choose between the truth and the lie. You may ask what will happen based on the choice made.

If you choose the lie, you choose, once again, to devolve. The lie will promise to unite while dividing you based on differences both inherent and contrived. The lie will tell you to deny the importance of commonality. The lie will cloud every issue with bold-sounding promises that lack the substance of fleeting intentions. And for what gain will you choose the lie? The lie will not serve you. It never has. You will become its slave. You will bow down to the earthly master of your choice and be granted the respect due the dust beneath the master's feet.

If you choose the truth, all truth will be revealed. You will receive the secrets that this universe and beyond hold. You will evolve in spirit and bring to this existence an understanding of the reality of the next. You will live in a world where no human being is the beast of burden for another. Freedom in this existence shines for every living soul and is only diminished when one is forced to stand in the shadow of another. Beware of any who profess comfort in shade that is shadow because you will be at the mercy of those providing false comfort.

There will come a time soon when you will be without the Gleau. Gone with it will be any proof of its existence other than the memory of any who experienced it. The lie will instruct you to ignore anything you have learned in the course of its existence. It will reveal a mystery to mankind, and you will be told to abandon that notion. How will you know then what to believe? As my answer was before, ask yourself three questions, and answer them with honest thought. Ask what you are asked to give. Ask what you are promised to receive. And ask when any one promise has offered more to all than what they were asked to give. If you find the answer to those questions, you will have found what the truth has revealed.

You have retained only partial memory of this same choice made in the past, but your history holds every lesson you need to make the choice to evolve now. Excuses masquerading as reasons will not save you, so pay attention to the insight you've been given. You can learn everything you are told, but everything you are told may not be worth learning. There will be many distractions to obscure the truth. When you discover that which connects this existence to the next, your choice will be simple.

I leave you now to that choice.

Sincerely,
Jase Albert Garrett

Brett finished and raised his eyebrows before speaking again. "I get the gist of it, but when does this choice have to be made?"

"Eons ago. Now. Tomorrow. I don't think when matters. I think the matter is that we haven't made the right choice yet even though we've been given every opportunity. It's time that we make positive use of the opportunity," Barbara answered her brother.

Ben smiled at Barbara. "Blindness does not obscure vision. It came to you," he said knowingly.

"I guess my job is to do what I've been doing and go one step farther. When I find the liar, I have to bring logic to bear," Redgie stated as a matter-of-factly with just a twinge of trepidation. Knowing the risks and dangers firsthand made this all the more necessary.

"I'll be there if you need me, Redgie," Ben reassured.

"I guess I'll go back to tending my chickens and visiting with my grandchildren. Tough job, but somebody has to do it," Lee announced, making light of the difficulty her task presented.

"It may not sound like so very difficult a mission to undertake, but the best way to turn a reality into a myth is by destroying its roots and silencing its witnesses. You, by your very existence, are a threat to the lie, and so are your children. And, unfortunately, so were your parents," Ben admitted.

Lee sat silent and dumbfounded for a moment. "You mean it wasn't just an accident?"

"An accident is simply an event where the cause, if determined, appears to be without intent. Intent is easily disguised as coincidence or happenstance," he tried to explain. "Some here chalk it up to fate and let the reasons remain a mystery."

"But why? Why were my parents a threat?"

"They weren't," Ben answered, wishing the next question would not be asked.

"Then why was there an accident?"

Ben took a breath and held it. Finally he spoke. "The accident was meant for all of you."

Lee was stunned. "I was just a little kid, for heaven's sake. I was no threat to anyone." A sudden new wave of guilt overtook her with waves of bright anger being consumed by sadness that clung to her chest like a heavy maroon cloud. Was she the reason her parents died?

"It was what you would wish, not you. It was the idea that was the threat."

"The Gleau? Are you saying that because of that stupid wish that I hadn't even made yet, my parents were killed?" Anger wouldn't let her tears flow.

"No," Ben said quietly, hoping he could dispel her reaction. "The notion was already there. The ability to perceive was already within every human being. The potential of that wish already existed, and it was because of your parents' love and sacrifice that it was manifested with Jase's help. It was their hope for the two of you."

"Then why am I alive? If this accident was meant for me, why am I still standing here?" she challenged.

"Because you were not the threat *then*. You are only a threat *now*, after the fact. The accident was just one of many negative events in this world that seeks to gain advantage by destroying the good. To cheat death makes evil suspicious. To sidestep it often goes unnoticed. As ones with the potential to make the Gleau a reality now, you and Jase sidestepped death unnoticed."

Lee was now listening intently, trying to make sense of why this all occurred. "But how? What force made this happen?" Ben had the attention of the other three in the room as well.

"Good," was Ben's single-word reply.

Lee's eyes were studying an empty spot in space as she tried desperately to put all the pieces of this puzzle together. "But who or what? How was this made possible?"

"Look at me, Lee," Ben said calmly.

She lifted her face to look at Ben, and what she saw made the appearance of the Gleau seem ordinary. It was clear that no one else in the room was able to see what was being revealed to Lee. Ben's form began to become translucent, almost ghostlike. Within this see-through Ben figure was another much smaller figure. And it spoke to her mind.

"Remember me?" it asked in silence.

Lee smiled and nodded to the little man who had spoken to her when she was on the swing. She replied in kind. "We both missed a great fried chicken dinner, you know."

The small figure winked just before Ben regained his solid form. "Even accidents come with a plan, and as we all know, plans can change at will. In its haste, evil failed to see the change," Ben said aloud.

Lee thought back to her discussion with Jase that day in the corn crib. Now she almost understood. This accident was going to happen, but plans changed. She said it herself; if she knew her children could be spared, she would agree to it. Somehow, her parents knew without knowing. Plans changed, and evil was kept unaware.

"Wait a minute," Brett jumped in. "Are you saying there are no real accidents?"

"Of course there are," Ben countered. "Gravity has no intent, but many have perished in a fall. Where fate can be questioned is when we try to determine if the fall was caused by a poor choice or a push."

"I guess that makes sense," Brett conceded. "But if pushed, was it still the fate of the fallen to fall, or the fate of the pusher to push?"

"Ah, now you are seeing the real battle," Ben spoke with approval. "Free will does not dictate fate, but it allows us to choose in that moment a path where a certain fate exists."

"Geez! It's another which came first, the chicken or the egg," Brett declared.

"Welcome to the complexity of reality," Ben added. "Just know that there are forces bent on negating free will, and it is essential in the evolution of the soul. Free will must have a choice based in the truth, or it does not exist. A choice between two lies is no choice at all."

"That's something I've understood since I was a child. And my grandparents understood it too," Redgie enlightened. "Granddaddy must have preached to me a thousand times not to take any fool's lie into my heart unless I wanted to become a slave to that fool."

"Your granddaddy was a wise man," Ben acknowledged.

"Yes, he was," Redgie heartily agreed. "He may not have had any formal education, but he was brilliant in ways they don't teach anymore. And my grandmamma was a great cook, but she said that man served food for thought that was a banquet!" he said wistfully.

"He asked why about things, didn't he?" Barbara directed to Redgie.

"That he did. And taught me to ask it as well," Redgie confirmed.

"That's something they don't encourage anymore," Barbara continued. "You're just supposed to believe only what you're taught and do as you're told. It's not Big Brother we should worry about anymore. It's Big Father, and he is intrusive and overbearing. And God forbid you question those who abuse authority or listen to those whose imaginations and sharp minds lead to discovery."

"You're right. The childish ego has been elevated," Redgie agreed. "We may have made huge technological advances in the last hundred years, but back then, *we* were bigger. I don't know about anyone else here, but I'm having a hard time looking up to the small-minded and self-serving who attempt to lead us now. Doesn't take a genius to see we're headed down the wrong path, but we're supposed to believe we are being led by geniuses."

"And that's why the truth is so important," Ben granted.

"I guess Shakespeare was right. Truth will out," Brett quoted. "Just hope it isn't too late."

"It's never too late," Ben insisted. "From the perspectives I've been shown, there is no late. There is only how far we have come and how far we have to go."

"Well, I hope it isn't much farther," Brett mused.

"The closer humanity gets to the truth, the more desperate evil becomes," Ben warned. "It will be ruthless in its mission to soft sell corruption and destroy the truth."

"I don't mean to be the only one here who isn't a hundred percent certain, but this truth, is it specific or general?" Brett continued.

"Both," Ben answered with confidence. "But even after this truth is given to the world, mankind must choose to accept it. And for the shadow dweller, this truth will be a light it won't tolerate."

"Wait a minute!" Lee exclaimed. "Now I know why he wanted me to write this down." Lee rummaged through a stack of papers, receipts, and recipes in a basket on the counter.

"Write what down? And who?" Brett questioned automatically.

"Jase did. When I spoke with him last night," she answered, still hunting for the scrap of paper.

Taken back a bit, Brett felt it necessary to remind Lee of certain realities in the form of a question. "Jase spoke with you last night after he was killed yesterday afternoon?"

"Here it is," Lee announced, locating what she had written down. Then to Brett, she explained. "Yes, I spoke with him last night," she insisted.

"Where exactly did you see him, Lee?" Brett asked, wondering if she had been watching *Ghost Hunters* again.

Coming to Lee's defense, Ben tried to explain. "This will make more sense later, but it was in a reality observed from a different perspective."

"Oh yeah, that clears things right up," Brett admitted with heavy sarcasm and threw his hands in the air in a gesture of confusion.

"Relax, Brett," Barbara directed her brother. "What did he ask you to write down, Lee?"

"Yeah, what does it say?" Redgie encouraged.

Lee read carefully from the paper. "There is a light within a man of light, and he lights up the whole world. If he does not shine, he is darkness."

The balance of the evening was spent in discussion of what wisdom these words might impart. As they thought many others would, they debated the contents of Jase's letter and what possible connection it might uncover. Ben listened as many necessary questions were generated. When those in the room looked to him for answers, he was quick to remind them that his talents, though extraordinary, were purposely limited.

It was close to midnight when the little impromptu party broke up. Brett and Barbara were the first to leave, promising to help Lee with Jase's arrangements when the time came. According to Ben, the as-yet-unidentified body of the Baker Beach shooting had been photographed, x-rayed, and sampled to the point where a cremation had already been scheduled. It was unanimously decided that the completion of Jase's work in this life should come before attending to the details of his death. Redgie's request to be included in the wake when the time came was wholeheartedly honored.

As she hugged each visitor good-bye, Lee felt no loss or loneliness at the prospect of them leaving. There was an unmistakable feeling of unity with these souls that transcended any distance of time or space that might come between them. The strength of contentment overwhelmed her as she watched Brett and Barbara's truck turn at the end of the drive, and Ben and Redgie enter the darkened barn.

PART VIII

Happy Birthday

NEARING HIS EIGHTY-SEVENTH YEAR ON this earth, Sturmisch took great comfort in knowing that as long as his human machine kept running into the future, he would always live. He had not failed to notice the years taking an ever heavier toll on a body given advantages few would ever know. He literally had the heart of a thirty-year-old man and the liver of another who had just turned forty. Much as he fought it, there was little else he could replace that time would not degrade as the core of his physical being seemed determined to rot. His mind, he felt, deserved at least two lifetimes to enjoy all that he had created. Patience had allowed his influence to seep into the public consciousness without struggle, and within mere days, they would recognize his true power. The baton would inevitably be passed, but Sturmisch knew the power would always be his.

Adam had given such an excellent speech at the Moscone Center to a wholly receptive crowd that Sturmisch could not deny his charisma. His plans to replace Adam changed as the polls did. He did offer Adam an out with a veiled threat of what he could reveal or worse. Of course, leverage Adam brought to bear with news of a witness to the setup at the bar and certain tapes in his possession countered that threat, and a mutual stalemate was honored. It was one of the few times that they met face-to-face and through the indelicate sludge that each displayed as a Gleau truths were told.

All would go exactly as he planned, or it would not go at all. Rather than see his life's work be destroyed, he had a Hail Mary waiting in the wings. Should a miracle of public conscience assert itself, at his direction chaos would become the norm, and martial law would be declared to keep the peace. When the dust settled and the prewritten accounts of culpability were issued, the opposition would be justly rounded up and dealt with. It would be just such an event where his cheerleaders of the phrase "That couldn't happen here" would be marched center field for a halftime show. It would become a nonevent with no victims, and his plan would proceed with his team winning the game decisively. It would definitely be a happy birthday this year.

In his quest to gather and maintain power, there was one place that Sturmisch dared never look while seeking it. Buried deep in his mind in a tiny forgotten corner was a truth he denied with vengeance. He had surrounded himself with the trappings of this physical world, but it wasn't enough to hide the fact that what he really wanted was never denied him by another man. He had toppled governments, caused untold deaths, ruled the world financial markets, found gain in the destruction caused by famine, poverty, and disease, and yet, what he ultimately sought was always just beyond his latest conquest. Maybe he chose to deny this fact because of its initial source. The father he called Mister delivered that truth in response to a challenge. In his youth, Sturmisch had boasted to his master that one day he would be a powerful man of influence over all men.

"No human can ever be truly powerful. He will always be just a man," Mister replied.

"I will prove you wrong, old man," Sturmisch claimed.

"You may try, my boy, but the only power you can ever hope to acquire will be that which you forcibly deny others, making it forever beyond your reach. Cutting off the head of another does not make you any smarter, nor does it make you grow two heads. You will become less and less as you subjugate more and more because no man can ever truly own another."

Well versed at a young age, Sturmisch sharpened his prideful tongue and corrected the old man. "You say that only because you have failed where I will succeed."

"No," the old man stated, knowing Sturmisch would discard this hard-learned lesson. "I say it because it is the truth."

Friday (October 26, 2012)

EE PLACED THE SMILING JACK-O'-LANTERN on the corner of the deck closest to the drive so the girls would see it when they arrived. A bounty of events had marked this day, most notably that it was almost a year to the day when Jase came walking into her life for the second time. After a protracted process of red tape, this morning she had received the delivery of his ashes accompanied by the only personal affect deemed worthy by the coroner: the dog tag that Lee had given to him. In her mind she could hear him laughing after announcing, "I'm back!"

Still in effect, the Gleau was doing what it could to reveal the ill intent that existed, but just as Ben and Jase both had predicted, revealing the truth did not subvert the will of those who chose not to believe it. Lee's wish was not as potent as she thought it might be. Maybe, just maybe, it would be a useful-enough tool to make the human animal become aware of the value of the human spirit, but the propaganda machine of the shadow dwellers in power was relentless. As it stood, too many were still being lured into the trap baited with the sweetest lies. The proffered temptations were getting more grandiose by the day to the point where loyalty to a particular view all but guaranteed a life of bounty at the expense of another. The argument never progressed past the point of what happened when those bearing the expense succumbed to death or the profound poverty of depletion. What then? Too few cared or even thought about that, it seemed.

It only made sense to Lee that if you didn't need to think about providing for yourself, what did you need to think about? The emotionally satisfied were happy with what sounded nice and didn't bother to think about how this miracle would be accomplished. They were content to accept the word of a proficient liar when it suited the selfish purpose of getting something for nothing. The elaborate ruse constructed to convince them of their superior intelligence also disguised the fact that they were being patronized into purposeful ignorance. Lee had seen it too often to think it was a mistake.

Less than a hundred years ago, an unsuspecting and trusting population had heard the same charismatic blather. They were told how wonderful they were, told they deserved all manner of necessities be provided for them, and told to abandon previous alliances and accept a new superior order. The horrific results of that historical exercise were being ignored. What was equally amazing was that in a land of opportunity and freedom, they were convinced those things were not enough. Fairness no longer meant a condition of impartiality and being just. Paradoxically, fairness was now dictated because it wasn't fair enough.

Unexercised intelligence had become to the brain what the appendix was to the intestines—useful at some point in our development, but now just a vestigial organ whose function was no longer essential to life. Toss the frontal and temporal lobes right in the garbage, and humanity would fit right in with this new nicer version of the human experience. But it wasn't nice. It was sad and barren and historically dangerous.

Breaking from thoughts less than pleasant, Lee took notice of movement in the barnyard. "Well, hello there," she spoke gently to the stranger approaching from the direction of the milk house. *How appropriate*, she thought as a tiny black kitten approached with caution. "I wonder where you came from," she asked herself. Lee squatted down, and the kitten with bright yellow eyes sidled up and permitted stroking. A meow that indicated both gratitude and hunger wasn't to be ignored, and Lee took her new charge to the kitchen. The kitten purred loudly as if it had read her mind and knew that its needs were about to be tended to.

She placed the baby on the floor and went to the refrigerator to find a suitable meal. A leftover chicken leg was located, and Lee turned to inform her inky guest of the menu. The kitten was not in view. "Where'd you go?" she said out loud. When she checked under the table, she heard a squeaky meow. As if led by instinct, the kitten was waiting patiently, crouched in the center of Semi's rocking chair. In that instant, Lee knew this was meant to be. This spooky little character had determined that it was home, and Lee would not argue. Spooky was home.

Emily and the tribe would be arriving late in the afternoon for the annual costume fitting, and Spooky would be a nice addition to the ambience of the affair. As this thought crossed her mind, her phone rang. It was Emily.

"Hey, Mom. We're on our way over. Do you have your television on?"

"No, I don't. I'm glad you're coming early, but what's up?"

"Just turn it on now. I'll be there in a few minutes. This is so cool! Bye," her daughter blurted out just before hanging up.

Closing the phone, she looked across the room at Spooky, back in the rocker, carefully washing his face with a paw. "I guess we'd better find out what all the fuss is about, huh, Spooky."

He winked one golden eye at her and went back to washing.

While changing and brushing her hair, Lee tuned in to KMIN to catch what had come out of the horse's mouth. A representative for the national network was recapping an event with significant sound bites included from the original broadcast in an onscreen box.

"A spokesman today from the Department of Neurologic Surgery at the Mayo Clinic in Rochester, Minnesota, made known some rather remarkable findings in the course of their usual work. What was first thought to be an equipment malfunction by the neurosurgical team was later determined to be something quite amazing.

"Whenever possible, procedures are digitally recorded for study. It was during such a surgery where the patient did not survive, due to complications unrelated to the procedure, that the anomaly was first noted in January of this year. Based purely upon conjecture and personal observation, the phenomena known as the Gleau has somehow made it possible to determine the physical existence and physiology of an identical body of less dense tissue that reverts to pure energy at the moment of complete separation from the host body. The separate body, which doctors have named the ethereal body, appeared to the naked eye to dissipate with the coexisting Gleau in cases where the patient did not survive. Due to the fact that we strive to avoid fatal outcomes, this anomaly remained purposely unremarkable until a patient coded during surgery, and cardiac restart was successful. The ethereal body became visible but, as the video demonstrates, was reabsorbed when normal heart rhythm was restored.

"Medical professionals were reluctant to make any comment about their observations until subsequent data could confirm that this was not a onetime event. As mortality is impossible to predict and avoided whenever possible, the appearance of the ethereal body is visible for less than a hundredth of a second, and its capture on video was unexpected. Slow-motion study of high-speed digital recordings capturing images at a rate of 3,000 fps are still being studied, but the initial conclusion is that our earthly bodies are hosts to another now documented living being of a nature not yet completely understood. Due to unfortunate cases where the outcomes were fatal, this event has been recorded a total of eleven times at the Mayo Clinic. Similar studies have begun at other major medical institutions to confirm these findings.

"It was further noted that recorded surgeries prior to the existence of the Gleau do not contain images of the ethereal body, so it has been determined that the Gleau is an essential mechanism in this discovery. This finding has garnered the interest of many other branches of the scientific community."

The network went to commercial, and Lee was silent while she absorbed all that she just saw and heard. She found the replay of the slow-motion image as beautiful as it was astounding. In a flash of thought, she also realized how medical science, technology, and the Gleau all had to be perfectly synchronized for this to be recognized. Something told her that more than simple chance was at work here.

"Wow," she said to her new feline kitchen companion. "What do you think, Spooky?"

"Who's Spooky?" a male voice asked from behind her.

Quite startled by the unexpected reply, Lee turned so quickly she nearly lost her balance. Her Gleau exhibited a coronal discharge of bright white, orange, and purple. "Ben! Geez, you nearly scared the life outta me!" she barked as much with surprise as authority.

Embarrassed by his own amusement, Ben apologized. "Sorry, Lee. Guess I should have just said boo."

"You nearly scared me to death, you big ghost!" Lee exaggerated, hoping humor would help dissipate the adrenaline shock to her system.

Ben moved to Lee's side and gave her a swift hug of apology that was returned in earnest. "Well, what do you think about this newest discovery?" he asked, all the while eyeing a tray of pumpkin-faced cupcakes.

"Here," she said, directing him to a chair. "Have a cupcake. I'm not sure what I think just yet. Cider or soda?" she inquired in typical Lee fashion.

"Cider please," Ben answered as a crunch of gravel in the lane indicated Emily's arrival.

Nearly tripping over her own feet and a tangle of child paraphernalia she had in tow, Emily entered the kitchen ready to celebrate more than All Hallow's Eve. "Isn't it something! Hey, Ben! So glad you're here. I've only got about nine hundred questions. Hey, Mom! Where can I put this stuff?"

Lee helped her daughter put aside her burden and welcomed her to a seat. Emily's barrage of questions continued. "So, Ben, any insider info about this latest discovery you'd care to impart?"

Ben smiled. "Have a cupcake. These are delicious," he deflected.

"Pffft!" Emily responded. "Don't you think this is huge? Finally, the very thing used to deny anything faith-based has proven that it exists! Science has vindicated faith!"

"Science has just been able to document what wasn't visible before. For those who choose to deny what it means, shadow dweller hypocrisy will kick in, and they will downplay anything that might interfere with man worshipping man. May I try a chocolate one, please?" Ben asked, nodding toward the tray of cupcakes.

"Well, aren't you just a killjoy." Emily laughed and handed him another. Attempting the delicate process of removing the cupcake paper from his cupcake with the precision of a forklift, Emily offered to help. "May I?" She made quick work of the paper removal, and Ben made quicker work of the cupcake as he popped it whole into his mouth. "He's stifling himself with cupcakes, I believe," Emily insinuated with a smirk.

"Ben's right," Lee addressed her firstborn. "This is just a key, and first you have to want to go through the door before you even think about using it in the lock."

"Couldn't have said it any better myself," Ben congratulated Lee.

"Thanks," Lee replied.

"So why even offer the key? The same sour-grapes crowd who now has the key in hand can look at the door and proclaim there is no great mystery beyond it and refuse to open it. I can understand why they would hesitate to prove me right, but why would they hesitate to prove me wrong?" Emily challenged.

"Two things: doubt and pride. Too many would rather eat dung than admit that their research disproved a stated hypothesis. And to prove you right or wrong would eliminate doubt and prove their pride false. And it is this false pride that the masters peddle here to maintain power over other men," Ben tried to clarify.

"I still don't get it," Emily said with exasperation. "We can certainly choose not to buy the limitations they peddle."

"Some think they can't afford not to. They are afraid of what might happen," Ben answered. "They may not understand the broader depths of reality, but they surely have seen and understand the consequences of digging any deeper than they've been told to. And it may not be noted officially, but the Gleau that has been decried as pure bunk by the shadowed ones is being used to identify traitors to their cause. When ridicule and insult don't put the unauthorized thinkers back on track, sterner measures are brought to bear. Their goal is to keep as many in the dark as possible."

"He's right, and it's just a step, Emily," Lee corroborated. "And each time we take a step, we are allowed to exercise our free will about whether or not to take that step. Free will is a gift from beyond the door, and the peddlers of darkness prefer to have us believe that they provide it. Too many people mistake the fact that just because the shadow dwellers can deny someone free will, they are somehow able to grant it as well." Lee was caught off guard when Emily said nothing. "Does that make sense?"

"Yes, it does. So this discovery is just another hint pointing to the same thing, I'm guessing."

"One of many hints," Ben agreed.

"So what happens now?" Lee proposed.

"Maybe Redgie has something to say about it," Ben said, pointing to the television.

"Well, I'll be flipped. I was just thinking about him earlier today," Lee remarked. She had been keeping track of his speaking engagements where, true to his word and Jase's request, he put himself in the unenviable position of asking the unpopular and direct questions and demanding logical and truthful answers. He had become Redgie Apple-Hayseed, planting questions in minds chock-full of organic fertilizer.

Lee watched attentively as a young woman armed with a microphone approached Redgie on the steps of a building he had just exited. She and a gaggle of her cohorts physically blocked his way down the steps and began a barrage of questions.

"Mr. Lewis, Mr. Lewis! Our viewers would like a moment of your time, if you could spare it," the young lady spoke into her microphone and then directed it at Redgie.

"I'll give you what time I have, certainly," Redgie obliged. "If you could follow me to my car, I can answer as we walk." The small crowd parted, and Redgie listened as he made his way to the parking lot.

"Can you give us your opinion on the news today from the Mayo Clinic? Do you think what they captured on film is actually the human soul?"

"Well, my opinion and my thoughts are two slightly different things." Redgie laughed.

The lady toting the microphone was less amused and more determined. "So do you think it's true or not?" She tried pinning him down.

"I think what I saw today was pretty amazing, but my opinion about the existence of the human soul remains the same, even if this method of discovery is found to be flawed."

"So you have doubts?" she pressed as they approached his car in the parking lot.

"Only about the thoughts, not my opinion," he said with his now trademark smile.

"So if their discovery changes, will your opinion change as well?" she persisted.

Redgie was growing weary of this news maker sparring with him to obtain a desired answer. "Young lady, I'm sorry, I don't know your name. Do you know for how long science has debated and still only theorizes about the properties and characteristics of gravity?" He didn't wait for an answer. "It wasn't until 1687 that we took enough notice of its effect to consider it worth published study. It's been around since at least the beginning of the universe. You would think that something as simple as gravity—something you and I experience every day—would no longer hold any mystery. But it does. They can't agree on the value of the gravitational constant G so the measure is approximate. They don't know if it is a force comprised of gravitons, gravitational waves, or if it exists at all according to Einstein's theory that it is a bend in the space-time continuum caused by the mass of an object. Science is also at a standstill with any conclusive answers about the Gleau, which, like gravity, we can all observe but is not fully understood by science. So let me get this straight." He paused. "You want me to doubt the very science that has now produced evidence of something that was said not to exist by virtue of that science? Man seems to forget that he did not invent this gathering of information and discovery called science. In fact, we are all part of it. I think they should concentrate on gravity a little more before they go dismissing what this new discovery is." Redgie waited for the next question as he opened his car door.

"My name is Carla," the young woman informed him with something slightly less than a frown. "But I'm not sure that gravity has anything to do with this situation."

Redgie did his best to keep his eyes from rolling. "My point is that debating the discovery doesn't change reality. When they explain it fully, gravity will still be the same, and I seriously doubt I will float away into the cosmos if Einstein was right, but I have my doubts about you. As for the soul, we tentatively have visual proof, but I don't need their proof. The human spirit is as logical as gravity."

Undaunted by thought, the lady reporter decided to go for broke. "So you think this has something to do with proving the existence of God?" There was a silent gasp among the other reporters as she dared to speak *that* word.

Redgie smiled, shook his head, and rested his arms on top of the open car door. "My dear Carla," he politely condescended,

"God doesn't need to be proved, only discovered. Like gravity, the proof is all around us, but gravity doesn't compete for the human soul, so it isn't a threat to the darkness here that seeks to dominate mankind through men. I'm far more inclined to trust in the God who gave me this universe and the brain and free will to make the most of it with this life than I am any man who offers false paradise at the expense of the lives of my fellow man."

The interview with Redgie was over, but the discussion wasn't quite finished. Carla turned her back to Redgie and walked away without as much as a thank-you for his time. To her cameraman in tow, she muttered, "I should have known. Idiotic religious freaks abound."

"You brought it up. And you have the freedom to say that here without repercussion," her cameraman spoke knowingly.

Giving him a questioning look, she added, "Of course I do. So what?"

"Try saying something like that elsewhere on this earth where freedom belongs only to the rulers of men, and you wouldn't be so lucky," he informed.

"Oh really. And just how would they know I said anything?"

"Because in those places, it would be my duty to honor my rulers and report you. When man is considered a god, that god hears all."

She eyed him with suspicion. "And just who were you before you got this job? Let me guess. Intelligence advisor to some ambassador, maybe?"

"Sergeant Kevin Prescott, United States Marine Corps, ma'am."

Lee muted the television when the station went to a break. "Wow. I'm surprised they didn't edit most of that out," she remarked.

"Redgie is controversy, and that's news. They left it all in there so that one of their experts can appear and negate any thought he may have provoked," Ben stated.

"Well," Emily began with a sigh, "what will keep people from giving up their free will? Too many think giving it up is getting them everything for nothing."

Ben smiled. "That has been the choice throughout our histories. The only way a man can ever hope to be a god here is to take away what only the God can give: free will. My people may not have had the benefit of formal doctrines, but it was a truth they understood because of the logical mind of existence. In the mind of total reality, the people are free. It is when man is trapped in the small mind of another human that his existence stays small and dark. Mankind cannot make one star brighter by dimming another. My forefathers understood that simple reality. Whether or not you understand the next realm is immaterial, but giving up freedom and the will it implies guarantees you never will."

"So where do we go from here?" Lee asked.

"We wait," Ben answered.

Omega

S TURMISCH LEFT HIS MONTANA LAIR twice during the month
of November, the second being his last. The first excursion
was by far more pleasurable for him than for those who
shared his company. When his Adam horse crossed the finish
line, Sturmisch was there in the winner's circle determined to
maintain his hold on the reins. His sharing in the victory was
more tolerated than welcomed, but Sturmisch allowed Adam his
moment in the sun.

Demonstrating barely a clue that his victory was carefully
crafted by generational undermining, mental manipulation, and
historical distortion, Adam was as close as he would ever be
to indicating gratitude to anything beyond himself. His praise
congratulated the recognition of *his* brilliance, *his* vision, and *his*
power. During this exaltation of those confirming his right to
this power, his Gleau took on the appearance of a full-body black
hole, absorbing the very existence surrounding him while issuing jagged bolts of lava red that cooled to a fluorescent pea-soup
green and flowed inward as if grasped by invisible hands desperately seeking freedom. The mesmerized crowd took little note of
his coat of grotesque color and rejoiced in this miracle of man
who would be their salvation.

Sturmisch watched from the sidelines as Adam mustered a
single tear to augment the exaggerated smile he bestowed upon
his fawning admirers. Adam caught sight of the old man in his
peripheral vision and knew he *had* to be proud that he pulled it off,
but secretly hoped he was jealous. The crowd before him cheered
after every sentence he uttered, and he let them. Expectant eyes
were glued to every gesture, every facial display, and every word.
These people weren't just supporters; he felt they *belonged* to him.

And as his property now, bought and paid for, he could do as he wished and deliver to them what he wished. Truth be known, they were now the least of his concerns. He got what he needed from them, and they were now expendable. Surely they did not believe that he possessed some magic wand to make all their troubles disappear, but he did have a pen that he would wield as a magic sword and make the largess they had come to expect disappear in the interest of true fairness.

The roar of the crowd was displaced momentarily by an amusing thought. As he beamed and waved, the thought of fairness made him chuckle. If he were to hand them each a million dollars, they would be grateful for less than a split second when he informed them that they were now part of the despised. He wondered how many would hand the million back to be in the good graces they expected the productive to be. They thought they had the power of their vote, but they sold it. And Adam now owned it and them.

Knowing Adam as well or better than he did himself, Sturmisch was content to let Adam think whatever he cared to at the moment. Basking in public glory was not the way a real god should conduct himself. A real god of men does not welcome the distraction of the limelight, nor does he shun it. He simply owns those in it.

As the dust of irregularity settled around the day of Adam's crowning moment, most of it was swept under the rug and forced into the bowels of what wasn't important. The stench of it all would hang in the air for a few weeks and be replaced by new concerns as humanity moved forward toward *the* day. Once again, Sturmisch was sure that when the fuse was lit, it would be any who opposed perfection who would shoulder blame for anything less. His personal congratulations expressed in a handshake and an unwanted pat on the back from Adam were exchanged without any photographic record, and he returned to the sanctity of his private hideaway to await the planned and necessary carnage.

Not yet official, Adam exercised his power with enthusiasm. Maintaining the thrill of the pursuit wasn't going to be easy, but it was what he required. The nuts and bolts and daily grind of responsibility were not his forte, so he sought Sturmisch's council to install surrogates to deal with the day to day and to rid himself of a current irritation.

The Gleau was becoming a memory before it ceased to be, at least in Sturmisch's thoughts. Subsequently, on a brisk afternoon in late November when Adam was granted a private audience with Sturmisch at his underground establishment, it was to allay any uncertainties that the Gleau or its perceived revelations would challenge Adam's reign. Or at least that's what Sturmisch was led to believe.

With his now required bodyguards in tow, Adam approached the designated coordinates of Sturmisch's bunker. Knowing there was little that impressed the old man, he made it a point to bring an offering of select teas that he doubted would be appreciated or, for that matter, consumed. Upon reaching the hidden entrance, there was barely a second or two of waiting, and the door slid open. With an uncharacteristic smile, Sturmisch welcomed Adam and bid him to enter alone. A small protest from Adam's escort was squelched by a wave of his hand, and the door slid shut before the protest was complete.

"Sticklers for protocol," Adam explained.

"Goes with the job," Sturmisch replied, no longer sporting his smile.

As they both seated themselves in the golf cart and proceeded down the dimly lit tunnel, Adam began relaying his concerns about his upcoming responsibilities.

"I've prepared a list," Sturmisch spoke with authority, brushing aside Adam's words. "You'll have no problems, and if you do, I will handle them."

"I knew I could count on you," Adam replied, doing his best to disguise the fact that he no longer considered Sturmisch a supporter but more a useful subject to do his bidding. Had Sturmisch sought truthfulness in the light surrounding Adam, it was hidden beneath a spillage of familiar deceit.

The tunnel opened to a large room with smooth concrete floors that met a series of steps and ramps leading to Sturmisch's work and well-appointed living areas. The two ascended several sets of steps and landings to what Adam assumed was Sturmisch's office and base of operations.

"Nice digs. Very James Bond nemesis-esque," Adam remarked.

Sturmisch said nothing. He handed Adam a typed list of names and the appointments they would fill. Adam glanced at it briefly, folded it, and tucked it in an inside-jacket pocket.

"I don't think the Redgie clown is going to be a problem any-more, and this Gleau nonsense has nearly run its course, so if you stick to my program, your job is done," Sturmisch informed flatly. Sturmisch never did mention to anyone his unexpected meeting with the giant Indian. As long as Adam did as he was instructed, Sturmisch was free to pursue the as-yet-denied technology he sought. If he could possess such a power, it would grant him a greater range to oversee the execution of his perfect world.

"Thanks," Adam responded with empty cordiality. "One more thing though, before I leave," he continued.

"What else could there be?" Sturmisch replied, readying him-self to be seated at his desk. He turned and directed his glance in Adam's direction. Adam was smiling and aiming the short barrel of a revolver at Sturmisch.

"What's that? A peashooter?" Sturmisch asked, feign-ing disinterest.

Mocking the old man, Adam turned the weapon slightly and read what was inscribed. "No. Actually, it's a Ruger SP101 .38 special caliber, or at least that's what it says on the label," Adam humored.

"And just what are you going to do with your peashooter?" Sturmisch asked, still not convinced that this was anything more than a bluff.

"I'm going to shoot a pea, I guess," Adam replied with open amusement.

"Seriously, put that thing away. You've got work to do," Sturmisch admonished.

"Yes, I do. And the first thing I'm going to do is save the world from you," Adam spoke, maintaining his smile, which was now closer to a smirk.

"Do as your limited judgment directs you, you fool! My demise will do nothing for you," Sturmisch insisted. "Do this, and you will be undone," he stated with an assurance of disdain.

"You don't get it, do you, old man," Adam posed as anything but a question. "I own the writers of the rules now. I can do anything I want and get away with anything I want. The keys of reality are mine now."

Sturmisch ignored what he was hearing and moved casually toward the open laptop on his desk. A loud crack echoed throughout vast space as hurtling lead struck the laptop and sent bits of plastic shrapnel flying. Reflex caused Sturmisch to withdraw instantly, and before the revolver's report was completely silenced, he set his venom upon Adam. "You ignorant ass! Do you really think that's all it takes? You can't destroy me or my work! What I've set in motion you cannot fathom!"

Adam smiled and pulled back the hammer, advancing the cylinder to the next round. "Oh, don't worry. I'm not going to destroy your work. I'm simply going to take advantage of it. And if you've taught me one thing with absolute certainty, it's that there can be only one god. Time for you to retire."

For the first time since he was a child, Sturmisch felt his humanity keenly. He had no words to dissuade the evil before him. In his mind, the irony of this situation made itself known. What better to combat evil than the evil it created? Sturmisch didn't hear the next shot.

He stood next to his desk, feeling no pain. He watched as Adam withdrew a handkerchief and massaged the stainless tool in his hand and walked to a crumpled figure on the floor. A lifeless hand was pressed around the revolver, and it was tossed aside. With a new visual clarity, he watched as Adam removed a pair of latex gloves and pocketed them. "You won't get away with this," Sturmisch spoke as Adam walked past the golf cart and headed toward the exit tunnel.

"No, he won't, but he can't hear you," said a familiar voice.

Without surprise, Sturmisch acknowledged Ben's presence with a glance.

"Welcome home," Ben directed at the diminished spirit standing next to him.

"Is it?" Sturmisch asked in true sincerity.

"Home? Yes, it is," Ben answered as Sturmisch receded and Twiford took form.

"So what happens now?"

"For you, I don't know." The physical world around them maintained its form, but from a distance beyond the dimensions of this one, a pinprick of light began to grow until its brightness seemed to make this physical world disappear.

"I'm drawn to that light," Sturmisch relayed, both amazed and reluctant.

"I'm not surprised," Ben replied.

"Before I go, may I ask you a question?"

"Certainly."

"If we are truly made in his image, why didn't I know this?"

Ben chuckled and smiled. "Sometimes the most learned in human form are the slow learners on this side. His image is consciousness and light, and we possess both of those qualities. Human form is like a school uniform."

"Wow," Sturmisch spoke with the reverence of a prayer.

What did you learn?" Ben asked as Sturmisch began walking toward the brilliance.

"Not enough," he stated humbly and disappeared into the light.